the Magnate

MICHELLE CELMER
JENNIFER LEWIS
LEANNE BANKS

MILLS BOON

Published in Great Britain 2015
by Mills & Boon, an imprint of Harlequin (UK) Limited,
Eton House, 18-24 Paradise Road, Richmond, Surrey, TW9 1SR

MISTRESS TO THE MAGNATE © 2015 Harlequin Books S.A.

Money Man's Fiancée Negotiation, Bachelor's Bought Bride and *CEO's Expectant Secretary* were first published in Great Britain by Harlequin (UK) Limited.

Money Man's Fiancée Negotiation © 2010 Michelle Celmer
Bachelor's Bought Bride © 2010 Jennifer Lewis
CEO's Expectant Secretary © 2010 Leanne Banks

ISBN: 978-0-263-25213-2
eBook ISBN: 978-1-474-00392-6

05-0515

Harlequin (UK) Limited's policy is to use papers that are natural, renewable and recyclable products and made from wood grown in sustainable forests. The logging and manufacturing processes conform to the legal environmental regulations of the country of origin.

Printed and bound in Spain
by CPI, Barcelona

MONEY MAN'S FIANCÉE NEGOTIATION

BY
MICHELLE CELMER

Bestselling author **Michelle Celmer** lives in south-eastern Michigan with her husband, their three children, two dogs and two cats. When she's not writing or busy being a mum, you can find her in the garden or curled up with a romance. And if you twist her arm really hard you can usually persuade her into a day of power shopping.

Michelle loves to hear from readers. Visit her website, www.michellecelmer.com, or write to her at PO Box 300, Clawson, MI 48017, USA.

To the ladies of Sister Night:
Karen, Janet, Susie, Toni and Cora.

Prologue

Melody Trent shoved clothes into a suitcase feeling a sense of urgency that was totally without merit. Ash wouldn't be back until late. He'd been working longer and longer hours lately. Spending less and less time with her. Honestly, she would be surprised if it didn't take a few days before he even noticed she was gone.

Emotion welled up in her throat and tears stung her eyes. She bit down hard on the inside of her cheek and took a deep, calming breath. It had to be hormones because she had never been a crier.

She would love to be able to blame her mother and her revolving bedroom door for this. She would like to think that she'd stayed with Ash for three years because her mother's longest marriage—and there were five in total—barely lasted nine months. She wanted to be different from her mother, better than her, and look at the mess it had gotten her into.

She looked over at the photo on the dresser of her and her mother. It was the only one Mel had of them together. She was thirteen, with the body of a ten-year-old. Scrawny, skinny and awkward, standing next to her voluptuous, beautiful mother. No wonder she'd felt so insignificant, so invisible. It wasn't until college, when she shared an apartment with another student who worked part-time as a personal fitness trainer, that she finally started looking like a woman. It took vigorous daily workouts and relentless weight training, but she finally had curves to speak of, and within a year men began noticing her and asking her out.

Her body was the bait, and sex the addiction that kept them coming around, that kept them interested, because what other reason would a man have to be with someone like her? She was smart, but in her own opinion not very pretty. She was content to sit at home and study, or read a good novel, when her peers only wanted to party.

That was why she and Ash had always worked so well. She was able to go to law school, and do all the other things she enjoyed, and never worry about how the rent would get paid, or where she would find money for her next meal. He took care of her financially, and in return all she had to do was take care of everything else. And the truth was, she didn't mind the cooking and cleaning and laundry. She'd been doing it nearly her whole life, as her mother had never taken an interest in anything domestic—God forbid she break a nail.

And of course part of the package was keeping him sexually satisfied, and at that she was a master. Only lately, the past six months or so, she could feel him pulling away from her. When they made love she felt as though his mind was somewhere else. No matter what she did, however kinky and adventurous to hold his attention, she could feel him slipping away.

When she missed her period she was sure it was a fluke. Ash had been pretty clear about the fact that he was sterile. And though their relationship had never been about love, it was mutually exclusive, so for almost three years they had never so much as used a condom.

But then her breasts started to feel tender, and her appetite suddenly became insatiable. She knew even before she took the pregnancy test that it would be positive. And of course it was. Ash had made it clear on more than one occasion that he didn't want to be tied down. But he was a good man, and she knew he would do the right thing. The question was, did she want to be stuck in a relationship with a man who didn't want her or her child?

If she left Ash, she would have to quit law school, though honestly, she'd lost her interest in the law a while ago. She just hadn't had the heart to tell Ash. He had invested so much in her education. How could she tell him it was all for nothing?

She had been in the shower, debating her next move, when Ash came in with the video camera. She felt exhausted, and depressed, and in no mood to play the vixen, and really saw no point. She had already pretty much decided what she had to do. There was no need to keep trying to impress him. Three years of playing the role of the perfect woman had left her utterly exhausted. But when he stepped in the shower and started touching her, started kissing her, more tenderly than he ever had before, she melted. And when he made love to her, she could swear that for the first time he actually saw her. The *real* her. She let herself believe that somewhere deep down maybe he loved her.

For two weeks she agonized over what to do. She let herself hope that he would be happy about the baby. Then he came home from work in a foul mood, ranting about Jason Reagart being forced to marry and have a child he hadn't planned or expected. He said how lucky he was to have a woman who respected his boundaries. She knew then that her fantasy about her, Ash and the baby was never going to happen.

That was last night. Today she was leaving.

She stuffed the rest of her things in her case, leaving the cocktail dresses and sexy lingerie behind. She wouldn't be needing them where she was going. They wouldn't fit in a few months anyway. She zipped it up and hauled both pieces of luggage off the bed. Her entire life in two suitcases and an overstuffed duffel bag. She was twenty-four with hardly anything to show for it. But that was going to change. She was going to have a child to love, and maybe someday she might meet a man who appreciated her for who she really was.

She lugged the bags to the front door then grabbed her purse from the kitchen counter. She checked to make sure the six thousand was safely tucked inside. It was money she had been gradually accumulating over the past three years and saving for a rainy day.

When it rained it poured.

Next to the stack of credit cards Ash had given her, Mel set a notepad and pen out so she could write Ash a letter, but the truth was, she didn't have a clue what to say. She could thank him for all he'd done for her, but hadn't she thanked him enough already? She could tell him she was sorry, but honestly, she wasn't. She was giving him his freedom. Wasn't that enough?

She didn't doubt he would find someone to replace her, and in a few weeks she would be just a distant memory.

She grabbed her bags and opened the door, took one last look around, then left that life behind for good.

One

Asher Williams was not a patient man by nature. When he wanted something, he didn't like to wait, and truth be told, he rarely had to. However, he was warned, when he enlisted the services of a private investigator, that finding a missing person could take time. Particularly if the person they were looking for didn't want to be found. That being the case, he was surprised when he received a call from him a mere two days later.

Ash was in a meeting with several of his colleagues and wouldn't normally answer his cell phone, but when he saw the P.I.'s number on the screen, he made an exception. He suspected it was either very good news, or very bad.

"Excuse me for just a minute," he told his colleagues. He rose from his chair and walked across the room, out of earshot. "You have news?" he asked, then heard the three words he had been hoping for.

"I found her."

In that instant he felt a confusing and disturbing combination of relief and bitterness. "Where is she?"

"She's been staying in Abilene, Texas."

What the hell was she doing in *Texas?*

That wasn't important now. What mattered was bringing her back home where she belonged. And the only way to do that was to go and get her. He was sure, with some convincing, he could make her see that he knew what was best for her, that leaving him had been a mistake. "I'm in a meeting. I'll call you back in five minutes."

He hung up the phone and turned to his colleagues.

"Sorry, but I have to go," he told them. "And I'm not sure when I'll be back. Hopefully no more than a few days. I'll let you know when I have more details."

The look of stunned confusion on their faces as he walked from the room was mildly amusing, and not at all unexpected. In all his time as CFO of Maddox Communications, Ash had never missed a meeting or taken a sick day. He had never been so much as five minutes late for work, and he honestly couldn't recall the last time he'd taken a vacation—much less one with two minutes' notice.

On his way into his office Ash asked his secretary, Rachel, to hold all his calls. "And cancel any appointments I have for the next week, just to be safe."

Her eyes went wide. "A *week?*"

He closed his office door and settled behind his desk, his mind racing a million miles an hour with all that he needed to do before he left as he dialed the P.I.'s number. He answered on the first ring.

"You told me it could take months to find her," Ash said. "Are you sure you have the right Melody Trent?"

"I'm positive it's her. Your girlfriend was in an auto accident. It's how I found her so quickly."

Melody Trent wasn't his girlfriend. By definition, she was his mistress—a warm body to come home to after a long day at work. He paid her law school tuition and living expenses and she offered companionship with no strings attached. Just the way he liked it. But it was no time to split hairs.

"Was she injured?" he asked, expecting, at worst, a few bumps and bruises. He truly was not prepared for what the P.I. said next.

"According to the police report, the driver, your girl-friend, was pretty banged up and there was one fatality."

Ash's stomach bottomed out and his mouth went dry. "How banged up?"

"She's been in the hospital for a couple of weeks."

"You said there was a fatality. What happened exactly?" He rose from his chair, began pacing as the P.I. gave him what few details he had about the crash. And it was bad. Worse than Ash could have ever imagined. "Is Melody being held responsible?"

"Fortunately, no. The police filed it as an accident. That doesn't mean there won't be a civil suit, though."

They would deal with that when and if the time came. "How is Melody? Do you have any details on her condition?"

"All the hospital would say is that she's stable. They'll only give details to family. When I asked to talk to her, they said she wasn't taking phone calls. That usually means that for whatever reason, the patient is unable to speak. My best guess would be she's unconscious."

Since Melody left him, Ash had been counting the hours

until she came crawling back to ask forgiveness, to say that she'd made a mistake. At least now he knew why she hadn't. Although that wasn't much of a consolation. And he would be damned if anyone was going to stop him from learning the truth. "I guess I'll just have to be family."

"You going to say she's your long-lost sister or something?" the P.I. asked.

"Of course not." He needed something a bit more believable. Something he could easily prove.

Melody was his fiancée.

The next morning Ash caught the earliest flight to the Dallas/Fort Worth airport, then rented a car and made the two-and-a-half-hour drive to Abilene. He had called ahead the afternoon before, setting up a meeting with the doctor in charge of her care. They told him that Melody was conscious and out of the woods, but that was the most they would say over the phone.

Once he got to the hospital he strode right past the registration desk. He'd learned a long time ago that if he looked as though he belonged somewhere, showed he was in charge, people naturally followed along, and no one tried to stop him as he stepped onto the elevator. He got off on the third floor, surprised to realize that he was actually nervous. What if Melody didn't want to come back to him?

Of course she would, he assured himself. Her leaving had obviously been a great error in judgment, and it would have only been a matter of time before she realized how much she missed him. Besides, where else would she go while she healed from her injuries? She needed him.

He stopped at the nurses' station and they paged a Dr. Nelson. He appeared less than five minutes later.

"Mr. Williams?" he said, shaking Ash's hand. The

department on his name badge was neurology, which likely meant that Melody had suffered some sort of brain injury. Which explained why she would have been unconscious. But did it mean her injuries were even more serious than he could have imagined? What if she never made a full recovery?

"Where is my fiancée?" Ash asked, surprised by the note of panic in his voice. He needed to hold it together. Barging in and making demands would only make this more difficult. Especially if Melody told them he actually wasn't her fiancé. He took a second to collect himself and asked, in a much calmer tone, "Can I see her?"

"Of course, but why don't we have a talk first."

He wanted to see Melody now, but he followed the doctor to a small family waiting room by the elevator. The room was empty, but for a television in the corner playing some daytime game show. He sat and gestured for Ash to join him.

"How much do you know about the accident?" the doctor asked.

"I was told that the car rolled, and there was one fatality."

"Your fiancée is a very lucky woman, Mr. Williams. She was driving on a back road when the crash occurred and it was several hours before someone drove past and discovered her there. She was airlifted here for treatment, but if the local EMS team hadn't worked so quickly, you would be having this conversation with the coroner."

A knot twisted his insides. It was surreal to imagine that he had come so close to losing Melody for good, and the thought of her lying trapped and alone, not knowing if she would live or die, made him sick to his stomach. He may have been angry that she left him, but he still cared deeply for her. "What was the extent of her injuries?"

"She suffered a subdural hematoma."

"A brain injury?"

He nodded. "Until two days ago she's been in a drug-induced coma."

"But she'll recover?"

"We expect her to make a full recovery."

Ash's relief was so intense, his body went limp. If he hadn't already been sitting, he was sure his legs would have given out from under him.

"Although," the doctor added, his expression darkening, "there were a few…complications."

Ash frowned. "What complications?"

"I'm sorry to have to tell you that she lost the baby."

"Baby?" he asked, the doctor's words not making any sense. Melody wasn't having a baby.

The doctor blinked. "I'm sorry, I just assumed you knew that she was pregnant."

Why would Ash even suspect such a thing when the radiation from childhood cancer had rendered him sterile? It had to be a mistake. "You're *sure?*"

"Absolutely."

The only explanation, Ash realized, was that Melody had been cheating on him. The knot in his gut twisted tighter, making it difficult to take a full breath. Is that where Melody had been going when she left him? To be with her lover? The father of her child?

And like a love-sick fool Ash had been chasing after her, prepared to convince her to come home. She had betrayed him, after all that he had done for her, and he hadn't suspected a damned thing.

His first reaction was to get up, walk out of the hospital and never look back, but his body refused to cooperate. He needed to see her, just one last time. He needed to know why the hell she would do this to him, when he had given her everything she had ever asked for, everything she could have ever needed. She could have at least had the decency, and the courage, to be honest with him.

He could see that the doctor was curious to know why, as her fiancé, Ash hadn't known about the pregnancy, but Ash didn't feel he owed him or anyone else an explanation. "How far along was she?" he asked.

"Around fourteen weeks, we think."

"You think? Didn't she say?"

"We haven't mentioned the miscarriage. We think it would be too upsetting at this point in her recovery."

"So she believes she's still pregnant?"

"She has no idea that she was pregnant when she was in the accident."

Ash frowned. That made no sense. "How could she not know?"

"I'm sorry to have to tell you, Mr. Williams, but your fiancée has amnesia."

The gripping fingers of a relentless headache squeezed Melody's brain. A dull, insistent throb, as though a vice was being cranked tighter and tighter against her skull.

"Time for your pain meds," her nurse chirped, materializing at the side of the bed as though Melody had summoned her by sheer will.

Or had she hit the call button? She honestly couldn't remember. Things were still a bit fuzzy, but the doctor told her that was perfectly normal. She just needed time for the anesthesia to leave her system.

The nurse held out a small plastic cup of pills and a glass of water. "Can you swallow these for me, hon?"

Yes, she could, she thought, swallowing gingerly, the cool water feeling good on her scratchy throat. She knew how to swallow pills, and brush her teeth, and control the television remote. She could use a fork and a knife and she'd had no trouble reading the gossip rags the nurse had brought for her.

So why, she wondered, did she not recognize her own name?

She couldn't recall a single thing about her life, not even the auto accident that was apparently responsible for her current condition. As for her life before the accident, it was as if someone had reached inside her head and wiped her memory slate clean.

Post-traumatic amnesia, the neurologist called it, and when she'd asked how long it would last, his answer hadn't been encouraging.

"The brain is a mysterious organ. One we still know so little about," he'd told her. "Your condition could last a week, or a month. Or there's a possibility that it could be permanent. We'll just have to wait and see."

She didn't want to wait. She wanted answers *now*. Everyone kept telling her how lucky she'd been. Other than the head injury, she had escaped the accident relatively unscathed. A few bumps and bruises mostly. No broken bones or serious lacerations. No permanent physical scars. However, as she flipped through the television channels, knowing she must have favorite programs but seeing only unfamiliar faces, or as she picked at the food on her meal tray, clueless as to her likes and dislikes, she didn't feel very lucky. In fact, she felt cursed. As though God was punishing her for some horrible thing that she couldn't even remember doing.

The nurse checked her IV, jotted something on her chart, then told Melody, "Just buzz if you need anything."

Answers, Melody thought as the nurse disappeared into the hall. All she wanted was answers.

She reached up and felt the inch-long row of stitches

above her left ear where they had drilled a nickel-size hole to reduce the swelling on her brain, relieving the pressure that would have otherwise squeezed her damaged brain literally to death.

They had snatched her back from the brink of death, only now she wondered what kind of life they had snatched her back to. According to the social worker who had been in to see her, Melody had no living relatives. No siblings, no children, and no record of ever having been married. If she had friends or colleagues, she had no memory of them, and not a single person had come to visit her.

Had she always been this…alone?

Her address was listed as San Francisco, California—wherever that was—some sixteen hundred miles from the site of the accident. It perplexed her how she could still recognize words and numbers, while photos of the city she had supposedly lived in for three years drew a complete blank. She was also curious to know what she had been doing so far from home. A vacation maybe? Was she visiting friends? If so, wouldn't they have been concerned when she never showed up?

Or was it something more sinister?

After waking from the coma, she'd dumped the contents of her purse on the bed, hoping something might spark a memory. She was stunned when, along with a wallet, nail file, hairbrush and a few tubes of lip gloss, a stack of cash an inch thick tumbled out from under the bottom lining. She quickly shoved it back in the bag before anyone could see, and later that night, when the halls had gone quiet, she counted it. There had been over four thousand dollars in various denominations.

Was she on the run? Had she done something illegal? Maybe knocked off a convenience station on the way out of town? If so, wouldn't the police have arrested her by now?

She was sure there was some perfectly logical explanation. But just in case, for now anyway, she was keeping her discovery to herself. She kept the bag in bed with her at all times, the strap looped firmly around her wrist.

Just in case.

Melody heard voices in the hallway outside her room and craned her neck to see who was there. Two men stood just outside her door. Dr. Nelson, her neurologist, and a second man she didn't recognize. Which wasn't unusual seeing as how she didn't recognize anyone.

Could he be another doctor maybe? God knew she had seen her share in the past couple of days. But something about him, the way he carried himself, even though she only saw him in profile, told her he wasn't a part of the hospital staff. This man was someone…important. Someone of a higher authority.

The first thing that came to mind of course was a police detective, and her heart did a somersault with a triple twist. Maybe the police had seen the money in her purse and they sent someone to question her. Then she realized that no one on a public servant's pay could afford such an expensive suit. She didn't even know how she knew that it was expensive, but she did. Somewhere deep down she instinctively knew she should recognize the clothes designer, yet the name refused to surface. And it didn't escape her attention how well the man inside the suit wore it. She didn't doubt it was tailored to fit him exclusively.

The man listened intently as the doctor spoke, nodding occasionally. Who could he be? Did he know her? He must, or why else would they be standing in her doorway?

The man turned in her direction, caught her blatantly staring, and when his eyes met hers, her heart did that weird flippy thing again. The only way to describe him was…intense. His eyes were clear and intelligent, his build long and lean, his features sharp and angular. And he was ridiculously attractive. Like someone straight off the television or the pages of her gossip mags.

He said a few words to the doctor, his eyes never straying from hers, then entered her room, walking to the bed, no hesitation or reserve, that air of authority preceding him like a living, breathing entity.

Whoever this man was, he knew exactly what he wanted, and she didn't doubt he would go to any lengths to get it.

"You have a visitor, Melody." Only when Dr. Nelson spoke did she realize he'd walked in, too.

The man stood silently beside her bed, watching her with eyes that were a striking combination of green and brown flecks rimmed in deep amber—as unique and intense as the rest of him.

He looked as though he expected her to say something. She wasn't sure what though.

Dr. Nelson walked around to stand at the opposite side of her bed, his presence a comfort as she felt herself begin to wither under the stranger's scrutiny. Why did he look at her that way? Almost as though he was angry with her.

"Does he look familiar to you?" Dr. Nelson asked.

He was undeniably easy on the eyes, but she couldn't say that she'd ever seen him before. Melody shook her head. "Should he?"

The men exchanged a look, and for some reason her heart sank.

"Melody," Dr. Nelson said, in a soothing and patient voice. "This Asher Williams. Your fiancé."

Two

Melody shook her head, unwilling to accept what the doctor was telling her. She didn't even know why. It just didn't feel right. Maybe it was the way he was looking at her, as if her being in an accident had somehow been a slight against him. Shouldn't he be relieved that she was alive?

So where were his tears of joy? Why didn't he gather her up and hold her?

"No, he isn't," she said.

The doctor frowned, and her so-called fiancé looked taken aback.

"You remember?" Dr. Nelson asked.

"No. But I just know. That man can't be my fiancé."

Tension hung like a foul odor in the room. No one seemed to know what to do or say next.

"Would you excuse us, Doctor?" her imposter fiancé said, and Melody felt a quick and sharp stab of panic. She didn't want to be alone with him. Something about his presence was just so disconcerting.

"I'd like him to stay," she said.

"Actually, I do have patients I need to see." He flashed Melody an encouraging smile and gave her arm a gentle pat. "The nurse is just down the hall if you need anything."

That wasn't very reassuring. What did they even know about this man? Did they check out his story at all, or take him on his word? He could be a rapist or an ax murderer. A criminal who preyed on innocent women with amnesia. Or even worse, maybe he was the person she had taken that cash from. Maybe he was here for revenge.

She tucked her purse closer to her side under the covers, until she was practically sitting on it.

The phrase *never show fear* popped into her head, although from where, she didn't have a clue. But it was smart advice, so she lifted her chin as he grabbed a chair and pulled it up to the side of her bed. He removed his jacket and draped it over the back before he sat down. He wasn't a big man, more lean than muscular, so why did she feel this nervous energy? This instinct to run?

He eased the chair closer to her side and she instinctively jerked upright. So much for not showing fear. Even in repose the man had an assuming presence.

"You don't have to be afraid of me," he said.

"Do you honestly expect me to just take your word that we're engaged?" she asked. "You could be...*anyone*."

"Do you have your driver's license?"

"Why?"

He reached into his back pants pocket and she tensed again. "Relax. I'm just grabbing my wallet. Look at the address on my driver's license." He handed his wallet to her.

The first thing she noticed, as she flipped it open, was

that there were no photos, nothing of a personal nature, and the second thing was the thick stack of cash tucked inside. And yes, the address on his license was the same as hers. She knew without checking her own license because she had read it over and over about a thousand times yesterday, hoping it would trigger some sort of memory. A visual representation of the place she'd lived.

Of course, it hadn't.

She handed his wallet back to him, and he stuck it in his pocket. "That doesn't prove anything. If we're really engaged, where is my ring?" She held up her hand, so he could see her naked finger. A man of his obvious wealth would have bought the woman he planned to marry a huge rock.

He reached into his shirt pocket and produced a ring box. He snapped it open and inside was a diamond ring with a stone so enormous and sparkly it nearly took her breath away. "One of the prongs came loose and it was at the jeweler's being repaired."

He handed it to her, but she shook her head. She still wasn't ready to accept this. Although, what man would offer what must have been a ridiculously expensive ring to a woman who wasn't his fiancée?

Of course, one quick thwack with the ax and it would easily be his again.

She cringed and chastised herself for the gruesome thought.

"Maybe you should hang on to it for now, just to be safe," she told him.

"No. I don't care if you believe me or not." He rose from his chair and reached for her hand, and it took everything in her not to flinch. "This belongs to you."

The ring slid with ease on her finger. A perfect fit. Could

it just be a coincidence? It was becoming increasingly difficult not to believe him.

"I have these, too," he said, leaning down to take a stack of photos from the inside of his jacket. He gave them to her, then sat back down.

The pictures were indeed of her and this Asher person. She skimmed them, and in each and every one they were either smiling or laughing or...*oh, my*...some were rather racy in nature.

Her cheeks blushed brightly and a grin quirked up the corner of his mouth. "I included a few from our *personal* collection, so there wouldn't be any doubt."

In one of the shots Asher wore nothing but a pair of boxer briefs and the sight of all that lean muscle and smooth skin caused an unexpected jab of longing that she felt deep inside her belly. A memory, maybe, or just a natural female reaction to the sight of an attractive man.

"I have video, as well," he said. She was going to ask what kind of video, but his expression said it all. The look in his eyes was so steamy it nearly melted her. "Due to their scandalous nature, I felt it best to leave them at home," he added.

Melody couldn't imagine she was the type of woman who would let herself be photographed, or even worse videotaped, in a compromising position with a man she didn't trust completely.

Maybe Asher Williams really was her fiancé.

Ash's first suspicion, when the doctor told him Melody had amnesia, was that she was faking it. But then he asked himself, why would she? What logical reason did she have to pretend that she didn't know him? Besides, he doubted that anyone in her physical condition could convincingly fabricate the look of bewildered shock she wore when the doctor told her Ash was her fiancé.

Of course, she had managed to keep the baby she was carrying a secret, and the affair she'd been having. After the initial shock of her betrayal had worn off, he'd felt nothing but seething, bone-deep anger. After all he had done for her—paying her living expenses and college tuition, giving her credit cards to purchase everything her greedy heart had desired, taking care of her for *three* years—how could she so callously betray him?

Coincidentally, just like his ex-wife. He hadn't had a clue then either. One would think he'd have learned his lesson the first time. And though his first instinct had been to walk out the door and never look back, he'd had an even better idea.

This time he would get revenge.

He would keep up the ruse of their engagement and take Melody home. He would make her fall in love with him, depend on him, then he would betray her, just as cold-heartedly and callously as she had him. And he wouldn't lose a single night's sleep over it.

"What was I doing in Texas alone?" Melody asked him, still not totally convinced.

Ash had anticipated this question and had an answer already prepared. "A research trip."

"Research for what?"

"A paper you were working on for school."

She looked puzzled. "I go to school?"

"You're in law school."

"I am?" she asked, looking stunned.

"You have a year to go before you take the bar exam."

Her brow furrowed and she reached up to rub her temple. "Not if I can't remember anything I've learned."

"I don't care what the doctors say," he told her, taking her hand, and this time she didn't flinch. "You'll get your memory back."

Her grateful smile almost filled him with guilt. Almost.

"So you just let me go on this trip, no questions asked?"

He gave her hand a squeeze. "I trust you, Mel."

The comment hit its mark, and the really pathetic thing was that it used to be true. He never would have guessed that Melody would do something like this to him.

"How long was I gone?"

"A few weeks," he lied. "I began to worry when you stopped answering your phone. I tried to find you myself, but that went nowhere fast. I was beside myself with worry, Mel. I thought something terrible had happened. I thought…I thought that you were dead. That I would never see you again." The fabricated emotion in his voice sounded genuine, even to his own ears, and Melody was eating it up. "The police were no help, so I hired a private detective."

"And here you are."

He nodded. "Here I am. And I would really like to hold my fiancée. If she would let me."

Melody bit her lip, and with gratitude in her eyes, held her arms out. She bought his bull—hook, line and sinker. This was almost too easy.

Ash rose from his chair and sat on the edge of her bed, and when he took her in his arms and she melted against him, soft and warm and a little fragile, he had a flash of something that felt like relief, or maybe satisfaction, then he reminded himself exactly what it was that brought them to this place. How deeply she had betrayed him. His first instinct was to push her away, but he had to play the role of the loving fiancé.

She let her head rest on his shoulder and her arms slipped around his back. The contour of her body felt so familiar to him, and he couldn't help wondering what it must have been like for her, holding a stranger. Some deep place inside him wanted to feel sympathy, but she had brought this on herself. If she hadn't cheated on him, hadn't stolen away like a criminal, she never would have been in the accident and everything would be normal.

As her arms tightened around him, he did notice that she felt frailer than before, as though not only had she lost pounds, but muscle mass. Their building had an exercise room and as long as Ash had known her, Melody had been almost fanatical about staying in shape. He wondered if this would be a blow to her ego.

But how could it be if she didn't even remember she *had* an ego? Or maybe that was something that was inborn.

Under the circumstances Ash didn't expect the embrace to last long, and he kept waiting for her to pull away. Instead she moved closer, held him tighter, and after a moment he realized that she was trembling.

"Are you okay?" he asked, lifting a hand to stroke her hair.

"I'm scared," she said, her voice small and soft. Melody wasn't a crier—in three years together he could recall only two times he'd even seen the sheen of moisture in her eyes—but he could swear that now he heard tears in her voice.

"What are you scared of?" he asked, stroking her hair and her back, pretending to comfort her, when in reality he felt that she was getting exactly what she deserved.

"Everything," she said. "I'm afraid of all I don't know,

and everything I need to learn. What if I'm never..." She shook her head against his chest.

He held her away from him, so he could see her face. Melody was a fighter. Much like himself, when she wanted something, she went after it with all pistons firing. It was what had drawn him to her in the first place. But right now, he couldn't recall ever seeing her look more pale and distraught, and he actually had to harden his heart to keep from feeling sorry for her.

She had brought this on herself.

"If you never what?" he asked.

Her eyes were full of uncertainty. "What if I can't be the person I was before? What if the accident changed me? What will I do with my life? Who will I be?"

Not the heartless betrayer she had been before the accident. Not if he had anything to do with it. He would break her spirit, so no other man would have to suffer the same humiliation he had.

A tear spilled over onto her cheek and he wiped it away with his thumb, cradling her cheek in his palm. "Why don't you concentrate on getting better? Everything will work out. I promise."

Looking as though she desperately wanted to believe him, she leaned her head back down and sighed against his shoulder. And maybe she did believe him, because she was no longer shaking.

"I'm getting sleepy," she said.

"I'm not surprised. You've had an eventful morning. Why don't you lie down?"

He helped her lie back against the pillows. She did look exhausted. Mentally and physically.

He pulled the covers up and tucked them around her, much the way his mother had for him when he was a boy. When he'd been sick, and weakened by the radiation, she'd somehow managed to be there every evening to kiss him goodnight, despite working two, and sometimes three jobs at a time to keep their heads above water. Until she'd literally worked herself to death.

Though Ash was declared cancer free by his thirteenth birthday, the medical bills had mounted. His father had been too lazy and most times too drunk to hold down a job, so the responsibility of taking care of them had fallen solely on his mother. And due to their debt, annual trips to the doctor for preventative care that wasn't covered by their insurance had been a luxury she couldn't afford. By the time she'd begun getting symptoms and the cancer was discovered, it had already metastasized and spread to most of her major organs. The news had sent his father into a downward spiral, and it was left up to Ash to take care of her.

Eight months later, and barely a week after Ash graduated from high school, she was gone. For years, he felt partially responsible for her death. Had it not been for his own cancer, they might have caught hers sooner, when it was still treatable.

The day of his mother's funeral was the day Ash had written his father out of his life for good. His aunt had contacted him several years later to let him know that his father had passed away. Advanced liver cirrhosis. Ash didn't go to the funeral.

By then Ash was living in California, and going to school. Like his mother, he worked two and three jobs to make ends meet. Despite that, he'd somehow managed to maintain a near-perfect GPA. After graduation he'd married his college sweetheart and landed a job with Maddox Communications, convinced he was living the American dream. Unfortunately things had not been what they seemed.

The day he was offered the position of CFO, what should have been one of the best days of his life, he'd learned that his wife was having an affair. She'd claimed she did it because she was lonely. He'd worked such long hours he was never there for her. She sure hadn't minded spending the money he earned working those long hours, though. Not to mention, when he *had* been home, the "I have a headache" excuse was a regular. The irony of it would have been laughable had he not been so completely devastated.

Granted, theirs had never been a particularly passionate marriage, but he'd thought they were relatively happy. Apparently not. And the worst part had been that he hadn't suspected a thing.

Ash had thought he was through with women for good, but only a few months after the divorce was final he met Melody. She was young and beautiful and bright, and he was fascinated by her spunk and enthusiasm. Probably because he saw much of himself mirrored back in her eyes.

They had come from similar humble beginnings, and, like him, she was determined to succeed. They'd started dating in early April. The last week of May when the sublet on her apartment expired, he'd suggested she stay with him until she found another place, and she just never left.

Since then they seemed to have an unwritten understanding. She made herself accessible to him in any capacity necessary with no strings attached. There were no sentiments of love or talk of marriage, no questions or accusations when he worked late or cancelled a date. In return he provided financial security.

At times, he couldn't help thinking he was getting the better end of the deal. Not only did he have a willing mistress at his disposal 24/7, he also had the satisfaction of knowing that he was helping her make something of her life. If his mother had someone like that, someone to take care of her, she might still be alive.

Helping Melody had, in his own way, been a tribute to his mother. An homage to her strength and character, and as far as he was concerned, Melody had betrayed her, too.

He gazed down at Melody and realized she was sound asleep. For several minutes he just watched her, wondering what could have driven her to be unfaithful to him. When had she changed her mind, and decided that she wanted more than what they had? And why hadn't she just told him the truth? If she'd truly wanted out, he would have respected that. He wouldn't have liked it, and he would have tried to talk her out of leaving, but he would have eventually let her go. No strings attached.

Instead she had thrown back in his face everything he had ever done for her.

"How is she?" someone asked, and Ash turned to see Dr. Nelson standing in the doorway.

"Sleeping."

"I just wanted to stop back in once more before I left."

"I'm glad you did. We never discussed when I could take her home. I'd like to make travel arrangements."

He gestured Ash into the hall. "If she continues to improve, I would say a week to ten days."

"That long? She seems to be doing so well."

"She suffered a severe brain injury. You can't necessarily see the damage, but believe me, it's there." He paused then added, "When you say home, I assume you mean California."

"Of course."

"You should know that flying will be out of the question."

"Not even in my company's private jet?"

"She had a brain bleed. The change in pressure could very literally kill her. Frankly, I'm not crazy about the idea of her being on the road for that long either, but I guess there aren't any other options."

Sixteen hundred miles trapped in a car together. Not his idea of fun. Besides, he wanted to get her home and settled before she remembered something. If she ever did.

"I was wondering," Ash said. "If she does regain her memory, how long will it take?"

"There's no definitive answer that I can give you, Mr. Williams. If she does regain any memories, it can be a slow and sometimes traumatic process. Just be thankful that she's doing as well as she is. It will just take time and patience."

Unfortunately he had little of either.

"Even if she doesn't regain her memories," he added, "there's no reason to expect that you two won't live a long and happy life together regardless."

Actually, there was one damned good reason. Whether she remembered it or not, Melody had crossed him. It was time she got a taste of her own medicine.

But to make this work, Ash had a bit of cleaning up to do first.

Three

When Melody opened her eyes again, Ash wasn't in the room. She had the sudden, terrifying sensation that everything that had happened earlier was a dream or a hallucination. Then she lifted her hand, saw the diamond on her ring finger and relief washed over her.

It was real.

But where did Ash go? She pushed herself up on her elbows to look around and saw the note he'd left on the tray beside her:

> Went to get your things. Back later to see you.
> XOXO
> Ash

She wondered where he was going to get them, then realized she must have been staying in a hotel when she'd had her accident. But that was more than two weeks ago.

Wouldn't they have discarded her things by now? Did hotels hang on to the items abandoned by their customers?

She hoped so. Maybe there was something among her things that would spark a memory, and she was interested to see this so-called research Ash had been talking about. Not that she didn't believe him. It was just that something about this whole scenario was…off.

If what he said was true, and she was only here for school, what was she doing with four thousand dollars hidden in the lining of her purse? Was she trying to bribe someone, or buy information? Had she gotten herself into something illegal that she had been afraid to tell him? What if her accident hadn't been an accident after all?

And even worse, what if the person she was trying to get away from was Ash?

She realized just how ridiculous that sounded and that she was letting her imagination run away from her. She'd seen the photos; they were obviously very happy together. She was sure that the expression she'd mistaken for anger when he'd first entered her room was just his reaction to learning that she didn't remember him. After all, how would she feel if the man she had planned to spend the rest of her life with forgot who she was? Then insisted that she supply proof of their relationship? That would be devastating.

There were other things that disturbed her, as well. It seemed as though the news that she was in law school would evoke some sort of emotion. If not excitement, then maybe mild curiosity. Instead she'd just felt…disconnected. As though he were talking about another woman's life. One she had little interest in. And in a way maybe she was.

She was sure that once she got home and back into a regular routine, things would come back to her. She would be more interested in things like her career and her hobbies. If she had any hobbies. She hadn't even thought to ask him. There were all sorts of things he could tell her about her life.

She heard footsteps in the hall, her spirits lifting when she thought it might be Ash, but it was only the nurse.

"I see you're awake," she said with her usual cheery disposition. "How are you feeling?"

"Better," she said, and it was true. She still had a million questions, but at least now she knew that when she was discharged from the hospital, she would have somewhere to go. There was someone out there who loved and cared about her.

"I saw your fiancé," the nurse said as she checked Melody's IV. "He's very handsome. But that just stands to reason, I guess."

"Why?"

"Well, because you're so pretty."

"I am?"

The nurse laughed. "Well, of course you are."

She made it sound so obvious, but when Melody had seen her reflection the other day, the only thing she noticed was that a stranger's eyes stared back at her. She didn't stop to consider whether she was attractive. It just didn't seem important at the time.

"I hear that you're in law school," the nurse said, jotting something down on Melody's chart. "I never would have guessed."

"Why is that?"

She shrugged. "Oh, I don't know. I guess you just don't seem the type. I think of lawyers as pushy and overbearing. You're not like that at all."

She wondered what she *was* like, but she was a little afraid to ask.

The nurse closed her chart and asked, "Is there anything you need?"

She shook her head.

"Okay, well, you ring if you need me."

When she was gone Melody considered what she said. What if she really wasn't cut out to be a lawyer? Would she be throwing all those years of school down the toilet?

But honestly, what did the nurse know of her? She was not going to plan the rest of her life around a comment made by someone who had known her for less than three days. And not at her best, obviously. Maybe when she was back on her feet and feeling like her old self she would be lawyer material again. A real shark.

Or, as she had considered earlier, maybe the accident had changed her.

There was really no point in worrying about it now. Like the doctor said, she needed to concentrate on healing. It was sage advice, because the sooner she got back to her life, the sooner she would get her memory back. And in the meantime she was sure, with a fiancé like Ash to take care of her, everything was going to be okay.

Ash stood in the impound lot at the Abilene police station, heart in the pit of his stomach, knees weak, looking at what was left of Melody's Audi Roadster. Suddenly he understood why everyone kept saying that she was lucky to be alive.

Not only was it totaled, it was barely recognizable. He knew it was a rollover accident, he just hadn't realized how *far* it had rolled, and the momentum it had gained by the time it hit the tree that had ultimately stopped it. The passenger's side was pretty much gone, completely crushed inward.

Had she hit the tree on the driver's side, there was no

doubt she wouldn't have survived. Also, Mel always drove with the top down, but apparently it had been raining, so when she flipped over there was at least something there to keep her from snapping her neck. Although just barely, because the top, too, was crushed, and at some point had come loose and was hanging by a single bolt.

He hated Melody for what she had done to him, but he wouldn't wish an accident like this on his worst enemy.

According to the police, she'd tried to swerve out of the way when she saw the bike. Unfortunately it had been too late.

He walked over and peered in the driver's side, immediately seeing what he was looking for. He tried the door but it was hopelessly jammed. With one hand he pushed the top out of the way then reached around the steering wheel and grabbed the keys from the ignition. He hit the release for the trunk, but it didn't budge, and he had no better luck with the key. If there was anything in there, she was going to have to live without it.

He turned to walk back to the entrance, then as an afterthought, walked back and snapped some pictures with his phone. The matter had already been reported to his insurance company, but it never hurt to be thorough and keep a record for his own reference.

When he was back in his rental car, he punched the address the P.I. had given him into the GPS and followed the commands until he was parked in front of a house about fifteen minutes from the hospital.

The house itself was tiny but well-kept, although the neighborhood left a lot to be desired. How could she go from a penthouse condo to living in what was barely a step above a slum? To be with her lover? If so, the guy had to be a loser. Although if she had come here to be with her lover, why hadn't he been at the hospital with her?

Well, if there was someone else there, he was about to find out.

There were no cars in the driveway, and the curtains were drawn. He walked to the front door with purpose, slid the key in, and opened it. The first thing that hit him was a rush of cool air punctuated by the rancid stench of rotting food. At that point he knew it was safe to assume that she lived alone. No one would be able to stand the odor.

Covering his face with a handkerchief, he walked through a small living room with outdated, discount-store furniture, snapping on lights and opening windows as he made to the kitchen. He saw the culprit right away, an unopened package of ground beef on a faded, worn countertop, next to a stove that was probably older than him. She must have taken it out to thaw right before the accident.

He opened the kitchen window, then, for the landlord's sake he grabbed the package and tossed it in the freezer. He was sure the contents of the fridge were similarly frightening, but since neither he nor Mel would be returning, he didn't feel compelled to check.

There was nothing else remarkable about the room, so he moved on to explore the rest of the house.

The bathroom counter was covered with various toiletries that he didn't recognize—and why would he when they didn't share a bathroom—but everything was distinctly feminine. He checked the medicine chest and the cabinet below the sink but there was no evidence that a man had ever lived there.

He searched her bedroom next, finding more old and tacky furniture, and an unmade bed. Which was odd because back home she always kept things tidy and spotless. He found a lot of familiar-looking clothes in the closet and drawers, but again, nothing to suggest she'd had any male companionship. Not even a box of condoms in the bedside table. He and Melody had at one time kept them handy, but not for quite some time. They were monogamous, and he was sterile, so there really never seemed a point.

She had obviously had unprotected sex with someone, or she wouldn't have gotten pregnant. It hadn't even occurred to him earlier, but now he wondered if he should go get himself tested for STDs. Melody had callously put her own health and his in jeopardy. One more thing to hold against her.

He searched the entire room, top to bottom, but didn't find the one thing he was looking for. He was about to leave when, as an afterthought, Ash pulled back the comforter on the bed and hit pay dirt.

Melody's computer.

In the past he would have never betrayed her trust by looking through her computer. He respected her privacy, just as she respected his. But she had lost that particular privilege when she betrayed him. Besides, the information it contained might be the only clue as to who she was sleeping with. The only explanation as to why she left him. She owed him that much.

He wanted to look at it immediately but he honestly wasn't sure how much longer he could stand the stench and he still had to pack Melody's things. Most of her clothes he would ship home and have his secretary put away, keeping only a smaller bag in Texas, to make his two-week trip story more believable.

He looked at his watch and realized he was going to have to get moving if he was going to get back to the hospital before visiting hours were over. Though he was exhausted, and wanted nothing more that to go back to the hotel and take a hot shower, he had to play the role of the doting fiancé.

He crammed her things into the suitcases he found stored in her bedroom closet, shoved everything into the trunk of his rental car to sort later, then headed back to the hospital, but when he got there she was sleeping. Realizing that he hadn't eaten since that morning—and then only a hurried fast-food sandwich before his flight boarded—rather than eat an overpriced, sub-par meal in the cafeteria, he found a family diner a few blocks away. It wasn't the Ritz, but the food was decent, and he had the sneaking suspicion he would be eating there a lot in the next week to ten days. When he got back to Mel's room she was awake, sitting up and clearly relieved and excited to see him. "I was afraid you wouldn't make it back."

"I said in my note that I would be back. I just had a few things to take care of." He pulled up a chair but she patted the bed for him to sit beside her.

She looked a lot better than she had earlier. Her eyes were brighter and there was more color in her cheeks, and as he sat, he noticed that her hair was damp. As if reading his mind, she said, "They let me take a shower. It felt *so* wonderful. And tomorrow they want me to start walking, to get the strength back in my legs."

"That's good, right?"

"The nurse said the sooner I'm up and moving around on my own, the sooner they'll discharge me." She reached for his hand, and he had no choice but to take it. "I can hardly wait to go home. I'm sure that once I'm there, I'll start to remember things."

He hoped not. At least, not for a while. That could definitely complicate things. "I'm sure it will," he told her.

"Did the hotel still have my things?" she asked hopefully.

"Hotel?"

Her brow furrowed. "I just assumed I was staying at a hotel, while I did my research."

He cursed himself for letting his guard down. The last thing he wanted was to rouse her suspicions. He swiftly backpedaled.

"You were. I just thought for a second that you remembered something. And yes, they did. Your suitcase is in the trunk of my car. I'll keep it at my hotel until you're released."

"What about my research? Were there papers or files or anything?"

"Not that I saw," he said, realizing that the lies were coming easier now. "But your laptop was there."

Her eyes lit with excitement. "There might be something on it that will shake my memory!"

"I thought of that. I booted it up, but it's password protected, so unless you remember the password…." He watched as Melody's excitement fizzled away. "Tell you what," he said. "When we get back to San Francisco I'll have the tech people at work take a look at it. Maybe they can hack their way in."

"Okay," she agreed, looking a little less defeated, but he could see that she was disappointed.

In reality, he would be calling work at his soonest convenience and with any luck one of the tech guys could walk him through hacking the system himself. Only after he removed anything pertaining to the baby or the affair, or anything personal that might jog her memory, would he let her have it back.

It would be easier to have the hard drive reformatted, but that might look too suspicious. He'd thought of not mentioning the laptop at all, but it stood to reason that since she was a student, she would have one.

He could have lied and said it was destroyed in the accident, but unfortunately it was too late for that now.

"Can you do me a favor?" she asked.

"Sure."

"Can you tell me about myself?"

"Like what?"

"My family, my friends, where I'm from. Anything."

The truth was, despite living together for three years, he didn't know a heck of a lot about Melody. If she had friends at school, she didn't mention them, and when she wasn't in school, he really wasn't sure what she did with her time, other than cooking his dinners, cleaning their condo and of course shopping. She had always kept personal things pretty close to the vest. Either that or he had just never thought to ask.

But she looked so hopeful, he had to come up with something.

"Your mom died before I met you," he told her. "Ovarian cancer, I think. You told me that you never knew your real father, but you'd had something like five or six stepfathers growing up."

"Wow, that's a lot. Where did I grow up?"

He struggled to remember what she had told him when they first met. "All over, I think. You said that she moved you around a lot. I know you resented it."

Just as he had resented so many things from his own childhood. The cancer not even being the worst of it. But he was in no mood to dredge that up. Besides, she had no idea that he'd been sick. It just never came up. He and Mel knew each other, especially in the biblical sense, but they didn't really *know* each other.

He'd been so sure that was the way he'd wanted it, so jaded by his marriage, he never considered that he might want more. Not until it was too late.

Four

Melody had this look, like the playground bully had just stolen her candy. "Wow. It sounds like I had a pretty lousy childhood."

Ash felt a jab of guilt for painting such a grim picture.

"I'm sure there were good things," he told her. "You just never talked about it much."

"How did we meet?"

The memory brought a smile to his face. Now, this was something he remembered. "A company party. At Maddox Communications."

"That's where you work, right?"

He nodded. "You were there with some cocky junior rep. Brent somebody. A real jerk. But the instant I saw you standing by the bar, wearing this slinky little black number, I couldn't look away. Hell, every man in the room had their eye on you. He was droning on, probably thinking he was hot shit because he was with the sexiest woman at the party, and you had this look like you were counting the minutes until you could send him and his overinflated ego packing. You looked over and saw me watching you. You gave me a thorough once-over, then flashed me this sexy smile."

Her eyes went wide. "*I* did that?"

Her surprise made him laugh. "Yeah. At that point I had no choice but to rescue you. So I walked over and asked you to dance."

"How did my date feel about that?"

Ash grinned, recalling the shocked look on the kid's face, the indignant glare as Ash led Mel onto the dance floor and pulled her into his arms. "He didn't look very happy."

"What did he do?"

"What could he do? I was CFO, he was a lowly junior rep. I could have squashed him. Although, if memory serves, someone else eventually did. I don't think he lasted long with the firm."

"So we danced?" she said, a dreamy look on her face.

"All night." Ash had been the envy of every man at the party. At the time he'd still been reeling from his divorce and the ego boost was a welcome one. It wasn't until later that he realized just how thorough of a *boost* she intended to give him.

"Then what happened?" she asked.

"You asked if you could see my office, so I took you there. The instant the door closed we were all over each other."

She swallowed hard, looking as scandalized as she was intrigued. And maybe a little turned on, too. "Then what?"

"You really have to ask?"

"We had *sex* in your office?" she asked in a hushed voice, as if she worried someone would overhear. "Right after we met?"

This from the woman who had never hesitated to tell him exactly what she wanted, when she wanted it, in the bluntest of sexual terms. Language that would make a lot of women blush. Or blanch.

He grinned and nodded. "On the desk, on the sofa, in my chair. Up against the plate-glass window overlooking the bay."

Her cheeks flushed bright pink. "We did it against a *window?*"

"You've always had voyeuristic tendencies." He'd never met a woman more confident, more comfortable in her own skin, than Melody. Though he would never admit it aloud, her brazen nature could be the slightest bit intimidating at times.

But obviously now something had changed. There was a vulnerability in her eyes that he'd never seen before. A hesitance she had never shown. Truth be told, he kind of liked it. And maybe it softened him up just a little. He may have supported Mel for the past three years, but he would never make the mistake of thinking that she depended on him. Had she not met him, she would have managed just fine on her own.

He'd forgotten what it felt like to have someone need him.

"I can't believe I slept with you on the first date," she said. "I can't imagine what you must have thought of me."

"Actually, with my divorce barely final, it was exactly what I needed."

"You were married before?"

"For seven years."

"Why did you split up?"

"I guess you could say it was due to a total lack of appreciation."

"What do you mean?"

"She didn't appreciate the hours I worked, and I didn't appreciate her screwing her personal trainer in my bed."

She sucked in a surprised breath, clearly outraged on his behalf. "She *cheated* on you?"

"For quite some time as I understand it." He wondered how Melody would feel if she knew she had done the same thing? Although, as far as he knew, never in *his* bed. But that was just geography. Cheating was cheating.

Melody tightened her grip on his hand. He hadn't even realized she was holding it. It occurred to him suddenly how cozy this little scenario had become. Too cozy for his liking.

He pulled his hand free and looked at his watch. "It's late. I should let you get some sleep."

"Did I say something wrong?" she asked, looking troubled. "Because if it bothers you to talk about your ex, we can talk about something else."

Frankly, he was all talked out. He wasn't sure what else to say to her. And he wished she would stop being so… nice. Not that she hadn't been nice before, but she'd always had an edge. A sharp wit and a razor-edged tongue. Now she was being so sweet and understanding, she was making it tough for him to hold on to his anger. To be objective.

"You didn't say anything wrong. It's just, well, it's been a really long day. Maybe I'm the one who's tired."

"I'm sorry, I'm being selfish," she said, looking truly apologetic. "I didn't even take into consideration how hard this has been for you."

"It has been a long couple of weeks not knowing where

you were," he said, which only made her look more guilty. "I'm sure I'll feel better after a good night's sleep."

"Go," she said, making a shooing gesture. "Get some sleep."

"Are you sure? I can stay longer if you want me to."

"No. I'm tired anyway. I'll probably watch a few minutes of television then fall asleep."

He had the distinct feeling she was lying, because honestly, she didn't look the least bit tired. But he wasn't going to argue.

"I'll be back first thing tomorrow," he assured her, rising from the edge of the bed.

"Thank you," she said, her expression earnest.

"For what?"

"Telling me those things about myself. It makes me feel a little less…lost. Even if it wasn't quite what I expected."

"You're welcome," he said, and leaned down to brush a kiss across her forehead. "I'll see you tomorrow."

As he walked from the room he heard the television click on. He couldn't help feeling the slightest bit guilty for leaving her alone, but he had a charade to plan.

It turned out that Ash didn't need the help of the tech guys at Maddox Communications to hack into Melody's computer. After only five or six tries, he figured the password out all by himself. His birthday. The fact that it was something so simple surprised him a little, but he was grateful.

His first task was to remove evidence of Melody's affair from her computer, only she must have been very careful because he found nothing, not even a phone number or an entry in her calendar, that suggested she was sneaking around.

As for the baby, there were a few doctor appointments

listed on her calendar, and the history in her Internet browser showed visits to several children's furniture store sites and a site called Mom-to-be.com, where it appeared she had been tracking her pregnancy—she was fourteen weeks and four days on the day of the accident—and blogging on a page for single mothers.

Apparently she had every intention of doing this alone. Was it possible that the father of the baby was nothing more than a one-night stand? A glorified sperm donor?

He skimmed the entries she had written, hoping to find a clue as to who the man was, or the circumstances surrounding their relationship. But after more than an hour of reading, all he'd learned was that the baby's father was, in her words, *not involved.* He noted that some of the earlier posts dated back to the weeks before she left him. It was also clear, by the tone of her posts, that she was very excited to be a mother, which surprised him.

She had always been so independent and career focused, he didn't think she even wanted a family. Of course, that was never something they talked about. Maybe because she knew that if she wanted children, she wouldn't be having them with him. Not naturally anyway. Knowing that he couldn't father a child of his own, he'd resigned himself to the idea of not having them at all.

What he found even more disturbing than the information about the baby was a file folder with electronic copies of her report cards. They dated back the past four semesters. Whenever Ash asked her about school, which admittedly wasn't very often, Mel claimed things were going great. Which was hard to believe now that he saw that she had been clinging to a low C average, when he knew for a fact that in her first year she'd never scored anything lower than an A minus.

It was as if she had lost her interest in the law. But if that was the case, why hadn't she said anything? It was true that they didn't normally talk about those kinds of things, but going to school for a career she no longer wanted seemed worth mentioning. Especially when he was shelling out the money for her tuition.

The more Ash looked through her files and read her e-mails, the more he began to realize that after three years together, he barely knew Melody. She lived a life that, outside the bedroom, had little to do with him. And though that was the way he'd always wanted it, he couldn't help but feel…indignant. And maybe a little angry with himself for not taking the time to get to know her better.

He may have been there for her financially, but even he had to admit that emotionally, he'd been pretty much vacant.

Which was exactly what they had agreed to going into this relationship, so he had no absolutely no reason to feel as though he had wronged her somehow.

If that was true, why did he feel like such a jerk?

Maybe his ex was right. Maybe he'd been too cold and distant. Maybe he used work as an escape from dealing with the ups and downs of his personal relationships. And maybe, like his ex-wife, Melody had grown tired of the distance. Tired of being alone.

Regardless of what she felt, that was no excuse to be unfaithful. If she wanted more, she should have leveled with him. Although for the life of him, he wasn't sure what he would have told her. If she had given him an ultimatum—a real relationship or she would find someone new—would he have been able to just let her go? A real relationship just seemed like so much work. More than he had time for.

But he was here now, wasn't he? He had *made* the time for this. Didn't that tell him something?

Sure it did, he just wasn't sure what. But he knew that at some point he was going to have to figure it out. Maybe it was simply that being with Melody had been very easy, and he wasn't quite ready to give that up.

Unfortunately, remembering how good things had been made her betrayal sting that much more.

Just as he promised, Ash was back at the hospital as soon as visiting hours began the next morning. He was dressed casually this time, in slacks and a silk, button-down shirt. And she could tell, as he walked into the room, a sly grin on his face, that he was holding something behind his back. Probably flowers.

"Wow, you look great," he said, and she knew he wasn't just saying it to be nice because the nurse had said the same thing.

"I feel really good," she admitted, and she was pretty sure it had a lot to do with him. Before he came to see her yesterday she had felt so depressed and alone. As though she had nothing to look forward to, no reason to get better. Everything was different now. She was engaged to be married, and had a home to return to. A whole life to explore and relearn. What more could she ask for?

"I got my appetite back in a big way. I just finished breakfast and I'm already anxious for lunch. Although I have to say, the food here leaves a lot to be desired."

"There's a diner a few blocks from here that has decent food. Maybe I can pick you up something for lunch, if it's okay with your doctor."

"I'll make sure the nurse asks him. I could go for a big juicy burger and greasy French fries."

"I didn't know you liked burgers and fries."

"What do I usually eat?"

"Salads and chicken mostly. Occasionally you'll have

red meat, but not more than once a week. You've always been extremely health conscious."

"Well, I keep seeing these fast-food ads and every time they show a burger my mouth starts to water. I'll worry about being health conscious when I'm out of the hospital." Which was a completely backward way of looking at it, she realized, but she didn't even care. Eating like a rabbit wouldn't build her strength and get her the heck out of here.

"A burger and fries it is then," he said, and he was still hiding whatever it was he was holding behind his back.

"So, are you going to show me what you've got there, or make me guess?" she asked.

"You mean this?" he asked, his smile widening as he pulled a laptop from behind him.

"Is that mine?" she asked and he nodded. "I thought it was password protected. Did you talk to the guys at work already?"

He set it in her lap. "I didn't have to. I made a few educated guesses and figured it out for myself."

She squealed with excitement. "Oh, my gosh! You're my hero!"

He regarded her quizzically, as if she had just said something totally off the wall.

"What?" she asked. "Why are you looking at me like that?"

"Sorry. I just never imagined you as the kind of a woman who would have a hero. You're far too self-sufficient."

"Well, I do now," she said with a smile. "And it's you."

She opened the laptop and pressed the button to boot it up, relieved that at least she recalled how. When the password screen popped up, she looked to Ash.

"Type in one, one, nineteen, seventy-five."

"What is it?"

"My birthday."

I guess it made sense that she would use her fiancé's birthday as a password. Unless she didn't want him getting into her files, which obviously wasn't an issue. She typed the digits in and the system screen popped up. "It worked!"

"You remember how to use it?"

She nodded. Like so many other things, navigating the computer just seemed to come naturally. She only hoped that the information it contained would spark other memories. Personal memories.

"I'm going to head down to the gift store and see if they have a *Wall Street Journal*," Ash said, and Melody nodded, only half listening as she began opening files on her desktop. "If they don't, I might try to find one at the party store around the block."

"'Kay," she said. "Take your time."

She started with her e-mail, thinking saved messages would hold the most information, but there weren't many. And of the dozen or so, most were from Ash. It seemed a little strange, especially being in school, that she didn't have more, but it was always possible she kept them on an off-site server for safekeeping. Especially if they were for her supposed research, and were of a high security nature.

Or maybe her imagination was getting the best of her again.

She opened her calendar next, going back for several months, and found nothing but her school schedule, a few theater and party dates with Ash, and of course her research trip, which according to this should have ended a few days after her accident. She also found a recent appointment with a wedding planner that they had missed, and realized that not only were they engaged, but apparently they had already set a date. One they would probably be forced to postpone now.

She quit out of her calendar and opened her photo file, but either she kept her pictures online or on a disk, or she wasn't a very sentimental person, because there were very few. Shots of herself and Ash, mostly. None of friends or fellow students. And none of family, which was no surprise since she didn't have any.

She did have a vast music library, and while she liked the various songs she sampled, she didn't relate them to any specific memories or events.

She went through file after file, but not a single thing, not even her school papers, looked familiar to her. She tried to be logical about it. She had barely been out of her coma for four days and the doctor had said it would take time. *Logically* she knew this, and she was trying to heed his advice. Emotionally though, she felt like putting her fist through the nearest wall.

"I hope you're not doing schoolwork already!" the nurse said as she walked in to check Melody's IV. Which was kind of a ridiculous notion, since not only would Melody not have a clue what work had been assigned, but even if she did, she wouldn't have any idea how to do it. She didn't remember anything about the law. But she had to cut the nurse some slack. It probably wasn't often she dealt with amnesia patients.

"I'm just looking at photos and things," Melody told her. "I was hoping I would remember something."

"That's a great idea! How's it going?"

"Nothing so far."

She hung a fresh IV bag and tossed the empty one in the trash by the sink. "Dr. Nelson would like to see you up and moving around today. But only with assistance," she added sternly.

Melody wouldn't dare try it alone. When she'd taken her shower earlier the nurse had to help her, and she had to shower sitting down. Her legs felt like limp spaghetti noodles and she was so dizzy she was having trouble staying upright.

"We could take a few practice steps right now," the nurse suggested, a not-so-subtle nudge, but Melody wasn't quite ready to put her computer aside.

"Could we maybe do it after lunch?" she asked.

"All right, but don't put it off too long. You need to rebuild your strength."

Melody knew that better than everyone else. And though walking might still be a challenge, she could feel herself improving by leaps and bounds. She gave most of the credit to Ash.

He'd given her something to fight for.

Five

After the nurse left, Melody went back to the photo file on her computer and opened a few of herself and Ash. When she looked at herself, it was still a bit like looking at a stranger. It was her, but not exactly her.

Her clothes were obviously expensive and quite form-fitting. The healthy eating must have paid off because she was very trim and fit—although now, after being in the coma, she looked a little gaunt. She seemed to like to show off her cleavage, which admittedly she had a fair amount of. She peeked under her hospital gown at her breasts and decided that she must own some pretty amazing push-up bras.

In the photos her hair was always fixed in a sleek and chic style that she couldn't help thinking must have taken ages in front of the bathroom mirror to perfect. So unlike the casual, wavy locks she was sporting now. Also, she wore a considerable amount of makeup and it was always flawlessly applied. She looked very well put together.

Just the thought of the time it must have taken to get ready each morning left her feeling exhausted. Maybe, when she was up and around again, she would feel differently. Although she couldn't help thinking she looked a bit...*vain.* But she was sure these photos represented only a small segment of her life. Who didn't like to look good for pictures? And she couldn't deny that she and Ash made one heck of a good-looking couple.

How would he feel if she didn't go back to being that perfectly put together woman? Would he be disappointed? Or did he love her for the woman inside?

The latter, she hoped. If not, would he be here by her side while she healed?

"Still at it?" the man in question said, and she looked up to find him standing at the foot of the bed. Ash was holding a newspaper in one hand and a brown paper sack in the other.

"You're back already?" she asked.

"Already? I've been gone almost two hours."

"Has it really been that long?" She would have guessed twenty-five or thirty minutes.

"I had to make a few calls to work, and I figured you wouldn't mind the time alone. Which apparently you didn't." He nodded to her computer. "Any luck?"

She closed the computer and shook her head, trying not to let it discourage her, or to dwell on it. "I've looked at pretty much all of it and I don't recognize a thing." She gestured to the bag he was holding. "What's that?"

"I stopped at the nurses' station on my way out this morning, and they called the doctor, who said there's no reason to have you on a restricted diet, so..." He pulled a white foam restaurant container from the bag. "Your burger and fries, madam."

The scent of the food wafted her way and her mouth instantly started to water. Now she knew why she was marrying Ash. He was clearly the sweetest man in the world.

"You're wonderful!" she said as he set it on her tray. "I can see why I fell in love with you."

He gave her another one of those funny looks, as though the sentiment was totally unexpected or out of character.

"What? Don't tell me I've never said I love you."

"It's not that. I just…" He shook his head. "I just didn't expect to hear anything like that so soon. I guess I figured you would have to take the time to get to know me again."

"Well, I sure like what I've seen so far." She opened the container top, her taste buds going berserk in anticipation. Her stomach growled and, up until that instant, she didn't even realize she was hungry. She automatically grabbed a packet of ketchup, tore it open with her teeth, and drizzled it over her fries. Ash pulled out a similar container for himself and set it beside hers on the tray, but his was a BLT with coleslaw. He sat on the edge of the mattress near her to eat.

The fries were greasy and salty, and by far the best thing Melody had eaten in days. Or maybe *ever*. And when she took a bite of her burger it was pure nirvana.

"How did your calls to work go?" she asked. "Are they upset that you'll be gone for a while?"

He shrugged. "Doesn't matter how they feel. They don't have a say in the matter."

She frowned. "I would feel awful if I got you in trouble, or even worse, if you got fired because of me."

"Don't worry. They aren't going to fire me. I'm the

best damned CFO they've ever had. Besides, they know that if they did let me go, their competitor, Golden Gate Promotions, would probably snap me up. The owner, Athos Koteas, would do just about anything for an edge. And that would be very bad for Maddox."

"Not if your contract has a noncompete clause," she said, stuffing a fry in her mouth. "Working for a competitor would be a direct breach. They could sue the pants off you. And I'm sure they would."

When she glanced up, Ash had gone still with his sandwich halfway to his mouth, and he was giving her that "look" again. Why did he keep doing that? "What? Do I have ketchup on my face or something?"

"Mel, do you realize what you just said?"

She hit rewind and ran it through her head again, stunned when the meaning of her words sank in. "I was talking like a lawyer."

Ash nodded.

"Oh, my gosh! I didn't even think about it. It just… popped out." A huge smile crept across her face. "I remembered something!"

Granted it was nothing important, or personal, but it was *something*. She tried to dredge up some other legal jargon, but her mind went blank. Maybe that was just the way it was going to be. Maybe it would come back in little bits and pieces. At that rate she would have her full memory back by the time she and Ash retired, she thought wryly.

"For the record," he said, "I did have a noncompete clause and they removed it when I refused to sign."

Maybe it was her imagination, but she had the feeling Ash didn't share in her happiness. It was as if he thought her remembering something was a *bad* thing.

It was just one more little thing that seemed…off.

She shook the thought away. She was being ridiculous.

Of course he wanted her to remember things. Didn't he? What reason would he have not to?

That, she realized, was what she needed to find out.

That had been a close call, Ash thought as he and Mel ate lunch. In hindsight, bringing her computer might not have been the brightest idea he'd ever had, but doing it today, instead of waiting until they got back to San Francisco, had sort of been an accident. He'd grabbed it on his way out the door when he left for the hospital. He didn't like the idea of leaving it in the room, for fear that it might be stolen. But as he climbed into his rental, the interior, at nine in the morning, was already about a million degrees. Assuming he would be in the hospital most of the day, it didn't seem wise to leave the laptop in the car, in the blistering heat.

What choice did he have but to bring it into the hospital with him, and as a result, give it to Melody? What if it did spark a memory? Was he willing to jeopardize his plans? He'd been up half the night removing personal information, so it seemed unlikely anything would shake loose a memory.

To confuse her, and hopefully buy himself a little more time, he not only removed things from the computer, but *added* a few things, as well.

To give her the impression they attended social functions together—when in reality they rarely went out socially—he added a few entries for fictional theater dates and parties. He also included a meeting with a wedding planner, which he thought was a nice touch. One they had regretfully missed because Mel had been missing.

The most brilliant switch, in his opinion, was her music. He knew from experience that some songs evoked specific memories or feelings. Like the knot he got in his stomach whenever he heard "Hey Jude" by the Beatles, the song that was playing the day he drove home to break the good news about his promotion and found his ex in bed with her personal trainer.

So, he deleted Mel's entire music catalog and replaced it with his own music library. Mel had always preferred current pop music, while he listened to classic rock and jazz. There wasn't much chance that would be jogging any memories.

Now he was wondering if that hadn't been enough. Or maybe the memories were going to come back regardless. Either way, he didn't want to panic prematurely. Remembering something about the law was still a far cry from regaining her personal memories.

He looked over at Melody and realized she'd stopped eating with nearly half her burger and fries still left.

"Full already?" he asked.

"Is there something you're not telling me?" she asked. "Something you don't want me to know?"

The question came so far out of left field he was struck dumb for several seconds, and when his brain finally kicked back in he figured it would be in his best interest to *play* dumb. "What do you mean?"

She pushed her tray aside. "I just get this nagging feeling that you're hiding something from me."

He could play this one of two ways. He could act angry and indignant, but in his experience that just screamed *guilty*. So instead he went for the wounded angle.

He pasted on a baffled expression and said, "God, Mel, why would you think that? If I did or said something to hurt your feelings…" He shrugged helplessly.

The arrow hit its mark. Melody looked crushed.

"Of course you haven't. You've been wonderful." She reached out and put her hand on his forearm. "You've done so much for me and I'm acting completely ungrateful. Just forget I said anything."

He laid his hand over hers and gave it a squeeze. "You suffered a severe head injury. You were in a coma for two weeks." He flashed her a sympathetic smile. "I promise I won't hold it against you."

Her smile was a grateful one. And of course, he felt like slime for playing on her emotions. For using it to his advantage.

Remember what she did to you, he told himself. Although, one thing he couldn't deny was that Melody was not the woman she'd been before the accident. In the past, she *never* would have confronted him this way with her suspicions. Yet, at the same time, she was much softer and compassionate than she used to be. Not to mention uncharacteristically open with her emotions.

When she told him she loved him he'd felt…well, he honestly wasn't sure *what* he'd felt. It was just…unusual. No one had said that to him in a long time. He and his wife had stopped expressing sentiments of love long before the final meltdown. The pain of their breakup had been less about lost love than the humiliation of her deceit, and his own stupidity for not seeing her for what she really was.

In the long run he honestly believed she had done him a favor, although he could have done without seeing the proof with his own eyes.

Even if Melody thought she loved Ash, she obviously didn't mean it or she wouldn't have cheated on him in the first place. Besides, their relationship wasn't about love. It was more about mutual respect and convenience. She was only saying what she thought she was *supposed* to say. She probably just assumed that she would never be engaged to a man she didn't love. But that was all part of the plan, wasn't it? To make her believe that they were in love. And apparently it was working.

He couldn't deny that in her current condition, he was having a tough time keeping a grip on the anger he'd felt when he learned about her pregnancy. He was sure that once he got her back home and she started acting like her old self, the wounds would feel fresh again. He would approach the situation with a renewed sense of vengeance.

He was counting on it.

Six days after Ash arrived in Abilene, after showing what Dr. Nelson said was remarkable progress, Melody was finally released from the hospital. An orderly wheeled her down to the front entrance, her heart pounding in anticipation of finally being free, and as they exited the building, a wall of hot, dry air washed over her.

She hoped their place in San Francisco had a courtyard or a balcony, because after being cooped up in the hospital for so long, she wanted to spend lots of time outside. She closed her eyes and breathed in deep, felt the sun beat down hot on her face as she was wheeled from under the awning to the curb where Ash waited with his rental car. It was barely 10:00 a.m. and it had to be pushing ninety degrees. The sun was so bright, she had to raise a hand to shade her eyes. She wasn't sure of the make of the vehicle, but it looked expensive.

Ash had dressed casually for the trip, in jeans and a T-shirt, and Melody didn't miss the group of nurses following him with their eyes, practically drooling on their scrubs.

Look all you like ladies, but he's mine.

Not that Melody blamed them for gawking. He looked hot as hell dressed that way. The shirt accentuated the width of his shoulders and showed off the lean muscle in his arms, and the jeans hugged his behind in a way that gave her impure thoughts. She could hardly wait until she was feeling well enough to have sex again. Right now, if she did anything marginally taxing, her head began to pound.

As soon as they reached the car Ash opened the door. A rush of cool air cut through the heat as he helped her from the chair to the front seat. The interior was soft black leather, and it had what looked like a top-of-the-line sound and navigation system. Ash got her settled in and helped with her seat belt, and as he leaned over her to fasten it, he smelled so delicious she wanted to bury her face in the crook of his neck and take a nibble. When he seemed convinced she was securely fastened in, with her seat as far back as it would go—just in case the airbag deployed and bonked her head, rattling her already compromised brain—he walked around and got in the driver's side. "Are you ready?" he asked.

"I am *so* ready."

He turned the key and the engine hummed to life, and as he pulled from the curb and down the driveway toward the road, she had this odd feeling of urgency. She felt that if he didn't hurry, the staff members were going to change their minds and chase her down like a fugitive, or an escaped mental patient, and make her go back to that awful room.

It wasn't until he pulled out onto the main road and hit the gas, and the hospital finally disappeared out of sight, that she could breathe easy again. She was finally free. As long as she lived, she hoped she never had to stay in a hospital room again.

He glanced over at her. "You all right?"

"I am now."

"You're comfortable?" he asked.

"Very." He'd brought her suitcase to the hospital and she'd chosen a pair of jeans and a cotton shirt to start the trip. She'd tried to find a bra she liked, but either they were push-up and squeezed her breasts to within an inch of her life or they were made of itchy lace, so she'd opted not to wear one at all. As long as she didn't get cold, or pull her shirt taut, it was kind of hard to tell. Besides, it was just her and Ash and he'd seen her breasts plenty of times before.

The jeans were comfortable, and although at one point she was guessing they were pretty tight, now they hung off her. Despite her constant cravings for food, her eyes were bigger than her stomach, but Dr. Nelson assured her that her appetite would return.

She'd opted to wear flip-flops on her feet and toed them off the instant she was in the car, keeping them within reach should she happen to need them.

Other than the dull ache in her temples, she couldn't be more comfortable.

"If you need to stop for any reason just let me know," Ash told her. "And if the driving gets to be too much we'll stop and get a hotel room."

"I'm sure I'll be fine." If it were at all possible, she wished they could drive straight through until they got to San Francisco, but it was a twenty-four-hour trip and she knew Ash would have to sleep at some point. Still, she wanted to stay on the road as long as possible. The sooner they got home, the better. She was convinced that once she was there, surrounded by her own possessions, her memories would begin to return.

Ash turned onto the I-20 on-ramp, hit the gas and zoomed onto the freeway, shooting like a rocket into traffic.

"This is pretty nice for a rental," she told him.

"It's not a rental," he said as he maneuvered left into the fast lane. "This is my car."

His car? "I thought you flew here."

"I did, but I wanted you to be comfortable on the way home so I arranged to have my car brought to Texas. It arrived yesterday morning."

That couldn't have been cheap. She'd never asked Ash about their financial situation, but apparently CFOs at San Francisco ad agencies made decent money.

"It looks expensive," she said. "The car, I mean."

He shrugged. "I like nice cars."

"So I guess you do okay? Financially."

He flashed her a side glance, one of those funny looks that had become so familiar this past week. "Are you asking how much I make?"

"No! Of course not. It's just, well…you wear expensive clothes and drive an expensive car. So I'm assuming you make a decent living, that's all."

"I do okay," he said, a grin kicking up one corner of his mouth, as though the idea of her even asking amused him. And she knew that if she asked exactly how much he made, he would probably tell her. It just wasn't that important.

All that mattered to her was how wonderful he'd been this week. Other than running an occasional errand, or stepping out to pick up food, Ash hadn't left her side. He got there every morning after visiting hours started and didn't leave until they ended at ten. She had been off her feet for so long and her muscles had deteriorated so much that at first walking had been a challenge. Because she was determined to get out of there as soon as humanly possible, Melody had paced, back and forth, up and down the corridors for hours to build her strength. And Ash had been right there by her side.

At first, she'd literally needed him there to hang on to, or to lean on when her balance got hinky. It was frustrating, not being able to do something as simple as taking a few steps unassisted, but Ash kept pumping her full of encouragement and, after the second day, she could manage with only her IV pole to steady her. When they finally removed her IV, she'd been a little wary at first, but realized she was steady enough walking without it. Yesterday she had been chugging along at a pretty good pace when Dr. Nelson came by to let her know she would be released in the morning. He had already discussed her case with a neurologist in San Francisco—one of the best, he said—and Melody would go in to see him as soon as they were home.

Melody's lids started to feel droopy and she realized the pain pills the nurse had given her right before she was discharged were starting to kick in.

Ash must have noticed because he said, "Why don't you put your seat back? It's the lever on the right. And there's a pillow and blanket in the backseat if you need them."

The man thought of *everything*.

It was plenty warm in the car, even with the air on, but the pillow sounded good. She reclined her seat then grabbed the pillow from the back and tucked it under her head. She sighed and snuggled into the buttery-soft leather, sure that her hospital bed hadn't been half as comfortable. She wanted to stay awake, to keep Ash company, but her lids just didn't want to cooperate, so finally she stopped fighting it and let them close. It couldn't have been ten seconds before she slipped into a deep, dreamless sleep.

Six

Melody woke, disoriented and confused, expecting to be in her hospital bed. The she remembered she'd been set free and smiled, even though her head ached so hard she was sure that her eyeballs were going to pop from their sockets.

"Have a good nap?"

She looked over and saw Ash gazing down at her, a bottle of soda in his hand. Only then did she realize they were no longer moving. She rubbed her eyes, giving them a gentle push inward, just in case, and asked, "Why are we stopped?"

"Lunch break."

She looked up and saw that they were parked in a fast-food restaurant lot.

"I was just going in to grab a burger. Do you want anything?"

"No, I'm good. But my head is pounding. What time is it?"

"After three."

She'd been asleep for *five* hours?

"It's probably the elevation. Do you need a pain pill?"

She nodded, so he opened the glove box and pulled out the prescription they had filled at the hospital pharmacy. "One or two?"

One pill wouldn't put her to sleep, and she would be able to keep Ash company, but gauging the pain in her head, she needed two. "Two, I think."

He tapped them out of the bottle and offered his soda to wash them down. "I'm going in. You sure you don't want anything?"

"I'm sure."

While he was gone she lay back and closed her eyes. She must have drifted off again because when the car door opened, it startled her awake.

Ash was back with a bag of food. He unwrapped his burger in his lap and set his fries in the console cup holder. It wasn't until they were back on the highway, and the aroma permeated the interior, when her stomach started to rumble in protest.

Maybe she was hungry after all. Every time he took a bite her jaw tightened and her mouth watered.

After a while Ash asked, "Is there a reason you're watching me eat?"

She didn't realize how intently she'd been staring. "Um, no?"

"You wouldn't be hungry, would you?" he asked.

She was starving, but she couldn't very well ask him to turn around and go back. "I can wait until the next stop."

"Look in the bag," he told her.

She did, and found another burger and fries inside.

"I kind of figured once you saw me eating you would be hungry, too."

"Just one more reason why I love you," she said, diving into her food with gusto.

She was only able to eat about half, so Ash polished off the rest. When she was finished eating the painkillers had kicked in and she dozed off with her stomach pleasantly full. A few hours later she roused for a trip to the rest stop, and as soon as the car was moving again, promptly fell back to sleep. The next time she opened her eyes it was dark and they were parked in front of an economy hotel. She realized that Ash was standing outside the open passenger door, his hand was on her shoulder, and he was nudging her awake.

"What time is it?" she asked groggily.

"After eleven. We're stopping for the night," he said. "I got us a room."

Thirteen hours down, eleven to go, she thought. Maybe this time tomorrow they would be home.

He helped her out and across the parking lot. All the sleep should have energized her, but she was still exhausted, and her head hurt worse than it had before. Maybe this trip was harder on her system than she realized.

Their bags were already inside and sitting on the bed.

"They didn't have any doubles left and there isn't another hotel for miles," he said apologetically. "If you don't want to share, I can sack out on the floor."

They had shared a bed for *three* years. Of course, she had no memory of that. Maybe he was worried that she would feel strange sleeping with him until they got to know one another better. Which she had to admit was pretty sweet. It was a little unusual being with him this late at night, since he always left the hospital by ten. But actually, it was kind of nice.

"I don't mind sharing," she assured him.

"How's your head feel?"

She rubbed her left temple. "Like it's going to implode. Or explode. I'm not sure which."

He tapped two painkillers out and got her a glass of water. "Maybe a hot shower would help."

She swallowed them and said, "It probably would."

"You can use the bathroom first."

She stepped in the bathroom and closed the door, smiling when she saw that he'd set her toiletry bag on the edge of the sink. He seriously could not take better care of her.

She dropped her clothes on the mat and blasted the water as hot as she could stand then stepped under the spray. She soaped up, then washed and conditioned her hair, then she closed her eyes and leaned against the wall, letting the water beat down on her. When she felt herself listing to one side her eyes flew open and she jerked upright, realizing that she had actually drifted off to sleep.

She shut the water off and climbed out, wrapping herself in a towel that reeked of bleach. She combed her hair and brushed her teeth, grabbed her dirty clothes, and when she stepped out of the bathroom Ash was lying in bed with the television controller in one hand, watching a news program.

"Your turn," she said.

He glanced over at her, did a quick double take, then turned back to the TV screen. "I thought I was going to have to call in the national guard," he said. "You were in there a while."

"Sorry. I fell asleep in the shower."

"On or off?" he said, gesturing to the TV.

"Off. The second my head hits the pillow I'll be out cold."

He switched it off and rolled out of bed, grabbing the pajama bottoms he'd set out. "Out in a minute," he said as he stepped in the bathroom and shut the door. Less than ten seconds later she heard the shower turn on.

Barely able to keep her eyes open, Melody walked on wobbly legs to the bed. She'd forgotten to grab something to sleep in from her suitcase, and with her case on the floor across the room, it hardly seemed worth the effort. It wasn't as if he had never seen her naked before, and if she was okay with it, she was sure he would be, too.

She dropped her towel on the floor and climbed under the covers, her mind going soft and fuzzy as the painkillers started to do their job.

At some point she heard the bathroom door open and heard Ash moving around in the room, then she felt the covers shift, and she could swear she heard Ash curse under his breath. It seemed as though it was a long time before she felt the bed sink under his weight, or maybe it was just her mind playing tricks on her. But finally she felt him settle into bed, his arm not much more than an inch from her own, its heat radiating out to touch her.

She drifted back to sleep and woke in the darkness with something warm and smooth under her cheek. It took a second to realize that it was Ash's chest. He was flat on his back and she was lying draped across him. At some point she must have cuddled up to him. She wondered if they slept like this all the time. She hoped so, because she liked it. It felt nice to be so close to him.

The next time she woke up, she could see the hint of sunlight through a break in the curtains. She was still lying on Ash, her leg thrown over one of his, and his arm was looped around her, his hand resting on her bare hip.

The covers had slipped down just low enough for her to see the tent in his pajama bottoms. It looked…well…*big,* and for the first time since the accident she felt the honest-to-goodness tug of sexual arousal. She suddenly became ultra-aware of her body pressed against his. Her nipples pulled into two hard points and started to tingle, until it felt as though the only relief would come from rubbing them against his warm skin. In fact, she had the urge to rub her entire body all over his. She arched her back, drawing his leg deeper between her thighs, and as she did, her thigh brushed against his erection. He groaned in his sleep and sank his fingers into the flesh of her hip. Tingles of desire shivered straight through to her core.

It felt so good to be touched, and she wanted more; unfortunately, the more turned on she became, and the faster her blood raced through her veins, the more her head began to throb. She took a deep breath to calm her hammering heart. It was clear that it would be a while before she was ready to put her body through the stress of making love.

That didn't make her want Ash any less, and it didn't seem fair to make him keep waiting, after having already gone through months of abstinence, when there was no reason why she couldn't make him feel good.

Didn't she owe him for being so good to her? For sticking by her side?

Melody looked at the tent in his pajamas, imagined putting her hand inside, and was hit with a sudden and overwhelming urge to touch him, a need to please him that seemed to come from somewhere deep inside, almost like a shadowy memory, hazy and distant and just out of reach. It had never occurred to her before, but maybe being intimate with him would jog her memory.

She slid her hand down his taut and warm stomach,

under the waistband of his pajama bottoms. She felt the muscle just below the skin contract and harden under her touch. She moved lower still, tunneling her fingers through the wiry hair at the base. He was so warm there, as if all the heat in his body had trickled down to pool in that one spot.

She played there for just a few seconds, drawing her fingers back and forth through his hair, wondering what was going on in his head. Other than the tensing of his abdomen and the slight wrinkle between his brows, he appeared to be sleeping soundly.

When the anticipation became too much, she slid her hand up and wrapped it around his erection. The months without sex must have taken their toll because he was rock hard, and as she stroked her way upward, running her thumb along the tip, it was already wet and slippery.

She couldn't recall ever having done this before— though she was sure she had, probably more times than she could count—but she inherently seemed to know what to do, knew what he liked. She kept her grip firm and her pace slow and even, and Ash seemed to like it. She could see the blood pulsing at the base of his throat and his hips started to move in time with her strokes. She looked up, watching his face. She could tell he was beginning to wake up, and she wanted to see his expression when he did.

His breath was coming faster now and his head thrashed from one side to the other, then back again. She was sure that all he needed was one little push…

She turned her face toward his chest, took his nipple in her mouth, then bit down. Not hard enough to leave a mark, only to arouse, and it worked like a charm. A groan ripped from Ash's chest and his hips bucked upward, locking as his body let go. His fingers dug into her flesh, then he relaxed and went slack beneath her.

Mel looked up at him and found that he was looking back at her, drowsy and a little disoriented, as if he were still caught somewhere between asleep and awake. He looked down at her hand still gripping him inside his pajamas. She waited for the smile to curl his mouth, for him to tell her how good she made him feel, but instead he frowned and snapped, "Mel, what are you doing?"

Mel snatched her hand from inside Ash's pajamas, grabbed the sheet and yanked it up to cover herself. He couldn't tell if she was angry or hurt, or a little of both. But Melody didn't do angry. Not with him anyway. At least, she never *used* to.

"I think the appropriate thing to say at a time like this is thanks, that felt great," she snapped.

Yep, that was definitely anger.

"That did feel great. The part I was *awake* for." Which wasn't much.

He knew last night, when he'd pulled back the covers and discovered she was naked, that sleeping next to her would be a bad idea. When he woke in the middle of the night with her draped over him like a wet noodle, limp and soft and sleeping soundly, he knew that he should have rolled her over onto her own side of the bed, but he was too tired, and too comfortable to work up the will. And yeah, maybe it felt good, too. But he sure as hell hadn't expected to wake up this morning with her hand in his pants.

Before the accident it would have been par for the course. If he had a nickel for every time he'd roused in the morning in the middle of a hot dream to find Melody straddling him, or giving him head.

But now he almost felt…violated.

Looked as if he should have listened to his instincts and slept on the damned floor.

The worst thing about this was seeing her there barely covered with the sheet, one long, lithe leg peeking out from underneath, the luscious curve of her left breast exposed, her hair adorably mussed, and all he could think about was tossing her down on the mattress and having his way with her.

Sex with Melody had always been off-the-charts fantastic. *Always.* She had been willing to try anything at least once, and would go to practically any lengths to please him. In fact, there were times when she could be a little *too* adventurous and enthusiastic. Three years into their relationship they made love as often and as enthusiastically as their first time when it was all exciting and new—right up until the day she walked out on him.

But when it came to staying angry with her, seeing her in such a compromised condition and knowing that she had no recollection of cheating on him took some of the wind out of his sails. For now. When she got her memory back, that would be a whole other story.

But that did not mean he was ready to immediately hop back into bed with her. When, and *if,* he was ready to have sex with her, he would let her know. He was calling the shots this time.

"I don't get why you're so upset about this," she said, sounding indignant, and a little dejected.

"You could have woken me up and asked if it was okay."

"Well, seeing as how we're *engaged,* I really didn't think it would be a problem."

"You're not ready for sex."

"Which is why I don't expect anything from you. I was perfectly content just making you feel good. Most guys—"

"Most guys would not expect their fiancée, who just

suffered a serious head injury, to get them off. Especially one who's still too fragile to have him return the favor. Did you ever stop to think that I might feel guilty?"

Some of her anger fizzled away. "But it's been months for you, and I just thought…it just didn't seem fair."

Fair? "Okay, so it's been months. So what? I'm not a sex fiend. You may have noticed that my puny reptile brain functions just fine without it."

That made her crack a smile. "It didn't seem right that you had to suffer because of me. I just wanted to make you happy."

Is that what she had been doing the past three years? Making him happy? Had she believed that she needed to constantly please him sexually to keep him interested? Did she think that because he paid for her school, her room and board, kept her living a lifestyle many women would envy, that she was his…*sex slave?* And had he *ever* given her a reason to believe otherwise?

For him, their relationship was as much about companionship as sex. Although, in three years, of all the times she had offered herself so freely, not to mention enthusiastically, had he ever once stopped her and said, "Let's just talk instead?"

Was that why she cheated on him? Did she need someone who treated her like an equal and not a sex object?

If she felt that way, she should have said so. But since they were stuck together for a while, he should at least set the record straight.

"The thing is, Mel, I'm *not* suffering. And even if I was, you don't owe me anything."

"You sure looked like you were this morning when I woke up," she said.

"Mel, I'm a guy. I could be getting laid ten times a day

and I would still wake up with a hard-on. It's part of the outdoor plumbing package."

She smiled and he offered his hand for her to take. She had to let go of the sheet on one side and it dropped down, completely baring her left breast. It was firm and plump, her nipples small and rosy, and it took all the restraint he could muster not to lean forward and take her into his mouth. He realized he was staring and tore his gaze away to look in her eyes, but she'd seen, and he had the feeling she knew exactly what he'd been thinking.

"Not suffering, huh?" she said with a wry smile.

Well, not anymore. Not much anyway.

"I honestly believe that we need to take this slow," he said. "If you're not physically ready, we wait. *Both* of us."

"Okay," she agreed solemnly, giving his hand a squeeze. "You mind if I use the bathroom first, or do you want it?"

"Go ahead."

She rolled out of bed and he assumed she intended to take the sheet along to cover herself. Instead she let it fall and stood there in all her naked glory, thinner than she'd been, almost to point of looking a little bony, but still sexy and desirable as hell.

Instead of walking straight into the bathroom, she went the opposite way to her suitcase, her hair falling in mussed waves over her shoulders, the sway of her hips mesmerizing him. He expected her to lift her case and set it on the bed, but instead she bent at the waist to unzip her case right there. She stood not five feet away, her back to him, legs spread just far enough to give him a perfect view of her goods, and he damn near swallowed his own tongue. He saw two perfect globes of soft flesh that he was desperate to get his hands on, her thighs long and milky white, and what lay between them…damn. Doing him must have turned her on, too, because he could see traces of moisture glistening along her folds.

He had to fist the blankets to keep himself from reaching out and touching her. To stop himself from dropping to his knees and taking her into his mouth. He even caught himself licking his lips in anticipation.

She seemed to take an unnecessarily long time rifling through her clothes, choosing what to wear, then she straightened. He pulled the covers across his lap, so she wouldn't notice that conspicuous rise in his pajamas, but she didn't even look his way; then, as she stepped into the bathroom she tossed him a quick, wicked smile over her shoulder.

If that little display had been some sort of revenge for snapping at her earlier, she sure as hell knew how to hit where it stung.

Seven

They got back on the road late that morning—although it was Melody's own fault.

She'd already had a mild headache when she woke up, compounded by the sexual arousal, but bending over like that to open her case, and the pressure it had put on her head, had been a really bad move. The pain went from marginally cumbersome to oh-my-God-kill-me-now excruciating. But it had almost been worth it to see the look on Ash's face.

She popped two painkillers then got dressed, thinking she would lie down while Ash got ready then she would be fine. Unfortunately it was the kind of sick, throbbing pain that was nearly unbearable, and exacerbated by the tiniest movement.

Ash's first reaction was to drive her to the nearest hospital, but she convinced him that all she needed was a little quiet, and another hour or so of sleep. She urged him to go and get himself a nice breakfast, and wake her when he got back.

Instead, he let her sleep until almost eleven-thirty! It was nearly noon by the time they got on the road, and she realized, with a sinking heart, that they would never make it back to San Francisco that evening. On the bright side she managed to stay awake for most of the drive, and was able to enjoy the scenery as it passed. Ash played the radio and occasionally she would find herself singing along to songs she hadn't even realized she knew. But if she made a conscious effort to remember them, her stubborn brain refused to cooperate.

When they stopped for the night, this time it was in a much more populated area and he managed to find a higher-class hotel with two double beds. However, that didn't stop her from walking around naked and sleeping in the buff. The truth was, when it came to sleeping naked she wasn't really doing it to annoy Ash. She actually liked the feel of the sheets against her bare skin. The walking-around-naked part? That was just for fun.

Not that she didn't think Ash was right about waiting. When she'd invaded his pj's yesterday morning she really hadn't stopped to think that maybe he didn't want to, that he might feel guilty that it was one-sided. If she wanted to get technical, what she had done was tantamount to rape or molestation. Although, honestly, he hadn't seemed quite *that* scandalized.

Really, she should be thrilled that she was engaged to such a caring and sensitive man. And she supposed that if the burden of pent-up sexual energy became too much, he could just take care of matters himself. Although deep down she really hoped he would wait for her.

Despite wishing she was in Ash's bed, curled up against him, she got a decent night's sleep and woke feeling the best she had since this whole mess began. Her head hardly hurt and when they went to breakfast she ate every bite of her waffles and sausage. Maybe just knowing that in a few hours she would be home was all the medicine she needed for a full recovery.

Ash spent a lot of the drive on the phone with work, and though she wasn't sure exactly what was being discussed, the tone of the conversation suggested that they were relieved he was coming back. And he seemed happy to be going back.

They crossed the Bay Bridge shortly after one, and they were finally in San Francisco. Though the views were gorgeous, she couldn't say with any certainty that it looked the least bit familiar. They drove along the water, and after only a few minutes Ash pulled into the underground parking of a huge renovated warehouse that sat directly across the street from a busy pier.

He never said anything about them living on the water.

"Home sweet home," he said, zooming past a couple dozen cars that looked just as classy as his, then he whipped into a spot right next to the elevator.

She peered out the window. "So this is it?"

"This is the place." He opened his door and stuck one foot out.

"What floor do we live on?"

"The top."

"What floor is that?"

"Six." He paused a second and asked, "Would you like to go up?"

She did and she didn't. She had been anticipating this day for what felt like ages, but now that she was here, back to her old life, she was terrified. What if she didn't remember? What if the memories never resurfaced? Who would she be?

Stop being such a baby, she chastised herself. Like Dr. Nelson had reminded her the day she was discharged, it was just going to take time and she would have to be patient. No matter what happened up there, whether she remembered or not, it was going to be okay. She was a fighter.

She turned to Ash and flashed him a shaky smile. "I'm ready."

She got out and waited by the elevator while Ash collected their bags from the trunk. He pushed the button for the elevator and it immediately opened. They stepped inside and he slipped a key in a lock on the panel, then hit the button for the top floor.

"Does everyone need a key?" she asked.

He shook his head. "Only our floor."

She wondered why, and how many other condos were on the top floor. She was going to ask, but the movement of the elevator made her so dizzy it was all she could do to stay upright. Besides, as the elevator came to a stop and the doors slid open, she got her answer.

They stepped off the elevator not into a hallway, but in a small vestibule in front of a set of double doors. Doors that led directly into their condo! They weren't a condo on the sixth floor. They *were* the sixth floor, and what she saw inside when he unlocked the door literally took her breath away. The entire living area—kitchen, dining room and family room—was one huge open space with a ceiling two stories high, bordered by a wall of windows that overlooked the ocean.

The floors were mahogany, with a shine so deep she could see herself in it. The kitchen looked ultramodern and she was guessing it had every device and gadget on the market. The furniture looked trendy but comfortable, and everything, from the oriental rugs to light fixtures, screamed top-of-the-line.

For a second she just stood there frozen, wondering if, as some sick joke, he'd taken her to someone else's condo. If they really lived here, how could she *not* remember it?

Ash set the bags on the floor and dropped his keys on a trendy little drop-leaf table beside the door. He started to walk toward the kitchen, but when he realized she wasn't moving, he stopped and turned to her. "Are you coming in?"

"You told me you do okay," she said, and at his confused look she added, "financially. But you do *way* better than okay, don't you?"

He grinned and said, "A little bit better than okay."

Her fiancé was loaded. She lived in a loft condo overlooking the ocean. It was almost too much to take in all at once. "Why didn't you tell me?"

He shrugged. "It just didn't seem that important. And I didn't want to overwhelm you."

"Oh, awesome idea, because I'm not the least bit overwhelmed *now!*" She was so freaked out she was practically hyperventilating.

"I take it nothing looks familiar."

"Curiously, no. And you'd think I would have remembered *this*."

"Why don't I show you around?"

She nodded and followed him to the kitchen, looking out the bank of windows as they passed, and the view was so breathtaking she had to stop. She could see sailboats and ships on the water and they had a phenomenal view of the Bay Bridge.

Ash stepped up behind her. "Nice view, huh?"

"It's…*amazing*."

"That's why I bought this place. I always wanted a place by the water."

"How long have you lived here?"

"I bought it after the divorce was final. Right before we met. You've lived here almost as long as I have. You've always said that your favorite room is the kitchen."

She could see why. The cabinets had a mahogany base with frosted glass doors; the countertops were black granite. All the appliances, even the coffeemaker, were stainless steel and it looked as functional as it was aesthetically pleasing. "Do I cook?"

"You're an excellent cook."

She hoped that was one of those things that just came naturally.

There was a laundry room and half bath behind the kitchen, then they moved on to the bedrooms, which were sectioned off on the right side of the loft. Three huge rooms, each with its own full bath and an enormous walk-in closet. He used one as a home office, one was the master, and the third he told her was hers.

"We don't share?" she asked, trying hard to disguise her disappointment.

"Well, you've always used this as an office and kept your clothes and things in here. I just figured that until things settle down, maybe you should sleep here, too."

But what if she wanted to sleep with him?

He's only thinking of your health, she assured herself. She knew that if they slept in the same bed they would be tempted to do things that she just was not ready for. Look what had happened in the hotel. And last night she had wanted so badly to climb out of her own bed and slip into his.

She walked over to the closet and stepped inside, looking at all of her belongings. She ran her hands over the shirts and slacks and dresses, feeling the soft, expensive fabrics, disheartened by how unfamiliar it all was.

"Well?" Ash asked, leaning in the closet doorway, looking so casually sexy in faded jeans and an untucked, slightly rumpled polo shirt, his hair stilled mussed from driving with the windows down, that she had the bone-deep feeling that as long as they had each other, everything would be okay.

"They're nice clothes, but I don't recognize them."

"It'll come to you, just—"

"Be patient, I know. I'm trying."

"What are you planning to do now?"

"Look through my things, I guess. It's weird, but it feels almost like I'll be snooping."

"If it's okay with you," he said, "I'm going to go to the office for a while."

They'd barely been back ten minutes and already he was going to leave her alone? "But we just got here."

"I know, but I'll only be a couple of hours," he assured her. "You'll be fine. Why don't you relax and take some time familiarizing yourself with the condo. And you look like you could use a nap."

She didn't want him to go, but he had sacrificed so much already for her. It was selfish to think that he didn't deserve to get back to his life. And hadn't the doctor suggested she try to get back into her regular routine as soon as possible?

"You're right," she told Ash. "I'll be fine."

"Get some rest. Oh, and don't forget that you're supposed to make an appointment with that new doctor. The card is in your purse."

"I'll do it right away."

He leaned forward and kissed her on the forehead, a soft and lingering brush of his lips, then he turned to leave.

"Ash?"

He turned back. "Yeah?"

"Thank you. For everything. I probably haven't said that enough. I know it's been a rough week, and you've been wonderful."

"I'm just glad to have you home," he said. He flashed her one last sweet smile, then disappeared from sight. Not a minute later she heard the jingle of his car keys, then the sound of the door opening and closing, then silence.

As promised, the first thing she did was fish the doctor's card from her purse and called to make the appointment. It was scheduled for Friday of that week, three days away at nine in the morning. Ash would have to drive her of course, which would mean him taking even more time off work. Maybe he could just drop her off and pick her up. She wondered if it was close to his work. The receptionist spouted off cross streets and directions, none of which Melody recognized, but she dutifully jotted them down for Ash.

With that finished, she stepped back into her bedroom, wondering what she should investigate first. There was a desk and file cabinet on one side of the room, and a chest of drawers on the other. But as her eyes swept over the bed, she was overcome by a yawn so deep that tears welled in her eyes.

Maybe she should rest first, then investigate, she thought, already walking to the bed. She pulled down the covers and slipped between sheets so silky soft she longed to shed all of her clothes, but this was going to be a short rest, not a full-blown nap.

But the second her head hit the pillow she was sound asleep.

Despite how many times Ash reminded himself what Melody had done to him, she was starting to get under his skin. He was sure that going to work, getting back to his old routine, would put things in perspective. Instead, as he rode the elevator up to the sixth floor, his shoulders sagged with the weight of his guilt.

Maybe it was wrong to leave Melody alone so soon. Would it have really been so terrible waiting until tomorrow to return to work? But he'd felt as though he desperately needed time away, if only a few hours, to get her off his mind. Only now that he was gone, he felt so bad for leaving, she was all he could think about.

Damned if he did, damned if he didn't.

The halls were deserted as he stepped off the elevator, but when he entered his outer office his secretary, Rachel, who'd single-handedly held his professional life together this week, jumped from her chair to greet him.

"Mr. Williams! You're back! I thought we wouldn't see you until tomorrow." She walked around her desk to give him a warm hug. He wouldn't ordinarily get physically affectionate with his subordinates, especially a woman. But considering she was pushing sixty and happily married with three kids and half a dozen grandchildren, he wasn't worried. Besides, she was sometimes more of a mother figure than a secretary. She reminded him of his own mother in many ways, of what she might have been like if she'd lived. However, no matter how many times he'd asked, she refused to address him by his first name. She was very old-fashioned that way. She had been with Maddox *long* before he came along, and probably knew more about the business than most of the hotshots working there.

"I decided to come in for a few hours, to catch up on things," he told her.

Rachel backed away, holding him at arm's length. "You look tired."

"And you look gorgeous. Is that a new hairstyle?"

She rolled her eyes at his less-than-subtle dodge. He knew as well as she did that her hair hadn't changed in twenty years. "How is Melody?"

"On the mend. She should be back to her old self in no time."

"I'm so glad to hear that. Send her my best."

"I will." Rachel knew Melody had been in an accident, but not the severity of it, or that she had amnesia. There would be too many questions that Ash just didn't have the answers to.

It was best he kept Melody as far removed from his life as he could, so the inevitable breakup wouldn't cause more than a minor ripple.

When rumors of her leaving the first time had circulated, the compassionate smiles and looks of pity were excruciating. He didn't appreciate everyone sticking their noses in his personal life, when it was no one else's business.

Rachel looked him up and down, one brow raised. "Did someone make it casual day and forget to tell me?"

He chuckled. "Since I'm not officially here, I thought I could get away with it."

"I'll let it slide this one time." She patted his shoulder. "Now, you go sit down. Coffee?"

"That would be fantastic. Thanks." He was so zonked that if he were to put his head down on his desk he would go out like a light. He'd slept terrible last night, knowing that Mel was just a few feet away in the next bed, naked. It only made matters worse that she insisted on walking around the room naked beforehand.

While Rachel fetched his coffee, Ash walked into his office. It was pretty much the way he'd left it, except his inbox had multiplied exponentially in size. He was going to have to stay all weekend playing catch-up. Just as he settled into his chair Rachel returned with his coffee and a pastry.

"I know you prefer to avoid sweets, but you looked as if you could use the sugar."

"Thanks, Rachel." He'd been eating so terribly the past week that one little Danish wasn't going to make much difference. Kind of like throwing a deck chair off the Titanic. Thankfully the hotel in Abilene had had a fitness room, and he'd used it faithfully each morning before he left for the hospital.

"I there anything else?" she asked.

He sipped his coffee and shook his head. "I'm good."

"Buzz if you need me," she said, then left his office, shutting the door behind her.

Ash sighed, gazing around the room, feeling conflicted. He loved his job, and being here usually brought him solace, yet now he felt as if there were somewhere else he should be instead.

With Melody, of course. All the more reason not to go home.

Ash picked up the pastry and took a bite. Someone knocked on his door, then it opened and Flynn stuck his head in.

"I see our wandering CFO had finally returned to the flock. You got a minute?"

Ash's mouth was full so he gestured Flynn in. He swallowed and said, "I'm not officially back until tomorrow, so I'm not really here."

"Gotcha." He made himself comfortable in the chair opposite his desk. "So, after you left so abruptly last week I tried to pump Rachel for information but she clammed up on me. I even threatened to fire her if she didn't talk and she said this place would tank without her."

"It probably would," Ash agreed.

"Which is why she's still sitting out there and I'm in here asking you why you disappeared. I know your parents are dead, and you never mentioned any relatives, so it can't be that. I'm guessing it had something to do with Melody." He paused then said, "Of course you can tell me to go to hell and mind my own business."

He could, and it was tempting, but Ash figured he owed Flynn an explanation. Not only was Flynn his boss, he was a friend. However, he had to be careful to edit the content. Maddox had some very conservative clients. Conservative, *multimillion-dollar* clients. If rumors began to circulate that his mistress of three years left him because she was carrying another man's love-child, it would only be a matter of time before word made it to someone at Golden Gate Promotions, who wouldn't hesitate to use it against Maddox.

Not that he believed Flynn would deliberately do anything to jeopardize the success of the company his own father built from the ground up, but despite the best of intentions, things had a way of slipping out. Like the affair that Brock, Flynn's brother, was rumored to be having with his assistant. Brock and Elle probably never intended that to get out either.

It just wasn't worth the risk.

"I found her," Ash told Flynn.

"You told me you weren't even going to look."

"Yeah, well, after a few weeks, when she didn't come crawling back to me begging forgiveness, I got…concerned. So I hired a P.I."

"So where was she?"

"In a hospital in Abilene, Texas."

His brow dipped low over his eyes. "A hospital? Is she okay?"

Ash told him the whole story. The accident, the drug-induced coma, all the time he spent by her bedside, then having to drive home because she couldn't fly.

Flynn shook his head in disbelief. "I wish you would have said something. Maybe there was a way we could have helped."

"I appreciate it, but really, there was nothing you could have done. She just needs time to heal."

"Is she back home with you now?"

"Yeah, we got back today."

"So, does this mean you guys are…back together?"

"She's staying with me while she recovers. After that…" He shrugged. "We'll just have to wait and see."

"This is probably none of my business, but did she tell you why she left?"

"It's…complicated."

Flynn held up a hand. "I get it, back off. Just know that I'm here if you need to talk. And if you need anything, Ash, anything at all, just say the word. Extra vacation days, a leave of absence, you name it and it's yours. I want to do anything I can to help."

He wouldn't be taking Flynn up on that. The idea of spending another extended amount of time away from work, stuck in his condo, just him and Melody, made his chest feel tight. "Thanks, Flynn, I appreciate it. We both do."

After he was gone Ash sat at his desk replaying the conversation in his head. He hadn't lied to Flynn; he'd just left out a few facts. For Flynn's own good, and the good of the company.

His mom used to tell him that good intentions paved the way to hell, and Ash couldn't escape the feeling sometimes that maybe he was already there.

Eight

Melody's quick rest turned into an all-day affair. She roused at seven-thirty when Ash got back feeling more tired than before, with a blazing headache to boot. After feeling so good the day before, the backslide was discouraging. Ash assured her that it was probably just the lingering aftereffects of the barometer and temperature change going from Texas to California, and she hoped he was right.

She popped two painkillers then joined him at the dining-room table in her sleep-rumpled clothes and nibbled on a slice of the pizza he'd brought home with him. She had hoped they could spend a few hours together, but the pills seemed to hit her especially hard. Despite sleeping most of the day, she could barely hold her head up. At one point she closed her eyes, for what she thought was just a second, but the next thing she knew Ash was nudging her awake.

"Let's get you into bed," he said, and she realized that he had already cleared the table and put the pizza away.

Melody stood with his help and let him lead her to the bedroom. She crawled in bed, clothes and all, and only vaguely recalled feeling him pull the covers up over her and kiss her forehead.

When she woke the next morning she felt a million times better. Her head still hurt, but the pain was mild, and her stomach howled to be fed. Wearing the same clothes as yesterday, her hair a frightening mop that she twisted and fastened in place with a clip she found under the bathroom sink, she wandered out of her bedroom in search of Ash, but he had already left for work.

The coffee in the pot was still warm so she poured herself a cup and put it in the microwave to heat, finding that her fingers seemed to know exactly what buttons to push, even though she had no memory of doing it before. While she waited she fixed herself something to eat. She spent a good forty minutes on the couch, devouring cold pizza, sipping lukewarm coffee and watching an infomercial advertising some murderously uncomfortable looking contraption of spandex and wire that when worn over the bra was designed to enhance the breasts and improve posture. She couldn't imagine ever being so concerned about the perkiness of her boobs that she would subject herself to that kind of torture.

She also wondered, if she'd never gone to Texas, and the accident hadn't happened, what she would be doing right now? Would she be sprawled on the couch eating leftovers or out doing something glamorous like meeting with her personal trainer or getting her legs waxed?

Or would she be in class? It was only mid-April so the semester wouldn't be over yet. She wondered, when and if she got her memory back, if they would let her make up the time and work she'd missed or if she would have to go back and take the classes over again. If she even wanted to go back, that was. The law still held little interest, but that could change. And what if it didn't? What then?

Worrying about it was making her head hurt, so she pushed it out of her mind. She got up, put her dirty dishes in the dishwasher alongside Ash's coffee cup and cereal bowl, then went to take a long, hot shower. She dried off with a soft, oversize, fluffy blue towel, then stood naked in her closet trying to decide what to wear. Much like the bras she had packed for her trip, everything she owned seemed to be a push-up or made of itchy lace—or both. Didn't she own any no-nonsense, comfortable bras?

It gave her the inexplicable feeling that she was rummaging through someone else's wardrobe.

She found a drawer full of sport bras that would do until she could get to the store and put one on. Maybe she'd liked those other bras before, and maybe she would again someday, but for now they just seemed uncomfortable and impractical. The same went for all the thong, lace underwear. Thank goodness she had a few silk and spandex panties, too.

She was so used to lying around in a hospital gown that the designer-label clothes lining her closet seemed excessive when all she planned to do was hang out at home, but after some searching she found a pair of black cotton yoga pants and a Stanford University sweatshirt that had been washed and worn to within an inch of its life.

Since she was already in the closet, she decided that would be the place to start her search for memory-jogging paraphernalia. But around ten, when Ash called to check on her, nothing she'd found held any significance. Just the typical stuff you would find in any woman's closet. She wondered if she was trying too hard. If she stopped thinking about it, maybe it would just come to her. But the thought of sitting around doing nothing seemed totally counterproductive.

Refusing to let herself get frustrated, she searched her desk next. She found papers in her hand that she had no recollection of writing, and an envelope of photos of herself and Ash, most in social settings. She'd hoped maybe there would be letters or a diary but there were none.

In the file cabinet she found pages and pages of school-work and other school-related papers, but nothing having to do with any specific research she'd been working on. In the very back of the drawer she found an unmarked file with several DVDs inside. Most were unmarked, but one had a handwritten label marked *Ash's Birthday*. Video of a birthday party maybe? Home videos could jog a memory, right?

Full of excitement and hope, she grabbed the file and dashed out to the family room to the enormous flat-screen television. It took her a few minutes just to figure out how to turn everything on, and which remote went with which piece of equipment. When the disk was in and loaded she sat on the couch and hit Play…and discovered in the first two seconds that this was no ordinary birthday party. At least, not the kind they would invite other people to. For starters, they were in bed…and in their underwear. Those didn't stay on for long though.

This was obviously one of those videos that Ash had mentioned. Although, at the time, she had half believed he was joking. She felt like a voyeur, peeking through a window at another woman's private life. The things she was doing to him, the words coming out of her mouth, made her blush furiously, but she was too captivated to look away. Was this the kind of thing Ash was going to expect when they made love? Because she wasn't sure if she even knew how to be that woman anymore. She was so blatantly sexy and confident.

Melody hated her for it, and desperately wanted to *be* her.

When the DVD ended she grabbed one of the unmarked DVDs and put it in the player. It was similar to the first one, starting out with the two of them in bed together. But this time after a bit of foreplay she reached over somewhere out of the camera's view, and came back with four crimson silk scarves that she used to tie a very willing Ash to the head and footboard.

Watching this DVD she discovered just how flexible she actually was. Physically and sexually. It was sexy and adventurous, and in a lot of ways fun, but it occurred to her as it ended that she wasn't particularly turned on. More curious than aroused. Not that she didn't enjoy seeing Ash naked. His body was truly a work of art. Long and lean and perfect in every way. It was the sex itself that was, she hated to admit, a little…boring.

She grabbed a third disk and put it in, and as it began to play she could tell right away that it was different. This one was set in Ash's bathroom, and he was filming her through the clear glass shower door. She was soaping herself up, seemingly lost in thought. He said her name, and when she turned she looked genuinely surprised to see him standing there holding the camera. After that he must have put the camera on a tripod because he came from behind it, already beautifully naked, and climbed in the stall with her, leaving the door open.

The tone of this video was completely different from the others. They soaped each other up, touching and stroking, as if they had all the time in the world. And unlike the others there was a lot of kissing in this one. Deep, slow, tender kisses that had Melody's attention transfixed to screen, actually licking her lips, wishing she could taste Ash there.

Missing was the sense of urgency, as if it were a race to see who could get who off first. Instead they took their time exploring and caressing, their arousal gradually escalating, until they both seemed to lose themselves. It was like watching a totally different couple, and this was a woman she could definitely imagine being. A woman she *wanted* to be.

The first two DVDs had been sexy, but they were just sex. There didn't seem to be much emotion involved. In this one it was clear, by the way they touched, the way they looked in each other's eyes, that they had a deep emotional connection. She could *see* that they loved each other.

On the screen Ash lifted her off her feet and pressed her against the shower wall. Their eyes locked and held, and the ecstasy on their faces, the look of total rapture as he sank inside her made Melody shiver.

She *wanted* that. She wanted Ash to kiss her and touch her and make love to her. She was breathing heavily, feeling so warm and tingly between her thighs that she wished she could climb through the screen and take the other Melody's place. They were making love in the purest sense, and she couldn't help thinking that if he were here right now she would—

"This one is my favorite," someone said from behind her.

Melody shrieked in surprise and flew off the couch so fast that the remote went flying and landed with a sharp crack on the hardwood floor several feet away. She spun around and found Ash standing behind the couch, a couple of plastic grocery bags hanging from his fingers and a wry grin on his face.

"You scared me half to death!" she admonished, her

anger a flimsy veil to hide her embarrassment. But it was useless because her face was already turning twenty different shades of pink. He'd caught her watching porn. Porn that *he* was in. What could be more embarrassing? "You shouldn't sneak up on people."

"I wasn't sneaking. In fact, I wasn't being particularly quiet at all. You just didn't hear me. I guess I see why."

On the television her evil counterpart was moaning and panting as Ash rocked into her, water sluicing down their wet, soapy bodies. Melody scrambled for the remote, but it took her a few seconds of jabbing random buttons before the DVD stopped and the screen went black. When she looked back at Ash he was still wearing that wry smile.

"What are you doing home? It's only—" she looked at the clock and could hardly believe it was after three "—three-fifteen."

Had she really been watching sex videos for almost two hours?

He held up the bags. "There's nothing here to eat but pizza so I stopped at the store after a lunch meeting. So you wouldn't have to go out."

"Oh. Thank you."

She waited for a comment about her watching the video, waited for him to tease her, but instead he walked past her and carried the bags to the kitchen. It was the first time she had seen him in a suit since the day he showed up at the hospital to claim her, and, oh, man, did he look delicious. There was something undeniably sexy about an executive who shopped for groceries. Of course, as turned on as she was right now, he would look sexy in plaid polyester floods and a polka-dot argyle sweater.

"I found the DVDs in my file cabinet," she said, following him, even though he hadn't asked for an explanation, or even looked as though he expected or required one.

He set the bags on the island countertop and started unpacking them. It looked as though he had picked up the basics. Milk, eggs, bread, a gallon of orange juice, as well as two bags full of fresh fruits and vegetables.

"I didn't know what they were when I found them," she said, stepping around to put the perishables in the fridge. "I was pretty surprised when I put the first one in."

One brow rose. "The *first* one?"

God, she made it sound as if she had been sitting there watching them all day.

"The *only* one," she lied, but it was obvious he wasn't buying it. Probably because he'd seen the DVDs strewn out on the coffee table.

"Okay, maybe I watched two…"

Up the brow went again.

"…and a *half.* It would have been three if I'd finished the one I was watching when you walked in."

He seemed to find her discomfort amusing. "Mel, watch as many as you like."

She wondered if he really meant that. "It doesn't… *bother* you?"

"Why would it?" he asked, looking very *un*bothered.

"Because you're in them, and they're very… personal."

He gave her a weird look. "You're in them, too."

"Yeah, but…it doesn't *seem* like me. It's like I'm watching someone else do all those things."

"Take my word for it, it was definitely you." He emptied the last of the bags so she balled them up, shoving one inside the other, and tossed them in the recycling bin under the sink.

"So," she said, turning to him. "The shower one is your favorite?"

He grinned and nodded, and she wondered if she could talk him into re-creating it someday soon. It only seemed fair, seeing as how she could no longer remember doing it.

"It was mine, too," she said.

"Why do you suppose that is?"

"I guess because it seemed more…*real*."

That brow rose again. "Are you suggesting that in the others you were faking it?"

"No! Of course not," she said, but realized, maybe she had been. The first two had been lacking something. They seemed almost…*staged*. As if she had been putting on a show for the camera. And there was no denying that, now at least, the hot sex and dirty talk didn't do half as much for her as watching them make love.

Had she been faking it in those first two?

"You look as though you're working something through," Ash said. He was standing with his arms folded, hip wedged against the counter. He narrowed his eyes at her. "*Were* you faking it?"

She hoped not. What was the point of even having sex if she wasn't going to enjoy it? "Even if I was, I wouldn't remember. Would I?"

"That's awfully convenient."

She frowned. "No. It isn't. Not for me."

"Sorry." He reached out and touched her arm. "I didn't mean it like that."

She knew that. He was only teasing and she was being too touchy. She forced a smile. "I know you didn't. Don't worry about it." She grabbed the last of the items on the counter, opened the pantry and put them away.

Ask looked at his watch. "Damn, it's getting late, I have

to get back. Thanks for helping put away—" He frowned and said, "Wait a minute."

He walked to the fridge and opened it, scanning the inside, all the drawers and compartments, as if he'd forgotten something, then he closed the refrigerator door and looked in the cabinet under the kitchen sink. He did the same thing to the pantry, then he turned to her and asked, "Do you realize what you just did?"

Considering the look on his face, it couldn't have been good. "No. Did I put everything in the wrong place or something?"

"No. Mel, you put everything in the *right* place."

"I did?" She wanted to believe it was significant, but at the same time she didn't want to get her hopes up. "Maybe it was a coincidence?"

"I don't think so. When it comes to your kitchen you're almost fanatical about keeping things tidy and organized. Everything in there is on the correct shelf, or in the right drawer. You even put the bags in the recycling bin when we were done and I don't recall telling you it was even there."

He was right. She hadn't even thought about putting them there, she just did it. Just like the law stuff. It just came to her naturally, by doing and not thinking.

Her heart started to beat faster and happiness welled up, putting a huge lump in her throat. "You think I'm remembering?"

"I think you are."

She squealed and threw herself into his arms, hugging him tight, feeling so happy she could burst. She realized, especially after watching those DVDs, just how many things she *wanted* to remember.

She laid her head on his shoulder and closed her eyes, breathing in the scent of his aftershave. It felt so good to be close to him. Even if he wasn't hugging her back as hard as she was hugging him. "Do you think it was the DVDs? Maybe watching them made me remember the other things?"

"Maybe."

She smiled up at him. "Well, then, maybe the real thing would work even better."

He got that stern look and she quickly backpedaled. "I know, I know. I'm not ready. Yet. It was just…an observation. For when I *am* ready." Which she was thinking might be sooner than they both expected.

He smoothed her hair back from her face and pressed a kiss to her forehead. "I think, when your brain is ready to remember things, it will. I don't think you can rush it. Every time you've remembered something it's been when you weren't thinking about it. Right?"

She nodded.

"So just relax and let it happen naturally." He looked at his watch, gave her one last kiss on the forehead, and said, "Now I really have to go."

She was disappointed, but didn't let it show. "Thanks for bringing the groceries. I suppose I should think about making something for dinner."

"Don't worry about feeding me. I'll probably be home late. I have a lot of work to catch up on."

Which was her fault, so she couldn't exactly complain. She walked him to the elevator instead, watching until he stepped inside and the doors closed.

This time it was definitely not her imagination. Knowing that she was remembering things troubled him for some reason, and the only reason she could come up with was that there was something that he didn't *want* her to remember. But she had no clue why, or what it could be. She thought about the money that she'd stashed in the pocket of one of the jackets in her closet. Was that the key to all of this?

She decided that if she had any more epiphanies or memory breakthroughs it would be best, for the time being anyway, to keep them to herself.

Nine

Ash took Friday morning off so he could take Mel to her appointment with her new neurologist. She had offered to have Ash drop her off and pick her up when she was finished, so he wouldn't miss more work, but the truth was he wanted to be there to hear what the doctor had to say.

It had been eerie the other day, watching her put the groceries away, only to realize that, right before his eyes, she was becoming herself again. She was remembering, no matter how small and insignificant a memory it had been. The point was, it was happening, and he wasn't sure he was ready.

Although since then, she hadn't mentioned remembering anything new. Not that he'd been around to witness it himself. Work had kept him at the office until almost midnight the past three days so he and Mel had barely seen each other.

The doctor gave her a thorough neurological exam,

asked a couple dozen questions, and seemed impressed by her progress. He suggested that she slowly begin adding more physical activities back to her daily regimen. Mel glanced over at Ash, and he knew exactly the sort of *physical activities* she was thinking of. And he knew, the second she opened her mouth, what she was going to say.

"What about sex?" she asked.

The doctor looked down at the chart, a slight frown crinkling his brow, and for one terrifying instant Ash thought he was going to mention the miscarriage. Had Dr. Nelson warned him not to say anything? Finding out about the baby now would ruin everything.

"I see no reason why you shouldn't engage in sexual activity," he said, then added with a smile. "I would caution against anything too vigorous at first. Just take it slow and do what you're comfortable with. I also suggest walking."

"I've been doing that. We live right by the water so I've been taking walks on the shore."

"That's good. Just don't overdo it. Start at ten or fifteen minutes a day and gradually work your way up." He closed her file. "Well, everything looks good. If you have any problems, call me. Otherwise, I won't need to see you back for three months."

"That's it?" Mel asked. "We're really done?"

The doctor smiled. "At this point there isn't much I can do. But only because Dr. Nelson took very good care of you."

He shook hers and then Ash's hand, and then he left. From the time they stepped into the waiting room, the entire appointment hadn't taken more than twenty minutes.

"That sure was quick," Mel said as they walked to

the reception desk to make her next appointment. "I was expecting CAT scans and EEGs and all sorts of tests. I'd thought I'd be trapped here all day."

So had he. Now that it was out of the way he was anxious to get back to work.

He drove her home and went up with her to grab his briefcase. He planned to say a quick goodbye and head out, but he could see by her expression that she wanted to "talk" and he knew exactly what about. Honestly, he was surprised she hadn't brought it up the second they got out of the doctor's office.

"Okay, let's have it," he said, dropping his briefcase beside the couch and perching on the arm.

She smiled shyly, which was weird because Mel didn't have a shy bone in her body. Or didn't used to. He couldn't deny that he liked it a little. "So, you heard what the doctor said, about it being okay to make love."

"When you're ready," he added, hoping she didn't think they were going to throw down right here on the living-room rug. Not that he hadn't been thinking about it either, after walking in to find her watching their home movies.

She had been so transfixed by the image of the two of them in the shower that she hadn't heard him come in. He'd taken his keys from the lock and gave them an extra jingle to alert her to his presence. When that didn't work he'd shut the door with more force than necessary, but she hadn't even flinched. He'd tried rustling the plastic bags he was holding, and determined at that point that it was a lost cause. She had been so captivated, it was as if the rest of the world had ceased to exist. Then he'd stepped closer to the couch, seen the rapid rise and fall of her chest as she breathed, the blush of arousal in her cheeks. She'd clenched the edge of the couch, looking as though she were about to climb out of her own skin.

The last time he'd seen her that turned on was when they had made that DVD.

In that instant he knew he wanted her, and it was just a matter of time before he gave in and let her have her way with him. But he'd wanted to wait and make sure everything went all right with her doctor appointment. And now he'd been given a green light.

When she didn't say anything, he asked, "Do you feel like you're ready?"

She shrugged. "I don't know. I guess I won't be sure until I try."

He waited for her to suggest that they try right now, but she didn't. Instead she asked, "Are you working late again?"

"Until at least nine," he said. "Probably later."

She sighed. "I'll be really happy when you're caught up and we can actually see each other for more than ten minutes in the morning before you walk out the door. And maybe one of these days I'll actually get to make dinner for you."

"Soon," he said, not sure if that was a promise he could, or *wanted,* to keep. He needed to keep some distance between them.

He waited for her to bring up the subject of sex again, but surprisingly, she didn't. "Anything else before I go?" he asked.

She shook her head. "I don't think so."

Oookay. With affirmation from the doctor, he expected her to all but throw herself at him. Why was she acting so…timid?

He walked to the door and she followed him. "Call me later and I'll try to wait up for you," she said.

"I will." He leaned down to brush a kiss to her cheek, but this time she turned her head and it was her lips he touched instead. He had kissed Mel at least a million times before, but this time when their lips met he felt it like an electric charge. Her sudden sharp intake of breath told him that she'd felt it, too. They stood that way for several seconds, frozen, their lips barely touching. He waited for her to make her move, but after several seconds passed and she didn't move, didn't even breathe as far as he could tell, he took matters into his own hands. He leaned in first, pressing his lips to hers.

Her lips were warm and soft and familiar and she still tasted like toothpaste. He waited for her to launch herself at him, to dive in with her usual enthusiasm, to ravage him with the deep, searching, desperate kisses that sometimes made him feel as though she wanted to swallow him whole.

But she didn't. In fact it took several seconds before he felt her lips part, and she did it hesitantly, as if she was afraid to push too far too fast. Even when their tongues touched it wasn't more than a tentative taste.

He'd never kissed her this way before, so tender and sweet. She didn't dive in with gusto, in what he had to admit sometimes felt more like an oral assault than a kiss. Not that it wasn't hot as hell, but this was nice, too. In fact, he liked this a lot.

It was so different, so *not* Melody. Even though he'd sworn to himself that he'd take this slow, he let himself be drawn in. Let her drag him down into something warm and sexy and satisfying.

He realized something else was different, too. Melody always wore perfume or body spray. The same musky, sensual fragrance that at times could be a touch cloying. Now the only detectable scent was a hint of soap and shampoo intermingled with the natural essence of her skin and her hair. Honestly, it was sexier and more arousing than anything she could find in a bottle.

And he was aroused, he realized. He was erect to the point of discomfort and aching for release. If her labored breathing and soft whimpers were any indication, he wouldn't have to wait long.

He deepened the kiss and her tongue tangled with his, and she tasted so delicious, felt so good melting against him, he was the one who wanted to ravish her. He had promised himself that he would make her wait a little longer, draw out the anticipation for another day or two, until he really had her crawling out of her skin, but at that precise moment, he didn't give a damn what he'd promised himself. He wanted her *now*.

Just as he was ready to make the next move, take it to the next level, he felt Mel's hands on his chest applying gentle but steady pressure, and he realized that she was pushing him away.

He broke the kiss and reluctantly backed off. "What's wrong?"

Melody's cheeks were deep red and he could see her pulse fluttering wildly at the base of her neck. She smiled up at him and said, a little breathlessly, "That was amazing. But I think it's all I can handle right now."

All she could *handle?* Was she kidding? Once Mel got started she was unstoppable. Now she was actually stopping him?

Ash was so stunned by her sudden change of heart that he wasn't sure how to act or what to say to her. She had never told him no. In fact, since he met her, he couldn't recall a time when he'd even had to *ask* for sex. She was usually the aggressor, and she had an insatiable appetite. There were even times when he wished they could take a day or two off.

Now, for the first time in three years, he wanted something that he couldn't have.

It was a sobering realization.

"I'm sorry," she said, and he realized she was gazing up at him, looking apologetic. "I just don't want to rush things. I want to take it slow, just like you said."

For a second he had to wonder if this was some sort of twisted game. Get him all hot and bothered then say no. But the thought was fleeting because the Melody gazing up at him wasn't capable of that kind of behavior. He was the one who had all but scolded her for touching him in the hotel room, the one who kept saying that they should take it slowly.

If anyone was playing games, he was, and he was getting exactly what he deserved.

"Are you okay?" she asked, her mouth pulled into a frown. "Are you upset with me?"

He desperately wished she was the old Melody again, so he could use this opportunity to hurt her. But in his mind they had inexplicably split into two separate and distinct people. The good Mel, and the evil Mel. And he knew that he couldn't hurt this Melody.

Jesus, he was whipped. He'd gone and let her get under his skin. The *one* thing he swore he wouldn't do.

"No," he said, pulling her into his arms and holding her. "I'm not upset. Not at all."

May as well enjoy it while it lasted, he thought, as she snuggled against him, burying her face in the crook of his neck. He knew, with her memory slowly returning, it was only a matter of time before the evil Mel was back and the good Mel was lost forever.

It was inevitable, but damn, was he going to miss her.

Leaving Mel and going in to work had been tough, but not as tough as it would have been staying with her. Sex had been the furthest thing from his mind the past couple weeks, but now, after one damned kiss, it seemed it was all he could think about. As a result, he was having one hell of a time concentrating on work.

He took an early lunch, early being noon instead of two or three, and though he didn't normally drink during work hours, he made an exception and ordered a scotch on the rocks. It helped a little.

On his way back to his office he ran into Brock Maddox.

"I was just going to call you," Brock said. "Can I have a quick word?"

"Of course."

He gestured Ash to his office, and when they were inside he closed the door and said, "Flynn told me what happened with Melody. I wanted you to know how sorry I am."

"Thanks. But she's actually doing really well. She had an appointment with her neurologist today and everything looks good."

"I'm relieved to hear it."

"Was that all?" Ash asked, moving toward the door.

"There's one more thing. As you've probably heard, we didn't get the Brady account."

"I heard." Brady Enterprises was a fairly large account, and the fact that they didn't get it was unfortunate, but Ash wasn't sure if it warranted the grim look Brock was wearing. As CFO, Ash knew they were financially sound with or without Brady.

"They hired Golden Gate Promotions," Brock told him.

"I heard that, too." It was never fun to lose, especially to a direct competitor, especially one as cocky and arrogant as Athos Koteas, but obviously Golden Gate pitched them an idea, and a budget, they couldn't refuse.

"Did you hear that they low-balled us out of the deal?" Brock asked, and when Ash opened his mouth to respond, he added, "Using a pitch that was almost identical to ours."

"What?"

"That's more the reaction I was hoping for."

"Where did you hear this?"

"I have an acquaintance over at Brady and she clued me in. She said it was even suggested that Maddox was stealing pitch ideas."

"Are we?"

The question seemed to surprise Brock. "Hell, no! That was *our* idea."

"So, how did Golden Gate manage to pitch the same thing? Coincidence?"

"Highly unlikely. The only explanation is that someone here leaked it."

If that was true, they had a serious problem. "What does Flynn think of this?"

"I didn't tell him yet."

As vice president, Flynn should have been told about this immediately. "You don't think he needs to know?"

"I wanted to talk to you first."

"Why? As CFO, this really isn't my area of expertise."

"Look, Ash, I'm not sure how to say this, so I'm just going to say it. You know that I've always liked Melody, but is it possible that she could have had anything to do with this?"

The question was so jarring, so out-of-the-blue unexpected, it actually knocked Ash back a step or two. *"Melody?* What would she have to do with this?"

"It just seems coincidental that right around the time we started laying out the framework for the pitch, meetings you were in on, she disappeared. I would understand completely if maybe you went home and mentioned things to her, never suspecting that she would leak it to our competitor. Maybe they made her an offer she couldn't refuse."

Ash's hands curled into fists at his sides, and had he been standing within arm's reach, he might have actually slugged Brock. "The idea that you would accuse Melody of all people of corporate espionage is the most ridiculous, not to mention *insulting,* thing I've ever heard."

"Considering the way she took off, it just seemed a plausible scenario."

"Yeah, well, you are *way* off base," Ash said, taking a step toward him, all but daring him to disagree.

Brock put his hands up in a defensive posture and said, "Whoa, take it easy, Ash. I apologize for offending you, but put yourself in my position for a minute. Like I said, I *had* to ask. There's a rumor that she didn't leave on the best of terms, so I figured—"

"So we're listening to rumors now? So should I assume that you're screwing your assistant?"

Brock's brow dipped in anger and Ash had the distinct feeling he'd taken this argument a step too far, then Brock's attention shifted to the door.

"Mother, would it really be too much for you to knock before you enter a room?"

Ash turned to see Carol Maddox standing in the now-open doorway. Small and emaciated but a force to be reckoned with nonetheless. And oh, man, she didn't look pleased. Of course, as long as Ash had known her, disappointment and contempt were the only two expressions that had ever made it through the Botox. In fact, he couldn't recall a single incidence when he'd seen her smile. She was probably one of the unhappiest, nastiest people he'd ever met, and seemed hell-bent on taking everyone else down with her.

"I need to have a word with you, dear," she said through gritted teeth, or maybe the Botox had frozen her jaw. Either way, she looked royally pissed off and Ash was in no mood to get caught in the crosshairs.

"I take it we're finished here," he said, and Brock nodded curtly.

As Ash sidestepped around Mrs. Maddox to get to the door, he almost felt guilty. The remark about Brock sleeping with Elle didn't seem to go over well with good ol' mom. But that was what he got for accusing Melody of all people of leaking company secrets.

Even if Ash had told her about the campaign—which he definitely hadn't—she was not the type to go selling the information to Maddox's rival. And somewhere deep down he would always resent Brock for even suggesting that she would.

Wait a minute…

He gave himself a mental shake. Wasn't he being a touch hypocritical? Why was he so dead set on defending the honor of a woman he planned to use, then viciously dump? This was the evil Mel they were talking about, right?

Because, although she may have betrayed Ash's trust, it would be against everything he believed to castigate someone for something they didn't do. And for this, she was completely innocent.

When he reached his office Rachel greeted him anxiously. "Oh, *there* you are. I've been calling you. Miss Trent called."

"Sorry, I forgot my cell in my desk. What did she want?"

"She said she needed to talk to you and she sounded frantic. *Completely* unlike herself. She asked to have you call her immediately on her cell phone."

Melody *wasn't* the frantic type, and that alone alarmed him. "Did she say why?"

"No. But I'm worried. She acted as if she'd never spoken to me before."

That was because, as far as she knew, she never had. "I'll call her right away."

He stepped into his office, shut the door and dialed her cell. She answered before it even had time to ring on his end, and the stark fear in her voice made his heart drop.

"Ash?"

"It's me. What's wrong?"

"I need you to come get me," she said, her voice quivering so hard he could barely understand her. His first thought was that maybe something had happened and she needed to be taken to the hospital.

"Are you hurt? Did you hit your head?"

"No, I just need a ride," she said, then he heard the sound of traffic in the background and realized that she must not be at home. She'd said something about taking a walk when he left for work. Had she maybe walked too far and couldn't make it back on her own?

"Mel, where are you?"

"The Hyde Street Pier."

The Hyde Street Pier? That was *way* the hell across town from their condo. There was no way she could have walked that far. "How did you get over there?"

"Can you just come?" she asked, sounding desperate.

"Of course. I'm leaving right now. I'm ten minutes away."

"I'll be in front of the Maritime store right on the corner."

Ash hung up the phone, grabbed his keys from his desk drawer, and as he passed Rachel's desk he said, "I have to run out for a while. I'll try to make it back this afternoon."

"Is everything okay?" she asked, looking concerned.

"I'm not sure." But he was about to find out.

Ten

Melody didn't have to remember her past to know that she had never felt so stupid or humiliated in her *entire* life.

She sat in the passenger seat of Ash's car, wringing her hands in her lap, wishing she could make herself invisible. At least she'd stopped trembling, and now that her heart rate had slowed her head had stopped hurting, and she wasn't dizzy anymore either. That didn't stop her from feeling like a total idiot.

"Are you ready to tell me what happened?" Ash asked gently, looking away from the road for a second to slide her a sideways glance.

"You're going to think I'm stupid," she said.

"I won't think you're stupid." He reached over and pried one hand free and curled it under his. "I'm just glad you're okay. You scared me."

She bit her lip.

"Come on, Mel."

"I got lost," she said quickly, immediately wishing she could take it back. But he didn't chastise or make fun of her, not that she thought he would. It didn't make her feel any less like a dope though. And to his credit, he sat there silently waiting for her to elaborate, not pushing at all.

"Remember I said I was going to take a walk?"

He nodded.

"Well, I felt so good, so full of energy, I guess I over-estimated my endurance a bit. I got about a mile and a half from home—"

"A mile and a half?" His eyes went wide. *"Mel!"*

"I know, but it felt so good to be in the fresh air, and it was mostly downhill. But then I started to get *really* tired, and the way back was all *up*hill. I knew I wouldn't be able to make it back, so I got on a bus."

"You knew which bus to take?"

"I thought I did. Unfortunately it was the wrong bus. It took me in the opposite direction of home, and by the time I figured it out I was *really* far. So I got off at the next stop and got on a different bus, but that one was going the wrong direction, too. It was such a strange sensation, like I knew deep down that I should know which bus to take, but I kept picking the wrong one."

"Why didn't you ask someone for help?"

"I was too embarrassed. Besides, I felt like I needed to do it on my own."

"And they say men never ask for directions," he said, rolling his eyes, and she couldn't help but crack a smile.

"I rode around for a couple of hours," she continued, "and finally got off at the pier. I had absolutely no idea where I was. I could have been in China for all I knew. Nothing looked familiar. And I guess...I guess I just freaked out. My heart was racing and I had this tightness in my chest, like I was having a heart attack. Then my hands started going numb and I felt like I was going to pass out and that *really* scared me. That's when I called you."

"It sounds like you had a panic attack. I used to get the same thing when I was a kid, when I went in for my treatments."

"Treatments?" she asked.

He paused for a second, then said, "Radiation."

She frowned. "Radiation? What for?"

"Osteosarcoma," he said, then glanced over and added, "Bone cancer."

He had cancer? She'd had no idea. Well, she probably *did*, she just didn't remember. "I know I've probably asked you this before, but when?"

"I was twelve."

"Where was it?"

"My femur."

"How long were you—"

"Not long. Eight months, give or take. They caught it early at my annual physical. A round of radiation and chemo and I was fine."

She was pretty sure it hadn't been as simple as he made it sound. Especially if he had been having panic attacks. "Do you worry… I mean, could it…come back?"

"If it was going to come back it would have a long time ago." He glanced over at her. "If you're worried I'm going to get sick and die on you, I'm probably more likely to be hit by a bus."

"I didn't mean that. I just…I don't know what I meant. The question just popped out. I'm sorry."

He squeezed her hand. "It's okay."

She could see that it was a touchy subject and she didn't want to push it. She just hoped he didn't think that it would ever stop her from marrying him. She was in this for the long haul, until death do them part and all that. And speaking of marriage…

"I was wondering," she said. "Is there a reason you wouldn't tell people at work that we're engaged?"

His shot a glance her way. "Why do you ask?"

"Well, when I called your office, and your secretary asked who it was, I said Ash's fiancée, and she sounded really confused."

"What did she say?"

"She said, *Ash's what?* and I said, *Ash's fiancée, Melody.* I got the distinct impression that she had no idea we were engaged."

"We just haven't officially announced it," he said. "I asked right before you left on your trip, then you didn't come back…." He shrugged.

"So you didn't say anything to anyone."

"It was the last thing on my mind."

"Well, I guess that explains the pictures and the videos."

"What about them?"

"I noticed that I wasn't wearing my engagement ring in a single one. So now I know why."

Melody looked over at him and Ash had a strange look on his face, as if he felt sick to his stomach or something.

"Is it okay that I said something to her? I mean, we have no reason not to announce it now. Right?"

"I've just been so swamped since we've been back, with everything at work, and the doctor's office. The truth is, it completely slipped my mind."

"But it is okay."

He smiled and squeezed her hand again. "Of course."

"Oh, good," she said, feeling relieved. "Since I kind of

already did. To your secretary anyway. Do you think we should plan some sort of engagement party? Or at least call the wedding planner?"

"I think you shouldn't worry about it until you've had more time to heal. There's no rush. Look at what happened today when you got too stressed."

He was right. She knew he was. It was just that she felt this need to get on with her life. This deep-seated urgency to move forward.

Give it time, she told herself. *Eventually you'll be yourself again.*

When they got back to their building, instead of pulling into the underground lot he stopped at the front entrance.

"You have your key?" he asked.

She pulled it from her jacket pocket and jingled it in front of him. "You're not coming up?"

"I really need to get back. You're okay now, right?"

Sort of, but she wasn't exactly looking forward to being alone. But she couldn't be selfish. "I'm okay. Maybe I'll take a nap."

"I'll call you later." He leaned over and kissed her, but not on the cheek or forehead. This time he went straight for her lips. He brushed them softly with his, and she could swear her already shaky knees went a little bit weaker.

"I'll see you later." She got out and shut the door and watched him zip down the block and around the corner. Incidentally, she didn't see him later. Well, not for more than a few seconds when he roused her with a kiss and said good-night.

From the light in the hallway she could see that he was still in his suit, and he had that fresh-from-the-office smell clinging to his clothes, so she knew he had just gotten home. She peered at the clock and saw that it was after midnight.

At least tomorrow was Saturday. They could finally spend some quality time together. Maybe they could take a walk down by the water and have a picnic lunch at the park. She wondered if they had ever done that before. She drifted off to sleep making plans, and woke at eight feeling excited.

She got dressed and as she brushed her teeth she caught the distinct aroma of coffee. She had hoped to be up first, so she could surprise him with breakfast in bed. Looked as though he didn't sleep in on the weekends.

She expected to find him in the kitchen reading the financial section, but he wasn't there. He wasn't in his bedroom either. Where had he gone?

She grabbed her cell off the counter and dialed his cell. He answered on the third ring. "Where are you?" she asked.

"Just pulling into the lot at work. I thought I would get an early start."

"It's Saturday."

"And your point is?"

"I just…I thought we could spend some time together today."

"You know I have a lot of catching up to do."

"What about tomorrow?"

"Working."

He was working on *Sunday?*

Or was he? What if all these late nights and weekends, he was actually somewhere else?

"Ash…are you having an affair?" The words jumped out before she could stop them, and the second they did she wished them back.

And Ash responded just as she would have expected.

Bitterly. "That's really something coming from…" He suddenly went dead silent, and for a second she thought the call had cut out.

"Ash, are you there?"

"Yes, I'm here, and no, I'm not having an affair. I would *never* do that to you."

"I know. I'm sorry for even suggesting it. I'm just… I guess I'm feeling insecure, and lonely. I never see you."

"I missed more than a week of work."

Which was her fault, so she shouldn't complain. That was more or less what he was saying. "I know. You know what, forget I said anything."

"Tell you what, I'll try to make it home in time for dinner tonight, okay?"

"That would be nice."

"I'll call you later and let you know for sure."

"Okay. I—I love you, Ash."

There was a sight pause, then he said, "Me, too. Talk to you later."

She disconnected, feeling conflicted, asking herself the obvious question. *Me, too?* Given the situation, wouldn't the more appropriate response be, *I love you, too?* Shouldn't he be happy that, despite technically knowing him only a couple of weeks, she knew she loved him? Or maybe he thought she was just saying it because she was supposed to. Maybe that was his way of letting her know that it was okay not to say it if she wasn't ready.

Or maybe she was just losing her mind.

She groaned and dropped her forehead against the cool granite countertop, which she realized was a really dumb move when her head began to throb.

Maybe the problem was that she just needed a purpose outside of Ash. She needed to get back to her education, back to law school. She needed a life. Maybe then she wouldn't care how little time Ash had for her.

If he really needed to be at work, why did Ash feel like such a jackass?

Mel was just going to have to learn that this was the way things were. The way it had *always* been. They had always led very separate lives. She was there when he had time for her, and when he didn't she filled her days with school and shopping. And she had never had a problem with that before.

It made sense that being stuck at home would drive her a little nuts. What she needed was a car, and her credit cards back. That should make her happy.

He rode the elevator up to his floor, feeling better about the whole situation, and wasn't surprised to see Rachel sitting there as he approached his office. She always worked half a day on Saturdays. Sometimes longer if there was a critical pitch in the works.

"G'morning, beautiful," he said and she just rolled her eyes.

"Coffee?"

"Please."

He shrugged out of his jacket and had settled behind his desk by the time she returned.

"How is Melody today?" she asked, setting his coffee in front of him.

"Better." He'd given her a very vague explanation of yesterday's event. He said only that she was out, and wasn't feeling well, and didn't think she could get back home on her own. Rachel hadn't said a word to him about his and Melody's supposed engagement. He didn't doubt that she was simply biding her time.

"I'm a little surprised to see you here," she said.

"Why? I always work Saturday."

"Well, with Melody still recovering…"

"She's okay. It's good for her to do things on her own."

Rachel shrugged and said, "If you say so." And before he could tell her to mind her own business she was gone.

Melody was a big girl, and she had always been extremely independent. Once she had a car, and money to spend, she would stop giving him a hard time.

Instead of working he spent the better part of the morning on the phone with his regular car dealership, negotiating a deal. Because he was a regular and valued customer the salesman even offered to bring the model he was interested in over for a test drive. Unfortunately they didn't have one in stock with all the options he wanted and had to ship it in from a dealership in L.A., but delivery was promised on Monday.

With that taken care of, he called to reinstate all the credit cards he'd cancelled when she left. With expedited delivery they would arrive around the same time as the car. By the time Rachel popped in at noon to let him know she was leaving, he was finally ready to start working.

"Stay home tomorrow," Rachel told him. "Melody needs you just as much as these clowns do. Probably more."

"Thanks, Dr. Phil."

She rolled her eyes and walked out.

Not ten minutes later Brock rang him.

"I need you in the conference room now," he said sternly. Considering his tone, this wasn't going to be a friendly chat, and Ash was not in the mood to get chewed out again. He couldn't even imagine what he'd done. Had Brock found something else to pin on Melody?

Dragging himself up from his desk, he headed down

the hall. The normally clear glass walls of the conference room were opaque, which in itself was not a good sign.

The door was closed, so he knocked.

"Come in," Brock snapped.

Jesus, he so didn't need this today. Ash sighed and pushed the door open, ready to tell Brock to go screw himself, and was nearly knocked backward by a roomful of people shouting, "Surprise!" at the top of their lungs.

He must have looked the part because after a beat, everyone started to laugh. They were obviously celebrating something, but he had no idea what. Had he gotten a raise that no one told him about?

On the conference table was a cake, then he noticed the hand-drawn banner draped from the ceiling.

Congratulations, Mr. Melody Trent.

Eleven

People started milling over to Ash, shaking his hand and congratulating him on his engagement. Brock and Flynn and Jason Reagert. Gavin Spencer, Celia Taylor and Celia's fiancé, Evan Reese. There were even a few public relations people, several creatives and a large group of his financial people from the fifth floor.

Everyone knew.

Dammit. So much for it not being a big stink when he dumped Melody.

Between handshakes someone stuck a drink in his hand and he took a long swallow. "You guys really didn't have to do this," he said.

"When we heard the news we knew we had to have some sort of celebration," Flynn said. "We wanted to invite Melody, but Rachel didn't think she would be feeling up to it."

Jesus, what a nightmare that would have been.

Rachel, the person he assumed was responsible for this fiasco, was on the opposite side of the room so it took him a few minutes to make his way over. When he did, she gave him a huge smile and hugged him. "Congratulations, Mr. Williams."

"You are so fired," he said, hugging her back.

She knew it was an empty threat, so she just patted his arm and said, "You're welcome."

Celia approached and handed him another drink. "I figured you could use it. I know you hate big productions like this."

"Thank you." He accepted the glass and took a long drink.

"I can't tell you how thrilled I am for the two of you," she said. "I know how hard the past couple of months have been. I'm so glad everything worked out. Have you set a date?"

He took another slug of his drink. "Not yet."

"I hope you're not planning to elope, or get hitched in Vegas. You know everyone here is expecting an invitation."

Well, then, everyone here was going to be very disappointed.

He finished his drink and someone gave him another, then someone else handed him a slice of cake. As desperately as he wanted to get the hell out of there, he was more or less stuck until the party wound down around three. And though he could have easily drunk himself into a stupor, he stopped at five scotches—although two were doubles. He wasn't drunk by any means, but tipsy enough to know he shouldn't be driving.

When everyone but the executives had cleared out, Ash figured it was finally safe to get the hell out of there. He hadn't gotten squat done. Not work anyway, and he was in no condition to go back to his office.

"I'm going to call a cab and head home," he told everyone.

"We're heading out, too," Celia said. "Why don't you let us drive you? You don't mind, do you, Evan?"

Her fiancé shrugged. "Fine with me. If you want, Celia could take you home in your car and I can follow. That way you won't have to take a cab into work."

"That would be great," Ash said.

Feeling pleasantly buzzed, he said his goodbyes to everyone else, and the three of them headed down to the parking garage.

When he and Celia were alone in the car and on their way to his condo she told him, "There's something we need to talk about."

"Is something wrong?"

"No. Everything is actually going great. But it's clear that the long-distance relationship Evan and I have is going to get tedious."

"But things are okay with you two?"

"Yeah. Things are so good, I'm moving to Seattle at the end of the year."

Ash hated to see her go, but he wasn't exactly surprised. She had fallen pretty hard for Evan. He just wanted her to be happy. "I guess this means you're leaving Maddox?"

"Technically, no. I'll be handling all of the advertising for Reese Enterprises as a consultant for Maddox. I'll just be doing it from Seattle."

"Wow, that's great."

"I told Brock and Flynn I was thinking of leaving, and they didn't want to lose me."

"That's because you've made them a lot of money. They know a good thing when they see it."

"I'm excited, but I'm going to miss everyone here."

"Who's going to take your place?"

"His name is Logan Emerson, he's going to start working with me Monday. I'll train him for a couple of weeks, then I'll be exclusively on the Reese account. I'm sure I'll be doing a lot of traveling back and forth until I make the move."

"Well, we'll miss you, but it sounds like an awesome opportunity."

They reached Ash's building and he directed her down into the parking garage, then they walked up to the street where Evan was waiting.

"Thanks for the ride," he said.

Celia smiled. "No problem. See you Monday. And say congratulations to Melody for us. We should all get together for dinner sometime, when she's feeling better."

"Definitely," he said, knowing that would never happen.

Ash waved as they drove off, then he went upstairs. The condo was quiet so he figured Mel was probably out for a walk, but then he saw her key on the counter. He walked to her room and looked in but she wasn't in bed, then he heard water turn on in her bathroom. He crossed the room, and since the bathroom door was open, he looked in.

Hot damn. Melody was in the shower.

He wondered if she might be in the mood for company. After watching her watch that video the other day, he had the feeling it could get very interesting.

He shrugged out of his jacket and tossed it on the bed, then kicked off his shoes.

He stepped into the bathroom, not being particularly stealthy, but Mel was rinsing shampoo from her hair so her head was thrown back and her eyes were closed. Suds ran down her back and the curve of her behind, and all he could think about was soaping up his hands and rubbing them all over her.

He waited for her to open her eyes, so she would see him there, but when she finally did she turned with her back to him. She grabbed a bottle of soap and poured some out into her hand then turned away from the spray and began soaping herself up. He had a fantastic profile view as she rubbed suds into breasts and her stomach and down her arms. It was far from a sensual display, but he was so hot for her, she might as well have been giving him a lap dance.

She finished her arms then her hands moved back to her breasts. She cupped them in her hands, her eyes drifting shut as she swirled her thumbs over her nipples. They hardened into two rosy pink points, and he could swear he saw her shudder.

Goddamn.

God knew he'd seen Mel touch herself before. So many times that, honestly, the novelty had sort of worn off. But this was different. Maybe because she didn't know he was watching. Because she wasn't putting on a show for him. She was doing it because it felt good.

She did seem to be enjoying it, and he was so hard his slacks were barely containing him. He watched, loosening his tie as she caressed herself. He tossed it across the back of the toilet and started unbuttoning his shirt.

Melody's hands slipped down off her breasts, then moved slowly south, stroking her hips and her stomach and the tops of her thighs. It was obvious what her final destination would be and he thought, *oh, hell, yeah.* Unfortunately she chose that moment to open her eyes and see him standing there.

She shrieked so loud he was sure the people living beneath them heard it.

"You scared me half to death!" she admonished when she realized it was just him. He half expected her to try to cover herself, but she didn't. Her cheeks did flush though. "How long have you been standing there?"

"Long enough to enjoy what I was seeing."

He could see that she was embarrassed, which made it that much more arousing.

"You know it's rude to spy on people," she said, then her hands came up to cover her breasts. "Tell me you don't have a video camera out there."

He chuckled. "No camera," he assured her, unfastening the buttons at his wrists. "And I wasn't spying, I was watching."

"Same thing."

"You make it sound like I was looking through a peephole in the wall." He tugged the shirt off and dropped it on the floor.

Mel watched it fall, and when she saw the tent in his pants her eyes grew larger. "W-what are you doing?"

He pulled his undershirt over his head and dropped that on the floor, too. "Taking off my clothes."

Her eyes strayed to his chest. He didn't think she realized it, but she was licking her lips. "Um…why?"

"So I can take a shower." He tugged off his socks then unfastened his pants and shoved them and his boxers down.

"With me?" she said, her voice suddenly squeaky and high-pitched, as if she'd been sucking helium.

"Unless you have someone else in there with you."

He crossed the room and pulled the shower door open, his hard-on preceding him inside. If Mel's eyes opened any wider they would fall out of her head.

"I thought we were taking this slow," she said, backing against the far wall, looking worried.

"Don't worry, we are." He stepped under the spray, slicking his hair back. "We're just doing it naked."

If they didn't make love that was okay with him; he just needed to touch her, get his hands on *some* part of her body. If she let him get her off, fantastic, if she returned the favor, even better. He was going to let her set the pace.

Mel stood in the corner watching him, chewing her lip. "This is going to sound stupid, because we've done this before, but I'm really nervous."

"That's why we're taking it slow." And if the anticipation killed him, well, he would at least die with a smile on his face. "So, tell me what you're ready for. What can I do?"

She thought about it for several seconds, then swallowed hard and said, "I guess you could…kiss me."

The logical place to start. He didn't want to corner her, so he took her hand and pulled her to him, so they were both under the spray. But when he leaned in to kiss her, the head of his erection bumped against her stomach. She jumped with surprise, then laughed nervously.

"Outdoor plumbing," he said with a shrug.

"I know, I'm being ridiculous. I'm sorry."

The weird thing was, he liked it. He liked that she wasn't trying to take charge, that for once he could be the aggressor.

"You know what, I have a better idea. Turn around." He grabbed the soap and poured some in his hand.

"What are you going to do?"

"Wash your back." She cast him a wary look, and he said, "Just your back. I promise."

She turned and faced the wall, bracing her hands on the tile as he smoothed the soap across her shoulders and down her back.

"Hmm, that feels nice," she said, as he used both hands to massage her shoulders, and he felt her begin to relax. He worked his way down, but as he got closer to her behind, she tensed again.

"Relax," he said, sliding his hands back up. "This is supposed to be fun."

"I'm sorry. I don't know why I'm so nervous. I wasn't like this in the hotel."

"Maybe it's because you knew you weren't able to do anything then."

She shrugged, and said without much conviction, "Maybe."

His hands stilled. "Why do I get the feeling there's something you're not telling me?"

"It's stupid."

He turned her to face him and she looked so cute, water dripping from her hair, her brow crinkled with the weight of whatever it was that troubled her. "If something is bothering you it's not stupid. If you don't tell me what's really wrong, we can't fix it." And he would *never* get laid.

"It's those videos."

"The shower one?"

She shook her head, eyes on her feet. "The other two. I know it was me, but it's *not* me anymore. That woman… she was just so confident and sexy. I don't think I can do and say the things she did. I can't be her anymore."

He shrugged. "So what?"

Her eyes met his, so full of grief and conflict that he felt his scotch buzz wither away. "I'm *so* afraid I'm going to disappoint you, Ash."

This wasn't one of the silly sex games she used to play with him, or even a mild case of the pre-sex jitters. She was genuinely distraught. He'd never seen her this confused and vulnerable before. Not even in the hospital.

"Mel, you *won't* disappoint me. That's not even a possibility."

She didn't look as though she believed him. She lowered her eyes but he caught her chin in his palm and forced her to look at him. "Listen to me. I don't want the Melody who was in those videos. I want *you*."

He realized it was probably the most honest thing he had ever said to her. He wanted her in a way that he'd never wanted the other Melody.

So why was he still expecting her to act like her? Did he think that, despite being nervous and wanting to go slow, she would just magically shed her inhibitions the instant he touched her?

He wanted her, God knew he did, but not if it was going to hurt or confuse her. It just wasn't worth it. Physically she may have been ready for him, but emotionally she just wasn't there yet. He was pushing too far too fast.

Jesus, when had he gone so soft?

He turned and shut off the water.

"What are you doing?" she asked, looking even more confused, not that he could blame her. First he said they should wait, then he all but molested her, then he put on the brakes again. At this rate he was going to give them both whiplash.

Just because he bought her a car, and planned to give her a couple of credit cards, was he back to thinking she owed him? She hadn't asked for anything.

"We're getting out," he told her.

"But—"

"You're not ready for this. And I'm really sorry that I pushed you. I feel like a total jerk." He didn't just feel like a jerk, he *was* one. He grabbed the towel she'd hung on the hook outside the shower and wrapped it around her, then he got out and fetched one for himself from the linen closet. He fastened it around his hips, and when he turned Melody was standing in the shower doorway, wrapped in her towel, watching him, her brow wrinkled.

"Everything okay?" he asked.

She nodded, but she didn't move.

"We should get dressed. And if the offer for dinner is still good I'd love it if you cooked for me. Or if you prefer we could go out. Your choice."

"Okay," she said, but didn't specify which one, dinner in or out. But before he could ask, she walked out of the bathroom.

He gathered his clothes from the floor and walked into her bedroom, expecting her to be getting dressed. Instead she was lying in bed, propped up on one elbow, the blankets draped about waist level.

She probably wasn't trying to look sexy, but damn it all, she did. At that moment he would swear on his life that she had the most beautiful breasts in the free world. And, God, did he ache to get his hands on them.

"Taking a nap?" he asked.

She shook her head, then she pulled back the covers on the opposite side of the bed and patted the mattress. "Get in."

Get in? Into bed?

Now he was the one who was confused. "Mel—"

"Get in," she said more firmly.

"But…I thought…I thought we were waiting."

"Me, too. Now come over here and get into bed."

Though he still wasn't sure what was going on, he walked to the bed, tossing his clothes in a pile on the floor. His skin was still damp and the sheets stuck to him as he slid between them.

Since he didn't know what she expected from him, he

lay beside her, mirroring her position. "Okay, I'm in. Now what?"

"Now you should kiss me. And this time don't worry about the plumbing. I want you to touch me."

Good, because he started getting hard the second he saw her lying there, and short of putting on pants, or lying on top of the covers while she stayed under them, there was going to be inevitable physical contact. The question was, how far was she willing to let this go?

"Just to be clear, so I don't cross any boundaries, are you saying that you want to make love?"

"Yes, I am. And I do. Right now."

Thank You, God.

She lay back against the pillows, gazing up at him, waiting for his kiss. He knew what the old Mel would expect. She would want it hard and fast and breathless. But this Mel didn't have a clue what she wanted, so he was free to do whatever he chose, like a painter with a clean canvas.

But maybe this time, it was a picture they could paint together.

Twelve

Ash leaned in to kiss her, his hand cupping her face so tenderly, and Melody knew she was safe with him. That she would always be safe.

She wasn't exactly sure what happened in the bathroom, but when Ash shut off the water and wrapped her in a towel, told her they were stopping, something inside her shifted. She knew in that second that she wanted him, that she was ready *now*. It was time to stop looking backward and focus on the future.

His lips brushed hers, so gentle and sweet, and whatever anxiety or fear remained dissolved with their mingling breath. It was the kind of perfect kiss that every girl dreamed about. And she had, she realized. She had been that girl. The memory was so near she could almost reach out and touch it. But she didn't want to think about anything right now, she just wanted to feel. And Ash was exceptional in that department.

His kisses roused her senses and his caresses trailed fire across her skin. It was as if he owned a road map to every erogenous zone on her body, and he explored each one until she felt crazy with want. He made her shudder and quake, taking her to the brink of mindless ecstasy then yanking her back the second before she could reach her peak.

He aroused her with such practiced skill it made her feel inept in her own efforts, but he never once gave the impression that her touch did anything but arouse him. And nothing could be more erotic for her than touching him all over. Learning him again. She discovered that his ears were exceptionally sensitive, because when she nibbled them he groaned and fisted his hands in her hair. And when she did the same to his nipple he dragged her face to his and kissed her so hard she felt breathless. What he seemed to like most though was when she straddled his thighs, took his erection in her hand, but instead of stroking, swirled her thumb in slow circles around the head.

"My God, that feels amazing," Ash said, his eyes rolling closed, his fingers curling into the sheets. It was unbelievably arousing, watching him struggle for control. Knowing she was making him feel that way.

"Did I used to do this to you before?"

He swallowed hard and shook his head. "I don't want to come yet, but if you keep that up I will."

"It's okay if you do." She wanted him to.

He shook his head and opened his eyes. They were glassy and unfocused. "Not yet. Not until I'm inside you."

Well, all he had to do was ask. She rose up on her knees and centered herself over him. When he realized what she intended to do, he asked, "Are you sure?"

She had never been so sure of anything in her life.

Her eyes locked on his, she slowly lowered herself onto his erection, taking him inside her inch by excruciating inch. She was sure that making love, no matter how often or how many times they had done it before, had never given her this soul-deep sensation of completeness.

"You're so *tight*," he said, his hands splayed across her hips, looking as though he was barely hanging on.

She rose up until only the head was inside her, then sank back down. Ash groaned as her body clenched down around him. He reached up and hooked his hands around her neck, pulling her down for a kiss. It was deep and reckless and more than a little wild. And in one smooth motion, he rolled her over so that she was the one on her back, looking up at him. And he was wearing a cocky grin.

She opened her mouth to protest the sudden change of dynamics, but at the same time he rocked into her, swift and deep—*oh, so deep*—and the sound that emerged was a throaty moan.

He pulled back again then rocked forward. Once, twice. Slooowly. Watching her face. This was just like the shower video, only better because she was actually feeling it. And it was everything she expected and more.

Faster, she wanted to say. *Harder.* But the words were getting lost somewhere between her brain and her lips. She felt paralyzed, poised on a precipice, and as he moved inside her, each thrust pushed her a little closer to the edge. Ash must have been able to tell that she was close. He picked up speed.

Her body began to tremble, then quake, then the pleasure took hold almost violently. It felt as though her body was turning in on itself. Toes curling, fingers clenching. She was still in its grip when Ash groaned and shuddered.

She was just starting to come around, to come back to herself, when he dropped his head on her shoulder. He was breathing hard, and she was having a tough time catching her breath, too.

Ash kissed her one last time then rolled over onto the mattress, drawing her against his side.

"Don't take this the wrong way," he said. "But that was without question the quietest sex we have ever had."

She knew from the videos that she had the tendency to be…*vocal,* during sex, but she just assumed she was saucing it up for the camera. She didn't realize she *always* acted that way. "I can try to be louder next time."

"Oh, no," he said quickly. "Quiet is good. I've stopped getting those I-know-what-*you*-did-last-night looks in the elevator."

She rose up on her elbow to look at him. "You're not serious," she said, but she could see by his expression that he was. Her cheeks flushed just thinking about it. He once said that she had voyeuristic tendencies, but come on. "I still have a hard time believing some of the things I did. And you know, I just assumed that when I got my memories back, I would go back to being the person I was before. But the truth is, I don't think I want to. I think I like myself better the way I am now."

"You know, I think I do, too."

She hoped he really meant that. That he wasn't secretly disappointed. "You don't miss the makeup and the perfect hair and the clingy clothes?"

"To be honest, I hadn't given it much thought. The clothes you wear look fine to me, and your hair is cute this way." He reached up and tucked a strand behind her ear. "As for the makeup, I never thought you needed it anyway."

"I think I was insecure as a child."

His brow furrowed. "You remember?"

"Not exactly. It's hard to explain. It's just a feeling I have. I look at the way I was and it's just so not me, so not who I am now. It makes me feel as though I was playing a role. Trying to be something that I wasn't. Which means I couldn't have liked myself very much, could I?"

"I guess not."

"Would it be okay with you if I bought some new clothes? Those lace push-up bras are like medieval torture devices. I'd honestly rather have smaller-looking boobs than suffer another day in one of those things."

He grinned. "You can buy whatever you need."

"I'll probably need you to take me, though. Since I'm not thrilled with the idea of taking the bus. In fact, I may never get on one again. You could just drop me off, and I could call when I'm finished."

"How would you feel about driving yourself?"

She thought about that and realized there was really no reason why she couldn't drive herself. She was off the pain meds and she wasn't getting dizzy any longer. "I guess I could. As long as you don't mind loaning me your car."

He got this adorable, mischievous grin. "I was going to wait until Monday when it got here to tell you."

"When what got here?"

"I wanted it to be a surprise, but I suppose I could tell you now."

"Tell me what?"

He jumped up, looking a bit like an excited little boy, and reached for his pants on the floor. He pulled his cell phone from the pocket, then flopped down on his stomach beside her. He tapped at the touch screen, but when she sat up and tried to see over his shoulder what he was doing, he rolled onto his back. "Just hold on."

He had such a sweet, goofy grin on his face, she was

dying to see what he was up to. When he finally handed her the phone there was photo of a car on the screen. A luxury mini-SUV in a rich shade of blue. "I thought your car was new," she said.

"It is."

"So why buy another one?"

He laughed. "For you. That's your car. Well, not that exact one, but one just like it."

"You bought me a car?"

"You need one, right?"

"Oh, my God." She threw her arms around his neck and hugged him. "Thank you!"

He laughed and hugged her back. "It's not that big of a deal."

"Maybe not to you, but it is to me."

"If you scroll left you can see what it looks at from other angles."

She sat back against the pillows, scrolling through the other shots he'd taken.

"It's so cute! I love it."

"It also has an excellent safety record. And I got the extended option package. It has everything."

She scrolled to the next page, but it wasn't of the car. It took her a second to figure out exactly what it was she was seeing, and when she did, her head began to spin.

One second Mel was all smiles, then her face went slack and all the color leeched from her skin. She lifted a hand to her mouth, as if she might be sick.

He sat up. "Mel, what's wrong?"

She shook her head and said, "I should be dead."

He looked down at his phone and realized she was no longer looking at her new car. She was looking at the photos he'd taken at the impound lot in Texas, of what was left of her old car. He had completely forgotten they were there.

"Crap!" He snatched the phone away, but it was obviously too late. He should have erased the damned things, or at least transferred them to his work computer. "I didn't mean for you to see those. I'm sorry."

She looked up at him, eyes as wide as saucers. "How did I survive that?"

"You were really lucky."

"Everyone kept saying that. But they always say that when someone has an accident and doesn't die. Right?"

He shrugged. "I guess sometimes they really mean it."

"Was it just the one picture, or are there more?"

"Half a dozen maybe. I'll erase them."

She held out her hand. "I want to see."

"Mel—"

"Ash, I *need* to see them."

"It'll just upset you."

"It will upset me more if I don't. *Please.*"

He reluctantly handed it back to her, and watched as she scrolled through the photos. When she got to the last one she scrolled back the other way. She did that a few times, then she closed her eyes tight, as though she was trying to block the image from her mind.

Letting her look had been a bad idea. He should have told her no and erased them. "Mel, why don't you give me—"

"I rolled," she said, eyes still closed.

"That's right. Into a ditch. Then you hit a tree. The doctor told you that, remember?"

Her brow wrinkled in concentration. "The interior was black, the instrument panel had red. Red lights. And the gearshift…" She reached out with her right hand, as if she was touching it. "It was red, too." She opened her eyes and looked up at him. "There was an air freshener hanging from the mirror. It smelled like coconuts."

There was no way she could have seen that kind of detail in the photo on his phone. She was remembering. "What else?"

"I remember rolling." She looked up at him. "I remember being scared, and hurting, and thinking I was going to die. It was...*awful*. But I do remember."

He wondered how long it would take before she remembered what else had happened, *why* she rolled into the ditch. Had she been conscious enough to know that she was miscarrying?

He put his hand on her shoulder. "It's over, and you're safe now."

She looked up at him. "There's something else."

He held his breath.

She stared at him for what felt like an eternity, then she shook her head. "I don't know. I know there's something there. Something I should know. It just won't come."

"It will," he assured her, hoping it never did, wishing she could just be content to let it stay buried.

Thirteen

Mel had a bad dream that night.

After a dinner of takeout Chinese that they both picked at, and a movie neither seemed to be paying much attention to, Ash walked Mel to bed.

He was going to tuck her in then go to his office and work for a while, but she took his hand and said, "Please stay." He couldn't tell her no. They undressed and climbed into bed together. He kissed her goodnight, intending it to be a quick brush of the lips, because he was sure that sex was the last thing on her mind. But her arms went around his neck and she pulled him to her, whispering, "Make love to me again."

He kept waiting for her demanding aggressive side to break through, but she seemed perfectly content lying there, kissing and touching, letting him take the lead. And he realized just how much he preferred this to the hot and heavy stuff.

Afterward she cuddled up against him, warm and soft and limp, and they fell asleep that way. It was a few hours later when she shot up in bed, breath coming in ragged bursts, eyes wild with fear.

He sat up beside her, touched her shoulder, and found that she was drenched in sweat. He felt the sheet and it was drenched, too. For a second he was afraid she'd developed a fever, but her skin was cool.

"I was rolling," she said, her voice rusty from sleep. "I was rolling and rolling and I couldn't stop."

"It was a dream. You're okay." He had no doubt this was a direct result of her seeing those photos and he blamed himself.

"It hurts," she said, cradling her head in her hands. "My head hurts."

He wasn't sure if it hurt now, or she was having a flashback to the accident. She seemed trapped somewhere between dream and sleep. "Do you want a pain pill?"

She shivered and wrapped her arms around herself. "I'm cold."

Well, lying between wet sheets wasn't going to warm her.

"Come on," he said, climbing out of bed and coaxing her to follow him.

"Where?" she asked in a sleepy voice, dutifully letting him lead her into the hall.

"My room. Where it's dry."

He got her tucked in, then laid there for a long time, listening to her slow even breaths, until he finally drifted off.

She apparently didn't remember the dream, or waking up, because she shook him awake the next morning and asked, "Ash, why are we in your bedroom?"

"You had a nightmare," he mumbled, too sleepy to even open his eyes.

"I did?"

"The sheets were sweaty so I moved us in here." He thought she may have said something else after that but he had already drifted back to sleep. When he woke again it was after eight, far later than he usually got up. Even on a Sunday. He would have to skip the gym and go straight to work.

He showered and dressed in slacks and a polo since it was Sunday and it was doubtful anyone else would be around the office, then went out to the kitchen. Mel was sitting on the couch wearing jeans and a T-shirt, her hair pulled back in a ponytail, knees pulled up with her feet propped on the cushion in front of her. If he didn't know better, he would say she wasn't a day over eighteen.

When she saw him she looked up and smiled. "Good morning."

He walked to the back of the couch and leaned over, intending to kiss her cheek, but she turned her head and caught his lips instead. They tasted like coffee, and a hint of something sweet—a pastry maybe—and she smelled like the soap they had used in the shower last night. He was damned tempted to lift her up off the couch, toss her over his shoulder and take her back to bed.

Maybe later.

When he broke the kiss she was still smiling up at him.

"Good morning," he said.

"There's coffee."

"How long have you been up?" he asked as he walked to the kitchen. She'd already set a cup out for him.

"Six-thirty." She followed him into the kitchen, taking

a seat on one of the bar stools at the island. "It was a little disorienting waking up in a bed I didn't fall asleep in."

"You still don't remember it?"

She shook her head. "I do remember something else though. The book I've been reading, I've read it before. I mean, I figured I had, since it was on the shelf. But I picked it up this morning after already reading almost half of it, and bam, suddenly I remember how it ended. So I went to the bookshelf and looked at a few others, and after I read the back blurb, and skimmed the first few pages, I remembered those, too."

This was bound to happen. He just hadn't expected it to be this soon. "Sounds like you've been busy."

"Yeah. I was sitting there reading those books, thinking how stupid it was that I could remember something so immaterial, and I couldn't even remember my own mother. Then it hit me. The picture."

"What picture?"

"The one of me and my mom, when I was thirteen."

He recalled seeing it in her room before, but not since they had been back. He didn't recall seeing it in her place in Texas either. "I remember you having one, but I don't know where it is."

"That's okay. I remembered. It just popped into my head. I knew it was in the front pouch of my suitcase. And it was."

Ash could swear his heart stopped, then picked up triple time. She remembered packing? "Your suitcase?"

"I figured I must have taken it with me on my trip."

"Right…you must have." Hadn't he checked her suitcases? So there would be nothing to jolt her memory? It was possible that he only patted the front pouches, assuming they were empty.

Oh, well, it was just a photo.

"I found something else, too," she said, and there was something about her expression, the way she was looking at him, that made his heart slither down to his stomach. She pulled a folded-up piece of paper from her back pocket and handed it to him.

He unfolded it and realized immediately what it was. A lease, for her rental in Abilene.

Oh, hell. He should have checked the damned outer pockets.

"I wasn't on a research trip, was I?"

He shook his head.

"I moved out, didn't I? I left you."

He nodded.

"I've been sitting here, trying to remember what happened, why I left, but it's just not there."

Which meant she didn't remember the affair, or the child. The limb-weakening relief made him feel like a total slime. But as long as she didn't remember, he could just pretend it never happened. Or who knew, maybe she did remember, and she was content to keep it her little secret. As long as they didn't acknowledge it, it didn't exist.

"You didn't leave a note," he said. "I just came home from work one day and you were gone. I guess you weren't happy."

She frowned. "I just took off and you didn't come after me?"

"Not at first," he admitted, because at this point lying to her would only make things worse. "I was too angry. And too proud, I guess. I convinced myself that after a week or two you would change your mind and come back. I thought you would be miserable without me. But you didn't come back, and I was the one who was miserable. So I hired the P.I."

"And you found out that I was in the hospital?"

He nodded. "I flew to Texas the next morning. I was going to talk you into coming back with me."

"But I had amnesia. So you told me I had been on a trip."

He nodded. "I was afraid that if I told you the truth, you wouldn't come home. I went to your rental and packed your things and had them shipped back here. And I…" Jeez, this was tough. They were supposed to be having this conversation when he was dumping her, and reveling in his triumph. He wasn't supposed to fall for her.

"You what?" she asked.

"I…" *Christ, just say it, Ash.* "I went through your computer. I erased a lot of stuff. Things I thought would jog your memory. E-mails, school stuff, music."

She nodded slowly, as though she was still processing it, trying to decide if she should be angry with him. "But you did it because you were afraid of losing me."

"Yes." More or less, anyway. Just not for the reason she thought. And if he was going to come this far, he might as well own up to all of it. "There's one more thing."

She took a deep breath, as if bracing herself. "Okay."

"It's standard procedure that hospitals will only give out medical information to next of kin. Parents, spouses… *fiancés*…"

It took a minute for her to figure it out, and he could tell the instant it clicked. He could see it in her eyes, in the slow shake of her head. "We're not engaged."

"It was the only way I could get any information. The only way the doctor would talk to me."

She had this look on her face, as if she might be sick. He imagined he was wearing a similar expression.

She slid her ring off and set it on the counter. At least she didn't throw it at him. "I guess you'll be wanting this back. Although, I don't imagine it's real."

"No, it's real. It's…" God, this was painful. "It's my ex-wife's."

She took a deep breath, holding in what had to be seething anger. He wished she would just haul off and slug him. They would both feel better. Not that he deserved any absolution of guilt.

"But you did it because you were afraid of losing me," she said, giving him an out.

"Absolutely." And despite feeling like the world's biggest ass, telling her the truth lifted an enormous weight off his shoulders. He felt as though he could take a full breath for the first time since the day he had walked into her hospital room.

"You can't even imagine how guilty I've felt," he told her.

"Is this why you've been avoiding me?"

Her words stunned him. "What do you mean?"

"All the late nights at work."

"I always work late. I always have."

"Do you always tell me you're at work when you really aren't?"

What was she talking about? "I've never done that. If I said I was at work, that's where I was."

"I called your office yesterday afternoon, to ask you about dinner, but you didn't answer. I left a message, too, but you never called back."

He could lie about it, say he was making copies or in a meeting or something, but the last thing he needed was one more thing to come back at him. "I was there. Brock and Flynn decided to throw an impromptu party. To celebrate our engagement."

Her eyes widened a little. "Well, that must have been awkward."

"You have no idea."

"I guess that's my fault, for spilling the beans."

"Mel, none of this is even close to your fault. I find the fact that you haven't thrown something at me a miracle."

"In a way, I feel like I should be thanking you."

"For what?"

"If you hadn't done this, I would never have known how happy I could be with you."

Not in a million years would he expect her to thank him for lying to her.

"But," she continued, and he felt himself cringe. When there was a but, it was never good. "If things stay the way they are, you're going to lose me again."

This was no empty threat. He could see that she was dead serious.

"What things?"

"You're always at work. You're gone before I get up and you come home after I'm asleep. That might be easier to stomach if you at least took the weekends off. I sort of feel like, what's the point of being together, if we're never together?"

The old Melody would have never complained about the dynamics of their relationship, or how many hours he worked. Even if it did bother her. And maybe that was part of the problem.

He couldn't deny that right before she left, he had been pulling away from her. He was almost always at work, either at Maddox, or in his home office. And it seemed that the further he retreated, the harder she tried to please him, until she was all but smothering him. Then, boom, she was gone.

Had it never occurred to him that he had all but driven her into another man's arms?

He knew that the sugar daddy/mistress arrangement wasn't an option any longer. She wanted the real thing.

She deserved it. But what did he want? Was he ready for that kind of commitment?

He thought about Melody and how she used to be, and how she was now. There was no longer a good Melody and an evil one. She was the entire package. She was perfect just the way she was, and he realized that if he ever were to settle down again, he could easily imagine himself with her. But relationships took compromise and sacrifice, and he was used to pretty much always getting his way, never having to work at it.

And honestly, he'd been bored out of his skull.

He wanted a woman who could think for herself, and be herself, even if that meant disappointing him sometimes, or disagreeing with him.

He wanted Melody.

"Mel, after everything I went through to get you back, do you honestly think I would just let you go again?"

Her bottom lip started to tremble and her eyes welled, though she was trying like hell to hold it back. But he didn't want her holding anything back.

He walked around the island to her but she was already up and meeting him halfway. She threw herself around him and he wrapped her up in his arms.

This was a good thing they had. A really good thing. And this time he was determined not to screw it up.

After seeing the pictures of her wrecked car, Melody's memories began to come back with increasing frequency. Random snippets here and there. Things like the red tennis shoes she had gotten on her birthday when she was five, and rides her mother let her take on the pony outside the grocery store.

She remembered her mother's unending parade of boyfriends and husbands. All of them mistreated her mother in some way or another, often physically. She didn't seem to know how to stand up for herself, when to say *enough,* yet when it came to protecting Mel, she was fierce. Mel remembered when one of them came after her. She couldn't have been more than ten or eleven. She remembered standing frozen in place, too frightened to even shield her face as he approached her with an open palm, arm in mid-swing. She closed her eyes, waiting for the impact, then she heard a thud and opened her eyes to find him kneeling on the floor, stunned and bleeding from his head, and her mother hovering over him with a baseball bat.

She hadn't been a great mother, but she had kept Mel safe.

Despite having finally learned that it was socially unacceptable, Mel had been so used to the idea of men hitting that when she'd started seeing Ash she'd always been on guard, waiting for the arm to swing. But after six months or so, when he hadn't so much as raised his voice to her, she'd realized that he would never hurt her. Not physically anyway.

When she admitted that to Ash, instead of being insulted, he looked profoundly sad. They lay in bed after making love and talked about it. About what her life had been like as a child, how most of her memories were shrouded in fear and insecurity. And as she opened up to him, Ash miraculously began to do the same.

She recalled enough to know that their relationship had never been about love, and that for those three years they had been little more than roommates. Roommates who had sex. She couldn't help but feel ashamed that she had compromised herself for so long, that she hadn't insisted on better. But they were in a real relationship now. They had a future. They talked and laughed and spent time together.

They saw movies and had picnics and took walks on the shore. They were a couple.

He didn't care that her hair was usually a mess and her clothes didn't cling. Or that she'd stopped going to the gym and lost all those pretty muscles and curves she'd worked so hard to maintain, and now was almost as scrawny as she'd been in high school. *Less is more,* he had said affectionately when she'd complained that she had no hips and her butt had disappeared. He didn't even miss the push-up bras, although he knew damn well if that had been a prerequisite to the relationship she probably would have walked.

He even forgave her for all the orgasms she had faked, during sex she didn't want but had anyway, because she was so afraid of disappointing him. And she was humbled to learn that there were many nights when he would have been happy to forgo the sex and watch a movie instead. He made her promise that she would never have sex if she didn't want to, and she swore to him that she would never fake an orgasm again. He promised that she would never need to, and in the weeks that passed, she didn't.

Despite all the talking they had done, there was still one thing that they hadn't discussed, something she had been afraid to bring up. Because as close as they had grown, there was still that little girl inside who was afraid to disappoint him. But she knew she had waited long enough, and one morning at breakfast, over eggs and toast, he gave her the perfect segue.

"Since your memory is almost completely back now, have you considered when you'll go back to school?" he asked.

She was suddenly so nervous that the juice she was drinking got caught in her throat. It was now or never.

"Not really," she said, then thought, *Come on, Mel, be*

brave. Just tell him the truth. "The thing is, I don't want to go back. I don't want to be a lawyer."

He shrugged and said, "Okay," then he took a drink of his juice and went back to eating.

She was so stunned her mouth actually fell open. All that worrying, all the agonizing she had done over this, and all he had to say was *okay?*

She set her fork down beside her plate. "Is that it?"

He looked up from the toast he was spreading jam on. "Is what it?"

"I say I don't want to be a lawyer and all you say is *okay?*"

He shrugged. "What do you want me to say?"

"After you spent all that money on law-school tuition, doesn't it upset you that I'm just going to throw my education away?"

"Not really. An education isn't worth much if you aren't happy in what you're doing."

If she had known he would be so understanding she would have told him the truth months and months ago. She thought of all the time she had wasted on a career path that had been going nowhere. If only she'd had the courage to open up to him.

"Do you have any idea what you might want to do?" he asked.

The million-dollar question.

"I think so."

When she didn't elaborate he said, "Would you like to tell me?"

She fidgeted with her toast, eyes on her plate. "I was thinking, maybe I can stay home for a while."

"That's fine. It isn't like you *need* to work."

"Maybe I could do something here, instead of an outside job."

"Like a home business?"

"Sort of." *Just say it, Mel. Spit it out.* "But one that involves things like midnight feedings and diaper changes."

He brow dipped low. He took a deep breath and exhaled slowly. "Mel, you know I can't—"

"I know. I do. But there's always artificial means. Or even adoption. And I don't mean right now. I would want us to be married first." He opened his mouth to say something but she held up a hand to stop him. "I know we haven't discussed anything definite, or made plans, and I'm not trying to rush things. I swear. I just wanted to sort of…put it out there, you know, to make sure we're on the same page."

"I didn't know you wanted kids."

"I didn't either. Not till recently. I always told myself I would never want to put a kid through what I went through. I guess I just assumed I would have a life like my mom's. It never occurred to me that I would ever meet someone like you."

A faint smile pulled at the corners of his mouth, but he hid it behind a serious look. "How many kids are we talking about?"

Her heart leaped up and lodged somewhere in her throat. At least he was willing to discuss it. "One or two. Or *maybe* three."

He raised a brow.

"Or just two."

After a pause he said, "And this is something you *really* want?"

She bit her lip and nodded. "I really do."

There was another long pause, and for a second she was afraid he would say no. Not just afraid. She was terrified.

Because this *could* be a deal breaker. She wanted a family. It was all she'd been able to think about lately.

"Well," he finally said. "I guess one of each would be okay."

By the time the last word left his mouth she was already around the table and in his lap with her arms around his neck. "Thank you!"

He laughed and hugged her. "But not until we're married, and you know I don't want to rush into anything."

"I know." They could hardly call three years rushing, but she knew Ash had trust issues. After his own cancer, then losing his mother to the disease, he'd had a hard time letting himself get close to people, then when he finally did, and married his wife, she had betrayed him in the worst way possible.

But Ash had to know by now that she would never do that to him. She loved him, and she knew that he loved her, even if he hadn't said the words yet.

It was a big step for him, but she knew if she was patient he would come around.

Fourteen

Ash sat at his desk at work, still smiling to himself about the irony of Mel's timing. Funny that she would pick today to finally broach the marriage and kids subject, when tonight he planned to take her out for a romantic dinner, followed by a stroll by the water, where, at sunset, he would drop down on one knee and ask her to marry him.

He hoped that if she had even the slightest suspicion of his intentions, he had dispelled that when he pretended not to be sure about wanting kids. Although admittedly, until recently anyway, he hadn't even considered it. He'd never planned to get tied down again, so it had just naturally never entered his mind. And his ex had never expressed a desire for children.

Now he knew, if they were his and Mel's, his life would never be complete without them. Natural or adopted.

He opened his top drawer, pulled out the ring box and flipped the top up. It wasn't as flashy as the ring he'd given his ex. The stone was smaller and the setting more traditional, but after Mel confessed how much she had disliked the ring for their fake engagement, he knew she would love this one. A sturdy ring, the jeweler had told him, one that would hold up through diaper changes and baby baths and dirty laundry. And with any luck that would be the scene at their condo for the next several years.

There was a knock on his office door. Ash closed the ring box and set it back in his drawer just as Gavin Spencer stuck his head in. "Am I bothering you?"

"Nothing that can't wait," Ash said, gesturing him in.

Gavin strode over and sank into the chair opposite Ash's desk. "It's getting really weird out there."

Ash didn't have to ask what he meant. The mood around the office had been tense for the past couple of weeks. He could only assume it was due in part to the security leaks. It wasn't openly discussed, but at this point everyone knew.

"That's why I stay in here," Ash said.

"You're lucky you can. You should try working with Logan Emerson."

"I did notice that he doesn't exactly seem to fit in."

"He kind of creeps me out," Gavin said. "It seems like every time I look up, he's watching me. Then I caught him in my office the other day. He said he was leaving me a memo."

"Did he?"

"Yeah. But I could swear the papers on my desk had been moved around. There's something not quite right with him. There are times when he doesn't even seem to know what the hell he's doing. Doesn't seem like a very smart hire to me. If it were my firm, you could bet I would do things differently."

But it wasn't. He knew Gavin dreamed of branching

out on his own, of being the boss, but talk like that could make some people nervous. Ash just hoped Gavin wouldn't undermine the integrity of Maddox and leak information to Golden Gate to suit his own interests.

Gavin's cell rang and when he looked at the display he shot up from his chair. "Damn, gotta take this. I've got a lead on a new client. I don't want to say too much, but it could be very lucrative."

"Well, good luck."

When Gavin was gone Ash looked at the clock. It seemed that time was crawling by today. It was still four hours until he picked up Mel for dinner. It was going to be tough sitting through the entire meal, knowing the ring was in his pocket. But he knew that the water was one of her favorite places, so that was where he wanted to do it. He'd timed it so that the sun would be setting and the view would be spectacular.

He'd planned it so precisely, there wasn't a single thing that could possibly go wrong.

Melody was running late.

She leaned close to the mirror and fixed the eyeliner smudge in the corner of her eye. Boy, she was out of practice.

Ash stuck his head in for tenth time in the past fifteen minutes. "Ready yet?"

"One more minute."

"That's what you said ten minutes ago. We're going to be late for our reservation."

"The restaurant isn't going anywhere. It won't kill us if we have to wait a little longer." It was their first real night out since the accident, and she wanted it to be special. She'd bought a new dress and even curled her hair and pinned it up.

"Mel?"

"Fine! Jeez." She swiped on some lipstick, dropped the tube in her purse and said, "Let's go."

He hustled her into the elevator, then into the car. Her new car sat beside his, and though she had been a little nervous at first being back in the driver's seat, now she loved it. She even made excuses to go out just so she could drive it.

Ash got in the driver's side, started the car and zipped through the garage to the entrance. He made a right out onto the street. Traffic was heavy, and Ash cursed when they had to stop at the red light.

"We're going to be late," he complained, watching for a break in the traffic so he could hang a right.

"What is it with you tonight?" she asked, pulling down the mirror on the visor to check her eyeliner one last time. "Are you going to turn into a pumpkin or something?"

He started to move forward just as she was flipping her visor up, and at the same time a guy on a bike shot off the curb and into the intersection.

"Ash!" she screamed, and he slammed on the brakes, barely missing the guy's back tire as he flew by in an attempt to beat the light.

"Idiot," Ash muttered, then he turned to look at her. "You okay?"

She couldn't answer. Her hands were trembling and braced on the dash, her breath coming in short, fast bursts. She suddenly felt as though her heart was going to explode from her chest it was hammering so hard.

"Mel? Talk to me," Ash said, sounding worried, but his voice was garbled, as if he was talking to her through water.

She tried, but she couldn't talk. Her lips felt numb and she wasn't getting enough air.

Out. She had to get out of the car.

The car behind them honked so Ash zipped around the corner.

He put his hand on her arm, keeping one eye on her and one on the road. "Mel, you're scaring me."

She couldn't breathe. She was trapped and she needed air.

She reached for the door handle and yanked, not even caring that they were still moving, but the door was locked.

Ash saw what she was doing and yanked her away from the door. "Jesus, Mel, what are you doing?"

"Out," she wheezed, still struggling to get a breath. "Get me out."

"Hold on," he said, gripping her arm, genuine fear in his voice. "Let me pull over."

He whipped down the alley behind their building then turned back into the parking garage. The second he came to a stop she clawed her door open and threw herself out, landing on her knees on the pavement. Her purse landed beside her and its contents spilled out, but she didn't care. She just needed air.

She heard Ash's door open and in an instant he was behind her. "Mel, what happened? Is it your head? Are you hurt?"

It was getting easier to breathe now, but that crushing panic, the instinct to run intensified as adrenaline raced through her bloodstream.

She closed her eyes, but instead of blackness she saw a rain-slicked windshield, she heard the steady thwap of the wipers. The weather was getting worse, she thought. Better get home. But then there was a bike. One second it wasn't there, then it was, as though it materialized from thin air. She saw a flash of long blond hair, a pink hoodie. She yanked the wheel, there was a loud thunk, then rolling—

"No!" Her eyes flew open. She was still in the parking garage, on the floor. But it happened. It was real. "I hit her. I hit the girl."

"Mel, you have to calm down," Ash said sternly, then she felt his arms around her, helping her up off the ground. Her knees were so weak, her legs so shaky she could hardly walk on her own.

"There was a bike," she told him. "And a girl. I hit her."

"Let's get you upstairs," he said, helping her to the elevator.

As the doors slid shut she closed her eyes and was suddenly overwhelmed by the sensation that she was rolling. Rolling and rolling, violent thrashing, pain everywhere, then wham. A sharp jolt and a pain in her head. Then, nothing. No movement. No sound.

Can't move.

Trapped.

"Mel."

Her eyes flew open.

"We're here."

Disoriented, she gazed around and realized she was back in the elevator, on their floor and he was nudging her forward. Not in the car. Not trapped.

He helped her inside and sat her down on the couch. He poured her a drink and pressed it into her hands. "Drink this. It'll help you calm down."

She lifted it to her lips and forced herself to take a swallow, nearly gagging as it burned a trail of fire down her throat. But she was feeling better now. Not so panicked. Not so afraid. The fuzziness was gone.

He started to move away and she gripped the sleeve of his jacket. "Don't go!"

"I'm just going to get the first-aid kit from the guest bathroom. We need to clean up your knees."

She looked down and saw that her knees were raw and oozing blood, and the sight of it made her feel dizzy and sick to her stomach.

She lay back and let her head fall against the cushion. She remembered now, as clear as if it had happened this morning. She was in the car, knowing she had to get help. She had to help the girl. But when she tried to move her arms something was pinning her. She was trapped. She tried to see what it was, thinking she could pry it loose, but the second she moved her head, pain seized with a vicelike grip, so intense that bile rose up to choke her. She moaned and closed her eyes against the pain.

She tried to think, tried to concentrate on staying conscious. Then she felt it, low in her belly. A sharp pain. Then cramping. She remembered thinking, *No, not there. Not the baby.*

The baby.

Oh, God. She had been pregnant. She was going to have Ash's baby.

The final piece of the puzzle slid into place. That was why she left Ash. That was why she ran to Texas. She was pregnant with Ash's baby, a baby she knew he would never want.

The relief of finally having the answers, finally seeing the whole picture, paled in comparison to the ache in her heart.

They could have been a family. She and Ash and the baby. They could have been happy. But how could she have known?

Ash reappeared and knelt down in front of her. He'd

taken off his suit jacket and rolled his sleeves to his elbows. "This is probably going to sting," he warned her, then he used a cool, damp washcloth to wipe away the blood. She sucked in a surprised breath as she registered the raw sting of pain.

"Sorry," he said. "This probably won't feel much better, but we don't want it getting infected. God only knows what's on the floor down there."

He wet a second cloth with hydrogen peroxide, and she braced herself against the pain as he dabbed it on her knees. It went white and bubbly on contact.

If she had known it could be like this, that they could be so happy, she wouldn't have left. She would have told him about the baby.

Now it was too late.

Ash smoothed a jumbo-size bandage across each knee. "All done."

"Is she dead?" Mel asked him, as he busied himself with repacking the first-aid kit. The fact that he wouldn't look at her probably wasn't a good sign. "Please tell me."

He sighed deeply and looked up at her. "It wasn't your fault."

So that was a yes. She pretty much knew already. And her fault or not, she had killed someone's baby. Someone's child. And she hadn't even had a chance to apologize. To say she was sorry. "Why didn't someone tell me?"

"The doctor thought it would be too traumatic."

She laughed wryly. "And finding out this way has just been a barrel of laughs."

He rose to his feet, the kit and soiled rags in hand. "He did what he thought was best."

It hit her suddenly that the doctor must have told him about the baby, too. He thought Ash was her fiancé. What reason would he have to hide it?

All this time Ash knew and he had never said a word. It was one thing to lie about engagements, and hide personal information, but this was their *child*.

"Is that why you didn't say anything about the baby, either?"

Ash closed his eyes and shook his head. "Don't do this. Just let it go."

"Let it go? I lost a baby."

He looked at her, his eyes pleading. "Everything has been so good, please don't ruin it."

"Ruin it?"

"Can't we just do what we've been doing and pretend it never happened?"

Her mouth fell open. "How can you even say something like that? I lost a child—"

"That wasn't mine!" he shouted, slamming the first-aid kit down so hard on the coffee table that she heard the glass crack. She was so stunned by the unprecedented outburst that it took a second for his words to sink in.

"Ash, who told you it wasn't yours? Of course it was yours."

He leveled his eyes on her, and if she didn't know better, she would think he was going to hit her. But when he spoke his voice was eerily calm. "You and I both know that's impossible. I'm sterile."

She could hardly believe what he was suggesting. "You think I had an *affair*."

"I had unprotected sex with you for three years, and with my wife for seven years, and no one got pregnant before now, so yeah, I think it's pretty damn likely that you had an affair."

He couldn't honestly believe she would do that. "Ash, since that night at the party, when we met, there has been *no one* but you."

"The party? I seriously doubt that."

He might as well have just called her a whore.

"If it *was* mine," he said, "why did you run off?"

"Because you had made it pretty clear that you had no desire to have a family, and you sure as hell didn't seem to want me. I figured it would be best for everyone if I just left. Frankly, I'm surprised you even noticed I was gone."

His eyes cut sharply her way.

Why was he being so stubborn? He *knew* her. He knew she would never hurt him. "Ash, I'm telling you the *truth.*"

"And I'm just supposed to trust you? Just take your word for it when I know it's impossible?"

"Yes. You should. Because you know I wouldn't lie to you."

"I don't believe you," he said, and it felt as though a chunk of her heart broke away.

"Why did you even bring me back here? If you thought I cheated on you, if you hated me that much, why not just leave me in the hospital? Were you plotting revenge or something?"

His jaw clenched and he looked away.

She was just being surly, but she'd hit the nail right on the head. "Oh, my God." She rose from the couch. "You *were,* weren't you? You wanted to get back at me."

He turned to her, eyes black with anger. "After all I did for you, you betrayed me. I've taken care of you for three years, and you repay me by screwing around. You're damn right I wanted revenge." He shook his head in disgust. "You want to know the really pathetic thing? I forgave you. I thought you had changed. I was going to ask you to marry me tonight, for real this time. But here you are, *still* lying to me. Why won't you just admit what you did? Own up to it."

Own up to something she didn't do?

The really sad thing was that she suspected, somewhere deep down, he believed her. He knew she was telling the truth. He just didn't want to hear it. When the chips were down, and things got a little tough, it was easier to push her away than take a chance.

"Is this the way it is with you?" she asked. "You find something really good, but when you get too close, you throw it away? Is that what you did to your wife? Did you ignore her for so long that you drove her away?"

He didn't respond, but she could see that she'd hit a nerve.

"I love you, Ash. I wanted to spend the rest of my life with you, but I just can't fight for you anymore."

"No one asked you to."

And that pretty much said it all. "Give me an hour to pack my things. And I would appreciate if I could use the car for a couple of weeks, until I can find another one."

"Keep it," he said.

Like a parting gift? she wondered. Or the booby prize.

She rose from the couch and walked to her room to pack, her legs still wobbly from the adrenaline rush, her knees sore.

But they didn't even come close to the pain in her heart.

Ash sat at a booth in the Rosa Lounge, sipping his scotch, trying to convince himself that he wasn't miserable, wasn't a complete idiot, and not doing a very good job of it.

Mel had been gone three days and he could barely stand

it. And now that he finally realized what an idiot he'd been, he wasn't sure how to fix it.

He knew he had to be pretty desperate at this point to arrange this meeting, but there were some things that Mel had said that really stuck in his craw, and he had to know, once and for all, if she was right.

He checked his watch again and looked over at the door just in time to see her come in. Her hair was shorter than before, but otherwise she didn't look all that different. She scanned the room and he rose from his seat, waving her over. When she saw him, she smiled, which was a good sign. When he'd called her and asked to meet she'd sounded a little wary.

As she walked to the booth he saw that she still looked really good, and, wow, really pregnant.

"Linda," he said as she approached. "Good to see you."

"Hello, Ash." His ex-wife leaned in and air kissed his cheek. "You look great."

"You, too," he said. "Please sit down."

He waited until she slid into the opposite side of the booth, then he sat, too.

The waitress appeared to take her drink order, and when she was gone Ash gestured to Linda's swollen middle. "You're pregnant. I had no idea."

She placed a hand on her stomach and smiled. "Six weeks to go."

"Congratulations. You're still with…" He struggled to conjure up a name.

"Craig," she supplied for him. "We just celebrated our second wedding anniversary last month."

"That's great. You look very happy."

"I am," she said with a smile. "Everything is going great. I don't know if you remember, but Craig owned a gym in our old neighborhood. I talked him into expanding and we just opened our fourteenth fitness center."

"I'm glad to hear it."

"How about you? What have you been up to?"

"I'm still at Maddox."

She waited, as if she expected more, and when there wasn't she asked, "Anyone…*special* in your life?"

"For a while," he said, wanting to add, *until I royally screwed up.* "It's complicated."

She waited for him to elaborate. And though he hadn't planned to, the words just kind of came out.

"We just split up," he heard himself tell her. "A few days ago, in fact."

"I'm going to go out on a limb and assume that you asking to meet me is directly related somehow."

His ex was no dummy.

"I need to ask you something," he told her, rubbing his hands together, wondering if maybe this wasn't such a good idea. "And it's probably going to sound…well, a little weird after all this time."

"Okay." She folded her hands in front of her and leaned forward slightly, giving him her undivided attention.

"I need to know why you did it. Why you cheated on me."

He thought she might be offended or defensive, but she looked more surprised than upset. "Wow, okay. I didn't see that one coming."

"I'm not trying to play the blame game, I swear. I just really need to know."

"You're sure you want to do this?"

No, but he'd come this far and there was no going back now. "I'm sure. I need to know."

"Let's face it, Ash, by the time you caught me with Craig, our marriage had been over for a long time. It was only a matter of time before I left. You just didn't want to see it, didn't want to take responsibility. You wanted to make me out to be the monster."

"I guess I still believed we were happy."

"Happy? We were nonexistent. You were never around, and even when you were you were a ghost. You just didn't want to see it."

She was right. They had drifted apart. He didn't want to see it. Didn't want to take the blame.

"I know it was wrong to cheat on you, and I'll always be truly sorry for that. I didn't want to hurt you, but I was so lonely, Ash. The truth is, when you caught us, and you were so angry, I was stunned. I honestly didn't think you cared anymore. I felt as though I could have packed my bags and left, and you wouldn't have noticed until you ran out of clean underwear."

All of this was beginning to sound eerily familiar.

"So I drove you to it?"

"Please don't think that I'm placing all the blame on you. I could have tried harder, too. I could have insisted you take more time for me. I just assumed we were in a phase, that we had drifted, and eventually we would meet back up somewhere in the middle again. I guess by the time it got really bad, it didn't seem worth saving. I just didn't love you anymore."

"Wow," he said. Drive the knife in deeper.

"Ash, come on, you can't honestly say you didn't feel the same way."

She was right. His pride had taken a much bigger hit than his heart.

"Is that what you wanted to know?" she asked.

He smiled. "Yeah. I appreciate your honesty."

She cringed suddenly and pushed down on the top of

her belly. "Little bugger is up under my ribs again. I think he's going to be a soccer player."

"He?"

"Yeah. We still haven't settled on a name. I'm partial to Thomas, and Craig likes Jack."

"I always thought you didn't want kids."

"It's not so much that I didn't want them, but it never seemed like the right time. And it was a touchy subject for you, since you thought you couldn't."

"*Thought* I couldn't?"

She frowned, as though she realized she'd said something she shouldn't have.

"Linda?"

She looked down at her hands. "I probably should have told you before."

Why did Ash get the feeling he wasn't going to like this? "Told me what?"

"It was in college. We had been together maybe six months. I found out I was pregnant. And before you ask, yes, it was yours."

"But I can't—"

"Believe me, you can. And you did. But we were both going for degrees, and we hadn't even started talking about marriage at that point. Not to mention that we had student loans up the yin yang. I knew it was *really* lousy timing. So I did what I believed was the best thing for both of us and had an abortion."

Ash's head was spinning so violently he nearly fell out of the booth. "But all those years we didn't use protection?"

"*You* didn't, but I did. I had an IUD. So there wouldn't be any more accidents."

He could hardly believe he was hearing this. "Why didn't you tell me?"

"I thought I was protecting you. Believe me when I say I felt guilty enough for the both of us. And even if I had wanted to keep the baby, I knew you wouldn't. I didn't want to burden you with that."

That seemed to be a common theme when it came to him and women.

So Mel had been telling him the truth. She had been through hell and lived to talk about it, she had lost a baby, *his* baby, and he had more or less accused her of being a tramp.

He could have been a father. And he would have, if he hadn't been so selfish and blind. Not to mention *stupid*.

He closed his eyes and shook his head. "I am such an idiot."

"Why do I get the feeling you're not talking about us any longer?"

He looked over at her. "Do you think some people are destined to keep repeating their mistakes?"

"Some people maybe. If they don't learn from them."

"And if they learn too late?"

She reached across the table and laid her hand over his, and just like that, all the unresolved conflict, all the bitterness he'd shouldered for the past three years seemed to vanish. "Do you love her?" she asked.

"Probably too much for my own good."

"Does she love you?"

"She did three days ago."

She grinned and gave his hand a squeeze. "So what the heck are you doing still sitting here with me?"

Damn, the woman was good at disappearing. He had no clue where she was staying and she refused to answer her phone. But this time Ash didn't wait nearly as long to call the P.I. and ask him to find her again. But when Ash gave him the make and year of her car, the P.I. asked, "Does the car have GPS?"

"Yeah, it does."

"Then you don't really need me. You can track her every move on any computer. Or even your phone if it has Internet. I can help you set it up."

"That would be great," Ash told him. It was about time something went right. And thank God this time she hadn't gone very far. Within hours he was pulling into the lot of a grocery store a few miles away from the condo.

The idea of a confrontation inside the store seemed like a bad idea, so he parked, got out of his car and made himself comfortable on her hood. There was no way she would be leaving without at least talking to him.

She came out of the store maybe ten minutes later and his heart lifted at the sight of her, then it lodged in his throat when he thought of all the explaining he had to do. And the confessing.

She had one bag in her arms and she was rooting around in her purse for something, so she didn't see him right away.

She looked adorable with her hair up in a ponytail, wearing jeans, tennis shoes and a pullover sweatshirt. He was finding it hard to imagine what he considered so appealing in the way she looked before the accident. This just seemed to be a better fit.

She was almost to the car when she finally looked up and noticed him there. Her steps slowed and her eyes narrowed. He could see that she was wondering how he'd found her, especially when she had been dodging his calls.

"GPS," he said. "I tracked you on my phone."

"You realize that stalking is a criminal offense in California?"

"I don't think it can be considered stalking when I technically own the car."

She tossed the keys at him so forcefully that if he hadn't caught them he might have lost an eye. "Take it," she said and walked past him in the direction of the street.

He jumped down off the hood to follow her. "Come on, Mel. I just want to talk to you."

"But I don't want to listen. I'm still too mad at you."

Mad was good as far as he was concerned. Since he deserved it. She could get over being mad at him a lot easier than, say, hating his guts. Not that he didn't deserve that, too.

She was walking so fast he had to jog to catch up to her. "I've been an ass."

She snorted. "You say that like it's something I don't already know."

"But do you know how sorry I am?"

"I'm sure you are."

"It's not that I didn't believe you about the baby. I just didn't want it to be true."

She stopped so abruptly he nearly tripped over his own feet. "Are you actually saying that you didn't want it to be yours?"

"No! Of course not."

"You really are an ass," she said, and turned to leave, but he grabbed her arm.

"Would you please listen for a minute? I could live with the idea that you'd had an affair, that you had made a mistake, especially when I was the one who drove you away in the first place. But knowing that the baby was mine, and I was responsible…" Emotion welled up in his throat and he had to pause to get a hold of himself. "If I had treated you right, showed you that I loved you, you never would have felt like you had to run away. All the terrible things you went through never would have happened. Everything, all of it, is *my* fault."

She was quiet for what seemed like a very long time, and he watched her intently, in case she decided to throw something else at him. God only knew what she had in the bag.

"It's no one's," she finally said. "We both acted stupid."

"Maybe, but I think I was way more stupid than you. And I am so sorry, Mel. I know it's a lot to ask, but do you think you could find it in your heart to give me one more chance? I swear I'll get it right this time." He took her free hand, relieved that she didn't pull away. "You know that I love you, right?"

She nodded.

"And you love me, too?"

She sighed deeply. "Of course I do."

"And you're going to give me another chance?"

She rolled her eyes. "Like I have a choice. I get the distinct feeling that you'll just keep stalking me until I say yes."

He grinned, thinking that she was probably right. "In that case, you could hug me now."

She cracked a smile and walked into his arms, and he wrapped them around her. Even with the grocery bag crushed between them, it was darned near perfect. *She* was perfect.

"You know, deep down I didn't really think it was over," she said. "I figured you would come around. And of course I would be forced to take you back. *Again.*"

"But only after I groveled for a while?"

She grinned. "Of course."

He leaned down to kiss her, when a box sitting at the

very top of the grocery bag caught his eye. There's no way that was what he thought it was....

He pulled it out and read the label, then looked down at Mel. "A *pregnancy* test? What is this for?"

She was grinning up at him. "What do you think?"

He shook his head in amazement. *"Again?"*

"I don't know for sure yet. I'm only four or five days late. But my breasts are so tender I can barely touch them and that was a dead giveaway last time."

"I don't get it. I'm *supposed* to be sterile from the radiation."

"You might want to get that checked, because for a guy who is supposed to be sterile, you seem to have no problem knocking me up."

He laughed. "This is nuts. You realize that even if there are a few guys left in there, the odds of us going three years unprotected, then you getting pregnant not once but *twice,* is astronomical."

She shrugged. "I guess that just means it was meant to be. Our own little miracle."

He took the bag from her and set it on the ground so he could hug her properly. He didn't even care that people were driving by looking at them as if they were nuts.

As far as he was concerned, the real miracle was that he had let her go twice, and here she was back in his arms. And she could be damned sure he would never let her go again.

* * * * *

BACHELOR'S
BOUGHT BRIDE

BY
JENNIFER LEWIS

Jennifer Lewis has been dreaming up stories for as long as she can remember and is thrilled to be able to share them with readers. She has lived on both sides of the Atlantic and worked in media and the arts before she grew bold enough to put pen to paper. Happily settled in England with her family, she would love to hear from readers at jen@jen-lewis.com. Visit her website at www.jenlewis.com.

For Julie, international woman of mystery and passionate San Franciscan, who's made living in England so much fun.

Acknowledgements:

Many thanks to the kind people who read the book while I was writing it, including Anne, Anne-Marie, Carol, Cynthia, Jerri, Leeanne, Marie and Paula, my agent Andrea and Senior Editor Krista Stroever.

One

Uh-oh. What now?

Bree Kincannon's father waved to her from across the ballroom. A self-conscious everyone-is-watching wave. She stiffened as he headed toward her, marching through the splendidly attired crowd. He'd left their table the moment dessert was done, heading out to see and be seen, as usual.

Bree, as usual, had settled into her chair to listen to the music and wait for the evening to end. She'd come only because the fundraiser was for one of her favorite charities.

Wary, she glanced up as her father approached, his silver hair gleaming in the ballroom lights. Then she noticed the tall man behind him.

Oh, no. Not another introduction. She thought he'd

finally given up trying to introduce her to every eligible bachelor in San Francisco.

"Bree, dear, there's someone I'd like you to meet."

A familiar refrain. She'd heard it a lot in her twenty-nine years, and it rarely led beyond an awkward first date.

Still, she rose to her feet and planted a smile firmly on her lips.

"Gavin, this is my daughter, Bree. Bree, this is Gavin Spencer. He's an advertising executive with Maddox Communications."

Gavin Spencer thrust out his arm. She politely extended her hand to meet his. "Nice to..." *Oh, goodness.* She looked up and her heart almost stopped. Thick dark hair swept back from a high forehead. The slightest hint of five-o'clock shadow enhanced chiseled features, which framed a wide, sensual mouth.

He was gorgeous.

"Meet me?" A twinkle of humor lit warm gray eyes.

"Uh, yes. Really nice to meet you." She snatched her hand back. Her palm was practically sweating. Her father must be nuts thinking a man like this might be interested in her. "Maddox has done some really good campaigns lately. The print ads for Porto Shoes were really eye-catching."

And perhaps I could use the word really *a few more times in quick succession.* She felt her face heat.

"Thanks, I worked on that campaign." A smile revealed perfect white teeth. His chin had a slight cleft. "Your father tells me you're a photographer."

Bree's eyes darted to her father. He had? Shock and pride swept over her. He never bothered to say a word about her *hobby,* as he'd called it once. "Yes. I enjoy taking photos."

"She just won an award," her father chimed in, his face beaming with bonhomie. "The Black Hat or something."

"Black B-Book," she stammered. "It's a commercial photography competition."

"I know what the Black Book Awards are." Gavin tilted his head. "That's quite an accomplishment."

Bree's father waved to someone across the ballroom, nodded his apologies and strode off into the crowd.

Leaving her all alone with the most breathtakingly handsome man in the room.

She swallowed, smoothed the front of her crinkled taffeta dress and wished she'd worn something less... hideous.

"What kind of photographs do you take?"

"Portraits, mostly." Her voice sounded reasonably steady, which was impressive under the circumstances. She was annoyed that this gorgeous man her father had forced on her was having such an effect on her. She always felt so out of place in these situations. "I try to capture people's personalities."

"That sounds like quite a challenge."

"It's mostly about timing. Picking the right moment." She shrugged. She couldn't explain it herself. "I think the technical term is that I have a knack for it."

His finely cut mouth widened into a smile and those dreamy gray eyes twinkled. "A knack generally implies the kind of talent that makes you stand out from the crowd."

"Well, I certainly don't stand out from this crowd." She swept her arm, indicating San Francisco's most elegant and well-heeled partygoers—and instantly regretted her foolish words.

Of course she stood out. As the frumpiest and most unexciting person there.

"Everyone here is trying so hard to stand out." Dimples appeared under his impressive cheekbones. "It's the people who aren't trying who are more interesting. Would you like to dance?"

"Dance?" Did he mean with him? No one ever asked her to dance at these things.

"Is there an echo in here?"

"No. I mean, yes. Yes, I'd like to dance."

For a split second she wished the polished parquet would swallow her whole. Which would be quite a big gulp. Of course he didn't want to dance with her. He was just being polite. No doubt he'd have appreciated it if she politely refused.

But he extended his arm, clad in a deep black suit— like every other man at the formal gala—and led her to the dance floor where a band, in white tie and tails, played the thirties classic "In the Mood."

Gavin swept her out into the middle of the floor and slid his arm around her waist. Her whole body shivered with awareness, even through all the layers of crunchy taffeta. The steps to the dance were probably lodged somewhere in her subconscious. Lord knows she'd been dragged to enough dancing classes as a kid.

The room rushed past her as Gavin twirled her into a spin. He chased the music across the room, guiding them effortlessly through the other dancers. His enticing masculine scent wrapped around her, hypnotic and intoxicating. Her feet followed his almost as if they were attached, stepping in time. Her arm barely reached around his broad shoulders—which was quite something considering she was five feet nine inches—but she seemed to float along with him, gliding on the soaring trombones and quick-stepping with the punchy trumpets, until the music slid to a close.

Breathless and blinking, Bree extricated herself from Gavin's strong arms. Was that really her whipping around the floor like that—with a man like him?

"You're a wonderful dancer." His breath felt hot on her ear.

"Me? It was all you. I just had to follow."

"That's an art in itself. I bet you half the women in this room would be fighting so hard to lead they'd trip me up."

Bree laughed. "Probably true."

"You have a beautiful smile."

"Six years of orthodontics will do that for you."

He laughed. "And a wicked sense of humor." He led her off the dance floor, toward the bar. Eyes swiveled to him from all directions—both male and female eyes. Apparently no one could keep their gaze off the most impressive man in the room.

And he walked with his arm threaded firmly through hers.

Bree blinked under the unfamiliar glare of attention. They probably all wondered what on earth he was doing with her.

Heck, she wondered, too.

Being an heiress, and a plain one at that, made it easy to figure out what a man wanted. Begins with *m* and ends in *y*. But this guy could probably marry any heiress in the room—and there were plenty of them here tonight.

What was so special about her?

A voice in her head told her to stop worrying about it and just enjoy the attention that was making her heart beat faster than it had in quite some time.

"Would you like champagne?" He turned to offer her a glass.

"Thanks." Why not? The dance alone was something to celebrate. She took a sip and let the bubbles tickle her tongue.

He leaned in until his sexy stubble almost brushed her cheek. "How come I've never met you before?"

"I don't go out much. I adopted my two cats from the Oakland Animal Society, though, so I wanted to come to their fundraiser tonight. Do you have any pets?"

He shook his head. "Don't have the time. I work long hours and travel a lot. I bet your cats were lucky to find you."

"I like to think so. Especially since Ali needs insulin shots every day. Animals with health issues are hard to find homes for."

"You're a caring person."

"Or a sucker." She smiled. "But a happy one. They're my babies."

An odd expression flickered across Gavin's face. Something in his eyes, really, since his chiseled features didn't move.

Was he wondering why he was wasting time with a cat-owning spinster in a puffy dress, while stunning women cast suggestive glances over their drinks at him?

She'd rather be home with her cats anyway. Being around Gavin made her nervous, had her analyzing every move he made. She'd be a lot more comfortable with a camera lens between them. He was definitely too good-looking. It couldn't be healthy for her insides to be fluttering like this.

"I'm here because a client bought a table for the agency. It's obviously a good cause but I don't like these dos much, either," he murmured. "Too many people. Long speeches. Chewy beef." His dimples appeared again.

A warm sensation filled her chest. "What do you like to do?"

He hesitated a moment. "Interesting question. I spend so much time working, sometimes I forget what else is out there." He smiled, sheepish. "Lately though, I find myself wanting to slow down, enjoy the ride a bit more. Maybe even…" He paused and shoved a hand through his hair, as if embarrassed. "Settle down and start a family." His mouth formed a wry grin. "I guess that sounds sappy."

"Not at all." The way he looked at her with those soulful gray eyes made Bree feel woozy. Could this guy be more of a fantasy? "I think it's perfectly natural. Everyone needs balance in their life."

"Speaking of which, would you like to dance again? This song is one of my favorites."

The band had struck up a sultry Latin tune. Adrenaline prickled through her at the prospect of moving in sync with this man again. Was he for real?

Gavin entwined his arms with Bree's and led her back to the dance floor. He wished he wasn't wearing the stiff suit so he could feel her soft skin against his. So far everything about Bree seemed soft—the big gray eyes half hidden behind her glasses, her pink-tinged cheeks, her pretty, kissable mouth. He suspected there was also a soft, lush body hidden somewhere under all that crispy gray taffeta.

Her father had implied that she was unattractive and undesirable, and that her continued spinsterhood was a social embarrassment to him. His own daughter, a burden he'd pay well to be rid of. Could Elliott Kincannon really feel that way about the sweet woman on his arm?

Pure pleasure rippled through him as he slid his arm around her waist. Yes, she definitely had the kind of body a man could lose himself in. Full breasts bumped gently against his chest as he pulled her close. Her brown hair was pulled back into a tight knot and he wondered what it would look like cascading over her shoulders.

He liked the way she moved, too. Soft—again—and yielding, allowing her body to flow with his. Light on her feet as he twirled her slowly to the gentle rhythms. As she spun around to meet him, her eyes sparkled and she flashed a sweet, shy smile.

He couldn't help but respond with a smile of his own.

If first impressions were correct, then Bree Kincannon could make a very nice Mrs. Gavin Spencer. She might not be the kind of girl men flocked around in a bar, but so what? He didn't need some nipped-and-tucked trophy wife to prove his manhood.

And Bree Kincannon came with some very real incentives. One million of them, in fact.

Their eyes met again and a needle of guilt pricked his heart.

Could he really marry a woman for money?

He'd busted his ass for ten long years trying to build a reputation as a top-flight account executive. Since his first day on the job he knew he wanted to open his own agency. Bring together top creative talent, innovative thinking and creative media buying that would take the advertising world by storm.

If you'd told him ten years ago that he'd still be working for someone else at age thirty, he'd have laughed in your face.

But life had done a little laughing of its own.

His dad's pension plan had gone bust and he'd bailed his parents out of a mortgage mess. In truth, though, he was glad he could help them. The biggest mistake of his life was being dumb enough to trust a renowned "investment advisor" with a large chunk of his precious nest egg—only to learn in the papers it had been squandered on racehorses and vintage violins.

Gavin tugged Bree closer, enjoying the soft swell of her chest against his. Her long eyelashes lifted to reveal shining eyes.

He liked those eyes and it wasn't hard work to imagine looking at them for the rest of his life. He had a good feeling in his gut about Bree Kincannon, and his gut rarely steered him wrong.

Finding a wife, or even a girlfriend, had never been a priority for him. Married to his job, that's what his friends joked. True, though. He really loved his work and was more than satisfied with the occasional fling. At least then, no one was disappointed.

If he went through with this crazy plan, he'd work hard not to disappoint Bree. He'd be a good husband to her.

He dipped her slightly, and she yielded to the motion, letting herself fall backward into his hand. Trusting.

She had absolutely no idea what was going through his mind. If she knew, she'd be appalled beyond belief.

But she wouldn't know. Ever.

She giggled as he pulled her back up. A rare flash of excitement flared in his chest. She was enjoying this and dammit, so was he. He twirled her around, holding her close, hand pressed to the inviting curve of her hip.

He had a good feeling about this whole thing.

Bree stood in front of the mirror in the powder room on the pretext of rearranging her hair. Really she just wanted to see what exactly Gavin Spencer was looking at with that gleam of interest in his eyes.

People always told her she had pretty eyes. Rather an odd observation, since she wore glasses. She lowered the frames—the nice, low-profile ones she saved for special occasions—and peered into her own eyes. They didn't look all that special to her. Maybe that's what people said when they couldn't think of something else to compliment. She pushed the frames back up her nose where they settled comfortably into place. People said she should wear contacts but they were far too much hassle for her taste.

Her hair was a disaster, as usual. Unmanageable, frizzy and fighting her every step of the way. She never should have taken out the hairsticks she'd managed to jam in earlier. With a struggle, she poked them back in and secured a messy bun.

There wasn't a lick of makeup on her face, but then she never wore it. She wasn't skilled at applying lipstick, blush and eyeliner, so on the rare occasions she'd attempted to use them, she ended up looking like a clown.

And the dress was awful. Her Aunt Freda had assured her it "hid her figure flaws." It could also hide an international terrorist organization and several cases of contraband whiskey in its crispy folds. The boat neck turned her somewhat decent cleavage into an intimidating mountain range.

She didn't look any better than usual. If anything, she looked worse.

So why did Gavin seem so…entranced by her? Like he couldn't take his eyes off her. He'd guided her around the room since the moment they were introduced. She kept expecting him to spot someone else and bid her adieu, but he didn't.

In fact, she half suspected he was standing right outside the ladies room waiting for her.

She blew out hard. Bright patches of color illuminated her cheeks in a way that wasn't entirely charming. Her eyes were certainly shining, though.

As well they might be. She'd never danced like that. Even in her imagination! How could she not feel like Cinderella at the ball?

Which was funny, really, considering she was one of the richest women in San Francisco. Of course she'd come by that money the old fashioned way—by inheriting it—so she wasn't proud of her wealth. Quite the opposite, in fact. She often imagined people clucking and muttering, "All that money, and look how little she's accomplished."

Her father certainly felt that way. Even said it once or twice.

She sucked in a long, deep breath and tucked a stray lock of wild hair behind her ear.

Bree Kincannon, you are a desirable and enticing woman.

Nope. Not convincing.

Bree Kincannon, you are a damned good photographer and a fantastic cat mom.

Better.

She half-smiled at her reflection, then wiped her smile away when she realized the sylph-like blonde beside her was staring. She quickly patted her hair and turned to the exit.

Outside there was no sign of Gavin. The little shock of disappointment surprised her. Then she chastised herself. Did she really expect a man like that to wait around for her like a faithful dog?

He was probably already dancing with someone else.

Surreptitiously she scanned the dance floor. Past midnight, so the crowd was thinning. All the men were dressed alike in black tie, but she knew she'd spot Gavin immediately. He had that kind of presence.

A tiny shimmer of relief trickled through her when she didn't see him.

But did that mean he'd left without saying goodbye? She'd probably never see him again. Why would he call her, of all people?

She lifted her chin and started to weave through the tables to where she'd sat with some of her father's duller business associates, which wasn't a very charitable way to think of them since they'd all been nice enough to pony up a thousand dollars per seat. She was relieved to see that they'd all left, and she lifted her beaded bag off the back of her chair and slung it over her taffeta-clad shoulder.

Another quick glance revealed no sign of Gavin. Cold settled in her stomach. So that was it. A lovely evening. A fantastic time.

Possibly the best night of her life.

She swallowed. No doubt everyone who'd stared at her on Gavin's arm was looking at her now, the same way they always did. Poor old Bree. Perennial wallflower.

She shuffled toward the exit. She usually got a cab home from these things as her father often stayed late to schmooze into the wee hours. Of course it was kind of pathetic that she still lived in the family mansion. But she loved Russian Hill, and the big attic studio she'd turned into her private apartment was filled with special memories of the happy years before her mom died. She used to paint there every afternoon, while Bree played on the floor near her easel.

Bree bit her lip. She was happy with her life. Really! She didn't need some tall, dark, handsome charmer to waltz in and stir up trouble.

She retrieved her coat from the cloakroom and slid it over her shoulders. She was just about to walk across the marble foyer toward the exit when her heart slammed to a halt.

Gavin. Tall and proud as a ship's mast, an earnest look on his chiseled features.

And he was talking to her father.

Bree frowned. How did they know each other so well? Her father usually bothered only with mega-wealthy entrepreneurs who could make him a fast and large buck. If Gavin was just an advertising executive—a challenging and interesting job, but still a job—why was her father leaning in to speak with him as if he was Bill Gates?

She pulled her coat about herself and started slowly toward them. They both looked up fast when they noticed her, which made a weird knot of anxiety form in her belly.

"Bree, darling!" Her father extended an arm. "Gavin and I were just talking about what a wonderful evening this was. And I have you to thank for forcing me to buy a ticket." He turned to Gavin. "Bree has a soft spot for animals."

Bree managed a polite smile.

"It was a great pleasure to meet you, Bree." Gavin's eyes met hers.

Instantly a flare of heat rushed to her face and her heart began to pound like a jackhammer. "Likewise," she stammered.

"Are you free on Friday? The firm is having a cocktail party at the Rosa Lounge to celebrate a new campaign. I'd love you to come."

Bree's mind spun. Friday night? That was a serious dating night. And he wanted her to meet all his business associates? Her mouth dried.

"Uh, sure. That would be nice." She blinked rapidly.

"I'll pick you up at your house, if that's okay."

"That would be great." She smiled as calmly as she could. "I'll see you then."

"See you later, darling." Her father shot her a tight smile. "I have some friends to catch up with."

"Sure, I'll get a cab."

Gavin stepped toward her. "I'll drive you home. Then I'll know where to come find you on Friday."

He summoned a porter to tell valet parking before Bree could protest.

She inhaled deeply, took his offered arm and walked outside. The light mist of rain that had followed her to the Four Seasons earlier had evaporated, leaving a clear moonlit night that illuminated the sturdy bank buildings across Market Street and gave them the grandeur of real Roman temples. Stars glimmered overhead as Gavin helped her into the passenger seat of his low-slung sports car.

They chatted about the new Louise Bourgeois exhibit at the Modern on the short drive home. Gavin admitted he went often to keep on top of emerging trends so he could impress clients. He was embarrassingly gorgeous *and* he knew about art?

She leaped out of the car in front of her house, heart pounding. Would he try to kiss her?

Impossible.

Or was it?

Terror streaked along her veins as he rounded the car toward her. He took her hand, which was sweating slightly. A shiver of heat shot right up her arm.

"Good night, Bree." He clasped her hand in both of his, warm and firm. Their gazes held and her lips quivered with a mix of anticipation and apprehension.

Then he tilted his head. "I'll pick you up at seven on Friday, if that's okay."

"Perfect. See you then." She flashed a smile, then turned and scurried for the door.

Once inside she literally collapsed against it. And a big, wide, goofy smile spread across her face.

She had a Friday-night date with the most handsome man in San Francisco.

And if she weren't so freaked out, she'd be pretty darn thrilled about it.

Two

"Gavin, sweetie, how are you?" Marissa Curtis assaulted him as he entered the Rosa Lounge with Bree on his arm. She wrapped her skinny arms around him and kissed him on both cheeks, overwhelming him with that eye-watering fragrance she always wore. "I've missed you this week. Were you in Cannes?"

"Yes. Had some meetings." He'd had a really good time at the film festival, and it had given him a chance to plan his campaign to win Bree Kincannon, who stood rather patiently beside him.

"Marissa, this is Bree. Bree, Marissa."

"Oh, lovely to meet you." The blonde smiled, revealing frighteningly white teeth. "Are you Gavin's sister?"

Gavin exploded into a laugh. "My sister? I don't even have a sister."

"Oh." Marissa tipped her silly head to the side, so her silky hair cascaded artfully over her shoulder. "I just thought…" She looked mischievously at Bree.

"That Bree and I look so alike we must be twins?" Gavin wrapped his arm around Bree. She was stiff as a board.

Catty Marissa was no doubt trying to imply that Bree couldn't possibly be his date. After all, she wasn't built like a twig and dressed in Prada.

"Bree's my date."

"Oh." Marissa's grimace widened. "How charming." She widened her eyes rudely. "Must dash. I see Jake. He said he'd bring me something nice back from Cannes."

Gavin turned to Bree. "Don't mind her. She's just insane."

Bree's sweet smile reappeared, giving him a warm feeling in his chest. He liked her smile.

"And you know, we do kind of look alike." He rubbed her shoulder. "We've both got dark hair and gray eyes. Or wait, are yours green?" On closer inspection, the irises hiding behind her metal-framed glasses looked like pale jade. "I couldn't see you properly the other night. It was so dark at the gala." They were close enough for him to enjoy her scent—subtle and fresh, like the rest of her.

"They're probably more gray than green." Bree shrugged. "Doesn't make much difference to me. I just use them for looking out of."

"And taking pictures. I looked up your Black Book photos. Those were some amazing portraits."

"Interesting faces." She smiled shyly, her lips rosy and inviting. "Made my job easy."

"Who were they?" Her crisp black-and-white image of the older couple, standing outside on a city street, their bold, cheerful countenances sunlit and their happy union obvious, rather haunted him since he'd seen it. Something about the photo made it hard to forget.

"I don't even know. Isn't that embarrassing? I'll be exposed as a fraud." She bit her lip. "They were just standing there outside the library, waiting for someone, I think. I asked if I could take their picture."

"I'd never guess you hadn't known them for decades."

"That's what everyone says." She shrugged. "It's a little weird, I guess."

"It's art." He grinned. She was starting to relax. Good. "Hey, Elle. Come meet Bree." He beckoned to Brock Maddox's assistant. The slim brunette pushed past two art directors to join them. "Bree's a photographer."

"Are you really?"

"Award winning," pronounced Gavin. "Can I leave Bree in your capable hands for a moment, Elle? I need to chat with Brock."

"Sure. First we'll get her a drink. Follow me to the bar." Elle led Bree off into the thickening crowd.

Gavin scanned the room for Brock. He'd had a great meeting in Cannes with a hot new Czech director who might be willing to shoot a campaign for the right price. Gavin wasn't sure Brock would go for Tomas Kozinski's "right price," but it was worth a try. He had a unique, hand-held style that made even the scenery come alive.

"Hey, Gavin, how's it going? Still getting cozy with the Rialto yacht people?" Logan Emerson materialized in front of him, wine glass raised.

Irritation prickled Gavin's neck. "Trying to."

"That account would be a really big score. I can already see those Rialtos sailing under the Golden Gate Bridge at halftime on Super Bowl night."

"That might be a tad predictable."

"I guess that's why I'm an account exec and not a copywriter." Logan chuckled and slapped him on the back.

Gavin inhaled. Something about this guy really bothered him, and it wasn't just his bad jokes. Logan Emerson had only been at the company a few weeks, but already he seemed to be underfoot all day long: in every meeting; loitering by the espresso machine; he even wandered into the damned men's room whenever Gavin entered. Sometimes, like now, he'd be all smiles and jollities, but most of the time he just stood there. Watching.

Maybe he was trying to soak up the Maddox modus operandi so he could beat the other account executives at their own game. Which wasn't such a bad thing. At least then Gavin wouldn't feel too bad about leaving Brock in the lurch when he quit to start his own company.

Hopefully soon.

He cast his eyes around the room and was relieved and pleased to see Bree, wine glass in hand, chatting with Elle.

So far, so good.

"Actually my undergrad major was English." Bree took a sip from her delicate glass. Elle had snagged some white wine, then ushered her into a relatively quiet corner of the sleek bar, where they could talk. Bree felt a bit intimidated by her at first. Elle was so polished and put together in a tailored suit that showed off her slim figure. Her brown hair was sleek as sable and her blue eyes shone with intelligence and good humor.

After a few minutes, though, she started to relax, answering questions that Elle seemed to have asked with genuine interest. "At the time I thought I might even pursue a PhD in English, but I took some time off to travel and changed my mind. Flaky, I guess."

Elle smiled. "Not flaky, thoughtful. A lot of people rush ahead with some big plan they've had in their mind for years, and end up painted into a corner doing something that isn't their passion. I have to admit, I've always been mad about photography. I took a lot of classes in high school and college, but I guess I've never been daring enough to try to publish or exhibit my pictures. What got you started in photography?"

"I'm embarrassed to admit this, but it was a total accident. My dad gave me a camera for my birthday four years ago. I actually think a client gave it to him as a gift, as he doesn't know anything about them, but it was a top of the line Nikon, with a set of extra lenses. The kind of thing even a professional photographer would salivate over. I started fooling around with it—taking pictures of old oak trees in the park, and interesting buildings around Russian Hill and the Marina District."

Elle nodded, her blue eyes alight with interest. Bree felt a warm connection to her, even though they'd just met.

"One day I was taking a picture of St. Francis of Assisi on Vallejo Street."

"Oh, yes. The one with all the doorways."

"You know how that woman in the blue coat is often there?"

"Feeding the pigeons. Yes, totally!" Elle smiled.

"Something about her intrigued me. She has such a sense of purpose. I have no idea why she's there and I'd never ask. I'm far too shy." She pushed a stray hair off her cheek. Somehow Elle had put her so at ease that she didn't feel shy at all. "But I wanted to see if I could take a picture of that quiet dignity she exudes."

"What did you say?"

"I just asked if I could take her picture." Bree grinned. "I know now that I should have offered her two dollars and a model release form, but I was clueless at the time."

"And she said yes."

Bree nodded. "So I took the picture. Took only a few seconds—just her, standing there in front of the smallest door, her coat buttoned up to her neck like always, with that flock of pigeons at her feet. The shots came out pretty well, so I printed one and entered it in a small show at the local library. My image won, and people started making a fuss, so I figured I'd keep snapping away."

"I'd love to see that picture."

"You're welcome to come up to my studio any time."

"Really?" Elle's eyes lit up. "I'd love to! I've never been in a real photographer's studio."

"Oh, I wouldn't call it that." Bree blushed. "But it does have a lovely view out over the rooftops. I'm around tomorrow, if you'd like to come by."

"Can I? I don't have to be anywhere until five. It would be so nice to see some photographs that aren't glossy product shots for a change." She winked conspiratorially.

"If I come in the morning, I could bring some pastries and coffee from Stella's."

"You're on. I can never say no to their bear claws. The address is 200 Talbot Street. The limestone behemoth with the wrought-iron gates. If you come around the right-hand side there's a separate entrance up to my studio."

"Planning a secret tryst?" Gavin's deep voice made her spin around. His gray eyes looked at her with amusement.

"Absolutely." Elle grinned. "I want to see Bree's work before she gets too famous to talk to me. Did you know she's been asked to shoot a portrait for *San Francisco Magazine?*"

"Is that true?" Gavin tilted his head.

"It is." Bree blushed again, wishing she were actually as cool as everyone seemed to think she was. "I'm shooting Robert Pattison. They had a tough time deciding between Annie Leibowitz and me. I suspect I was cheaper." Gavin's dimples appeared. "They just called me out of the blue. Saw my pictures in Black Book."

"That's awesome." Gavin's rich voice rang with admiration. "I'd like to see your photos, too."

"Form a line, form a line," joked Elle, raising her glass. "But seriously, Robert Pattison? I wish I was a jet-setting photographer and not a lowly administrative assistant." She did a mock pout.

Bree very much doubted that Elle was just a "lowly administrative assistant." She waved and chatted with everyone as if she was the owner of the company, not the owner's right-hand woman.

"Hang tough, Cinderella. You'll get to go to the ball

one day. But in the meantime, you'd better find your boss. I haven't seen him anywhere."

"I'll go track him down. Nice to meet you, Bree, and I'll see you tomorrow."

Elle marched smartly off into the crowd.

"Brock has been a bit distracted lately." Gavin leaned in until his delicious masculine scent stole over her. "A lot going on."

The clang of a spoon hitting a glass snagged their attention.

Bree turned to see a gray-haired man in a conservative suit, wreathed in smiles. Amazingly, the entire room fell silent.

"It's our oldest client," murmured Gavin. "Walter Prentice. We're here to celebrate the launch of a new campaign for his company planned by Celia, one of our account execs. It's going really well."

"It's a great pleasure to spend an evening with the most impressive creative talent in the entire United States." The older man's voice carried through the crowded space. "In the years my company has worked with Maddox Communications, I've been pleased to get to know many of you as personal friends. I've just learned that Flynn Maddox and his lovely wife, Renee, are expecting their first baby. I'd like you to join with me in celebrating their new family with a champagne toast."

Already waiters carried trays full of champagne glasses around the room.

"Flynn is Brock Maddox's younger brother. He got back together with his wife recently after a long separation." Gavin's warm breath tickled her ear.

"How lovely." Bree smiled and accepted a sparkling

glass of bubbly. "And very sweet of your client to make a fuss."

"He's a nice guy. Very family oriented. Been married to his wife, Angela, for forty years."

"Impressive. Nearly all my dad's friends are divorced. Some of them several times."

"That's a shame." Gavin sipped his champagne. "Marriage should be for life—otherwise what's the point?"

His earnest gaze met hers—and made her gulp champagne too fast. "I'm sure you're right. But I've never been married, so I have no idea what it's really like." Her words came out a bit rushed. It was downright freaky to be discussing marriage on a first date, let alone a first date with a man like Gavin Spencer.

"Me, either." He grinned, boyish and charming. "But I hope that when I do tie the knot, it will be the kind of marriage I'll toast with champagne forty years later."

Bree tugged her eyes away. Okay, she must be dreaming. This couldn't possibly be real. There was no such thing as a gorgeous, dashing and successful man who wanted to stay married to one woman for life.

Was there?

Walter Prentice raised his filled champagne glass. "A toast to the happy couple! May their family be blessed with many years of happiness, and not too many sleepless nights." He grinned. "My own children have brought me so much joy. I know that Flynn and Renee will be fantastic parents."

He looked down, then directly at a tall, black-haired man, who Bree guessed might be Flynn. "You know our company slogan—family is everything. Well, it's not just a slogan, it's a way of life." He raised his glass.

The room buzzed with cheers. "Oh, my gosh, that really is their slogan, isn't it?" Bree laughed. "I've seen their ads on TV."

Gavin's gray eyes twinkled. "I guess sometimes believing your own publicity isn't such a bad thing. Hey, there's Brock. Come meet the big boss."

Bree's eyes widened as he slid his fingers to the small of her back to guide her across the room, claiming her as his date in front of everyone—friends, coworkers, clients. Almost as if he was showing her off.

She fought the urge to pinch herself. Any minute now she'd wake up in her own bed, with Faith and Ali stretched, purring, on the duvet next to her. But until then she'd better keep a smile on her face.

Never a morning person, Bree had barely managed to drag herself out of bed by the time Elle showed up at her door. She and Gavin had stayed at the party until nearly 1 a.m. Once again, he'd dropped her home without dropping a hint about coming in.

And without trying to kiss her.

"Hey, Bree!" Elle kissed her on the cheek like they were old friends. "I brought your bear claw and some coffee. I bet you need it after last night. Gavin must have introduced you to everyone in the room." She handed Bree a to-go cup full of steaming coffee.

"He may have even introduced me to some of them twice. It was all a blur after about ten o'clock. Come in." She ushered Elle into the bright room. Ornate Victorian paned glass covered one wall and part of the sloped ceiling, creating the bright studio light that gave the space its name.

"Oh, my lord, look at the view." Elle put the paper

bakery bag on the small dining table and moved to the window. "I bet on a clear day you can see Japan from here."

"Almost." Bree grinned. "I do love watching boats in the bay."

"I guess you'll miss the view when you move in with Gavin." Elle lifted a brow.

Bree froze. "What? There's nothing going on between Gavin and me. I only just met him."

"Really?" Elle's eyes widened. "I got the definite impression that you two were a serious item."

"He was being very…solicitous, but I only met him the night before."

"You're kidding me." Elle's eyes narrowed. "I know you and I only just met, so I shouldn't even ask this, but you've kissed, right?"

"Not even a peck." A prickle of embarrassment ran over her. If she were cute like Elle, he probably would have tried. "I think he's just being friendly."

"But he kept putting his arm around you." Elle cocked her head. "That's not the kind of thing you do with a friend. Nope. He's definitely after you. Probably just taking it slow."

Bree shrugged, hoping the heat in her face didn't show. "Let me get some plates."

They chatted about the house and the neighborhood while they ate their pastries and sipped the strong coffee. After they ate, Bree showed Elle some of her photos.

"You have an amazing eye. In each picture there's something of the essence of the individual. I know how hard that is to capture. I can't take a decent portrait to save my life. I'm lucky if their eyes are open."

"I wish I could offer some tips, but I'm afraid I'm not sure how I do it."

"Genius. Talent. All those things I don't have as a photographer." Elle smiled. "It's not hard to see why Gavin's crazy about you."

"Oh, stop! First of all, he's not crazy about me. Second of all, he hasn't seen my photos."

"Yes, he has. He was showing everyone the Black Book in the office on Friday."

"Was he really?" Bree bit her lip.

"One word. Besotted." Elle crossed her arms. "A man in love. Sometimes it happens that fast."

"Oh, come on. What could Gavin possibly see in me? I'm definitely not the type men fall head over heels for."

"What makes you say that?"

"Well, let's see. My hair has a mind of its own, which changes with the barometric pressure. I need to lose weight. And the only famous person I bear a resemblance to is one Duncan Kincannon, Tenth Laird of Aislin. You can see him halfway down the stairs in the main hall, wrapped in a gilt frame."

Elle giggled. "I bet Gavin loves your sense of humor."

"That's about all there is to love."

"What nonsense! Though…" She tipped her head to one side and pressed a figure to her lips. "If you don't mind my saying so…I can see a little room for improvement."

Bree cringed inside her baggy college sweatshirt. "More than a little room, I'm afraid."

"You're lovely as you are, but you could be lovelier.

I spent a summer working at a froufrou spa in Santa Barbara. I learned all kinds of brilliant tricks there."

"Like what?"

"Your hair. It's curly, right?"

"I think frizzy is a better description."

"No, seriously, will you take it down for a sec?"

Bree pulled the ponytail band from her hair with shaky fingers. The heavy mass fell—frizzily—over her shoulders.

"Oh, yes. You've got lovely ringlets in there. We just have to set them free."

"How do you do that?"

Elle smiled mysteriously. "We need to gather a few tools."

It was nearly four in the afternoon by the time Elle was satisfied with her work. They'd spent an hour in the sun while Elle filed and polished Bree's nails, and they waited for artfully applied lemon juice to scorch highlights into Bree's hair.

Next, Elle conditioned her hair. She'd rinsed, then applied yet more conditioner—gloppy handfuls of it—and made Bree swear she'd never let her hair dry without conditioner on it again.

While Bree dripped conditioner onto the wood floors, Elle rifled through her wardrobe, tut-tutting and holding items up to Bree's complexion. In despair, she marched Bree—hair still damp—out the door and down to Union Street, where she encouraged her to try on, and ultimately buy, three very expensive new bras and several mix-and-match pieces from a trendy boutique. Elle made the whole thing so enjoyable, Bree felt as if they were BFFs out for an adventure rather than two women who'd only met the night before.

Once coordinating shoes were found, they hurried back to the apartment where Elle applied a loose powder all over her face, "to brighten you up a bit," as she said. She brushed light blush over Bree's cheekbones, and smudged gray-green shadow around her eyes. A touch of rose-pink lipstick gave a subtle punch to her color, without making her look like a clown.

"Your hair's finally dry." Elle arranged it about her shoulders. "Why don't you look in the mirror?"

Half afraid of what she'd see, Bree made her way across the studio—no small feat in the heeled ankle boots Elle had talked her into.

A long mirror hung behind the bathroom door, and she inhaled as she pulled it open.

She squinted for a moment, looking the image up and down. Then she laughed aloud. "Who is that woman in my mirror?"

"It's you, babe."

"Not possible. This woman is trim and elegant, and has silky ringlets with blond highlights."

"It's all you. Standing up straight is a big part of it. Tall girls like you often stoop because you're afraid to stand out. If you do those yoga poses I showed you just once a day, you'll really see a difference in your posture."

"It never would have occurred to me that clothes which fit could make me look thinner!"

"You have a gorgeous, curvy figure and you should show it off."

"Who knew?" Bree grinned at her reflection. "And

I swear on my life, I'll never let my hair dry without conditioner again."

"That's my girl. So, when are you seeing Gavin next?"

Three

Gavin called on Sunday and invited Bree to a gallery opening on Tuesday night. A photography show. Said he wanted her opinion of the artist's work.

Naturally, she said yes.

For the opening she chose a wrap dress in a dark eggplant color that was subtle and dramatic at the same time. The cut flattered her hourglass figure—who knew she had one?—and made an asset of her height. For the first time in years, she wore heels, which probably made her about five foot eleven. She'd bravely "washed" her hair using only conditioner and it had come out shockingly well—a mass of shiny ringlets. As she sparingly applied some of the subtle makeup Elle had left for her, she wondered how Gavin would react.

At seven o'clock on the dot she heard a knock on the private door to her studio.

Heart pounding, she crossed the slippery wood floor as gracefully as possible in her heels and pulled it open.

"Hi, Br—" Gavin's mouth fell open.

"Hey, Gavin." She smiled. "How was work today?"

"Great. It was really good." He blinked, and peered at her curiously. "You look different."

"Just a little." She shrugged and turned into the loft. Part of her wanted to laugh out loud. "New dress."

"It looks stunning on you." His voice was deeper than usual. He looked devastating himself, in dark pants and a white shirt with a barely visible gray stripe.

"Thanks. Let me get my bag." She slung the small beaded vintage purse, which used to belong to her mom, over her shoulder. "I'm looking forward to the exhibit."

"Me, too." She turned to see him staring at her, a furrow between his brows.

"Something wrong?"

"Oh, no." He blinked. "No, nothing at all." He glanced lower, taking in the soft drape of her new dress over her hips. Her skin hummed under his hungry gaze.

He does find me attractive.

The feeling was utterly new, a strange and surprising thrill. She pulled her shoulders back, trying to maintain the posture Elle had showed her, and to hide the fact that her pulse was still pounding and her palms sweating, despite her composed appearance.

Gavin cleared his throat. "My car's downstairs."

They walked into the Razor gallery arm in arm. She was only a couple of inches shorter than him in her new heels. Eyes, once again, turned to stare. But this time they weren't glares of female indignation that she—lowly and insignificant plain Jane—was on Gavin's arm.

No, this time the men were looking, too.

Bree tossed her curls behind her shoulders as she accepted a glass of white wine. "Shall we look at the images?"

Even her voice sounded sultrier, as if overnight she'd morphed into a more sophisticated version of herself.

They looked closely at the photographs. Large digital prints of people, mostly at parties and nightclubs, the colors highly saturated and intoxicating. "I can almost hear the music," she said, looking at a couple entwined on a dance floor, perspiration gleaming on their barely clad bodies.

"That's why I like Doug's images. They invoke the other senses. I'm hoping he'll do a vodka campaign I have in mind. It's hard to make a flat piece of paper say 'drink me,' but I think this guy could pull it off." He pointed the artist out to Bree—a short, skinny guy with numerous piercings, a goatee and an air of manic enthusiasm.

"Now, he looks like an artist," she whispered. "Maybe I need to pierce my nose. What do you think?" She tilted her head, fighting the urge to grin.

"Definitely not. Your nose is absolutely perfect already." Gavin's warm gray gaze rested on her face. Her skin sizzled slightly under the heat of his admiration. "Your eyes are green."

"Yes." She blushed. "I got contacts." Elle had talked her into trying tinted ones.

"They're cute. And I can see you better without glasses in the way."

"Aren't we here to look at art? I'm starting to feel self-conscious."

Though she had to admit it was a good feeling to be admired. When Gavin went to get them fresh glasses of wine, a tall man with spiky blond hair approached her and made small talk about the images.

The look on Gavin's face when he returned was priceless.

He had to get Bree out of here.

Gavin tried not to scowl at the punk who'd horned in on her while he turned his back for a moment. He recognized the guy, a Finnish video editor with a tinny laugh. They'd worked together on a storyboard. "Hey, Lars. How's it going?"

"Good, Gavin. Good." He turned his gel-crusted head back to Bree. "So you're a photographer, too?"

"Yes." Bree smiled sweetly. Gavin hadn't noticed how full and lush her lips were before. Lust mingled with irritation in his veins. "Well, kind of. I haven't actually done a professional shoot yet."

"Bree and I were just heading out to dinner." His statement was more of a growl than he'd intended.

Every man in the room was looking at her. And who could blame them? The richly colored dress draped her curves in a way that should be illegal. In her heels she was probably the tallest women in the room, and with the regal tilt of her head and her cascade of shiny gold-tipped curls, she shone like a goddess.

"I'd love to take a quick peek at the images in the next room. Lars was just telling me about them. They're portraits of the artist's friends."

Gavin decided he'd like to tell Lars a thing or two.

But he resisted the primal urges surging in his blood. "Sure, let's go look."

He slid his arm through Bree's, claiming her, and guided her across the floor. He couldn't resist scowling at one dark-haired charmer who shot Bree a look so flirtatious it was downright tacky.

"Oh, look at this sweet couple," she exclaimed. He peered into a small square-framed image. A pair of teenage lovers were wrapped in each other on a park bench.

Gavin could readily imagine being in such a clinch with Bree. Her lush curves called out to him, urging his palms to explore their hills and valleys.

Arousal surged through him, and he tugged his gaze from Bree's breathtaking cleavage back to the artwork at hand. "Very nice," he murmured.

She tossed her cascade of curls behind her shoulder. He could almost swear her hair looked totally different last time he'd seen her. It had been tied back—maybe that was it.

It wasn't just the hair. Something was very different about Bree. She'd been pretty in a quiet and unassuming way when they'd met. Now she was undeniably a knockout. Even the way she carried herself seemed altered. Before, her shoulders were rounded, apologetic. Now she threw them back proudly.

Her stiff evening gown had concealed her body at the gala. This drapey number revealed it in tantalizing detail—her backside was a work of art all by itself. His fingers itched to pull at the bow tied her waist and unwrap the delicious present in front of him. "Are you hungry?"

Because I know I am. And not for food.

And her father was going to give him a million dollars to marry her? He'd approached the renowned venture capitalist to discuss an investment in his proposed business, and Kincannon had shocked him with his own proposal: one million dollars and his still-unwed daughter. Gavin's first instinct had been to refuse, but he agreed to meet her. Now, his good fortune seemed almost unbelievable. And he certainly didn't want to blow it by letting some wiseass muscle in on his prize.

"Uh, sure. What did you have in mind?" She blinked, those rich green eyes shining in a way they hadn't behind her glasses. "There's a good Thai place about a block away."

"Perfect. Let's go." He wrapped his arm firmly around her waist as they moved back to the main gallery. No way would he let another guy get his hooks into Bree Kincannon.

He shot a warning stare around the room. Hands off. She's mine.

Her hips shifted from side to side under his arm, stirring heat in his groin. His pursuit of Bree was fast morphing from a business proposition into a personal quest. He couldn't remember the last time he'd been so aroused by a woman.

At the restaurant he requested a quiet table in the back room—a gold spangled festival of Thai kitsch—where they could talk undisturbed. He admired the rear view as he helped Bree into her chair.

She shook out her napkin. "The pad thai's really good."

"I'll get that then." He didn't feel like reading the menu. He was far more interested in looking at her. A tiny silver heart hung from a fine chain around her neck, dancing dangerously near the enticing cleft between her breasts.

Now all he had to do was convince Bree he should be her future husband.

He poured some San Pellegrino into her glass. "Have you always lived in San Francisco?"

"We used to spend summers in Napa Valley when I was little, before my mom died, but other than that, yes. I've lived in the same house in Russian Hill since I was a baby."

"That's a lovely neighborhood."

"I suspect that's what my ancestors said when they built the house a hundred years ago. It's lasted through several earthquakes and is big enough for me to share with my father without us driving each other nuts, so I'm very fond of it."

"Is it strange still living at home with your dad?"

"I'm used to it, so it's not at all strange to me. I'm sure some people think it's a bit pathetic and that I should strike out on my own." She sipped her water. "I suppose I will someday. When the moment is right."

Phew. Gavin didn't much fancy sharing a house with the old man. Especially since Elliott Kincannon was about to become his benefactor.

"Does your family live in San Francisco?" Her innocent question tugged him back to the present.

"San Diego, but I moved away from home when I was seventeen and never looked back. My dad wanted me to follow family tradition and join the military. He was furious when I applied to UCLA and got a full scholarship to study marketing. We had a big blowup and I left that night."

"How awful! Did you patch things up?"

"It took about four years for him to give up his dreams of seeing me in a dress uniform covered in medals, but he's happy that I'm successful doing something I like."

"That's all that matters, really, isn't it? My dad couldn't understand why I kept taking jobs at nonprofit organizations that paid me less than my age. I enjoyed the work and was glad to help. And since I already had a nice place to live, I didn't need to rake in big bucks."

"You're lucky. I had a tough time right out of school. I was ready to take on the world and become CEO of General Electric, and my boss kept wanting me to file his papers and answer his phone instead."

Bree laughed. "Trust me, it's not much different at a nonprofit. Though there are less people so you have to pitch in more. I think it's good to start at the bottom— then you get a chance to watch how other people do things."

"And learn from their mistakes."

"That, too." Her bright smile flashed again, sending a charge of excitement through him. "Do you like working for Maddox Communications?"

"Sure. It's one of the top agencies on the West Coast. We have some of the biggest clients in America."

She cocked her head slightly. "Hmm, those are awfully generic reasons to like a place."

"I like Brock and Flynn Maddox, too. They inherited the family business from their dad, but they've done a lot with it."

Was it wise to tell her he wanted to strike out on his own? Probably not. Then she might start wondering if he was more interested in her funds than in her.

They gave their orders to the waiter, who quickly returned with their beers.

"I suspect my dad is disappointed that I don't want to be a venture capitalist." Bree raised her brows. "He can't understand why anyone would do something unless there's a profit involved."

"Crazy." Gavin managed to keep a straight face.

"I swear, I think the reason he never married again is that he couldn't find anyone richer than himself to marry!"

Bree laughed, and Gavin forced himself to join in. He had to make sure she *never* found out about her dad's proposition. "What do you think is a good reason to get married?" He poured some beer into her glass.

Bree looked up, as if studying the patterned ceiling for an answer. "Love, I suppose. What other reason could there be?"

His stomach clenched slightly. "Have you ever been in love?"

"Not since third grade. Randy Plimpton broke my heart so badly when he sat with Jessica Slade at the end-of-year picnic that I never recovered." A mischievous sparkle lit her eyes.

"That sounds devastating. I can see how you'd never trust your heart to a man again."

"That's how I felt. I guess that must explain why I've never even had a real boyfriend." Her cheeks colored slightly.

"That Randy has a lot to answer for. On the other hand, if you'd had a serious boyfriend you might have married him. Then you wouldn't be sitting here sipping Thai beer with me." He raised his glass.

"I guess there's a good side to everything." Bree

clinked her glass against his and took a sip. Her adorable nose wrinkled. "I don't drink much, either. I've led a very dull life, really."

"Perhaps that's all about to change."

Bree's eyes widened. "Do you think?"

"I do. I have a funny feeling about it." He cocked his head and let his gaze drift over her face. Her lips parted slightly, moist, as if they'd like to be kissed.

Which hopefully they would be in the very near future.

Bree took a tentative sip of the golden liquid, then blinked as she swallowed it down. "You know what? I'm ready for change. I'm tired of sitting on the sidelines of life. I'm ready to get out and enjoy it more."

Their pad thai arrived, steaming and fragrant with basil. They ate in silence for a few moments. Then Gavin decided to head deeper into dangerous territory.

"I've had girlfriends before, but never one that I thought was 'the one.'"

"I wonder how it's different. If you just *know* a person is the one you'll spend the rest of your life with." Her smooth brow wrinkled slightly. "That must be an amazing feeling."

"I hear it happens fast."

Her brows rose. "Love at first sight?"

"Something like that. The person just clicks with you."

Bree inhaled deeply, which drew his gaze to her bosom. Gavin's arousal thickened at the sight of her full breasts under the clingy dress.

She looked up at him, eyes soft. "I hope I'll find that one day. You know, someone I can feel totally comfortable with."

Maybe you already have.

Gavin tilted his head. "It could be the kind of thing that sneaks up on you as you get to know the person."

"You mean like one minute they're a friend and the next...you can't keep your hands off them?" She giggled.

"I'm sure that happens to people all the time." Her laugh tickled something deep inside him. "Probably just when they least expect it."

Gavin dropped Bree home and said goodbye with a restrained peck on the cheek. She didn't invite him in, though she looked as if she wanted to. He wanted to keep things slow and steady, rather than rush in too hot and heavy and possibly scare her off.

For their next date, he invited her to a jazz concert at the Palace of Fine Arts. For dinner he brought a carefully packed picnic from the gourmet store near his apartment, and a bottle of champagne. Bree, resplendent in a midnight blue dress and sparkly silver earrings, blushed with delight as he spread a blanket under a huge shade tree on the grounds and unpacked the food. The weather was warm and calm.

"I've always wanted to come for a picnic here," she exclaimed. "It's got to be one of the most romantic spots in the city."

He looked up from the feast he was unpacking. "Tonight seemed like the perfect opportunity."

"Look at the way the sunset lights up the lagoon." The expanse of water shimmered like liquid gold. Around them other couples and groups laughed and dined and took in the beauty of the spring evening. "The city has so many interesting places. You could live here for decades and never visit them all.

"And what a shame that would be." Bree unwrapped a lacquer box filled with stuffed grape leaves. "Ooh, one of my favorites. I swear the Kincannons must have Greek ancestry somewhere. We're all crazy about Greek food."

"You fit right in with the architecture then. Or is this Roman?" He glanced up at the heavily ornamented Corinthian style columns that adorned the massive buildings nestled around the lake.

Bree laughed. "They were built in 1915 for the World's Fair here in San Francisco. I'd call them World's Fair Classical. I love how 'over the top' they are. The original buildings were made of paper, and only meant to last a year. They proved pretty sturdy and by the time they started to fall down decades later, everyone was so attached to the place that they decided to rebuild it permanently."

The fading sun gleamed in her curls, lighting up the gold highlights. Her skin shone, cheeks still pink with excitement. He wanted to kiss her right now….

But he resisted. "How do you know so much about everything?"

"Just curious, I guess. And I have lived here my whole life."

"Do you plan to spend the rest of your life here?" He wasn't entirely sure why he asked. Did he want to find out if she had a life plan already mapped out, and if so, if she'd be happy to reconfigure it for him?

She frowned slightly, then smiled. "I don't know. I guess it all depends on where life takes me."

"As a photographer you can work anywhere."

She laughed. "I still don't think of myself as a photographer. I've only been offered one professional assignment so far. I haven't even done it yet. What if it's a disaster?"

"It will be fantastic. Is this the one for *San Francisco Magazine?*"

"Yes. It's next week. Robert Pattinson, for crying out loud! I'm paralyzed with nerves."

"You move very well for someone with paralysis." He offered her a dish of stuffed olives, and she smiled and took one. "Do you have to fly to New York for the shoot?"

"No, he's coming here for a movie premiere. At least if everything goes as planned. Maybe he'll cancel at the last minute." She tucked a curl nervously behind her ear and bit her lip.

"He won't cancel. He's a professional. And you'll do an amazing job. Just think, soon your picture will be pirated all over the internet."

"Oh, stop! I just hope I don't annoy him, or drop my camera or something. It's got to be film, not digital. I think that's one of the reasons they asked me."

"They asked you because you're amazingly talented and they know everyone will be talking about the pictures. Just relax and try to enjoy it." He stroked her arm. Her dress was silky soft jersey material that draped lusciously over her curves. Heat flared in his groin and he had to resist the urge to let his hand trail over more of her delicious body.

All in good time, he promised himself. He needed at least a few dates with her under his belt before he made any kind of…move. Though the temptation to make one right now was killing him.

Especially when she shifted, and the fabric of her dress pulled tight for a moment over her tantalizing breasts.

Ouch. His pants suddenly felt tight.

Her eyes sparkled as she sipped her champagne. "I'm excited about the concert. I've been going to jazz concerts regularly over the past year. I'm really starting to get the music."

He smiled. "Then you can teach me. All I do is enjoy it."

"That works, too. It's so nice to meet someone who likes doing so many of the things I enjoy."

"I love walking around with you. You know so much of the city."

Her eyes brightened. "I'd be happy to roam around more of it with you."

He offered her some marinated chicken in a pita and she put it on her plate. "Where do you recommend?"

"How about the Marina? Or the Painted Ladies— the Victorian houses, of course, not the hookers—near the park? Alcatraz is pretty wild. Have you ever been there?"

"No, and now I can't wait to go to each and every one of them."

Why hadn't he kissed her yet? Bree examined her carefully made up face in the mirror. Gavin was due any minute—again. They'd seen each other every other day for the past two weeks, walked nearly a hundred miles around the city, eaten countless meals and even— gasp!—held hands.

But not a single kiss on the lips. He brushed her cheek

lightly with his lips when they said goodbye, but that was it.

Maybe he wasn't attracted to her, after all?

She should be exhilarated after her shoot. Despite a late start, everything had gone smoothly and the proofs were to die for. The star was every bit as charming and polite as she'd imagined, and she'd managed not to blush and stammer like a teenager in his presence. She even showed him her portfolio so he'd have some idea of who the heck was taking his picture, and he'd asked all kinds of questions and seemed genuinely enthusiastic about her work.

She should be over the moon. Her first professional assignment was safely under her belt and she had another date with the most gorgeous man in San Francisco.

So why did she feel so…uneasy?

Gavin *seemed* to be interested. Something twinkled in his eyes when he looked at her, and she'd caught him sneaking glances at her cleavage, which had been on display more over the last couple of weeks than ever in her life.

He laughed at her jokes and appeared intrigued by all the odd anecdotes she'd picked up over the years. At one point, in the quiet gloom of an abandoned Alcatraz cell, she could almost swear he was going to step forward and kiss her. Tension hummed in the air like whispered voices of the people who'd been captive there. Her skin tingled at his nearness and she hoped with bated breath that he'd reach out to her.

But he didn't. And once again, after the ferry ride back, he said goodbye by pressing his lips gently to her cheek.

Good old Bree. Not really the kissable type. Perhaps

he saw her more as a friend. Or a sister, even, as that catty woman at his office party had suggested.

A sharp knock on the door tugged her back to the present. Her heart pounded under her latest clothing purchase, a stylish blouse with fine green and gray stripes. She added an extra hint of gloss to her lips for luck. Maybe he'd notice them and want to put his own lips on them tonight. If not, she might have to take matters into her own hands.

As if she had the nerve for that.

She pulled open the door and, as usual, her lungs squeezed with excitement and a big goofy grin pulled at her lips. "Hi, Gavin."

"Hi, Bree." The chaste cheek kiss he gave her still made her knees weak. How could a man smell so good after a long day at the office? Like wind and sea air and adventure. He'd changed into a pale blue shirt and faded jeans that hugged his thighs like a lover. "How do you feel about a walk to the Coit Tower on Telegraph Hill?"

"Great." Yeah, just great. The most popular proposal spot in the city and she was going to go there and maybe hold hands if she got lucky.

Unless…

She swallowed hard. No. Gavin Spencer was not going to propose to her tonight. This was the twenty-first century, not the eighteenth. A man did not ask a woman to marry him after accompanying her on a few bracing walks.

"There's a neat little Italian restaurant nearby, too, so we could grab some dinner."

"Sounds lovely." Her reply came out sounding a bit forced.

Gavin cocked his head. "Are you sure? Because we don't have to go if you don't want to."

"No, really, I'd love to." She reached down to grab her bag.

"And I was thinking that afterward, if you'd like, you could come back to my place for a nightcap."

"Oh. Sure, that would be great." Suddenly she was all breathless excitement. Her cheeks heated. He surely wouldn't ask her back to his place unless he intended to…

Butterflies unfurled in her stomach. What exactly did he have in mind? Possibly quite a bit more than a kiss.

"Let's go." He held out his hand and she took it. The door slammed behind her with a resounding thud.

They walked briskly through the streets to Telegraph Hill, where the pale spire of the tower rose above the surrounding houses. The climb up the hill toward the tower left Bree panting. "I can't believe you haven't even broken a sweat."

"I work out regularly." Gavin squeezed her hand. "I enjoy a good climb. Want me to carry you?" He raised a dark brow.

"The situation isn't that desperate yet. But there are steps inside the tower, too. I may take you up on it then." At the top of the hill, they admired the view of the Bay Bridge and Gavin suggested that maybe they'd climbed far enough.

"No way. You think I can't hack it, don't you?" She flexed her muscles under her new striped shirt. "I'd be a lousy date if we didn't even make it in to see all the murals. Did you hear the rumor that the tower was designed to look like a giant fire hose nozzle? Supposedly the lady who donated the land and the money to build the tower was a big fan of the local firehouse."

Gavin chuckled. "I can see a resemblance. I'm sure Sigmund Freud would have some other suggestions for things it looks like."

"You're not the first person to have made that observation, either. A giant phallic symbol rising over San Francisco. On that note, shall we go in?" She grinned and Gavin chuckled.

Inside the rotunda of the tower, he slid his arm around her waist as they looked at the murals painted during the depression: rural scenes of people picking crops, a San Francisco street scene complete with a pickpocket and a nasty car accident, a poor family panning for gold while a rich family looks on. "These were all painted during the depression, to provide work for artists, under the Works Progress Administration."

She enjoyed the warm sensation of his big arm around her, heating her skin through her thin blouse. "I know. Aren't they're stunning? I guess something good comes out of even the worst disasters."

"That's a very positive perspective. I fully approve." He squeezed her slightly as he turned to answer. Their faces hovered close for a second. Bree held her breath, sure he was going to lean in and kiss her...

But he peeled his arm gently from around her waist and moved away to peer at a detail in one of the paintings.

She rocked back on her boot heels and sucked in air. If he didn't make a move soon, she was going to go out of her mind.

After they had a delicious dinner and walked the short distance back to Russian Hill, Bree eased herself into the passenger seat of Gavin's sports car with a growing sense of anticipation and terror.

What if he *didn't* try anything? She might just die.

Gavin's gray gaze drifted from her hot cheeks to her rather dramatic cleavage and back again, with enjoyment that made excitement sizzle in her belly.

She could hardly believe how intimate and easy their conversation had become over the last few dates. Weren't men supposed to be difficult and mysterious and hard to understand? Gavin was easier to talk to than her girlfriends.

His apartment was in a tall white building on Stockton Street, and they parked in the lot underneath.

"This is very convenient." Bree pressed the elevator button that Gavin said would take them from the garage up to his apartment. "I hardly feel like we're in San Francisco. Shouldn't you have to throw on the parking brake and hike up a hill to get home?"

Gavin grinned ruefully. "Until I met you, I'd been missing out on a lot of the city's charm. I moved in here so I'd be close to work. I've been in this apartment since I first came from L.A. five years ago."

Gavin stepped into the small elevator after her, his nearness intimate in the cramped space. He'd rolled up his sleeves to reveal muscled forearms. His skin was tanned, dusted with dark hair. She wondered what those arms would feel like wrapped tight around her waist—right now.

Heat unfurled in her belly at the thought.

She glanced shyly at him as the door opened.

"We're here. It's the third door on the right. Not nearly as stylish as your studio, I'm afraid."

Bree walked down a hallway lined with identical blue

doors. She watched Gavin's strong fingers turn the key in the lock, and a shimmer of exhilaration slid through her as he opened the door into his apartment.

Gavin held the door for Bree to walk in ahead of him and she could swear she felt his eyes on her backside as she stepped over the threshold. His interest in her put a swing in her hips that she'd never felt before.

The front door led into a living room dominated by a black leather sofa. A glass coffee table held three neat advertising magazines and a TV remote.

"Would you like a drink?" Gavin headed for the small kitchen. "I have white wine, vodka and rum."

"I think I'd better go for wine. I'm not used to the hard stuff." Just being around Gavin made her light-headed. She followed him into a neat galley kitchen with gleaming appliances. "Your apartment is very tidy."

"We can thank the maid for that. I'm not home all that much. I've been working flat out on the Prentice account lately. They're running a new campaign starting next month."

"I can't imagine working such long hours. You must be exhausted."

Gavin poured wine into two glasses and handed her one. "Not really. You get used to it. I enjoy the work— it's energizing for me."

She took the glass and smiled. "You're lucky to have found work you like so much."

"Trust me, I know it. We're both lucky that way. Here's to your promising career as one of the West Coast's hottest young photographers." He raised his glass and Bree clinked hers against it.

"I'm not sure I'm really young enough for that title."

"Of course you are. Don't be ridiculous." Then a mock frown darkened his brow. "Unless you're seventy and have a really good plastic surgeon."

Bree laughed. "This is California. You should probably check my driver's license."

"Nah. I'll take my chances and drink to California's most beautiful photographer instead." He sipped his wine and peered at her with those seductive gray eyes.

"Now you're just exaggerating."

"Not at all." His eyes swept over her, scorching her skin all the way from her exposed neck to where her new expensive jeans encased her thighs. "You're certainly the most gorgeous woman in San Francisco, and I can say that with some authority since I meet a lot of models in my line of work. They'd all fade into the background with you around."

Bree bit her lip. What a flatterer. He did working in advertising—and she'd better not forget it. Still, he was very convincing.

She sipped her wine. The tart, cool liquid zinged over her tongue. Maybe he really did think she was pretty. She pushed her shoulders back the way Elle had shown her and tossed her curls behind her shoulders.

"Come sit on the sofa."

Gavin led her back into the living room. His blue striped shirt revealed his broad shoulders and, tucked into his faded jeans, emphasized his trim waist and a very cute butt. Desire sizzled in her belly as she imagined what he looked like underneath. All their hiking around the city had revealed him to be extremely fit.

She tore her gaze from his physique as he turned around and gestured for her to sit. She lowered herself carefully onto the leather couch and crossed her legs.

Once again she felt Gavin's eyes on her cleavage. Heat swelled in her breasts and thickened her nipples, making them hum with sensation.

Usually she hated her large breasts. They were always in the way, making her feel large and ungainly. But in her new, perfectly fitting bra, they were transformed into a pleasant and desirable part of a body she was forming a new relationship with.

Since she'd met Gavin, she felt comfortable—sexy—in her own skin. For the first time in her life.

He put his glass down on the table. Feeling a sense of impending…something, Bree set hers next to it.

Her skin prickled as he drew closer. His scent, masculine and seductive, crept over her. She could see the shadow of stubble on his skin—he'd definitely have to shave twice a day to lose it. A tiny smile lifted the corners of his wide, sensual mouth.

Oh, boy.

Bree sucked in a breath as lips moved closer. *He's going to kiss me.*

Her heart beat hard against her ribs.

For an agonizing instant, their faces hovered so close she could feel the heat from his skin against her cheek. Panic rushed through her, laced with longing so deep it ached in her bones.

Then his mouth brushed softly against hers.

Four

Bree shuddered as sensation crashed through her. Gavin's big, strong hands pulled her close as he deepened the kiss. His fingers pressed into her back, revealing the urgency of his own need.

Their tongues met in a jolt of electricity and she enjoyed the rough rasp of his chin against hers. She writhed on the smooth leather, desire filling her body like a bottle that might overflow.

Her hands found their way to Gavin's shirt front, where she ran her fingertips over the cotton, feeling the muscle beneath.

A moan issued from his mouth and echoed through her. His thickly muscled arms pulled her close until her nipples brushed against his chest. Arousal thrummed low in her belly, pounding in a way she'd never felt before. Her hands were now on his back, roaming and testing the hard muscle, grasping at his shirt while he kissed her—hard and fast.

When they finally came up for air, Bree found herself blinking and breathless.

"Wow." The single, low syllable fell from Gavin's moistened lips.

Bree exhaled hard. "*Wow* is right." Her whole body stung and tingled with stray sensations all the way down to her toes.

She'd kissed men before, but it had never felt anything like this. Usually there was some groping and fumbling, and she'd even had rather disappointing sex on two occasions, but she'd never known anything like this crazy jumble of emotions and feelings that swept through her like madness.

She reached for her wine and took a bracing gulp. Anticipation glowed between them in the quiet apartment. It wasn't total silence, though—the rapid beating of her heart warred with the ticking of a nearby clock.

Bree blew a lock of hair out of her face. "I guess that's what they call chemistry."

Gavin's mouth quirked into a smile. "No question. And I suspect if harnessed correctly it could solve all the world's energy problems."

"Less dangerous than nuclear fission, too."

"Or so we think." His storm-gray eyes swept over her. Her skin tingled as atoms snapped in half under his gaze. "Further experimentation is required."

Bree inhaled slowly, her breasts rising inside the caress of her bra. "If it's for the cause of science, we can hardly refuse." Her lips hummed with the desire to meet his again.

Gavin leaned in, his soft breath warming her skin for a second before his mouth slid over hers. Their tongues tangled and their hands grew bolder. Bree's fingertips slid beneath the waist of his pants and pulled at his shirt. She gasped when he brushed her nipple, and he cupped her breast, testing its weight in his palm.

Bree pulled his soft shirt loose in the back and reached under it, touching his skin. It was hotter than she expected, and the muscles of his back flexed under her fingertips.

His thumb slipped inside her blouse and strummed her nipple through her bra. She arched and moaned through their kiss in response.

Leaning into him, she let her fingernails rake over the hard muscle on either side of his spine. She'd never felt such a powerful male body. Heat simmered in her core as she felt the sheer strength of him, so different from the skinny boys she'd known in the past.

With a deft hand, he unbuttoned her blouse and pushed it aside until her breast was bared—or at least her bra. Her lips reluctantly gave up his mouth as Gavin pulled back.

Bree's eyes opened to see his gaze resting on her cleavage. The fine lace of the pretty bra gave the vista an erotic flavor. Thank goodness she wasn't wearing one of her old, white "over-the-shoulder-boulder-holders." She owed Elle big time for her fashion and beauty tips.

Gavin's chest rose as he inhaled and sighed. "This is the best view I've seen in a long time."

"And I bet you can see pretty far from this high floor."

"Rooftops and seagulls have nothing on the hills and valleys I see right now." His gaze scorched her skin.

Then his fingers tugged at her blouse and pulled it off completely. Bree wriggled out of the sleeves, until she was naked from the waist up.

Well, a bra counted as naked, didn't it?

She certainly felt naked under his hungry gaze.

Gavin lowered his mouth to her breast and licked her nipple through the satiny fabric. Bree's belly quivered at the sensation. His hand roamed over her back, sliding under the bra strap, then releasing the clasp with practiced ease.

She sucked in a breath as he pulled the black satin and lace from her, leaving her totally exposed.

"You are unbelievably hot." His eyes rested on her chest as he said it, which made her laugh. Her breasts weren't used to such frank and enthusiastic worship, and she couldn't help enjoying it.

"I don't think it's fair that only one of us gets to enjoy the view." She reached for his shirt buttons and pushed the shirt back to reveal ripped, tanned muscle. "Ah, much better."

A fine line of silky dark hair ran between his thick pecs, heading down below his leather belt. Bree's breath caught in her throat as she saw the thick bulge beneath the buckle.

On instinct, her hand slid down to touch him through the denim of his jeans. Hard and powerful, his raw arousal made her blink.

"I think we'd be more comfortable in the bedroom." Gavin's low voice sent a shiver of awareness through her.

"Okay." Her voice may have quavered a bit but he didn't seem to notice.

After a smoky head-to-toe glance that threatened to

light her skin on fire, he took her hand and led her into his bedroom.

He switched on a soft light, which threw out just enough illumination to reveal dark blue sheets on a wide wooden bed with sleek modern lines. Blinds covered the floor-to-ceiling windows. Gavin shrugged off his shirt—which was barely on to begin with—and held out his hands. Bree walked into his inviting embrace.

Her skin hummed under his exploring fingers. Breathless and a little nervous, she reached for his belt buckle. She wasn't experienced but she knew she shouldn't sit back and wait for him to do everything. He was probably used to temptresses like that woman at the party, who could drive a man to heights of distraction with one flick of a manicured fingernail.

She was surprised when the thick leather belt came easily through the thin buckle. Her knuckles grazed his thick erection, which throbbed under her touch.

He really wants me. She still could hardly believe it. How could everything have turned around so quickly?

One minute she was plain old Bree Kincannon, going about her usual dull but pleasant existence. Now she was standing in a strange man's apartment in her underwear, apparently on the brink of making love.

Love?

No. No one had said anything about love. Still, she couldn't deny that she felt a special connection with Gavin. And he obviously felt it, too. Isn't this what falling in love must be like?

"Oh!" She let out a little exclamation of surprise as he unzipped her jeans. He slid them down her thighs, caressing her skin with his mouth as he went, leaving her in only her lace-edged panties.

"You're breathtaking," he murmured.

Bree tried to hold up her end by undoing his jeans. Her eager fingers fumbled with the button and Gavin helped her slide them over his tight backside and down his thick, powerful thighs.

Oh, my. She'd never seen thighs like that. At least not outside an underwear commercial. Heart in her throat, she tugged at his dark gray boxers and couldn't help gasping as his arousal sprang free.

Gavin guided her gently onto the cool sheets and tugged her panties down over her thighs.

Now she really was naked. Excitement and fear prickled in her veins.

He climbed over her, his big muscled body making hers seem almost insubstantial, and lowered himself carefully onto the bed beside her.

A gentle kiss on the lips soothed her rattled nerves. Gavin's broad fingers roamed over her belly, leaving tingles of sensation in their wake. She tensed up slightly as he strayed between her thighs, but she parted her legs and let them in.

His fingertip probed into her warmth and she sucked in a breath as it found a sensitive spot. Her hips twitched slightly as he moved his fingers, stimulating secret places no one else had cared to explore.

Eyes closed, an expression of pleasure lighting his chiseled features, Gavin looked more heartbreakingly handsome than ever. Bree's heart squeezed. Could he be the one?

She'd more or less given up hoping that Prince Charming would come sweep her off her feet. Every little girl has that dream, but a grown woman of twenty-nine has learned that most frogs don't improve all that much upon kissing.

Ooh. She wriggled as Gavin's fingers sent a shockwave zinging through her. A tiny moan escaped her lips. Gavin's eyes opened a crack, and a wicked smile played at the edges of his sensual mouth.

Hot and slick under his touch, she felt more aroused than ever in her life. Gavin eased closer, until their bodies pressed together all the way from his broad shoulders to his sturdy thighs. Then he raised himself up onto a powerful arm, rolled on a condom with expert ease, and climbed over her.

She couldn't help an involuntary shudder as he entered her. All her nerve endings were alive and buzzing. Eyes closed, she gave herself over to the sensation. Her fingers dug into the hard muscle of his back as he slid inside her, slow and gentle, opening her like a secret chamber left unexplored for far too long.

Once inside her, Gavin released a throaty moan—a sound of relief mingled with pleasure. He started to move, and Bree's hips automatically joined in the dance, just as her body had flowed with his so readily on the dance floor at the charity gala. Maybe they were meant to be together….

She let the delicious thought flow through her as she followed him into a new realm of pleasure. Gavin's hands roamed over her body, squeezing and enjoying every inch of her, as they moved together. She explored the muscled ridges of his back and the firm curve of his backside.

Desire fluttered in her chest—and in all kinds of places she didn't know existed—as Gavin deftly shifted them into different positions. Heat pulsed through her and her thoughts jumbled and scattered as primal sensation shoved thought aside. Her body cleaved to his, writhing and twisting, steamy and slick.

She arched under him, taking him deeper, her breath coming in unsteady gasps, until suddenly everything exploded.

Or imploded.

Her body convulsed and twitched as tidal waves of wringing pleasure crashed through her bloodstream.

Then a low groan filled the air and she felt Gavin's arms wrapped around her like a vice. He throbbed inside her, sending further sparks of nuclear fission to her fingers and toes.

"Wow." His voice, thick and rough, echoed her exclamation after their kiss.

"Uh-huh," she murmured back, half amazed that she could still use language. Her brain seemed to have switched off for a few moments there. She opened her eyelids a tiny bit and her gaze locked onto Gavin's. His gray eyes dark with passion, he gazed at her, wrapped up in her completely.

Bree's chest tightened, filled with too much emotion. Gavin Spencer was too much for her. Way too much. Sweet, kind, caring, thoughtful—and ridiculously handsome. Things like this didn't happen to her. She was boring old Bree, the one you could always count on in a pinch because you knew she'd be free.

Or was she?

Maybe, after Elle's clever alterations, and with the help of Gavin's experienced touch, she'd truly morphed and changed into someone new. Someone exciting and desirable, whose life would now unfurl and brighten like a flower after the rain.

"I've never met anyone quite like you, Bree." Gavin rested his head on the pillow, peering at her through sleepy, half-closed eyes.

"Me? There's nothing special about me." She kicked herself for giving in to the familiar urge to run herself down.

A frown furrowed Gavin's brow. "Everything about you is special." He stroked her chin with his thumb. "You're warm and kind and caring. You're clever and creative and artistic."

Bree swallowed. She'd heard those before. They were the kind of compliments her starchy aunts offered, usually after critiquing her posture and lamenting her lack of marital prospects.

"And you're the best looking woman in San Francisco."

"Only in San Francisco?" She couldn't help teasing. His smoky gaze roamed over her naked body making her feel like the most beautiful woman on earth.

"Definitely in the whole Bay area. And the State of California. And the entire West Coast."

Bree mock pouted. "And there I was hoping for the Midwest, as well."

"I haven't spent much time there so I'm not an authority." His narrowed gaze twinkled with mischief.

"Never mind then." She tossed her curls. Gavin took one in his fingers and tried it on like a ring. "That's rather suggestive," she murmured.

"Perhaps that's my intention." He cocked his head slightly.

She bit her lip to stop a naughty smile sneaking across her mouth. "Shouldn't we get some sleep? Tomorrow's a workday."

"Actually, I'm on vacation. Had to use it or lose it."

"Lucky you."

"But if you have a busy day, I quite understand." He twirled her curl softly around his finger.

"Actually, I don't." She didn't have any plans at all, in fact.

"Then I have an idea." His brow furrowed again. "A big idea. A crazy, mad, wonderful idea."

Curiosity prickled through Bree. "What?"

He shifted until he was sitting up. "I'll be right back."

With a navy towel around his waist, Gavin strode to the study.

Crazy.

Definitely crazy, but the idea had seized him. Maybe because everything about Bree felt so right. Their lovemaking was sensational. Bree was every bit as passionate and erotic as he'd imagined, and that unbelievable body of hers…. He frowned at the erection already getting started again.

Mad.

No question he was mad. Everyone would tell him that. Heck, Bree would probably tell him that. They'd only known each other for two and a half weeks. But sometimes the universe was on your side and everything came together, like the time he won the big Stayco account.

No. This was nothing like the time he won the Stayco account. That was a business relationship. This would be a lifetime commitment.

His chest tightened. A lifetime with Bree. Right now that seemed very appealing.

In the study, the display on the digital clock gave

off just enough illumination for him to see the drawer handles.

Yes, the one million dollars offered by her father was an enticement. But it wasn't the only one, not by any means. It was more like a pearl necklace around the neck of a beautiful woman: it enhanced her appeal, rather than overshadowed it.

Wonderful.

That's how things could be if everything went according to plan. He and Bree could buy a nice house somewhere—maybe even Russian Hill, he'd always liked that area.

He could finally start his own company and settle into an exciting yet comfortable existence as a man in charge of his own destiny.

Excitement swelled inside him. He pulled open the top drawer and reached into its dark interior. Past the paper clips and stapler, his fingertips settled on a smooth leather box. He picked it up. The gold embossed around the edges glowed in the green light from the clock. He'd had no idea what to do with this ring when he was given it, but suddenly it seemed like just another perfectly fitting piece in the puzzle of his life.

He flipped open the lid to reveal a lovely Art Deco ring, three flawless diamonds—a large one flanked by two smaller ones—in a pretty setting. Most people probably would have sold it, but he couldn't do that. It had belonged to his grandmother, one of the most amazing people he'd ever met. She'd encouraged his creative ambitions, taking him to drama class and music lessons, paying for summer arts camp when his parents had disapproved.

She'd left him the ring in her will. At the time he'd

wondered why, but now he knew. She wanted him to give it to the woman he loved.

Gavin drew in a ragged breath and plucked the ring from its satin bed. Would Bree be offended by the offer of a used ring? She was an heiress, after all, able to buy whatever she wanted without a thought.

The ring glittered as he examined it. Bree wasn't flashy or pretentious, he thought. Deep down, he suspected the sentimental value of a ring might be more important than its market price.

He had no idea if it would fit, but that would be easy enough to fix. He left the box on the desk and tucked the ring into his palm.

Bree lay on the bed, curls sprawled on the pillow, the sheet draped over her delicious body. She smiled as he stood in the doorway. Adrenaline surged through Gavin's body—how would she react? Might she reject him out of hand? Then his plans would lie in ruins and he'd have to tell her father he'd failed to hold up his part of the bargain.

Her dark lashes flickered as she looked at him, expectant, probably wondering why he stood over her, hesitating, one hand behind his back. The ring prickled against his skin, hard facets of diamond goading him to ask her his burning question.

He walked to the bed and sat down on the covers next to her. The heat from her skin warmed him and eased the tension in his limbs. "Bree, I know we haven't known each other long." His voice sounded oddly gruff. Her eyes widened. "But sometimes life offers you a rare opportunity, something you weren't expecting and couldn't even have hoped for." He swallowed. "Bree, will you marry me?"

Five

Bree blinked. Obviously she was asleep and dreaming.

But it felt so real.

Gavin sat next to her on the bed, muscles honed by the soft lamplight, a towel wrapped around his waist like a toga. In his fingers, something sparkled. A ring. Just like in fairy tales when the handsome prince gets down on one knee and...

"I know it's sudden." His voice interrupted her thoughts. "I'm sure you're surprised. I am, too. I had no idea I could develop such strong feelings for a woman so quickly."

Chest tightening, Bree pushed herself up onto one elbow. "I'm not dreaming, am I?"

Gavin's handsome features creased into a smile. "No,

you're not. I'm as real as you are." He caressed her thigh through the sheet. Her skin hummed under his touch.

"And I'd like you to be my wife."

She swallowed. Gavin Spencer wanted to marry her? This couldn't be real. For a start, they'd known each other less than three weeks. Plus, he was gorgeous, a drop-dead knockout who must have women trailing after him wherever he went. Why would he want to be stuck with one woman for the rest of his life—least of all her?

"It's too sudden, isn't it?" He tilted his head.

"No. I mean, I don't know." She had no idea how to respond. Did she want to marry him? All the nerves and muscles in her body—especially those newly awakened by the evening's activities—sang *yes!* in a harmonized chorus.

But the old Bree muttered something quite different. *Beware. Something's off here. It's too soon. He's too good to be true.*

Bree drew in a long breath, which didn't help steady her racing nerves. "I don't know what to say." Her voice came out high and squeaky.

"'Yes' would work." Gavin's gray eyes sparkled, much like the glittering ring in his palm. Odd that it lay flat in his hand. Didn't men in the movies usually hold it between their fingers?

But this wasn't a movie. It was her life. Which had suddenly taken such a strange turn that she hardly knew who she was anymore, let alone how she should react.

"But we only just met. You don't know me." What if he married her, then realized she was just boring old Bree, not the fantasy woman he'd built up in his mind? "You probably think I'm a lot more exciting and interesting than I really am."

Gavin cocked his head. "You should have more faith in yourself." He eased closer on the bed and rested his free hand at her waist. "We've spent hours talking and you're undoubtedly the most thoughtful, intelligent and interesting person I've ever met."

"Am I really?" The question flew out before she could stop it. How embarrassing to go fishing for a compliment like that.

"No question about it. And that's not all. I'm entranced by your beauty, too."

"Oh, come on." She blushed. "I'm hardly a head turner."

"That's where you are so wrong. Heads turn wherever you go."

Bree bit her lip. Elle's makeover had apparently had its intended effect. She'd never attracted so much attention in her life as she had in the past couple of weeks. Even the time she'd accidentally worn two unmatched shoes to school on Awards Day.

"I'd be a good husband."

"I'm sure you would."

But doubts still niggled. Why was he trying so hard to sell himself? Couldn't they date for a while and test each other out more?

"I'd cherish and honor and ravish you." A mischievous gleam lit his eyes. A flash of desire echoed in Bree's belly. "Why don't you just try it on?" He shrugged, as if it was something casual. Try on an engagement ring and see how the whole engagement experience feels.

Bree shrugged, trying to conceal the odd mass of feelings roiling in her stomach.

"Why not?" Her squeaky voice betrayed her apprehension.

Gavin held the ring for her. She raised her hand. She rarely wore jewelry at all, and never on that finger. Everyone knew it was bad luck to put anything but an engagement ring on it. She'd never really expected to put a ring on that finger, resigned as she was to her quiet life with her cats.

Now a new realm of possibilities glittered, facets shimmering in the dim light. She poked out her naked finger, clutching the sheets about her with her other hand. A shiver of fear and excitement slashed through her as the cool metal touched her skin. Would it be too small? She wasn't a petite little thing, though her hands were probably the most delicate part of her. Would it stick firm over a knuckle and refuse to budge?

That would be a sign.

But it slid on, smoothly, all the way to the right spot.

"A perfect fit." Gavin's triumphant gaze fixed on hers.

"It is. How did you manage that?"

"Pure luck. And I think it's a message from the universe that it fits so well." He stroked her hand where the ring glittered on her finger. "I don't know how you'll feel about this, but it's a special ring. It belonged to my grandmother, who was married to the love of her life for fifty-seven years."

The three stones sat in a pretty setting. Looking at it now, she could see it was probably designed in the twenties. "It's lovely."

The ring buzzed a little against her skin. She wasn't sure how she felt about wearing someone else's wedding ring. It seemed to underscore the sensation that she'd accidentally stepped into someone else's life.

"My grandmother was very special to me. She gave me the ring in her will so I could give it to my wife one day. I can't believe how well it fits you. Like it was made for you."

Bree gulped. Now that the ring was on her finger, did that mean she'd said yes? "It's beautiful. Are you sure you want to part with it?"

Gavin held her hand. "I don't want to part with it. I want it on the finger of the woman I love."

Bree's stomach clenched. The word *love* hung in the air like a flash of smoke from a magic trick.

That's what had been missing, why the whole proposal had felt rather odd, forced—because he hadn't told her he loved her.

Until now.

"I love you, Bree." He caressed her hand with his thumb. "It's a new love, untried and untested, I'll admit. But I've never felt like this about anyone before. Something in my gut, in my heart, tells me that you're the woman for me."

The conviction in his voice wrapped around her like a cloak. Did she love him? She had no idea what love was even supposed to feel like. Arousal and desire sizzled through her like steam, no denying that. And Gavin was sweet and charming and intelligent and fun. And completely hot.

All the things she would have looked for in her dream husband. If she was looking for a husband. Which she certainly should be, according to pretty much everyone she knew. She was just so used to being suspicious, to doubting the motives of any man who came near her because he might be more interested in the Kincannon coffers than in her.

"There's something special between us, isn't there?" His voice interrupted her thoughts.

"Yes, there is." Bree frowned. The connection between them crackled right now, as she sat on the bed, her hands in his. She'd never felt so comfortable with a man, so safe. She'd certainly never felt so desirable and intriguing. "I do feel it."

She looked down at the three diamonds twinkling on her finger.

"Will you marry me?" Gavin's simple question, asked with hope in his wide gray gaze, blew away any last traces of resistance.

"Yes. I will." Exhilaration—and terror—flashed through her as she said the words. But she also felt a fierce conviction that this was right. Strange—and sudden—as it was, their pairing was meant to be.

Gavin wrapped his arms around her and held her tight. The warmth from his body mingled with hers and possibly for the first time in her life—at least since her mother died—she felt totally protected and cared for.

And loved.

As they pulled onto the Golden Gate Bridge in Gavin's car, Bree snuck a glance backward at the city. When she returned, she'd be a married woman. Mrs. Gavin Spencer. They were getting married right over the bridge in Sausalito.

Gavin had wanted to get married as soon as possible. No guests, just the two of them—and Bree's cats. Gavin had sweetly insisted that they come, too, since they were members of the family. One of his former clients owned a boutique hotel with a terrace overlooking the city that hosted small weddings quite often. He'd promised to provide the wedding officiant, a photographer and two witnesses.

The whole thing had been arranged so fast. The only holdup was the prenup—Gavin had insisted on one, maybe to prove that he wasn't a gold digger. She found the whole thing embarrassing. Didn't it imply that they might one day get divorced? She didn't want to think about that. Still, he'd managed to get one drawn up and signed in less than a day, and now here they were, barely forty-eight hours after his proposal.

Gavin turned to look at her. "Nervous?"

"A little." It was all happening so quickly. And a wedding without any friends and family seemed odd.

Still, despite some reservations, Bree had to admit it made sense. She didn't want the kind of big society wedding her father would have insisted on, which would take a full year to plan and involve more fuss than a royal inauguration. Better to do it this way, quickly and privately. Oddly, her father hadn't protested their impromptu plans the way she'd expected. He'd seemed quite unsurprised by her news and happy for both of them. Which wasn't so odd, really, since he'd undoubtedly introduced her to Gavin in the hope that she'd finally find a mate. Finally she'd managed to accomplish something her father approved of! Or at least she would have soon.

Very soon.

"Sausalito's a fun place to escape to. Even though it's just across the bridge, you feel like you're a million miles away." His warm grin tickled something inside her. Gavin looked even more breathtaking than usual today. A casual black shirt rolled up over his powerful forearms, faded jeans, his thick, dark hair slightly tousled. She could hardly believe she was sitting next to him, let alone driving to Sausalito to marry him.

The diamond ring still glittered on her finger. She hadn't taken it off since he'd put it on to test the size.

"We can live in my condo until we find a place. But I think we should get a house, so there will be plenty of room for you to have a big studio. What do you think?"

"I don't know what to think." She smiled. "I've never lived anywhere but the house I'm in now. I'm open to anything. I can always rent a separate studio for my business."

"No way. We'll find a house with a great studio for you. And a view of the bay is a must, since you're used to enjoying one."

How rich was he? He talked as if he had all the funds in the world at his disposal. Or did he expect her to pay for their new house? Odd how they were about to walk down the aisle but they hadn't discussed even the most basic practical matters.

Except the prenup. And those often weren't worth the paper they were written on anyway. If he hadn't insisted, she wouldn't even have thought of it. If she couldn't trust her husband, who could she trust? She wouldn't let money rule her life.

They drove through the low hills of the Gateway National Recreation area, then climbed up into the steep and picturesque streets of Sausalito. He pulled up in the circular driveway of a small Mediterranean style building with blooms bursting from pots and beds in every direction.

"The wedding's booked for six o'clock tonight, so we'll have plenty of time to get ready."

"Tonight?" Panic flashed over Bree. For some reason she assumed they'd have at least a day to…to what? If they were getting married, might as well get on with it.

Still, she'd barely had a chance to get used to having a "fiancé" yet, and they were going to run down the aisle *tonight*. Kind of funny how he'd just gone ahead and made all the plans—and she'd let him.

Gavin climbed out of the car, then came around to open her door. She stepped out onto the gravel on shaky legs. He slid a palm across the base of her spine, which sent waves of heat—as well as anxiety—shivering through her. "Tonight will be our wedding night." His smoky gray gaze smoldered with possibilities.

Bree blinked and blew out a shaky breath. "So it will."

He squeezed her hand. "I can't wait to be your husband, Bree."

"I can't wait to be your wife." She squeezed back, and happiness swelled in her chest, pushing away the anxiety. He was so open and affectionate, on top of all the other things she adored about him. Did anyone have a right to be this lucky?

Then she froze. "But what am I going to wear?"

"Anything you like. We have all afternoon to shop."

Though Bree was nervous about her ability to pick a flattering dress without Elle, she found one quite easily at a stylish shop down near the docks. The silvery-white, tea-length gown in shimmering satin draped elegantly over her curves. Sky-blue heels proved an oddly perfect match. At a local jeweler, they chose engraved wedding bands for the ceremony. Back at the hotel, she was visited by a bubbly hairdresser who piled her curls into a chignon fastened with pearl-tipped pins. Bree put on the sparkly pearl and diamond earrings they'd picked together. Gavin insisted on paying for everything, and her transformation into a blushing bride gave him obvious delight.

"You're breathtaking." He came up behind her as she put the finishing touches on her lipstick. His face appearing next to hers in the mirror made her smile.

"You're pretty smashing yourself." She glanced at his crisp, black satin bowtie. The elegant tuxedo only enhanced his matinee-idol good looks.

"We do make a nice looking couple." He slid his arms around her satin clad waist.

"And we do fit well together." She didn't look at all big or ungainly next to him—at over six feet, he made her feel perfectly proportioned. She wriggled under his tempting, warm touch. "In fact, I rather wish we didn't have to leave the room."

"It'll be worth it." He pressed a soft kiss to her cheek. Her skin, already hot and made up with blush, flushed deeper under his lips. "And we'll have all night to celebrate." Gavin's throaty whisper echoed through her, a promise of sensations she was quickly becoming addicted to. "Are you ready?"

"As ready as I'll ever be."

Panic and excitement tingled to Bree's toes and fingers as they stepped out onto the hotel's terrace. Glorious sunshine lit up the simple gazebo where the officiant waited for them. Gavin tightened his reassuring grip on her hand, and shot her an encouraging glance. Petunias spilled from carved pots and planters, and ribbons festooned the table holding the official paperwork.

The hotel's manager walked up to them, followed by a pretty blonde holding a boutonniere for Gavin. "Welcome, and congratulations on your special day." The speech sounded a little canned, Bree thought, then cursed herself for the petty thought. They were just being polite, and trying to make them feel at home.

She glanced out at the impressive view over the bay, where sailboats scudded over the dark water. It was a lovely spot to get married. Perfect, even. Besides, the whole point was to join herself to this wonderful man and begin an exciting new chapter in her life.

Still, her breathing came a little shallow as they walked toward the gazebo where the officiant stood waiting.

Could something that came together this quickly and easily really be permanent? Despite Gavin's strong and soothing hand in hers, Bree found herself pestered by doubts.

Maybe Gavin thought he was marrying the ringleted temptress Elle had turned her into, rather than the real her. What would happen when he discovered he'd married a dull mouse rather than the exciting woman of his dreams?

"I love you, Bree." His whispered words banished her worries like a strong breeze.

"I love you, too, Gavin." She rasped the words back with conviction. How had he known to turn and reassure her at just the right moment?

Because he was perfect—for her.

A few pleasantries were exchanged, and before she had a chance to gather her wits, the ceremony was underway.

"Do you, Bree Kincannon, take this man to be your lawfully wedded husband, to have and to hold, to cherish and love, as long as you both shall live?"

"I do." She spoke the words clear and loud, determined not to let any lingering doubts become evident to the witnesses, even if they were strangers. Gavin said his vows with a reassuring, deep voice and an expression of honest enthusiasm that almost made her laugh aloud.

"You may now kiss the bride."

In front of the assembled strangers, Gavin eased his arms around her waist, pulled her close, and kissed her—gentle, yet firm. Heat shimmered through her from head to toe.

"We're married," he whispered. "I've never felt so excited and happy in my whole life."

"Me, either." Bree spoke the truth. A whirlwind wedding to the most gorgeous man she'd ever met was unquestionably the high point of her quiet life so far. "It's all happened so quickly, I can't quite believe it."

"When something's right, it's like all the forces in the universe converge to make everything come together. That force has been in motion since the moment I met you."

"Even though I was wearing that horrid gray dress?"

Gavin laughed. "An ordinary dress can't hide the light that shines from inside you, Bree. I could tell right away that you were special. And then when we danced…" He let out a low whistle that tickled a laugh from down deep in her belly. "We're definitely going out dancing later." Then he hesitated. "Or maybe tomorrow. It's our wedding night and I have some very detailed plans for it." A slightly raised brow made desire quiver in Bree. The promise of sensual pleasure thickened her nipples under her silky dress.

She almost slid her hand inside his jacket to enjoy the hot hard muscle she knew lay under his elegant tux.

Then she remembered they still stood in the middle of the hotel terrace, under the professional gaze of the "witnesses."

She glanced around and took a step back. "Perhaps we should go somewhere more private?"

Back in their comfortable suite, which also featured breathtaking views of the bay, Gavin had the whole evening arranged down to the finest detail. Even the cats were settled near the sofa with gourmet meals and plush cushions. A knock on the door confirmed that everything was happening according to plan.

"That must be dinner." He kissed Bree's sweet lips one more time before heading for the door to their suite. He'd secretly placed an order for the hotel's finest meal, for them to enjoy in the privacy of their suite.

Only the best for Bree. Not because she was an heiress and accustomed to it anyway, but because he truly did want to cherish her, and to see that pretty face light with its familiar glowing smile.

"I'd just assumed we'd go out." Bree glanced at the door.

"On our wedding night? I prefer privacy." He shot her a teasing glance.

The waiter wheeled in a cart laden with pretty

Mediterranean pottery, then congratulated them and left. Bree lifted the lid of the first dish to reveal a rush of steam and the tempting scent of delicate hors d'oeuvres, two of each, an array of tiny pastries and bite-sized morsels.

He fed them to Bree, and she returned the favor, both of them laughing. When had he ever done anything this simple—this silly—with a woman, and had such a great time?

Never. That's when.

Bree's easy, drama-free approach to life was so refreshing. Even if one million big ones weren't currently winging their way into his bank account, he'd be very pleased with his choice of a life partner.

The soup was creamy vichyssoise sprinkled with fresh chives. Tender steak tips, baby vegetables and new potatoes in a rich gravy made a satisfying main course, and he was sure he couldn't eat another thing until they uncovered the desserts—tiny éclairs and profiteroles, delicate tarts and hand-decorated cakes. He licked cream off Bree's lips and toasted their marriage with a glass of Moet.

"I think we should retire to the bedroom." He picked up the champagne and their two glasses. "We'll be more comfortable there."

He waited while she stood, looking radiant, glowing like a movie star in her wedding finery. So different from the quiet, almost apologetic woman he'd met that first night at the gala. She'd blossomed magnificently since he met her. Eyes darted toward her wherever they went, taking in her statuesque beauty, and she looked quite comfortable and assured under the gaze of all those envious males.

The bed was turned down, fresh white sheets gleaming in the soft light. Bree settled herself gingerly on the edge and accepted the offered glass of champagne.

Gavin sat down next to her and pulled a pearl-tipped pin from her chignon. "Rapunzel, Rapunzel, let down your hair."

She giggled. "Wouldn't it be a shame to undo all the hairdresser's hard work?"

"But I can't run my hands through your tresses when they're all piled up on your head." He pulled out another pin, this one with a spray of baby pearls around a tiny diamond. A single coiled ringlet tumbled free.

Bree tugged gently at one end of his bow tie. It slid apart and she pulled the black silk loose from his collar. "Two can play at that game." Her green eyes glittered, pupils wide and dark.

The flame of desire burning deep inside Gavin all day roared through his muscles. But he kept his cool and slowly pulled another pin from Bree's shiny updo. A thick lock of luscious dark hair fell to her shoulder.

Bree reached for the button on his collar and pulled it loose. She undid the next one and ran a cool finger along his chest between his pecs.

Arousal snapped inside him. He lifted the fallen lock of hair and found the delicate shoulder strap of her dress. Pushing it aside, he kissed her shoulder and neck, inhaling the rich scent of her and burying his face in her hair. "Bree, you drive me crazy."

"Crazy enough to make you marry me, apparently."

"I'm the luckiest man alive." He found the zipper on the side of her dress and tugged it down gently. "To have the woman of my dreams right here in my arms."

Or in his hands. He let them roam, shameless and hungry for the touch of her after a day of restraint. His palms cupped her full, heavy breasts, sending desire pounding through him like a drumbeat. He slid his hands to her hips, to enjoy the lush curves draped in seductive satin. Breathing ragged, he pressed a hot kiss to her mouth.

Bree pushed herself against him, breasts crushing against his chest, her hands tangling under his jacket. "Your clothes are in the way," she gasped, when they broke for air.

She shoved his jacket off onto the floor and yanked at the last buttons on his shirt, then pushed it back over his shoulders.

Half blind with desire, Gavin helped Bree out of her shimmering dress until she lay sprawled on the bed, a vision of lush skin and delicate white lace underwear. Her hair tumbled about her face in gorgeous disarray.

Her tugged her bra straps down one at a time, then unhooked the bra to reveal her tight, pink nipples. He eased her panties down inch by inch, enjoying the soft curves of her hips and thighs. Her skin tasted honey sweet, like nectar against his tongue.

Bree wriggled under his teasing tongue until she reached up and grabbed him around the waist. They met, skin to skin, in a delicious collision. Hard and ready, he kissed her as she welcomed him into her slick warmth.

She arched her back and made a tiny sound as he sank into her, a murmur of pure pleasure that filled him with joy. "I love you, Bree," he rasped, meaning every word.

"I love you, too." Their bodies tangled along with

their words, hot and heartfelt, in a dance that celebrated their whirlwind affair and wedding.

No matter how it started, this romance would take them both to the stars.

Six

Breakfast in bed followed by slow, lazy lovemaking was a great way to start the day. Bree brushed croissant crumbs from the sheets, then trailed her fingers over Gavin's chest. Oddly enough, being married to him felt totally natural. Maybe all the hot, sticky sex had somehow glued them together.

"Why are you laughing?" His chest rumbled under her fingers.

"Private joke."

"Shouldn't those be shared between husband and wife?" He cocked a brow at her.

"I don't know. I've never been married before." She grinned.

"Me, either. I think that means we get to make up all the rules as we go along. Rule one, we should take a shower together."

Bree smiled. "That shower is big enough for two." Gavin whisked her off the bed and carried her in his arms into the shimmering white marble bathroom. He opened the glass door of the shower and adjusted the controls, all while holding her crooked between his arm and knee.

"You're making me feel downright dainty."

"You're downright delicious." He nipped at her neck with his teeth and laid a trail of kisses to her mouth. Warm water splashed from the gold faucets and spattered them both with tiny droplets. Bree licked some off his chest. His skin tasted salty and savory, and soon she was on her feet, kissing him hard, with water raining down over both of them.

They lathered each other with silky jasmine scented soap and rinsed by hand, until each individual body part was squeaky clean. With Gavin's hands on her, and his eyes greedily reveling in the way the water cascaded between her breasts, she felt like a goddess.

Desire shimmered in every cell of her body, keeping her in a constant state of peak arousal. Gavin was as hard as a Renaissance statue, built with curves and angles every bit as artistic. Water poured over his olive skin and trickled along the line of dark hair that enhanced the sculpted muscles of his chest.

His hands roamed over her, soapy and slick, treasuring her like a precious object. She still couldn't believe her luck. Apparently he couldn't get enough of her. And the feeling was entirely mutual. She'd never imagined wanting to spend a whole morning kissing and making love—after a full night of the same. The sheer pleasure that tingled through her was an addictive drug that made her crave Gavin's skin on hers.

They teased and touched and licked each other until the intensity of the arousal became overwhelming. Groaning with sheer relief, Gavin entered her and they both reached their climax almost immediately, under the soft rain of water.

"You're perfect, Bree. Perfect," he moaned, shuddering in her arms as they leaned heavily against the tiled wall. It was all Bree could do to stay upright. Her muscles had turned to water and her brain was too light with joy to form thoughts.

"You're…amazing." She couldn't even come up with a description for the man who'd turned her life inside out and made her…happy. Happier than she'd ever imagined possible. Dreams really did come true, just when you least expected it.

They spent that day and the next enjoying the sights of Sausalito. A boat ride on the bay, an exquisite French meal and a night of dancing in a steamy local club.

Everywhere they went people seemed to smile at them as if they glowed with some special newlywed happiness. Which they probably did.

It's all too good to be true. He's too good to be true.

Whenever the sneaky doubts crept around the edges of her brain, Bree banished them with a swat. It was just the old insecurities creeping back, the years of being an ugly duckling, attractive to men only for her money.

But Gavin didn't need her money. He seemed to have no interest in it at all. He was successful in his own right. She could be as poor as a church mouse and it didn't make any difference to him.

She laughed aloud. Gavin, marching up one of the

punishingly steep hills next to her, turned and squeezed her hand. "This time I won't even ask why you're laughing."

"Why not?"

"Because I know." A broad smile lit his handsome face. "I feel exactly the same way."

Back in San Francisco, Bree went to her apartment to pack a few necessities into her car and bring them to Gavin's. His apartment was roomy enough for all of them—her cat Faith wound herself around Gavin's legs, purring, then settled happily into a sunny spot by the living room window. Even the more reserved Ali seemed calm and quickly claimed a big soft armchair as her new home.

Now they officially lived together.

"Do you realize I never had the opportunity to live in sin?" She poked him gently with her finger as they lay in his bed, after their first night in their temporary home.

"I'm so sorry to have deprived you. I'm sure we can come up with some other sins to indulge in."

"Isn't it odd how nonchalant my dad was about the whole thing? He didn't seem at all surprised when I told him we were getting married. He must really like you. He hasn't introduced me to a man in a long time."

"He knows a good son-in-law when he sees one." Gavin's gray eyes twinkled.

"It's particularly amazing that he didn't mind us running off to Sausalito to get married without any big fanfare. He's usually such a snob about how things are done."

"Maybe he's just glad to see you happily settled." Gavin twirled a lock of her hair.

"I suppose so. Maybe it's a weight off his mind that I won't be a bitter spinster living in the garret of his house for the rest of his life." She grinned. "I much prefer being a happily married woman."

"Well, your happily married husband needs to get to work." Gavin eased away from her. Already her skin buzzed with protest, missing the contact with his.

"I'm not sure I can stand to be away from you all day." She pouted and pulled the sheets over her.

"We could meet for lunch." Gavin climbed out of bed and strode across the room, all toned muscle and easy grace. "That might be enough to prevent withdrawal from setting in."

"No. I'll be stoic." Bree tossed her head against the pillow dramatically. "I know your work is important to you and I don't want to be a distraction. Which of your big accounts are you working on today?"

An odd expression flickered across Gavin's face as he reached for his shirt. "Hmm. Not sure. All thoughts of Maddox Communications have fled my mind."

"You'd better hunt them down before Brock Maddox realizes. I'm glad I've met all the people you work with. Now, when you tell me about your day, I'll know exactly who you mean."

"Yeah." Gavin seemed distracted. Probably getting his head back into business after their weekend of sensual escape. She wasn't going to be the kind of wife who demanded her husband's full attention twenty-four hours a day. She intended to be supportive and practical, and make sure she focused on her own business, as well.

A long, happy sigh escaped her lips. "I think I'll

spend the day photographing couples." She shot him a smile. "They've always been my favorite subject. Now that I'm one half of a couple, I'm even more excited about capturing the glow they share."

"Do they usually say yes when you ask?"

Bree thought for a moment. "Yes. The happy ones do. It's the unhappy ones who don't want their picture taken and recorded for all time."

"Then I hope you meet a lot of happy couples today."

"None of them will be as happy as me, that's for sure."

Bree sank back into the sheets after Gavin kissed her goodbye and left for work. Maybe after strolling the streets with her camera for a couple of hours, she'd head over to the lab to do some printing. There, in the dark, she could have a silly grin on her face all day and no one would care.

She glanced at the clock—almost nine! Advertising companies must get off to a leisurely start in the morning. Her dad was usually in the office by seven at the latest. But banking was different, and the stock market marched to an entirely different rhythm.

Speaking of rhythm, was that the phone? The sound of tingling music pulled her attention to the living room. She was sure he hadn't left the radio on. She climbed out of bed and pulled on her light robe. The music continued and she followed the sound to its source, where a green light flashed on a slim cordless phone on Gavin's desk.

Should she answer it? This was her house now, too. Still, it wasn't the house line. Gavin must have a separate one for business. She probably shouldn't answer it. For a start, she'd have to explain who she was, since hardly anyone even knew she and Gavin were married yet. Probably better to let the machine get it.

While she hesitated, Gavin's recorded message started to play, followed by a beep. She turned to leave the room, since it really was none of her business. The voice stopped her in her tracks.

"Morning, Gavin, or should I call you 'son'?" Her father's familiar gruff chuckle chilled her. Her dad was calling? Well, why not? She turned back to the phone to pick it up.

"The money's making its way into your account as I speak. One million big ones. I executed the wire transfer five minutes ago."

Rooted to the spot, Bree frowned at the phone. What on earth was he talking about? Dread crept over her, inch by cold, cruel inch.

"You're a fast mover, I'll give you that. I thought you'd have six months of courtship ahead of you. Bree's a prickly character where men are concerned, but I can see you swept her right off her size tens."

Her mouth fell open and her stomach dropped.

Her feet were only size nine. Not that it mattered.

Her throat closed and her heart started to pound.

"So now you can open your own business and support her in the style to which she's accustomed. I'm sure the two of you will be very happy." His chuckle sounded more like a malevolent cackle. Bree's hands shook, but she couldn't bring herself to grab the phone and ask what was going on.

She didn't need to. It was painfully obvious what had happened.

Her father had paid Gavin to marry her.

The click and dial tone snapped in the air like a fired bullet. The red light now flashing on the sleek phone told her this wasn't a figment of her imagination.

It was all fake. Every loving word, every kiss, every caress.

She shook her head as her brain rejected the idea. Hair tumbled into her eyes, and her breathing came heavy and ragged.

Money? Why did he want her money? He had a good job—didn't he? He must. She'd met all his coworkers. Still, there probably weren't too many people who couldn't use another million dollars.

One million dollars. So that was her value. Pretty high, all things considered.

A racking sob exploded through her. Why one million? Why not two? Or just two hundred thousand? Or twenty? Or a slice of pie from Stella's bakery?

She crumpled to the floor. It was hardwood, and her shins and elbows hit hard as she came down. The sharp pain didn't mean much, though, as agony soaked through her from the inside out.

How could you be so foolish as to think he wanted you just for yourself?

"Idiot!" She yelled the word aloud, and it bounced off the clean white walls.

She'd been suspicious at first. Wary. Prickly, as her father so astutely observed.

But her doubts and fears had capitulated under his volleys of kisses and flattering words. In less than two weeks he'd seduced her up the aisle, all for the promise of a nice, fat, financial reward.

Bree curled up into a ball on the hard, shiny floor. What now? She couldn't go home and face the father who'd sold her like an unfashionable antique he no longer wanted in his collection.

She certainly couldn't face her friends. She'd proudly called each one of them from their Sausalito hotel room to announce her newly married state. They'd mostly sounded so surprised—and why not? Obviously no one in their right mind would marry boring old Bree Kincannon unless there was a tempting added incentive.

Did everyone at his office know?

No. She drew in an unsteady breath. Unlikely. This must be a private deal between him and her father. It wasn't the kind of thing you'd want people getting wind of. Marrying a woman for money was…sleazy, to say the least, by today's standards.

Bree eased herself into a sitting position and hugged her legs. Likely she was the only person who knew, outside Gavin and her father, of course.

And right now it was her little dark and dirty secret.

Tears rolled over her cheeks and splashed in dark spots on her green silk robe. The one she'd bought to bring out the green in her…contact lenses.

A growl of fury slid between her teeth. She'd let Elle doll her up and convince her she could attract a man like Gavin, when all along…

Was Elle in on it? The thought washed over her like an icy wave. She'd been an "instant friend," in a way that might make more savvy people suspicious. Had she been goaded by Gavin into turning his frumpy future bride into a woman who wouldn't embarrass him too much in company?

Bree bit her knuckle. It made sense. Gavin had

introduced her to Elle and set the whole thing up. Bree snatched up the phone and was both angry and unsurprised to see Elle's name right there in the contacts list. She punched the button to dial and rose to her feet, fury flashing through her.

"Elle Linton."

"It's Bree." Her voice was dark and rasped.

"Bree?" Elle sounded surprised. "How are you?"

"How am I?" Bree turned and paced, trying not to let raw fury shut down her brain. "Let's see. I just found out that my new husband married me for money. How do you think I should be?"

"What?" Elle's voice rang with fake surprise.

"Don't pretend you weren't in on it. I know why you put so much effort into defrizzing my hair and finding me new clothes. Gavin put you up to it."

"I have no idea what you are talking about. Are you okay? You sound a little—"

"Crazy?" Bree snorted. "Yes. I believe you're right. And no, I don't think I'm okay. In fact, I've never felt less okay in my life."

"Hold on a minute, please."

Bree resisted the urge to slam down the phone. But of course she wouldn't hang up on someone—she was dependable old Bree and that would be rude.

"Sorry about that." Elle's breathless voice grated against her ear. "My desk is right outside Brock's office and not at all private. I'm in the ladies' room now. I still don't have a clue what you're talking about."

"Of course you do. I phoned you myself from Sausalito to tell you my happy news." The last two words dripped with venom.

"I know, and I'm thrilled for you both."

"Why, are you getting part of the money?" Ugly scenarios unfolded in Bree's mind.

"What money? Slow down, Bree, I don't know what you're talking about."

"The money my father paid Gavin to marry me."

The following silence sucked the last breath from Bree's lungs. Now that she'd said it aloud, to another person, the awful reality of what had just happened seemed literally unbearable. She paced into the bedroom, where the sheets were still warm and wrinkled from their most recent tryst.

"I don't believe it." Elle's shocked whisper came at last.

"You didn't know?"

"I swear it. I know Gavin from work, but not personally."

"Your number is programmed into his phone."

"I'm Brock's assistant. He calls me all the time to set up meetings."

"So you had no idea about any of this."

"Not the slightest clue, Bree."

"You've never lied to me about anything?"

A moment of silence followed. Elle's voice was subdued, quiet, when she spoke again. "Not about this. I was sure Gavin genuinely liked you. Where did you get this idea about the money?"

"Oh, just the message my own dear father left for him about the wire transfer."

"Bree, I'm so sorry. I had no idea."

"Why did you sound so hesitant when I asked if you'd lied?" Another pause made suspicion crackle through Bree's brain.

"I have a secret of my own." Elle's whisper startled

her. "I wish I didn't because it's making lies part of my daily life." Silence hung in the air for a moment. "I'm having an affair with my boss."

"With Brock Maddox?" Bree didn't hide her surprise.

"Yes. I certainly never intended to, but things happened, and now…it's complicated. I wish I could tell you more, but it's better if I don't."

"I'll bet." Bree shook her head, trying to clear her tangled thoughts. What next?

"Do you love him?"

Elle's blunt question shocked her. "No."

"Not even a little?"

"I loved him madly until about four minutes ago. Does that make things clearer?"

"You can't switch love on and off. No one knows that better than me." Elle's voice was shadowed with regret. "You must still love him somewhere, underneath your anger and hurt."

"I'm sure I do. I'm dumb like that."

"Gavin's a good man. There's got to be something more to the story. Maybe this little discovery doesn't have to spoil everything. It could turn out to be a hiccup you can get past."

"That he took money to take me off my dad's hands? That's a lot to get past."

"Why don't you give him a chance?"

Could she? The possibility lit up Bree's brain like the lights on the Golden Gate Bridge. Could everything work out anyway? Could they live happily ever after and go whistling off into the sunset together?

Fresh tears pricked her eyelids and slid over her cheeks.

She swallowed hard. "Elle, you don't understand. This is what I've been so afraid of my whole life. I've always known men were only interested in me for the money I inherited from my mother. I fell so hard for Gavin because I was sure he was different. But he's no better than the rest. Worse, in fact."

"Maybe he really loves you, in spite of the money. Every time I saw him look at you, I could swear he had adoration written all over his face. I've never seen him like that before, and as you can imagine, he's never short of women flocking around him. I wouldn't say this if I didn't believe it, but I really think he loves you."

Bree cursed the way the possibility opened inside her like a ray of fresh hope. "I guess there is a really tiny possibility that you could be right."

"He gets a very good salary and bonus—I should know, since I file all the records. He certainly wouldn't need to marry you for money. I think you should stick around and figure out what's going on before you throw away a good chance for happiness. Sometimes life is more complicated than we want it to be, but that doesn't mean it's not worth the trouble."

"I'm not sure I can philosophize right now, but I won't do anything rash." Bree frowned. "At the very least, I want to hear his side of the story."

"And maybe your relationship will end up stronger after you get through this."

"I very much doubt it, but I'll try to keep an open mind." Bree ran a hand through her tangled hair. "Don't tell anyone."

"I won't tell a soul. Trust me, due to some unfortunate circumstances, I've become very, very good at keeping secrets."

Bree put the phone back in its base. She carefully deleted the message from her father, and wiped her fingerprints from the shiny surface like a criminal, despite the fact that she was apparently the only innocent party in San Francisco.

When the phone rang again, she snatched it up, terrified of discovering yet more shocking secrets about her new husband.

Her husband. The word that had filled her with such joy a short while ago now filled her with sadness and regret.

It was the hotel in Sausalito on the phone. Their wedding photos were ready and had been mailed to them. Oh, joy. Pictures of her grinning like a lovesick fool on the arm of a man who swept her off her oversize feet just to fatten his wallet.

The big question was what to do when he came home tonight.

Seven

The sound of Gavin's key in the lock almost made Bree squeeze her eyes shut for a moment, but she didn't want to smudge her mascara. She'd just finished putting it on so she'd be sure not to cry.

"Hi, sweetheart." His warm, rich voice rang through the apartment.

"Hi," she called back, willing herself to sound bright and enthusiastic, as if she had no idea she'd been bartered for cold cash. "How was your day?"

"Pretty good." Gavin hung his suit jacket in the closet and approached her, arms outstretched. She tried not to steel herself against his hug. Instead she stuck her arms out and approached him with shaky knees. "How was yours?"

"Fine." One way to describe the worst day of her life. "I made lasagna for dinner," she proclaimed, turning away before he could scrutinize her expression. She was still working on keeping it serene.

"Mmm, fantastic. I was too busy to eat lunch so it's lucky we didn't make plans."

"Something big going on at Maddox?"

"In a way." His voice had a funny tone to it that made her turn around.

"Oh?"

"Me, leaving." A sheepish grin snuck across Gavin's face. One that just a few hours ago she would have found adorable.

She froze. "Leaving Maddox Communications?" One million dollars was not enough to retire on. Not in San Francisco, at least. Maybe he just planned to kick back and live off her fortune?

She turned and marched to the kitchen to check on the lasagna. The dish had helped get her focus off Gavin this afternoon. Might as well use it as a distraction now.

"You're shocked, aren't you?" Gavin followed her into the small galley kitchen. His physical presence filled the doorway and she fought a stray surge of desire.

"Well, yes. I thought you liked it there." She didn't look up. Instead she busied herself with taking the dish out of the oven.

"It was a good place to build my reputation. But now I'm ready to strike out on my own." He eased up beside her and slid his arms around her waist.

"Careful. This dish is hot." She tried to wriggle away from him, hating the way her stomach tingled under his fingers.

"Then don't look so irresistible. It's not fair to wear a dress like that and then not let me touch you."

Arousal rippled inside Bree at the touch of his hand

on her hip. Curse him and this stupid dress. Another of the ones Elle had talked her into buying. Dark blue with a swirly skirt of clingy jersey.

"I just don't want to burn myself." *I've already been badly burned today.*

"All right, I'll set the table."

"I already did." She had everything planned and organized to perfection. She'd had plenty of time on her hands, after all, because the idea of photographing couples had quickly lost its charm. "Why don't you sit down? It's almost ready." She managed to keep her voice calm and even bright. Who knew she had such powers of deception?

She served the food with a smile. Gavin's admiring gaze took in her hard work primping this afternoon. She'd wanted to look good so he wouldn't know that inside she was in tiny pieces. "Why are you leaving Maddox Communications?"

Gavin's smile broadened, and took on a conspiratorial air. "To start my own company."

Bree swallowed as she sat down hard. Everything was becoming crystal clear. She called on an inner strength she hoped was in there somewhere. "What kind of company?"

"My own advertising shop. Boutique, top-notch creative, specializing in cutting-edge brands." The confident sparkle in his eye both aroused and infuriated her.

"Isn't that a risky endeavor? It must be hard to raise the money for a venture like that." She cocked her head, maintaining her placid demeanor.

Gavin's smile faded slightly, which gave her a moment of grim satisfaction. "Yes, no doubt it is, but I have years of experience now and I'm confident in my ability to make this endeavor succeed." He reached across the table and she let him take her hand and squeeze it. "With you by my side, there's no way I can fail."

His words rang hollow in the still air. Words that—if spoken yesterday—would have filled her with giddy pride. Today they sounded phony. A cliché. A lie.

Of course, in a way, he spoke the truth. It's hard to fail if the endeavor is underwritten by one of the most successful investors in San Francisco—who'd handed over the money as a reward for taking his daughter off his hands.

"So, are you bringing clients with you from Maddox?"

Gavin paused, fork hovering above his plate. "Much as I'd love to, I don't think that would be ethical."

"You wouldn't want to do anything unethical." Like, say, marry for money. "Much better to do things the honest, old-fashioned way." Like, say, marry for money. In the grand scheme of things, what he'd done wasn't all that outrageous. She'd bet nearly every single one of her ancestors had married for money. That would explain why there was so darn much of it in her bank account. Wait, was she trying to make excuses for him?

"Where do you plan to look for clients?"

"There are a couple who moved away from Maddox that I intend to pursue. And since I've put out the word I'm going out on my own, I've had some serious interest."

"Oh. How long have you been telling people you're starting your own company?" Hope bloomed in her chest. Perhaps this was something he'd been working on for some time that had nothing to do with her and her money. Maybe he was independently wealthy.

Maybe he really did love her.

Pathetic how she still shamelessly hoped for that.

"Just the last couple of days. I've been planning it for a long time but I was waiting for some things to come together."

"Oh." She stuck her fork into an innocent lettuce leaf. So much for her pathetic hopes. "How nice that they finally came together." She shot him a somewhat steely glance.

He didn't even notice—he just beamed at her. "It's the culmination of a lifelong dream. I've wanted my own company since I was a boy. At the time I had no idea it would be advertising, but that's what really gets my juices flowing."

Much to her chagrin, Gavin still got hers flowing. His excitement and enthusiasm were infectious. She almost wanted his company to be a big success just so she could enjoy that winning smile that lit up his chiseled features.

But she couldn't resist needling him a bit more.

"Juices are fun, but what about cash flow? Will things be tight while you get it off the ground?"

Gavin hesitated and looked at her as if surprised by her question. And really, why would an heiress ask the man she loved about money? Couldn't she just haul out some bags of gold bullion?

Then he leaned back in his chair, a satisfied look on his face. "I've got good start-up funds. Enough to rent a nice office space, pay good people and keep things going for at least six months even if it takes that long to land a client."

"Wow. You do have it well planned."

"It helps that I've got one of the best art directors in the country ready to come on board. Wait until you meet Tom, I know you'll like him. He does fine-art photography, too—collage mostly—and you'll recognize his work as soon as you see it. He's going to bring a couple of key people from the agency he's at now."

"I bet they won't be too happy."

Gavin shrugged. "Advertising is a bit of a dog-eat-dog world. Agencies form, merge, gain clients, lose clients. It's all part of the business. You're only as good as your biggest client."

"And who do you hope to snag as your biggest client?"

Gavin cocked his head and gave her a cheeky glance that tickled her insides. "You'll laugh if I tell you."

"I could use a good laugh."

He hesitated a moment. "No. Let me surprise you when I really do win them."

"Great. I love surprises." He didn't seem to notice the slight edge of sarcasm that crept into her voice. How could he string her along like this? How could he sit there and eat dinner so casually, when their whole marriage was a farce? Did he really intend to spend the rest of his life with her, or was she a temporary fundraising measure until he got his company off the ground?

Then he'd probably kick her to the curb and bring in a slender blonde who'd look better on his arm at the awards ceremonies.

No doubt that's exactly what he had in mind. He wasn't going to spend the rest of his life saddled with a dumpy nobody. Not once he really had his own money and didn't need hers.

She shoved a bite of lasagna into her mouth, to stem the flood of angry words to her tongue. Part of her wanted to let him have it—tell him she knew and how disgusted she was that he'd tricked her into marrying him. For a single sharp instant she fantasized about standing up now and yelling right at him. Ending everything, right now, and watching his startled reaction.

But common sense got the better of her. She couldn't bear to spew out all her hurt and shame. That would only give him power over her. He'd probably tell her she was all wrong and that he truly loved her and, sucker that she was, she'd probably believe him.

No. She had a better plan. Play him at his own game.

She'd make him think everything was working out perfectly. His happy little wife was sitting at home tinkering with her photos while he took the world by storm. She'd play along, encourage and support him, pretend to love and adore him the way he obviously expected.

Then, just when he was least prepared, she'd tell him she knew the truth and boot him out of her life.

"Great lasagna, Bree."

"Thanks." She forced a wide smile. "I like it with béchamel sauce instead of ricotta. More authentic, I think."

"I can't believe that on top of everything else you're an amazing cook, too."

"It's nothing. I enjoy cooking. You should tell me all your favorite meals so I can make them for you." Maybe that would make him truly fall in love with her.

Food was supposed to be the way to a man's heart. After money, of course.

Revenge would be sweet if he did actually fall for her before she revealed her secret.

"I love seafood." Gavin's gray eyes sparkled. "And barbecue. We'll have to set a grill up on the balcony. I scorch some mean shrimp."

"Sounds delicious. Perhaps when we buy our house we can set up an outdoor dining room." She smiled sweetly.

"I love that idea. I've been too lazy to entertain living here on my own. I usually go out. But when we have a real home, we'll have to have friends over often." He leaned forward, obviously enjoying his vision of their future.

It did sound fun. Friends gathered for a casual, outdoor meal. What a shame none of it was real. They were both just playing along, pretending, maintaining a charade.

"This salad dressing is sensational." He sucked a trace of the rich concoction off his fork, a gesture that caused an unpleasant sizzle deep inside her.

How could you still be attracted to him?

"It's the olive oil. I buy it fresh in Sonoma from an old guy there who has the most amazing orchard. Nothing tastes like it."

"We'll have to go there together."

"Absolutely."

"Still, it's not just the oil, it's the blend of spices. You have a real talent."

"Oh, I have all kinds of hidden talents." She tossed the curls she'd nurtured into shiny ringlets and smiled coyly. "You have no idea." She certainly was surprised that she'd managed to keep her cool so far. Maybe she did have undiscovered facets that this whole disastrous misadventure would polish to a shine.

Like a capacity to exact the perfect revenge on the man who'd made her worst nightmare come true.

That night, when Gavin's hands found her body under the covers, she yielded to his touch. It wasn't hard. In fact, it would have been almost impossible not to. Desire still throbbed inside her like an incurable ache. A day ago she might have called it love, or something foolish like that, but now she recognized it for the pure physical urge it was.

She wrapped her arms around his sturdy torso and let herself enjoy the sweet warmth of his skin against hers. She'd been so very lonely today. Would it hurt to enjoy sex before she went back to hating him?

As they moved together she let herself enjoy the sensation as a dance—pleasure that crept through every inch of her. Didn't people do this all the time and mean nothing by it?

He'd have been suspicious if she pushed him away. Not that she even had the willpower to do that.

When he kissed her on the mouth, she found herself kissing back with passion, unable to stop. Her climax pounded through her, making her clutch him tighter.

It doesn't mean anything, her mind protested, over the louder drumbeat of her blood. *You'll forget him.*

She would try, anyway.

Gavin donned his best power suit for a day of key meetings. For some reason, being married gave him an extra edge of stability—almost like a foundation— that made it easy to go out and take on the world. He'd noticed Bree seemed a little nervous lately—on edge, even. Perhaps she was worried about him stepping out on his own. Hopefully he'd soon be able to reassure her by obtaining clients.

Of course he could reassure her right now by mentioning that he had ample start-up funds, but he wasn't quite sure how she'd react to his deal with her father.

Guilt trickled through him like acid. He wished he could have pulled this off without the money, but you couldn't start a business without capital.

He'd make it up to her by being a devoted husband.

He kissed Bree after eating the delicious breakfast of bacon, eggs and fresh rolls that she'd made him. For some reason, she was dressed to the nines, in a pretty green dress that accentuated her curves. "You look beautiful, as always. I'll see you at the party tonight."

She cocked her head, her curls falling over one shoulder. "What party?"

"I thought I told you. There's a big shindig tonight to celebrate winning the new Reynolds Automotive account."

A shadow crossed her face. "No, you didn't say a word."

"Hmm. I wasn't sure quite how Brock would react to the news of me leaving. Maybe I half thought he'd have tossed me out on my ear by now."

"I'm surprised he hasn't." She cocked a brow.

"He said he trusts me. They've had some strange things going on at the agency lately, a mole of sorts, leaking information to a rival agency, and I've been helping him try to solve the problems it's caused. I also helped to win the Reynolds account, so he wants me to do some more work on that before I go."

"Nice to have a boss who thinks so highly of you." Gavin glanced up. He almost thought he heard a note of sarcasm in Bree's voice. No. It couldn't be. Her lovely smile lit up the room.

"Yeah. I'm sure some people think I'm crazy to leave, but everything reaches its natural limit eventually."

"Even a marriage?" She looked him directly in the eye in a way that spiked his blood pressure slightly. Maybe all the changes were making her feel insecure.

He quirked a smile. "'Till death us do part.' That's the only natural limit I can see." He kissed her soft cheek. Did she stiffen slightly as he hugged her?

It was a shame he had to leave right away. He had a breakfast meeting with the marketing director of Argos Shoes, an account he'd give almost anything to win. He was even prepared to eat breakfast again, since he hadn't wanted to disappoint Bree by turning down the fantastic meal she'd prepared to surprise him.

"Death, yes, I suppose you're right." Her green eyes surveyed him with a slightly unsettling look. "Hopefully that's a ways off, but I suppose you never know."

"You're in a rather grim mood this morning."

She shrugged, which had the dangerous effect of pulling the green fabric tighter over her spectacular breasts. Gavin shoved down a surge of desire welling inside him. "I'd better get out of here before I get distracted and miss my meetings. Bye, my love."

He kissed her and headed for the elevator. If things went well today, his new agency would be off to a flying start, and he'd be able to put Bree's fears to rest.

* * *

Bree sagged against the door after it closed behind Gavin. She hadn't hidden her emotions too well this morning. She'd donned the full makeup and the fancy dress, preparing a good breakfast and smiling like a store mannequin, but she couldn't seem to hide the hurt and fear roiling just below her manicured surface.

Making love—no, having sex—last night hadn't helped. The intimacy only reminded her of everything she'd lose when she pushed Gavin out of her life. She'd been happy alone because she'd never known anything different. Now she'd be agonizingly aware of all the pleasures of couplehood she'd be missing out on.

Ali brushed up against her legs. "I know, Princess, it's time for your shot. You're still my first love. I shouldn't have asked for more." Her stately fifteen-year-old cat paused, as if agreeing. "And at least I'll still have you and Faith when he's gone." She reached down and stroked Ali's soft back. "That will be more than enough."

She kicked off the stupid heels she'd put on to clack around the apartment as Little Mrs. Perfect. How had she let herself get duped into this? And now she had to put on the "perfect wife" act at a party with all his friends and coworkers? She wanted to cry.

Heck, maybe she would go ahead and have a cry. It couldn't hurt. That way she could get it out of her system and grin like a loon all night on the arm of the lying Gavin Spencer.

After Bree's odd behavior that morning, Gavin decided to go home and pick her up so they could arrive at the party together. He worried that she felt overwhelmed by her new life, and he felt guilty for announcing his dramatic career change so soon after their wedding. He probably should have given her a bit more time to get comfortable. And given that some of his coworkers were a bit testy about his announcement, he decided it might be better if they went to the party together so she didn't show up and get grilled by anyone before he got there.

"You look gorgeous, as usual." He had to pause for a moment, just to take in the vision of Bree standing in their apartment door. Her ankle-length dress, covered in tiny black-and-white stripes, flowed over her curves like water down a waterfall.

"Thanks. I did some shopping today." Her green eyes glittered hard as she gazed at him. Or possibly he was just imagining it. All the upheaval in his professional life must be making him testy. Bree seemed taller than usual, and a glance down confirmed that she wore sleek black-and-white pumps that added about three inches to her already impressive height. "Lucky I'm over six feet or I'd be standing in your shadow." He grinned.

She smiled tightly. "Now that I'm married, I don't have to worry that no one will dance with me because I'm too tall."

"An excellent point." She did look gorgeous. Her height served only to emphasize her Greek-goddess good looks, especially with her magnificent ringlets cascading over her shoulders. She must have spent hours getting ready.

Now that he thought about it, she'd been dressed to the nines even for their dinner at home last night. "You don't have to look breathtaking every minute, you know. It's okay to relax and wear whatever feels comfortable."

She cocked her head, which sent her curls tumbling over one breast. "Do you think I should wear that dress I had on when we met?"

He grinned. "Okay, maybe not that one. But I don't want you thinking you have to dress up all the time."

"Not a problem. I just dress how I like." She lifted her chin, tall and proud.

"As long as it's for your own pleasure, it's all good with me." Who wouldn't want a woman who looked as fantastic as this? He couldn't understand why no one had snatched her up before him. Her father must be nuts to think she needed his help in finding a husband.

He'd transferred the money, though. Gavin had seen it in the new account he'd opened just for this purpose. One million dollars—seven fat figures—right there on the screen of the computer under his name. Could life get any better than this?

He extended his arm to Bree, who threaded hers elegantly through it. "Let's go take the world by storm."

The Iron Grille restaurant on the first floor of the agency building throbbed with music, and waiters in white tie swirled through the crowd with trays of hors d'oeuvres.

"Oh, Gavin!" He grimaced at the site of nutty Marissa barreling toward him on her high heels, stringy blonde hair flying. He certainly wouldn't miss her. "Go on, tell me in secret. Which clients are you stealing, darling?"

"Marissa, I believe you've met my wife, Bree."

Marissa glanced at Bree, managing to look down on her, despite the fact that Bree was several inches taller. "Congratulations on your big catch, darling." Then she turned her evil gaze back to Gavin. "Or should I be congratulating you, sweetheart? I hear Bree's from old money."

Bree's mouth dropped open. Even he was rendered speechless. "Marissa, you're lucky you're a talented logo designer, or no one would put up with you."

"So true!" She grinned. "But come on, who are you stealing? Or are you the infamous mole everyone's been hunting for all year?"

He was in danger of losing his cool if he didn't get away from this woman. "Bree, let's go find a drink. I'm starting to need one." Bree looked panicked—not surprising. Marissa had that effect on people.

"Oh, go on and get your drink, handsome." Marissa waved heavily ringed fingers at him. "Logan doesn't think you're the mole anyway. And he would know."

The mention of his second least favorite Maddox employee stopped Gavin in his tracks. "Logan? What does he have to do with anything?"

"Didn't you know?" She pursed her lips with thinly concealed glee. "He's not an account executive at all. He's a private detective."

"That explains a few things about his performance." Gavin frowned. "Did Brock hire him to find the source of the leaks?" He couldn't believe he had to learn this from Marissa. Why hadn't Brock himself told him?

"You betcha, babe. And from your adorable surprise, I can see he didn't trust you with that information. You must have been on his list of suspects." She shot Bree a supercilious smile. "You watch out for this one, darling. There's more to him than meets the eye." She winked at him. "Though what meets the eye isn't half-bad."

Then she turned on her heels and vanished into the crowd.

Bree stood staring after her.

"Brock should get rid of her. A loose cannon like that is a danger to the company."

"So, apparently, is a mole. What did she mean by that?" Bree wasn't smiling or looking amused.

"Someone's been stealing company secrets and leaking them to the competition. It's been going on for a few months, and no one has any idea who it is."

"It sounds like Brock thought it might be you." Worry—or was it suspicion?—danced in Bree's green eyes. A nasty feeling crept through Gavin.

"I suppose he had to suspect everyone, though I assure you I'd rather die than betray my employer."

Bree simply cocked her head and narrowed her eyes. "I wonder if he thinks your leaving is a betrayal."

"No. People come and go in this business all the time. Par for the course."

Bree simply closed her lips in a tight smile. Did she really think he was capable of undermining the company? What was going on with her? "I think we both need some wine. Or maybe champagne."

"I couldn't agree more."

Gavin spent the rest of the party reassuring people that he had no intention of stealing Maddox clients for his new company. Some were surprised he was even there. Everyone was whispering about Logan Emerson being a private detective, but no one knew if he'd uncovered the spy.

At one point, Elle grabbed Bree by the hand and whisked her away. She explained that they were going out for some girl talk, and she'd escort Bree home. This was rather a relief for Gavin, since Bree seemed unusually tense. On top of the drama of his own departure and the hushed mutterings about the in-house traitor, the party was unusually exhausting. After only half an hour, he ducked out and headed upstairs into the Maddox offices to box up the last of his stuff. He was more than ready to leave Maddox Communications behind and start fresh.

He grinned at the weary security guard as he got off the elevator on the sixth floor. "Is the place locked? I might need you to let me in. I handed in my key."

"Mr. Maddox told me you'd be coming by. He's inside himself."

"Brock is in the office?" Odd. Gavin had noticed he wasn't at the party.

"Been there all evening. Sent out for dinner a while back, but told me to make sure he wasn't disturbed by anyone except you. Sent out for a bottle of whiskey, too." The elderly security guard raised his wiry brows.

Gavin frowned. What was going on? He couldn't take much more of this intrigue. He pushed into the open offices. "Brock?"

"Back here." His boss's voice was gruff. "Come on in."

He crossed the dark office to the light pooling out of Brock's door. Tension hung in the air like day-old cigar smoke. Inside the office, Brock sat in his big, leather chair behind the antique desk, his face uncharacteristically haggard.

"I didn't know my leaving was going to have such a dramatic effect on you," Gavin quipped.

"Trust me, you're the least of my problems."

"You do know I'm not the spy, don't you?"

Brock rubbed a hand over his face. "Believe me, it would be easier if you were."

Gavin strode across the room and pulled up a chair. "You know who it is?"

Brock drew in a deep breath. "Sure do. The gumshoe I hired finally found irrefutable evidence." An odd expression flickered across his face.

"The suspense is killing me."

"It's Elle."

Gavin frowned. "Your assistant?"

"Do you know any other Elles?"

"But she was at the party just now, downstairs. Bree left with her." Panic gripped his heart. Exactly what was going on here?

"I haven't yet told her that I know."

"Why not?"

"We're lovers." Brock picked up a crystal tumbler and took a hearty draught of the gold liquid.

Gavin sank back in his chair. "Holy—"

"What surprises you more—the fact that I'm having an affair with my assistant or the fact that she's a corporate spy?" He lifted a black brow and leveled his piercing blue gaze at Gavin.

"But why?"

"I'll give you the benefit of the doubt and assume you're asking why she was spying. You won't believe this. She's Athos Koteas's granddaughter."

Athos Koteas ran Golden Gate Promotions, Maddox's long-time rival on the San Francisco ad scene. The enmity dated back decades and had intensified lately, since competition for good clients was tighter than ever. "You really think they sent her here to sabotage your business?"

"I know it. And I've been fool enough to give her access to all our files, even the most confidential, as well as my bed. She's been undermining our operations and giving Golden Gate a top crack at all our clients for months."

Gavin blew out a long, hard breath. "I assume you're going to fire her."

"Right now I don't know what the hell to do." His blue eyes glittered with pain. "You think you know someone, and then…" He rubbed a hand over his brow.

A curse fell from Gavin's lips. "You know, I introduced Elle to Bree. They've even spent time together on the weekends. Now I'm worried she may have tricked Bree into something." That might explain why Bree looked so tense earlier.

"I have no idea what kind of damage she's done, and all the while I thought…" Brock growled. "I don't know what I thought. Women. You'd better watch out, Gavin. You never quite know what's going on in their minds."

Eight

Bree was pacing the apartment when Gavin arrived home shortly before midnight. Elle had tried to console her and convince her that Gavin was worth a second chance, but right now she was in too much pain to do anything but try to get through the night.

"Hi, Bree." Gavin closed the door behind him. Tall and majestic in his dark suit, he looked as strikingly handsome as ever. Was that fair?

"Hi, Gavin." Her voice cracked slightly, so she forced a bright smile. "How was the rest of the party?"

He frowned. "Very interesting. What exactly did you and Elle talk about after you left?"

She froze. Had Elle told Gavin that she knew about his deal with her father?

"I ask because Brock has discovered that Elle is the

spy at Maddox." He threw his jacket down on a chair and marched into the room.

"What?" Bree's head spun. The neat puzzle of her new life was breaking apart and she no longer had all the pieces.

"Brock had a private detective working in-house. He's been tracking and tailing the staff for weeks, undercover as an account executive. A very bad account executive, I might add. I kept wondering why Brock didn't fire him." He pulled a soda from the fridge and popped it open. "Want one?"

"No," she managed. "Elle is a crook?" Her voice came out high and squeaky.

"I don't know if she's broken any laws, but she's certainly broken Brock's trust."

"But they're..." She felt her face heat. Maybe Gavin didn't know about Elle's intimate relationship with Brock.

"Having an affair. He told me that, too. Maybe she planned it that way so he'd be less likely to suspect her."

Bree found herself staggering backward to the sofa where she sat down heavily. Wearing high heels all the time was a bad idea when the world kept tilting beneath you. She blinked, conscious of the green contact lenses she never took out. It was hard work being Little Mrs. Perfect.

Especially when everyone you liked and trusted turned out to have an ulterior motive.

Gavin walked toward her. "Did she extract any information from you?"

"Elle?" Bree racked her brain. "I don't think so. What kind of information might she have wanted?"

"About the Maddox accounts, I imagine."

"I don't know anything about them. How would I?"

He turned and paced across the room. "Could be she wants information about my new agency. I'm going to be more competition for Golden Gate. Did she ask about my plans?"

"She didn't, but even if she had, I don't know anything about them, either." There was a trace of bitterness in her voice. He hadn't mentioned his big plans to her until after he'd secured the funding for them by marrying her.

"True." He shoved a hand through his dark hair, and she cursed the sting of arousal that heated her belly. "What kinds of things did you talk about?"

"Girl stuff." *You.* "Nothing about business at all."

"I suppose that's something." He took a swig of his soda. "Let's put all this intrigue behind us and move on to more important things."

Bree sat stiffly, wondering what they would be.

"First of all, we haven't kissed since I came in the door." He rose from the chair and before she could protest he'd picked her up off the sofa, whirled her around and planted a big, hot kiss on her lips that turned her insides upside down.

When he pulled back he was grinning. Breathless, heart pounding, Bree struggled to be put down. How could she still be aroused by him? Her nipples tightened and heat cascaded over her, settling between her thighs. She felt breathless and unsteady.

All because of a man who didn't care one bit about her.

He set her down gently on her precarious heels. "The

really good news is that I have my first client. I got the call while I was at the party. Crieff Jewelers wants me to put together a campaign for them, to run in the top glossies."

"That's fantastic!" Bree couldn't help the expression of genuine glee. How could she be happy for him after all she'd learned? "You've worked hard for it." Marrying a virtual stranger was pretty hard work, after all.

"And I'd like you to be the photographer."

Her heart leapt. "You're kidding."

"Not even a little bit. I've seen your work and you're a top-notch talent."

Bree blinked. Did he really admire her photography, or was that just part of the act? Surely he wouldn't risk his first real client if he didn't think her work was up to scratch.

Unless there wasn't a real client and this was just a ruse to butter her up.

Crieff Jewelers, though. They were probably the most highbrow and expensive jeweler in the entire Bay area. The kind of place her dad would go for some custom cufflinks. And they were known for particularly sleek and eye-catching ad campaigns. Ideas and imagery began to dance in her mind.

But did Gavin really want her work, or just some free photos? She decided to put him to the test. "I'm a professional photographer. You'd have to pay me." She shot him an arch smile.

Gavin looked slightly taken aback, but he took her hands and squeezed them. "Of course you'll be paid. Ten thousand for the day's shoot, an additional thousand for each hour after five. It's the top rate at Maddox." He actually looked kind of anxious, as if he really wanted her to say yes.

"Then I'll do it." A smile flooded her face. How could she not be excited about an opportunity like this? It would be fun, however it came about. Something new and unexpected to add to her portfolio, and who knows, maybe a whole new direction for her budding photography career.

Gavin planted a soft kiss on her mouth that intensified the rush of feelings flooding through her. "We're a great team, babe."

Her heart sank. They were only a team as long as she could keep up this pretense of a happy marriage. Sooner or later the façade of wedded bliss would come crumbling down, and she had no idea how she'd extricate herself from that wreckage. His smile would certainly fade when she caused an embarrassing scandal asking for a divorce—if you even needed one after so little time. He wouldn't pay her fee, either, after her ruthless father demanded his money back.

Bree jumped up from the table and ran for the bathroom as tears threatened. The worst part was, she dreaded the prospect of hurting him, of crushing his dreams the way he'd destroyed hers. She blotted her mascara with a tissue and sucked in a deep breath. *You're supposed to be getting revenge, remember?*

Bree beamed with excitement as Gavin welcomed the clients to the full-service photo studio they'd hired for the day. The team from Crieff, a man and a woman, were young and hip. They'd e-mailed Bree snapshots of some of the pieces, and she'd sent back sketches of ideas, which they'd loved. Two sleek models sat at the other end of the studio, ready to wear the gems against an assortment of clingy black clothes Bree had borrowed from her new favorite boutique. The store had been happy to help, possibly because Bree had bought armfuls of clothing from them to augment her new image.

Gavin's new assistant passed around mint tea and freshly made lemonade, as well as coffee while they chatted about Bree's ideas. She felt oddly relaxed and professional. Having Gavin by her side, confident and beaming, didn't hurt. Why did he have to be so darned… happy?

Then again, why wouldn't he be? His big dream was coming true. It was hard not to share his exhilaration— she had to keep reminding herself she was just a pawn in his game.

She styled the models with the help of a professional hair stylist and a makeup artist, and took shot after shot. The results were fantastic—exactly what she hoped for—especially some rather arty black-and-white ones she talked them into, using real film instead of digital for a film-noir effect.

"She's a genius. Where did you find her?" The man from Crieff slapped Gavin on the back as they looked at some proofs on a laptop.

"I'm a very lucky man. She's my wife." He grinned at Bree. She glowed for a moment before remembering why she was his wife—so he could be here, getting slapped on the back by clients.

It would probably be better if she'd never found out. Right now she'd be glowing with happiness while having the time of her life, working a professional photography job with the love of her life by her side.

Revenge be damned. She couldn't live this lie any longer. It was time to tell Gavin she knew the truth.

"They loved the shots!" Gavin exclaimed, not for the first time, as they marched along Market Street after the shoot. Warm sunset tones lit up the old stone facades of the buildings.

"Yep. They seemed pretty happy." A contented smile snuck across her face.

"You really should consider a career in advertising photography." He squeezed her. They were walking along with their arms around each other, presenting a façade of wedded bliss for all to see.

"Maybe I will." *Just not with you.*

"You looked as if you were really enjoying the challenge. You did a fantastic job saying just the right thing to the models to get the look right. That's not easy, you know."

"It was fun. I could see myself doing some magazine work." She tossed her curls. She really could! Despite its downside, this episode with Gavin had boosted her confidence in herself and her capabilities.

"I think this calls for a big celebration dinner, so I made reservations at my new favorite restaurant, Iago's." Iago's was an especially fancy dining spot that Bree had heard her father talk about.

"Why not? Sounds like the perfect spot for a big-shot advertising company president to eat."

"That's what I'm thinking." Gavin's warm grin almost—almost—melted her resolve. Then she let the words of that overheard message replay in her head. *One million big ones.* That's what their whole "romance" was really about.

It was time to put her plan into action, which required a few organizational steps. "I need to go home and change."

"That's okay, we've got forty-five minutes. I figured you'd want to freshen up. You're such a stylish dresser." His gray eyes drifted over the simple black pantsuit she'd worn.

Bree Kincannon, a stylish dresser. She had been, lately. How funny.

Panic snuck through her as she realized she needed him out of the house so she could pack her things and get the cats into their crates. "Gavin, would you do me a huge favor and pick up a box of prints from my dad's house while I get changed?" That would take a good forty-five minutes, and he wouldn't have time to come home. "Give me the address of the restaurant. I'll meet you there."

"Sure. Here it is." He fished a sleek black matchbox out of his pocket, and handed it to her. She glanced at the address. Good, she could park in the public lot nearby.

She drew in a deep breath to steady her nerves. "It's a big blue plastic box to the left of my desk. I can't believe I forgot it." She didn't really need the box—her collection of prints that didn't quite make the cut—but this was her chance to get some time alone. To plan her escape. Heck, maybe he'd even run into her dad and they could have a nice round of congratulations….

Right before she blew their nasty little plot out of the water.

Gavin escorted her into the city's most exclusive new restaurant. Well-heeled diners, many in elegant evening clothes, sat at tables decorated with fresh flowers. Golden light shone through a wall of windows with a lovely view over the water. His hand on her lower back guided her through the forest of floor length tablecloths to the table with the best view of all, on a tiny balcony jutting out toward the bay.

"You must know people to get this table," she whispered.

"Only the best for my beautiful bride."

Bree's stomach clenched. This atmosphere of hushed refinement was hardly the place to make a scene. Maybe she'd better wait until they got home before she confronted him.

No, she had the whole thing planned. Her car was packed and her cats sitting quietly in their crates, with the windows cracked to give them air. She had a two-week supply of Ali's medicine and Faith's special food.

Terror unfurled inside her. Could she really do this? Just take off?

She drew in a deep, shaky breath, which caused her breasts to swell in the oh-so-stylish green dress she'd donned for the occasion. She wanted Gavin to remember her looking good, right before she brought the guillotine down on all his neat plans.

Gavin pulled back her seat, the perfect gentleman as always. She eased herself into it and spread the fine linen napkin on her lap. The waiter poured champagne and described the creative dishes on special.

"You were fantastic today." Gavin rested a warm gaze on her face. If she hadn't known better she'd think it was genuine admiration. "You had such an easy way with the clients. Some people are very nervous around them."

"I was trained from an early age." The heiress thing. She'd learned to converse comfortably with everyone from royalty to the staff, while mastering the alphabet. "Comes in handy sometimes."

"And you were so calm, even though we all knew we had only one day for the shoot."

"I knew we'd get it done."

"I wish there were more photographers like you around." He grinned and raised his glass. Why did he have to be so gorgeous? The smile sneaking across her mouth should be fake, but it wasn't. She just couldn't help it. Gavin was infuriatingly likeable.

"Why, so you could hire them instead of me?" She raised a brow and winked.

"Why do that, when I can keep it all in the family?" He reached across the table and she gave him her hand. "Isn't it just too perfect?"

"Yes, it's just too perfect." She struggled to keep emotion out of her voice.

Gavin's eyes sparkled with excitement about his new venture, not passion for her. Everything was too neat and pretty and nice to be real.

Because, of course, it wasn't.

The waiter served the artfully prepared appetizers. Bree picked up her fork, but her stomach was not interested in food and anxiety boiled in her gut.

Now. Tell him now.

But how could she, when he beamed with such pure happiness? She was usually the one to smooth everything over and soothe the proverbial troubled waters. She preferred to ease hurt feelings and make everyone feel better—even at her own expense. She was good old Bree, who you could always count on in a crunch.

Or at least she used to be.

Before dreams she'd never known she had all came true—and then fell apart within a week in the most cruel and hurtful way possible. Pain stabbed her chest, goading her into action.

She looked up from her sautéed shrimp. "Gavin, when exactly did you know you'd fallen in love with me?"

A tiny frown appeared on his forehead. "Hmm, what an interesting question."

"Was it when you first saw me, in that frumpy gray dress with no makeup and my wild-haystack hair?" She maintained a pleasant expression. "When I was so nervous I could hardly speak?"

He cocked his head. "No, I don't think it was right then."

"So why did you ask me to dance?"

"Why not?"

"Well—" she swallowed "—it's just that men usually only ask me to dance when they're interested in my money." She leveled a serious gaze at him. "I'm used to that. Somehow it all seemed different with you."

"Because it was different with me. I'm attracted to you, not your wealth." He took a sip of champagne. For a split second she thought she saw a flicker of unease cross his chiseled features. "I'm attracted to you for who you are."

Hurt welled inside Bree. How could he maintain a pleasant expression while telling such outright lies?

"But you were more attracted to me once I…changed my image."

"I wouldn't say that." A cute, rueful grin tugged at his

mouth. "Okay, maybe I would. You really are a knockout when you dress the part, Bree."

"I know that now. Though I really should give Elle all the credit. She's the one who transformed me from a frizzy-haired wallflower into the belle of the ball. Quite the fairy godmother, really. And I even got the handsome prince in the end, too."

Gavin frowned. "Elle transformed you? What is she up to? Ever since Brock told me she's the spy, I know there's far more to her than meets the eye. You should be careful around her. Who knows what she was trying to get out of you. You didn't give her any financial information, did you?"

"Of course not." *No, we wouldn't want her getting her hands on the money you want for yourself.* Tears welled inside her, but she held them back. Not yet. There'd be plenty of time for crying later. "But I did like her. And trust her. I'm a trusting person, or at least I used to be." Her voice cracked.

"She's broken your trust?"

Bree drew in a slow, steady breath. "Not her. Someone else."

Gavin frowned. "Who?" He leaned forward. "Just tell me and I'll go sort them out. I don't want anyone hurting your feelings." His gray eyes fixed on her face with probing intensity.

"You."

The single word fell from her lips and hung in the air for a moment.

Gavin's frown deepened. "I don't understand."

"No? Maybe you'd understand if I mentioned a certain number with six zeros."

He put his fork down on the tablecloth, still staring straight at her, and shoved a hand through his dark hair.

"I overheard a message my father left on your machine, thanking you for taking me off his hands—for a sizeable price, of course, since obviously no one would want to be stuck with me for nothing." Her voice rattled with the tears that wanted to come, but she forced herself to stay steady.

"He offered to help me start my own business. It's a simple investment on his part." He had the decency to look alarmed.

"Don't lie to me." She raised her voice. "I heard what he said. He was surprised you managed to seduce me into it so quickly. Usually I'm more sensible than that." She pulled her wedding and engagement rings from her finger, struggling to get them over her knuckle. "I've had plenty of men sniffing around my money and pretending to like me, so usually I can spot them a mile off. You were different, though. Far better looking, for one thing."

She took a final glance at his fine, handsome face. The kind of face she could have happily photographed and kissed for a lifetime—if it weren't the face of a scheming traitor.

"I am different. I'm not interested in your money."

"You took it, though, didn't you?"

"Your father's money." His voice was gruff. "Yes, I took it. Because I wanted to start my own business. I'd been waiting a long time and suffered some financial setbacks that made it impossible until your father offered me the chance—"

"To take advantage of a going-out-of-business sale on his spinster daughter." She blinked back tears. "Now

I know why you were in such a rush to get married. Why you didn't want a long engagement with an announcement in the papers, or even a real wedding. None of that was important to you because it wasn't about our marriage—or us—at all. It was all about money. Well, I'm not here to be given away, even with a million dollars." Her voice rang out, shattering the hushed refinement of the exclusive restaurant as she rose to her feet and threw the rings at him. They bounced across the tablecloth and disappeared as her chair crashed to the wood floor.

She rushed for the door, bumping into a table on the way and almost dragging the tablecloth with her, unsteady in her high heels. Panting, tears now running down her cheeks, she shoved her way out the door and ran for the fire stairs, clattering down until she reached street level.

Gavin wasn't behind her. Had she hoped he'd rush after her, try to convince her it was all a big mistake? She should have known better.

Their fairy-tale romance was a farce and the broken pieces of her dreams could never be put back together again.

It was almost completely dark when she reached the street, and she stayed in the shadows away from the streetlamps until she got to her car, parked two blocks away. Her hands shook as she fumbled in her bag for the keys, but Ali and Faith greeted her with mewing and purrs. "I'm here, ladies. We're making our escape together."

She settled into the cold leather seat and started the engine. Something tight gripped her heart as she pulled out into the late rush-hour traffic and headed for the freeway.

It was over.

With any luck, she'd never see Gavin again. Maybe one day she'd even forget him.

No. She'd never forget him. How could she forget someone who had tricked her into pledging her whole life to him?

How could she forget the firm warmth of his arms around her? The powerful touch of his fingers on her skin, or the soft enticement of his kiss?

"Damn him!" She pounded her fist on the wheel. Why did he have to introduce her to pleasures she'd never dared hope for? He should pay for that.

He would. She knew he would. Even if there wasn't a big scandal.

Her father would be sure to ask for the money back. He wasn't going to pay a million dollars for a marriage that had lasted less than a month. Elliott Kincannon was far too shrewd an investor for that.

No. Gavin would have to pay it all back, his business would fold and soon he'd be begging Brock Maddox to take him back.

Guilt speared through her, and she cursed herself for it. Deep down she still wanted him to succeed and be happy. And why not? That's the kind of sucker she was.

She let out a howl of anguish, spilling her pain into the night air.

What a fool she'd been, to think someone could love her for herself.

Nine

Gavin's gaze followed the rings as they bounced across the tablecloth, onto the floor. Slightly dazed, he ducked down and groped on the floor to retrieve them. Bree's angry words rattled in his skull.

Yes—there it was—the triple diamond his grandmother had left him. He palmed it and sat up, relieved. "Bree—"

She'd gone. He scanned the room, but she seemed to have vanished into the understated decor. He stood, ring still clutched in his hand.

"Can I help you, sir?" A waiter hurried over.

"Where did she go?"

"Your companion?"

"Yes!" Glancing about, he saw only the faces of strangers.

"I'm afraid I didn't see." He leaned closer. "Perhaps she's in the ladies'."

Gavin frowned. "I don't think so. I'd better pay the check." Urgency prickled under his skin.

"The entrées won't be a minute, sir."

"No, but…I have to go." People were staring. He reached into his pocket and pulled out three fifties. Hopefully that would cover it.

Damn, the other ring. He got down on the floor and peered around at the polished wood. The engraved gold band inscribed with both their initials sat quietly near a table leg. He snatched it up and pocketed it before climbing to his feet.

"Is there a problem, sir?" The maître d' approached, concern written on his dark brow.

"No problem at all. Just that something's come up." He cleared his throat. He could feel the curious stares and hear the whispered innuendo of the guests around him. He slid the crisp bills into the hand of the maître d' and murmured, "Keep the change."

Still stunned and not quite sure what was happening, he marched for the door. Out on the street he looked both ways. No sign of her. A cold fist of anxiety clenched in his gut. Why was she so upset? Was it really such a big deal that he'd accepted an…investment from her dad?

He shoved a hand through his hair. Of course it was a big deal. She thought he'd married her *just* for the money.

Guilt soaked through him, with a chaser of shame. It had seemed like a happy chain of events, leading to a favorable outcome for everyone involved. But he'd lost perspective on how it had all started.

How would her dad react? Gavin wondered if Elliott

Kincannon knew she'd found out. Maybe he could talk her out of causing a big scandal. That wouldn't be good for any of them.

And if she broke off the marriage, Kincannon might demand the one million dollars back.

Gavin stopped dead still, right in the middle of the road. A car swerved around him and he leaped to the sidewalk. He'd already spent a good chunk of the money on the lease for the new offices. And given a deposit to the contractor renovating the conference room. The money wasn't even his to give back anymore.

He marched through the lamp-lit streets. The apartment wasn't far, so he hadn't bothered with the car. He and Bree enjoyed their evening strolls after they went out to dinner or a gallery opening. She knew a lot about the city's architecture and history, and was always pointing out interesting nooks and crannies he'd never noticed before. The city had really come alive for him since he'd met Bree.

A pang of regret stung his chest. How awful that she'd found out like this. He could just picture her overhearing that message. She must have been devastated. If only he could find her and explain that he really did care about her and not about the money.

The elevator seemed to move like molasses on the way up to the apartment. What if she was already gone by the time he got there? He'd have to track her down at her father's house and he didn't relish seeing the old man's face if there was a whiff of scandal in the air. Still, no need to panic, he'd find her, tell her he really loved her, and everything would be okay. He hoped.

He knocked on the door. It was her home too, now. He didn't want to barge in if she was crying.

No answer. He slid his key in the lock and opened the door softly.

"Bree?"

The apartment was dark. He flicked on a light and waited for the sleek shadow of Bree's friendlier cat to appear, but nothing moved. "Faith? Where are you, Ali?"

Dread settled over him like a cold morning fog. The cats were gone, too. She couldn't possibly have had time to come back and get them already, so she must have taken them with her. He strode to her closet and flung it open. To his surprise, he found it still filled with her clothes, most of them new, some with the tags still hanging on them.

So she wasn't gone for good. Unless she had planned to abandon her new look along with him.

A nasty feeling goaded him back out the door and into the parking garage. He needed to get to the Kincannon mansion and win her back. And he needed to get there before the old man heard about their public breakup from someone else.

Usually a slow driver, Bree fought an urge to speed on the freeway. The lights of cars in the opposite lane danced like fireflies in the darkness, dazzling her and adding to her confused state of mind. She slowed down as a light mist of rain blurred the windshield and her phone rang.

Probably Gavin. She wasn't going to answer it. She let it ring and go to voice mail. Then it started ringing again. Again she let it go to voice mail. But the ringing continued and Ali started to mew in protest.

"It's okay, sweetie. We'll pull over and I'll tell that

jerk to stop bothering us." She pulled into a gas station and picked up the call, which was probably the sixth in succession.

"Stop calling me, I don't want to—"

"Bree, it's me, Elle."

She stiffened. "What do you want?" It came out just as rude as she intended. Now that she knew Elle was some kind of corporate traitor, she saw her new "friend" in an entirely different light. "Are you going to tell Gavin where I'm going?"

She'd told Elle her escape plan after the party. Before she'd learned about Elle's darker side.

"I still think you should rethink this whole thing." She heard Elle draw breath. "When are you planning to leave?"

"I'm already gone." She said it with grim satisfaction. "I'm on the road right now."

"Still going to Napa?"

"I'm really regretting telling you my plans since I've learned you're a spy."

"What?"

"Don't pretend you're innocent. Brock's detective found out."

Elle was silent on the other end of the call.

"And I'm still wondering if Gavin asked you to give me a makeover so I'd look better on his arm when he married me for money." She was proud of her steady voice.

"He had nothing to do with it. I swear. I do agree that it's a bit mercenary of him to take money from your father, but he's a guy, you know?"

"Well, I don't need one, then. I got along just fine without a man until now. And I'm getting rid of these damned green contact lenses, too." She popped the left one from her eye and tossed it into the backseat. Uh-oh. The world was blurry—which seemed appropriate, but made driving dangerous.

She reached into the glove compartment and was relieved to find her familiar old pair of spare glasses. The second contact hit the floor and she pushed the thick frames up the bridge of her nose. "I think a lot of the *improvements* I've made in my life lately were anything but. And what were you thinking, getting involved with Brock Maddox? It's bad enough that he's your boss, but you're spying on him, as well?"

"It's complicated." Elle's voice was barely a whisper. "I wish I could explain, but—"

"Save it. I've got enough problems of my own." She shoved a hand into her tangled curls. "The worst part is, I feel guilty." She could hardly believe she wanted to share her feelings with Elle after all she now knew, but she couldn't seem to stop herself.

"Why?"

"Because I'm ruining Gavin's pretty little dream-come-true plan to open his own agency. My dad will take the money back and it will all fall apart."

"I wouldn't worry too much about Gavin. He'll land on his feet. These big shots always do."

"You sound experienced in this area."

"Trust me, I am. What are you going to do?"

"No idea." And even if she did know, she wouldn't tell Elle. Here she thought she'd found a new best friend— they'd had so much fun together—and she'd turned out to be even more of a dark horse than her husband.

Husband. What a concept.

"The first thing I'm going to do is have the marriage

revoked or annulled or declared null and void—or whatever you do after a quickie wedding. I can't be the first whirlwind bride in California to have woken up in the morning and wondered what hit her."

"I still think you're wrong to give up on Gavin."

"Elle, a man marrying me for money is exactly what I've dreaded since I was a kid. It's not something I can forgive."

"I guess we all have our issues."

"Too right."

"Just don't forget to leave the conditioner in your hair." She could hear a hint of humor in Elle's voice. "It makes a big difference, doesn't it?"

"I admit it does. Has it made me happier?" She let out a snort of laughter. "I think I was better off frizzy. And on that note, I have an escape to make and two hungry cats to feed."

She hung up the phone before Elle could protest and switched it off. Not that Gavin had called. He probably didn't even care enough to come after her. He was probably out there trying to figure out how to save the money—since that's all he really wanted in the first place. He was likely over at her old house right now, glad-handing her father and attempting to turn things around. Who knew? Maybe it would even work. She'd always mattered less than money to her own father, who made no secret of it.

Bree pushed a stray tear from her cheek and wiped a sudden fog off her glasses before she pulled back onto the freeway. At least up in Napa she'd be away from everything and everyone, and could figure out what to do next. Maybe she'd move right away from San Francisco. Everyone here would be laughing at her once word got out. It was bad enough before, being a dumpy heiress. But to be one who got tricked into marrying a gold digger…well, that was more than she could handle. Perhaps she'd just go live in the hills as a hermit.

Hermits could have cats, couldn't they?

Gavin parked his car down the road from the Kincannon house. He could see lights on in the ground-floor windows, but the upper ones, where Bree had lived, were dark. Still, maybe she was downstairs, talking to her father.

He approached the carved front door of the mansion. His muscles burned with the urge to hold her. He wanted to explain that it wasn't as bad as she thought, that he really cared about her and not the money.

The door opened with a creak, and he was oddly surprised to see Elliott Kincannon himself behind it, dressed in a dark smoking jacket, like the nineteenth-century aristocrats he obviously modeled himself on.

"Ah, Gavin." He waved him inside. "How are things with Bree?"

So he didn't know.

"Not so good, I'm afraid." Gavin straightened his back. "She found out about our…arrangement."

"Upset, was she?" Elliott Kincannon led him into the front hallway, over the black-and-white marble floor, past polished wood columns and gleaming oil portraits. "I'm sure she'll recover."

Gavin drew a deep breath. The old man's uncaring attitude irked him. Then he grew angry with himself. Hadn't he also assumed he'd quickly find her and talk her around? Now he couldn't even find her. Panic surged inside him. "Is she here?"

"Here?" Elliott Kincannon swiveled on his heel and raised a brow. "Of course not. She lives with you now. I'd imagine she's ensconced in your palace in the sky."

Gavin frowned at the odd reference to his apartment. No doubt those who owned mansions looked down on those who didn't—even if they knew them to be millionaires.

"We were having dinner at Iago's, and then she told me she'd found out the truth and she took off. She was really upset." Gavin shoved his hands into his pockets. He suddenly hated standing there talking, wasting time. Bree could be headed anywhere.

Kincannon's stare hardened. "She waltzed out of Iago's? I hope she didn't make a scene."

"She threw her rings at me." Gavin took dark satisfaction in telling him this—Kincannon's cold nonchalance was getting under his skin. "Then she stormed out of the restaurant."

Bree's father looked appalled. "People must have seen."

"I'm sure they did."

"Word could get out. The family name might be dragged into the press."

Heaven forbid. How had Bree survived the first twenty-nine years of her life with this man?

"I hoped she'd be at the apartment, but she's gone and so are the cats. I thought she might be here."

"Well, she isn't. And she'd be most unwelcome if she turned up here. A married woman belongs with her husband. You must find her immediately before a scandal starts."

"I'm trying. Do you have any idea where she might

have gone?" A sense of urgency built in his chest. The thought of Bree, out there somewhere, upset and angry and hurting, grew inside him like a hot, uncomfortable flame. "Where does she usually go to get away?"

"Bree never goes anywhere." Kincannon knocked back a tumbler of golden liquid. "Just sits up there with her cats or putters about doing her little charity jobs. That's why I had to go out and hunt her down a husband myself. She was nearly thirty. People were talking."

"Bree's a very special woman." Gavin bristled with indignation at this man's dismissive attitude toward the woman he loved.

Yes, loved. There was no other word to describe the powerful surge of emotion rolling through him.

"Find her and smooth things over before the social pages get wind of this. I can just imagine the gossip if people think I paid to have my own daughter married off."

"Even though you did." Cold fury lashed inside Gavin. He felt like taking the million dollars and throwing it back in this man's expressionless, hard face.

But now wasn't the time for that. He had to find Bree before she got too far away. With her unlimited means, she could get on a plane to anywhere in the world. And then how would he track her down?

"I'll call you when I find her." He turned and marched for the door.

"You'd better find her tonight. If I see any whiff of this in the papers tomorrow..."

"You'll what?" Gavin turned and shot him a confrontational stare. This man was used to rolling over people and making them sweat—and to making his daughter feel inadequate and unworthy. "Bree's the important person here. She's upset, and justifiably so. It's my fault, and I intend to put it right."

If he could only find her.

But he couldn't. She'd disappeared into the misty coastal air. Gavin phoned everyone he knew and quite a few people he didn't. After four days, he was getting desperate.

His college friend Phil Darking was an editor at the local paper, and Gavin even went to see him, in case he'd heard anything on the gossip grapevine.

Phil had the gall to laugh. "Your wife's done a runner and you're calling the papers to ask where she is? Isn't it supposed to be the other way around? What if I use you as the headline tomorrow? It's a slow news day, you know."

"I just want to find out where she is. I've talked to everyone in town. I'm really worried, Phil."

"You think she's going to jump off the Golden Gate Bridge?"

"No, she's far too sensible for that." Why did people think this was funny? "I love her, Phil. She doesn't know that and I need to tell her."

"You married her without telling her you love her?"

"Of course I told her, but now she doesn't believe me. She thinks I married her for her money."

"Which would be quite understandable. Do you know just how rich those Kincannons are?"

"I don't care how rich they are. I don't care about anything except getting her back. I don't even care about the damn agency I've spent five years planning. I'd scrap the whole thing just to have her here right now, and I'm not kidding."

The realization shocked him. Five years of dreaming and scheming meant nothing compared to the prospect of spending his life without Bree. She'd been gone four long, agonizing days. Four mornings without her smile. Four evenings without her kisses. Four nights without her arms around him. He couldn't take much more of it.

"You've got it bad."

"Tell me about it. I've hired a private detective, I've called anyone I even think might know her, and gone to visit all of her relatives. I've been haunting all her favorite places in the city, but she's just disappeared. No one has even the slightest idea where she is." He blew out hard and looked up at his friend. "I'll do anything to get her back, Phil."

"Anything?" Phil's voice had a funny edge to it.

"Anything."

"I LOVE YOU. COME BACK TO ME."

The bold black print splashed across the front page of the *San Francisco Examiner* on newsstands all over the city. Gavin felt equal measures of embarrassment and excitement as he strode along a crowded street. The air hummed with the zing-zing of a passing cable car and his chest filled with hope. He'd already received a phone call from a popular local TV show, wanting him to come on and tell his story. Much to his surprise, he'd readily accepted.

He'd done the interview that morning. "Yes, I'm afraid I did accept money from my wife's father. I saw it as an investment in my new business." He'd cleared his throat and glanced down at the microphone pinned to his tie. Hot lights had brought out pinpoints of sweat on his brow, and the three cameras pointing right at him hadn't helped much, either.

"Yet you didn't tell your wife anything about it." The heavily starched blonde leaned in until her mascara-clad lashes were almost brushing his cheek.

"No, I never told her. And that's what makes the whole thing wrong. She's my wife and we should confide in each other about everything."

"And she was hurt when she found out."

"She was devastated." Gavin's voice thickened. "After she learned about the money, she decided I only married her for the cash, and that I didn't care about her."

"Is that true?"

Gavin stiffened his shoulders and reminded himself it was a leading question, not an accusation. "Nothing could be further from the truth. I love Bree. She captivated me from the first moment I met her. She's a lovely, talented, sweet, brilliant and funny woman, and I want to share the rest of my life with her."

"Spoken like a man in love." The gruff voice of the male cohost drew Gavin's attention to the side. "And is it true that you've given the money back?"

"Yes. Every penny of it." Pride swelled in his chest. He'd arranged the reverse transfer the previous afternoon. He'd had to throw in a big chunk of his personal savings to cover the money he'd already spent on the new agency. He'd also sent a personal note to Elliott Kincannon, apologizing for his role in the scheme and for any subsequent publicity. Frankly, though, he felt the old man deserved any wind that blew up his well-tailored coattails.

"I'm hardworking and ambitious enough to support Bree without any extra help. I know that now. Whether I can still make a go of my own agency, or whether I go to work for someone else, I'll continue to do my best work for my clients. Since I've met Bree, I've changed my perspective on everything. Work is still important to me, but I've discovered the joys of companionship. I'd never been so happy in my life, as I was during these last few weeks with Bree. I miss her more than I can describe."

"Aw." The female host had patted his leg. "Aren't you adorable? I'd marry you myself if you weren't already hitched to this lucky girl." She'd turned to one of the three large cameras pointing right at them. "Bree, do come back to him, won't you?"

But she hadn't.

Bree's muscles ached slightly every morning since she'd arrived in Napa. Maybe because she spent much of the day walking in the hills, trying to keep moving and keep her mind off a certain scheming and duplicitous man.

Faith rolled and stretched on the sheets next to her. "Morning, baby." She stroked the cat's soft fur. Sun shone through the delicate blinds on the window and illuminated the pale yellow walls of the pretty bedroom. She hadn't been here in years, though of course it was maintained in her absence like the other properties in the estate. Her mom used to love it here in the summers when she was little, and they often came to watch the grape harvest. As far as she could remember, her dad had never been here, not even once. It was one of more than thirty properties on the family rosters, and he was probably barely aware of its existence. That made it a great place to hide out.

But despite the glorious weather, the lovely surroundings and all the peace and quiet anyone could wish for, she still felt rotten.

And it was all Gavin Spencer's fault.

She heard a noise in the other room. A flopping sound.

She eased out of bed and went to investigate. Something lay on the doormat just inside the kitchen door. Mail? She hadn't told anyone she was coming here. Well, except Elle, but she'd hardly be sending letters. Perhaps people had noticed someone was living here and started to include her on the local "all residents" mailing lists.

It was a plastic envelope from a popular courier service. She ripped it open to find a folded tabloid newspaper. Affixed to the front was a sticky note that simply said, "And turn on the local TV news."

Bree frowned. She pulled the sticky note off the front of the paper and squinted at the large headline. "I LOVE YOU. COME BACK TO ME."

Her stomach clenched and something painful and bright opened inside her.

Ten

Don't get carried away. Bree scolded herself as the blurry black-and-white words danced in front of her eyes. *It's not like it's Gavin talking to you.* Ridiculous that she should even make a mental connection.

Still, something prickled through her—hope, or fear—as she turned back into the cottage and looked around for her glasses. When she found them on the bedside table, her hands trembled as she picked them up.

She pushed her glasses up her nose and scanned the page. Her jaw dropped as she read on.

"San Francisco is abuzz with the mysterious disappearance of newlywed heiress Bree Kincannon."

She gasped. Disappearance? That made it sound as if something suspicious had happened to her. Was Gavin in trouble?

"She hasn't been seen since last Thursday, when she took off after telling her new husband she'd found out he'd been paid to marry her."

A claw of panic gripped her. How did they know?

"Apparently Bree's father was so keen to marry his daughter off to a suitable husband, he paid the young executive one million dollars to take her off his hands." She cringed. It was bad enough to have such a terrible thing happen, but to have the whole world know...

Tears sprang to her eyes. Who would be cruel enough to show this to her?

She remembered the sticky note urging her to turn on the TV news. Some hidden core of self-preservation told her not to. Did she really want to see herself mocked and gaped at on TV, as well?

She glanced back at the paper. "Since her sudden departure, Bree's husband, Gavin, has been distraught." Bree tugged the paper closer. "Desperate to find his new wife, he approached the papers himself, asking for help."

Bree's mouth fell open. Then it snapped shut. Of course he was. He didn't want to lose the million bucks, so he needed to hunt her down and talk her round before Daddy Warbucks snatched the cash back.

She let out a long, loud sigh and threw the paper down. Even the bold headline, "I LOVE YOU. COME BACK TO ME," read entirely differently in light of the large sum of money involved. One million dollars was worth a little public embarrassment to most people, and obviously Gavin was no different.

Her dad must be hitting the ceiling. He hated publicity. He adhered to the old credo that a man's name should appear in the papers three times during his life—his birth announcement, his wedding announcement and his obituary. Oh, and maybe the occasional impressive business merger. Certainly not a tacky headline about how he paid someone to marry his dumpy daughter.

She would laugh, except somehow tears kept welling up, and now they'd made a big wet patch on the cheap newsprint. Ali rubbed against her leg and she leaned down to pet her. She saw the sticky note where it had fallen on the floor.

"I don't want to watch TV, Ali. It'll be even worse. Why can't he just leave me alone?"

Ali mewed in agreement and wrapped her tail delicately around Bree's calf. Still, curiosity goaded her into the tiny bedroom, to where a small but quite new television sat on a dresser. "I must be a glutton for punishment," she murmured as she turned it on. "Or just silly. I'm sure there are far more interesting things going on in the Bay area than an unhappy heiress running off."

Sure enough, the first channel showed people chugging some sports drink in a commercial, the second followed the blow-by-blow action of a local prize fight, and the third offered some cubic zirconia rings in a two-for-one deal.

"See? I'm getting an exaggerated sense of my own importance. No one cares about me at all."

Except Gavin. The words snuck up from somewhere in her conscience.

"Him least of all," she said aloud.

Then a thought crept over her. Had he brought the paper himself? Who else would care if she got his message? Perhaps he was out there somewhere, lurking in the rows of vineyard grapes behind the cottage, ready to spring on her and talk her back into his bed.

Never.

She crossed her arms, which were clad in a very unfashionable plaid work shirt she'd found in the closet. Probably from some farm manager who'd used the cottage for a while. These arms weren't going anywhere near Gavin Spencer again.

Oversize cubic zirconia still sparkled on the screen, and she wondered if the ring he'd given her was really an heirloom from his grandmother or a fake he'd bought off the television. When you married a woman for money, it really didn't make sense to throw in anything valuable.

It had been a pretty ring, though. She thought of it falling to the restaurant floor, among stray breadcrumbs and dropped napkins. She still could hardly believe she'd had the guts to do that. Totally unplanned, too! She'd been so upset and angry she hadn't even given a thought to the big scene she was making. It was probably her fault as much as his that the papers had caught onto the story.

The amazing deal on fake diamonds segued into a vacuum-cleaner commercial. Then the local news logo popped up.

Turn it off, now!

Her mind marched toward the set, but her feet stayed firmly planted on the floor.

"Heiress Bree Kincannon is still missing, more than five days after her tearful breakup from her new husband." A hideous picture of her filled the screen. The photo was at least five years old, because she recognized the awful plaid taffeta ball gown her aunt had talked her into wearing to some parties one season. With a goofy updo and a strand of big pearls, she looked every bit the lovelorn heiress.

Ouch. And why was she always an "heiress"? Why not "photographer Bree Kincannon," or even a plain old "San Francisco native" or something?

Her inner monologue screeched to a halt as Gavin appeared onscreen. Dressed, as usual, in a sleek dark suit, heartbreakingly handsome.

She let out a whimper, then cursed herself for it. At least no one was around to hear her. One advantage of being a hermit.

"Yes," Gavin said, leaning into a mike, "I'm worried. She's been gone almost a week. No one has heard from her. Of course I'm concerned."

"Do you think she's extra vulnerable because she's an heiress?"

Gavin looked confused for a moment.

The reporter drew closer. "Do you think she might have been kidnapped?"

Gavin's lips parted in astonishment. "I don't think so, but…" He frowned. "I suppose we can't rule out anything until she comes back. That's why I'm so desperate for word of her whereabouts." He shoved a hand though his hair in that cute way he did when he was thinking. "Bree, wherever you are, please, call me right now. I don't know what to do without you. You're everything to me."

The picture faded away into a story about penguins at the zoo. Bree stood staring, openmouthed, at the television.

She could almost swear from the look on his face that

he meant every word. Her heart beat hard and painful against her ribs, swollen and ready to burst.

"Don't let him do this to you!" she cried aloud. Already he'd turned her into the kind of maniac who ranted to herself. Still, what if he truly did think she'd been kidnapped, or worse? She didn't want him actually worrying about her.

Maybe she should call and leave a message on his phone.

A message on his phone. That's what started this whole mess in the first place. Why did everything have to be so complicated and awful?

The harsh doorbell ring jolted her hard. No way could she go to the door now, cheeks streaked with tears. Even if it was just the mailman, he might have seen the news. She wouldn't be able to go to the store for eggs without people staring. She snapped the TV off.

Again the doorbell rang, harsh and insistent.

"Go away." She hissed the words, not intending for them to be heard.

"Bree." A deep voice boomed into the cottage. It reverberated across the living room and into the bedroom where she stood.

Gavin.

The breath rushed from her lungs and her knees felt weak. *Stay silent. He can't see you here. He'll go away.*

But every nerve ending in her body stung with the urge to rush to the door.

"Bree, are you there? It's me, Gavin."

She closed her eyes and tried not to breathe.

"I miss you terribly." His words echoed through the

silent cottage. "I haven't been able to sleep since you left."

She knotted her hands together as his words wrapped around her. She hadn't slept much either. It was hard to sleep alone once you got used to having a warm, well-muscled body next to you.

Remember, it's the money he's after, not you. The icy blast of memory kept her feet rooted to the floor.

"I gave the money back."

Her chin shot up. Had he really?

"I didn't want it anymore. I can't believe I took it in the first place. I was just so caught up in the idea of going out on my own that I didn't think about how it would look to you."

"Because you thought I wouldn't find out." The words flew out of her mouth—barely more than a whisper—before she could stop them.

"Bree, you *are* there!" He rattled the door handle. "Let me in, please. I have so much apologizing to do." The urgency in his voice tugged at her heart.

"What if I don't want to hear it?" she said weakly. It took all her strength not to rush right into his treacherous arms.

"I'm just so glad you're safe." His relief rang across the space. Suddenly the wall between them seemed too much a barrier for her to bear. Bree found herself walking across the wood floor, silent in her tube socks. When she reached the doorway, she peered around the molding toward the front door, which had two frosted glass panes. She could see the tall shadow of a man—a very particular man—blocking the light behind them.

She stopped. Once she opened the door and got a

look at him, she might lose all ability to think straight. "Did my dad demand the money back?"

"No. He demanded that I get *you* back. He's not a man who acknowledges the possibility of failure." Humor echoed in his deep voice.

"I guess that's why you're here, then." She spoke flatly.

"No! I'm here because I want you back. I *need* you back. Bree, I never imagined I could be so dependent on another person for my happiness. Ever since you left, I've been miserable." Emotion reverberated in his gruff voice. "Please open the door. I don't think I can survive another moment without seeing your face."

Bree's heart squeezed. Then she remembered the tear streaks, her unstyled hair, her plaid shirt, sweats and tube socks. "I'm not at all sure you'll like what you see."

"Trust me, if it's you, I'll like it."

"I'm not glammed up."

"All the better. Nonstop glamour was a bit exhausting." Laughter hovered around his voice.

Bree walked very slowly to the door, still not at all sure whether she was going to open it. Her feet seemed to be moving of their own accord with the rest of her going along for the ride. When she reached the door she put her hand on the brass knob and hesitated.

Gavin was there, less than a foot away. She could see his tall silhouette on the other side of the decorated panes, and she could almost feel the heat of his skin even through the wood and glass. Her blood heated and a strange prickling sensation ran all over her. "If I open it, will you promise not to touch me?"

She was afraid of the power he had over her. Too

handsome for his own good and far too charming to be safe. He could talk anyone into anything, which was of course how he made his living.

"I'll put my hands in my pockets. Is that okay?"

She swallowed and nodded. "Yes." She turned the knob slightly, and put her other hand on the key.

The click of the latch made her heart jump, and she pulled the door open very, very slowly. Bright noonday light shone in, and her eyes found themselves staring at a white T-shirt stretched over a thickly muscled chest.

Sure enough, his hands were buried in the pockets of his dark pants. She allowed her eyes to creep up slowly toward his face, up his muscled neck to that angled jaw. Across his sensual mouth, caught hovering on the brink of a smile, to his assertive nose.

Gray eyes twinkled with anticipation. His dark hair was tousled, one lock hanging over his forehead. If anything he looked more gorgeous than ever. The urge to rush into his firm embrace was almost overwhelming….

But not quite.

"You and my father cooked this whole scheme up before we even met, didn't you?"

His lashes lowered in a sheepish expression. "That's true."

"Who came up with it?"

Gavin inhaled, broad chest rising under his white T-shirt. "I'm afraid he did. At first I thought he was joking. I was introduced to him at the gala and we chatted about my ambitions, just casual talk. Then he started asking more and more questions about me—where I was from, where I went to school, what I wanted to accomplish."

"No doubt he was making sure your origins wouldn't embarrass the great Kincannon name." She spoke drily.

A smile tugged at his mouth. "No doubt. I think he liked that I come from a long line of army generals."

"The Kincannons were a warlike people. Some say they still are." She fought her own smile. "So he came right out and asked if you'd consider marrying me for the right sum?"

Gavin looked down at the doorstep. "Yes. Like I said, I thought he was joking at first. Then he introduced me to you and we hit it off. When he and I talked later on that night, he assured me he was perfectly serious and that I was off to an excellent start."

Bree's chest tightened. "Do you have any idea how humiliating this is for me?"

"I can see now that it was totally wrong, but at the time... I don't know, it seemed kind of—old school. Like your dad."

"Biblical, even. A sort of dowry." She narrowed her eyes.

"Yeah." He winced. "Kind of like that. I guess the idea of all that money to start my own business made me look past the more unsavory aspects of the situation." He let out a sigh. "I'm really, really sorry."

Her chest tightened. "Don't be. You're very far from being the only man who might be tempted into marriage by the promise of a million dollars. I guess I should consider myself lucky he at least picked someone good-looking."

The hint of a smile hovered at the corner of his mouth again. "I'll take that as a compliment."

"Oh, come on, you know you're handsome." She

twisted her mouth and surveyed him. "That's probably why you were so confident you'd pull it off. You must have women eating out of your hands."

He glanced down to where his hands were still thrust into his pockets. "Not right now."

"You keep them there. Those hands are dangerous." She crossed her arms over her plaid-covered chest. "But I'm glad to finally hear the truth. I bet you were pretty alarmed when you met me. You probably thought I'd be a willowy blonde in a slinky black dress."

"I'm very glad you're not. I prefer curvy brunettes." Mischief sparkled in his eyes.

Something fluttered in her chest, but she resolved to keep steady. "Did you really think, that first night, that you'd go through with it?"

Gavin frowned. "I didn't think all that much. I just enjoyed our dance and knew I wanted to see you again."

"You moved in fast. Swept me right off my feet."

"You weren't the only one getting swept off your feet. I knew right away that you were special."

She swallowed hard. "I prefer the truth."

"That is the truth." He looked pained. "Though I don't honestly know how to make you believe it after everything that's happened. All I can say is that I gave back the money because I realized it doesn't mean anything to me without you."

His words wrapped around her as his gray gaze challenged her to argue.

"But what about your business? Will you have to close it?"

He shrugged. "Quite possibly, but I couldn't enjoy running it anyway if it meant losing you."

She raised a brow. "That's true on one level, at least. I bet my dad would demand the money back if you didn't get me to toe the line."

"It's a moot point now. I don't want it. I'd never take money from him or anyone again unless I earned it honestly." His sincere expression tugged at her heart. "I've been ashamed of myself ever since I realized how much I hurt you. I was an idiot, and I can only hope you find it in your heart to forgive me."

She glanced down at her chest. "I'm not even sure where my heart is, let alone whether I can find anything in it. It's been a stressful week."

"For me, too. I've been utterly miserable without you."

His serious expression almost made her laugh. "Oh, come on, I'm sure you've been far too busy wheeling and dealing to spend time moping over me."

"I've been far too busy running around trying to find you to do any wheeling and dealing. I was beginning to think you'd moved abroad. It's much harder finding a runaway heiress than a regular person with a job they have to show up at."

She let out a sigh. "Yes, poor little rich girl crying her eyes out at her luxurious Napa Valley hideaway. I guess it's no wonder the press make fun of me."

"No one's been making fun of you, but a lot of people are worried. I've been fielding phone calls from all over the world, some of them less than pleasant. You have a lot of friends."

"I do?"

"Unquestionably. One guy from Colombia was so angry I thought he was going to threaten me."

She smiled. "Oh, that's Pedro. We were in theater club together in college. He's a sweetie."

"And a girl from New York gave me a thorough dressing-down and told me I was a cad."

She chuckled. "That'd be Lacey. She's very out-spoken."

"And your aunt Freda…" He blew out a breath. "She doesn't mince words, either."

"So you can't wait to call them all back and tell them not to worry, you tracked Bree down and everything's hunky-dory again."

"Actually, I couldn't care less about them." He narrowed his eyes and stared right at her. "There's only one person I care about." His hands twitched in his pockets, as if he could barely stop himself from pulling them out. "She's right here and she's the most important person in the world to me."

Ali twisted around Bree's legs. "Careful, you're making my cat jealous. I don't think she's going to let you in."

Gavin looked down at the cat. "Come on, Ali, give a guy a break."

Ali stuck her tail in the air and marched back inside.

"Hmm." Bree cocked her head. "That response could be interpreted a number of ways."

"I think she means 'Come on in' in cat lingo."

"Either that or 'Get lost, punk.'" A grin flashed over her face.

"I guess I can't blame her if it's the latter, but I do hope you'll be more forgiving." He glanced down at his hands. "And maybe let me take my hands out of my pockets."

"Oh, okay. Just watch where you put 'em." She gave his bronzed forearms a suspicious look.

"I'll make sure they behave." His hands emerged from his pockets and hung innocently by his sides. "Though I'll warn you, they're pretty darn desperate to wrap themselves around you."

Bree bit her lip to hide a smile. "I did miss you, a little bit."

"Only a little bit, huh?"

She held up a thumb and finger, close together. "Maybe this much."

"I missed you so much it still hurts, even now that I'm here with you."

"I could get you an aspirin."

"A hug would work better." His charming, slightly arrogant grin made her smile and annoyed her at the same time. Of course he expected his charm to work on her.

And of course it did. "You might as well come in. I don't want the neighbors to see you loitering."

Gavin glanced over his shoulder. There wasn't a single house in view. "Good point. The crows might talk."

"We don't want them leaking anything to the press." Her whole body tingled and crackled with anticipation. Gavin's large, masculine presence in the room seemed to fill it and make it smaller. He smelled delicious— outdoorsy and slightly leathery, with a hint of sweat.

She liked making him sweat. "I suppose you expect me to forgive you."

He looked right at her. "I won't ask that of you. I'd rather move forward instead. I love you, Bree. I know you might not believe that after everything that's happened, but losing you has only made me more painfully sure. I ache for you like I need my next breath. The days are dull and pointless without you. Even work doesn't seem exciting anymore, without you there to share it."

Bree's chest expanded. "That photo shoot was pretty fun." *Even though I was going half-crazy trying to hide the hurt.*

"Everything we did together was fun. Just going out for coffee and a walk in the park, or lying in bed watching the sun rise. I want to watch the sun rise with you, Bree. Tomorrow and every day after that. If you'll take a chance on me again."

His voice thickened, heavy with emotion, and she felt it echo through her. Odd thoughts flickered through her mind.

"I'm sorry I threw your grandmother's ring on the floor."

"It's okay, I have it." He reached into his pocket again. "I would really like it to go back on your finger."

She noticed with some satisfaction that he was still wearing his ring.

He followed her gaze to his left hand. "I never took it off. I know our marriage got off to a rocky start, but I still believe in us, Bree. I believe in my heart that we're meant to be together."

"Are you saying my dad was a psychic?" She couldn't resist teasing him.

"He might well be. They call him The Guru in financial circles. Maybe his prescience extends beyond spotting the next hot businesses to invest in."

His wicked grin tickled something inside her. "He must be livid about the publicity."

"I'm sure he is." He shrugged. "But I didn't care

about him. I only cared about finding you. I'm sorry if the press embarrassed you, but I wanted everyone to know I was looking."

"Pretty sneaky of you to send me that newspaper to soften me up."

He frowned. "I didn't send a paper. I just drove right up and came to your door."

"How did you know I was here?"

He looked sheepish again. She saw his Adam's apple move as he swallowed. "Elle."

Bree blew out hard. "I swore her to secrecy! Of course, that was before I found out she had a dark side. I can't believe she told you."

"She took pity on me. I'm deliriously grateful to her."

"She must have sent the paper. I made the mistake of telling her the town I'd be in. She seemed really keen to get us back together. Why would she care one way or the other?"

"Maybe she just thinks we're perfect for each other." He leveled a wary gray gaze at her. "She wouldn't be the only one."

Bree took in his handsome face, so filled with hope and desire. "Perfect for each other. That's a tall order. We do fit together pretty well, though. Some of the puzzle pieces turned out to have some splinters on them, but I guess we could file them off together."

His gaze darkened and his lips curved into a smile. "I can think of some creative ways to do that."

"I'll just bet you can." She raised a brow. "Promises, promises." Her breasts felt heavy and her belly already rippled with desire. Just being around this man was dangerous. But it was the kind of danger she no longer wanted to resist.

She took a step toward him. Gavin looked as if he wanted to devour her whole. Even with her makeover stripped away, she felt…sexy and irresistible.

"Can I touch you?" His voice was low, breathy.

"Okay."

Eleven

Suddenly Gavin's mouth was on hers, and her arms wrapped around his sturdy back. Bree clung to him as if she would never let him go.

The days of hurt and loneliness fell away as she sank into his warm embrace. Gavin devoured her, his kiss hungry, like a man who'd been starving for days. His fingers roamed into her hair and over her curves as he hugged her tight.

When they finally came up for air they were both gasping. "I've never felt so rotten in my life as the past few days without you," breathed Gavin. "I knew I was crazy about you, but I didn't know how much until I lost you."

"My head is still spinning." Bree leaned her cheek on his shoulder. "Everything's been moving so fast since the minute we met. I've been so happy and so sad in such a short space of time."

"I think it's time we slowed right down and savored the moment together." Gavin picked up one of her hands and kissed it. "Possibly in bed."

Bree giggled. "I like the way you think." She tipped her head to the bedroom where she'd been hiding from him so recently.

They hurried across the small cottage, anticipation stinging Bree's skin. Already Gavin's fingers plucked at the buttons on her plaid shirt, and his breathing became ragged. Desire darkened his gray eyes as he slid the shirt back over her shoulders to reveal…her dreariest white cotton bra.

"You're so beautiful," he rasped. "And your eyes are so much prettier without the green contact lenses. They're softer and warmer and…" He let out a sigh. "I like the natural you best of all."

He slid the shirt back over her shoulders and caressed her skin as if she was an object of fine art. Heat flared in her belly. Under Gavin's admiring gaze she did feel beautiful. Her whole life she'd felt slightly inadequate and disappointing, until she met him. Under his keen attentions she'd blossomed into a confident woman, aware of her own attractions.

For a few days, that had all withered away. Yes, she'd maintained confidence in herself as an independent person, able to look after her needs and survive without anyone around to care for her. Now, as Gavin's eager hands roved over her breasts and belly, and played in her hair, she morphed back into the desirable woman he'd awakened.

A fine haze of dark stubble shaded Gavin's sculpted

cheeks. He looked tired and haunted, but passion flashed in his gray eyes. She slid her fingers under his T-shirt and over his warm skin. "I didn't think I was ever going to do this again." Her heart squeezed. She hadn't fully acknowledged all she'd lost when she left. Now the raw ache of loneliness rose to the surface and rolled away.

"I couldn't acknowledge that possibility." Gavin's hands crept lower, inside the waistband of her gray sweats and over her hips. "Our bed felt so cold and empty without you. All I could think about was finding you and bringing you home."

"You've found me."

"But suddenly bringing you home doesn't seem so urgent." He nuzzled against her cheek, and his stubble tickled her skin. "Because wherever you are feels like home."

Bree sighed. "I know exactly what you mean. I'd never really considered leaving the house I grew up in. It had always been my sanctuary, the place where I cherished my happy memories and maybe even hid from the world. Once I met you it didn't matter anymore. I just wanted to be with you, to live with you and share everything."

Her fingers had found their way to the button of his pants, and popped it free. She tugged down the zipper, urgency flaring in her blood.

Gavin unhooked her bra and pulled it away from her chest, replacing its close contact with his hot mouth. He eased her onto the bed, licking and sucking until her skin buzzed with arousal. She pushed his pants down over his strong thighs, and together they wriggled out of the last of their clothes.

He groaned with raw pleasure as her breasts pressed

against his bare chest. He was hard as the brass bedpost and his erection pressed against her thigh, fueling her own intense arousal.

Their kissing became even more fevered, and Gavin was pulling Bree gently onto the bed when the familiar chime of his phone filled the air.

"Oh, no," rumbled Gavin. "Let's ignore it."

"It might be important," breathed Bree. "You do have a business to run."

"Or it could be the press." Gavin winced. "Speculating on where you are."

"The missing heiress." She giggled. "I guess we could tell them I've been found. Though I rather like being mysterious."

"That settles it." Gavin drew her closer into his arms. "Forget about the rest of the world. Nothing matters but you and me."

The ringing stopped as they collapsed onto the mattress together, Gavin's arms firmly around her waist. Bree wriggled against him, enjoying the tantalizing closeness of his hard body.

Then the phone started to ring again.

Gavin groaned. "How can I answer the phone in this condition?"

"But if you don't answer it, you may never get out of this condition." Bree shot a glance at his all-too-obvious arousal. "I could lean over and answer it for you." Bree narrowed her eyes. "But I'm wary about picking up your phone these days."

Gavin cocked a brow. "I'd much rather you answer it while I'm right here so we can talk. I don't want you getting upset and running out on me just when I least expect it."

"Well, when you put it that way…" Bree reached down and fumbled with his pants on the floor until she found the phone. Heart pounding a little, she answered.

A crisp female voice responded. "Hello, this is Lazer Designs. We're inquiring about the address to send the contract?"

"One moment." Bree repeated the question for Gavin.

His eyes widened. "Tell them the apartment."

Bree gave them the address. The voice at the other end said, "Wonderful, and if you could pass on to him that we'd like the entire package—print, radio and television."

"I'll let him know. Thanks." She turned to Gavin. "Lazer Designs wants the entire package."

Gavin let out a whoop of joy. "Yes! I told them the whole situation, about me giving back the money and having to scale back my start-up operation. I even told them I had to give up my lease on the office, which is why they're calling about the address. I guess they decided to go with me anyway."

"They know you're the best." Bree beamed with pride.

"With this contract I'll be able to go full steam ahead. It's a big furniture company with stores in fifteen major cities. They'll keep me busy and fund operations and overhead for a good six months." He turned to her with a smug smile. "Without a penny of your dad's money."

"See? You didn't need it anyway. All you needed was the confidence to go out on your own."

"And you by my side."

"Literally, and figuratively." They lay skin-to-skin

on the soft bed. "And I believe we were in the middle of something before we got interrupted."

"I apologize for the interruption." Gavin layered soft kisses along her collarbone. "Pleasure before business from now on, at least for today. I love you. And I'm very, very hot for you."

"I can tell." She whispered the words into his neck. "And I'm pretty nuts about you, too. I'd have to be to take you back after everything that's happened."

"I'll make it up to you." He nipped at her neck and blew hot breath over it. Sensation flashed over her, tingling to her toes. "Starting right now."

He caressed and kissed her all over as she writhed on the mattress. When she was almost ready to cry out with the force of her desire, he entered her, slowly and carefully, until he was deep inside her. His groan of deep, heartfelt relief sent a smile to her lips. "Welcome back," she whispered. "I've missed you."

"Don't ever leave me again." Gavin buried his face in her neck. "I couldn't stand it."

"Me, either," she breathed. "Maybe we could just stay right here, forever."

They moved together, enjoying each other's bodies until the sun set outside the window. Then they took a break for dinner, before enjoying each other some more.

It was two full days before they set out on the road back to San Francisco.

"I guess flexible hours are one of the benefits of having your own business," said Bree as she loaded her bag into her car. "You can take off whenever you feel like it."

"As long as you're with me." Gavin kissed her and

slammed the trunk. "I hate that we have two cars to drive back. I'll be right on your tail the whole way."

She laughed. "That's almost challenging me to try to lose you."

"You go ahead and try. This time I won't let it happen. On a purely practical level, I need you to shoot the print ads for my new client."

"Well, if it's a professional commitment I suppose I'll have to behave."

Gavin frowned. "You never did put your wedding ring back on."

"Does that make me a bad bride?"

"Unquestionably. But since I rather pressured you into putting them on last time, I'll just give you the rings to do what you like with." He fished in his pocket and pulled out the trio of diamonds and the engraved band.

They sparkled in his palm.

"I want to wear them." Conviction unfurled in her chest. With none of the doubt that had given her pause last time. "I'm glad to be your wife and I want the world to know it." She slid the rings onto her finger, where they settled comfortably against her skin. Then she bit her lip. "I need to speak to my dad. Maybe he thought he was trying to help me, but that kind of interference just isn't right."

"We might never have met without his inter-ference."

"I know, but he treats me like a child. Why couldn't he have introduced us and then just left us alone to see what happened?" She cocked her head and narrowed her eyes. "Or would you have lost interest without that initial enticement?"

"Nope." Gavin fixed her with his steady gray gaze. "I knew there was something special about you the moment I danced with you."

A smile crept across her mouth. "The feeling was mutual."

"And you're right. Your dad shouldn't be interfering in your life. You're a grown woman. We'll go see him this afternoon."

Bree gulped. "Well, we don't have to literally confront him…."

"Yes. We do. You do. And I think I do, too. He needs to know that what he did was wrong. That he shouldn't be sticking his fingers in other people's lives. Otherwise who knows what he'll try next? He'll be trying to run our marriage from his downtown office."

Bree bit her lip. "You're right. He has so many ideas about how things should be done. He'll try to pick out our china for us and demand that our children are named after Kincannon ancestors, in the family tradition. I'm named for Briony Kincannon MacBride, born in 1651. We must stop him before he insists on naming our child Elliott."

Gavin grinned. "That would be a serious matter. Let's get moving."

Back in town they dropped off their bags and freshened up, then set off for the Kincannon mansion. Gavin wanted to get over there before Bree had a chance to get nervous and back out. A phone call to the housekeeper had confirmed that her father was at home, catching up on work in his study. Bree told her to keep their visit a secret, so she could set the agenda for a change.

"He's going to be mad about the publicity." Bree twisted her fingers together as they climbed the stone steps to the mansion.

"He'll get over it." Gavin rubbed her back. "Stay strong."

Lena, the housekeeper, gave Bree a warm hug and almost wept with happiness to see her back. "We were all so worried. The papers said you'd disappeared." She shot a stern glance at Gavin. "You be more careful with Bree."

"Trust me, I will," he said with conviction. Lena rewarded him with a smile, and ushered them upstairs.

Gavin tensed slightly as Bree knocked on the tall wood-paneled door of Elliott Kincannon's office. Bree, however, held her chin high and entered boldly when he said, "Come in."

"Hi, Dad." Gavin watched Bree falter for a moment as her father's stunned expression turned to a dark glower.

"You're back." Kincannon frowned, then rose and rounded the desk. "I'm glad you're unharmed." He shot a dark look at Gavin, who willed himself to remain silent. He could think of a few things to say to Elliott Kincannon, but this was Bree's moment.

She stared directly at him. "Why did you feel the need to pay someone to marry me?"

Kincannon cleared his throat. "I wanted to see you comfortably settled."

"And you didn't think that would ever happen without a financial incentive?" Bree cocked her head, causing her curls to fall over one shoulder.

"You're twenty-nine. I was becoming concerned."

"That I'd be an embarrassment to you." She spoke softly. "That people would whisper about how Bree Kincannon is getting older and no one wants to marry her."

"Of course not. I…" Her father had an uncharacteristically speechless moment.

"I've had offers, Dad. Several, in fact—some from men I'd barely met. When you have money, there are all kinds of people who'll happily marry you just to get their hands on it. If I wanted someone who'd marry me for my money, I could handle that all by myself in no time." She drew in a breath. "I was waiting for someone who'd marry me *without* wanting my money. Someone who was interested in *me*."

Kincannon shot a glance at Gavin, then looked back at Bree. "I imagine Mr. Spencer's gallant gesture of throwing my one millions dollars back in my face demonstrates to you that he is a man of such caliber."

"It helped. We'll never know what would have happened if you hadn't offered him the money, but at least I know he still wants me without it." Bree took a step toward Kincannon, who stood like a statue, dressed in a fitted pinstriped suit even in the privacy of his own home.

"Dad…" She reached out her hands and picked up one of his. "I really do believe you meant well. That you wanted me to marry a nice man and be happy. I don't blame you for trying to micromanage the situation, since that's just how you're used to dealing with things." She swallowed. "But please, in the future, let me make my own choices and live my life the way I see fit."

Kincannon nodded, his stern face clouded with emotion. "I'll do my best. It won't be easy, though." A smile lifted his wry mouth. "As you've observed, I am used to running the show."

"Well, Gavin and I are going to run our own show from now on. We'd very much like you to take a strong supporting role, but we also look forward to figuring things out on our own."

"Understood." His expression contained a mix of warmth and pride. It was obvious that he respected Bree for standing up to him.

Gavin cleared his throat. It was time for him to say his piece. "I apologize profusely for my role in the whole financial transaction. I should have refused immediately when you mentioned it. My gut instincts certainly told me to, but—like you—I saw a certain symmetry to the proposition. Perhaps we men are just too inclined to turn everything into a business deal. Anyway, I regret my role in hurting Bree's feelings, especially since I knew almost immediately that she was the woman for me—money or no money."

He looked at Bree and saw tears glisten in her eyes. His chest tightened and he fought the urge to tug her into his arms. "I'll just have to spend the rest of my life proving that to her."

"I have a feeling that you'll prove it very nicely." Elliott Kincannon crossed the room and took Gavin's hand in both of his. "Say what you will, I'm a good judge of character, and I liked you straightaway. I won't say there haven't been some moments when I changed my mind—" he arched a brow "—but I stand by my original opinion that you'll make an excellent husband for my daughter. I wish you both a happy marriage, and a long one. Longer than the brief years I shared with Bree's lovely mother. I never did meet another woman worthy of my hand."

Bree's tears finally rolled from her eyes. "Oh, Dad, I still miss Mom, too. You never speak about her."

"Still hurts too much, I'm afraid." He rubbed Bree's arm. "A love like that comes only once in a lifetime. I'm just lucky to have enjoyed it when I did." He glanced up at Gavin. "I am relying on you two to give me grandchildren, of course."

"We figured." Gavin winked at Bree. "But we're picking the names."

Kincannon let out a guffaw. "Bree told you about our family tradition?"

"I'm afraid so, and we intend to make new traditions of our own." An idea occurred to him. "Starting today. I'd like to take both of you out to dinner to celebrate a new beginning for all of us."

He looked at Bree for a response. She grinned enthusiastically. "Sounds great."

Gavin turned to her father.

"You're on." Then Kincannon lifted a brow. "But are you sure you can afford it? We Kincannons have expensive tastes."

"I don't," protested Bree. "Our favorite Thai restaurant isn't expensive at all. I bet you'd like it, too, Dad, if you were brave enough to try it."

"Perhaps it's time for me to broaden my horizons."

"Off we go, then." Gavin wrapped his arm around Bree.

She smiled and returned the gesture. He enjoyed the warm sensation of her arm tucked firmly around his middle. "And this time we're all sticking together. No secrets and no surprises."

"I promise." Gavin couldn't resist lowering his lips to hers for a stolen kiss. The delicate scent of her skin overwhelmed him as he pressed his lips to hers. He wanted to hold her in his arms forever.

The sound of Elliott Kincannon clearing his throat jerked him out of the romantic moment. "Save the mushy stuff for later, kids."

"Okay, Dad. We'll do our best. We were apart for nearly an entire week, though, so we have some catching up to do."

"I'm sure you'll manage."

"Yes, we will." Gavin seized the moment to gaze into Bree's beautiful gray-green eyes. "We have an entire lifetime to enjoy each other."

As Kincannon marched past them out the door, they heard the words "Indeed. And frankly I think I deserve a little credit."

But they were too busy kissing to reply.

Epilogue

"I'd almost suspect you of trying to keep me away from our home." Bree eyed her husband suspiciously. After nearly six months of marriage he still managed to intrigue her sometimes. They'd been walking around San Francisco all afternoon, from the Presidio clear across to Fisherman's Wharf, and he kept finding new places for them to go.

"Me? I just want to buy you a new pair of earrings. Is that a crime?" Gavin's gray eyes glittered with amusement.

"You've already bought me a new dress, a pair of shoes, some utterly wicked lingerie and silk stockings complete with lacy garters. Anyone would think you were trying to dress me up for something."

He shrugged. "I enjoy shopping sometimes. Business has been so good lately, why not enjoy the rewards?"

"I do appreciate the generosity—and I'm desperately proud of your success—but I'm kind of ready to go home." Their new house still needed a lot of work, but already it had become a sanctuary from the bustle of daily life. High on a hill, with its little garden and breathtaking view across the bay, it promised to be perfect—after a few more months of renovation drama.

"Well, if you insist." Gavin smiled mysteriously.

Bree stopped in her tracks on the pavement. "I'm actually allowed to go home?"

"Sure, why not?" His handsome face beamed with good humor. "We can go home and kick back with a glass of wine. It's Sunday tomorrow, after all."

"Phew." Bree hoisted a glossy shopping bag onto her shoulder. Gavin was carrying three others. "I was beginning to think you'd march me around the city all weekend."

"Just one thing first, though. We have to stop by my office on the way."

Brew blew out an exasperated sigh. "I knew there would be something."

"Important paper I forgot." The twinkle in his eye made her suspicious. "But don't worry, we'll get a cab."

Gavin told the cab to wait outside the small brownstone he'd found to house modest offices on the third floor. Once inside, Bree was surprised to find a bottle of champagne chilling in a silver bucket.

"Who put this here?" She touched the condensation droplets on the frosty bucket. "It's still ice-cold."

"Who cares?" Gavin uncorked the bottle and poured it into two flutes. "Let's drink it."

Bree frowned and glanced about. Everything else looked the same. Cluttered desk, piles of correspondence, big leather sofas for clients to wait on. Still, she took the offered glass and sipped. "Mmm, that's delicious."

"I agree. Just what the doctor ordered after a long day of shopping. Now get changed."

"You're very bossy all of a sudden. What's going on?"

Gavin just gave another mysterious shrug. "I'll bring your bags into the conference room so you can have some privacy." He swept up the colorful bags and carried them to the long walnut table.

"Privacy?" Bree frowned, a growing feeling of excitement—or dread—swelling inside her. "We're married."

"I know. Let me know if you need help putting on the lingerie." With a mischievous smile he closed the door behind him, leaving her alone with their purchases.

When she emerged, smoothing her new jade-green dress, a big grin lit his face. "Would have looked better with earrings, but not half-bad."

"Oh, you!" She put her hands on her hips. "What's going on? Is that cab still downstairs? If so, let's grab him before he leaves. I'm not sure I can walk more than a block in these shoes." She stuck out one of her new suede Manolos.

"Then let's go." Gavin grabbed her by the arm and pulled her down the stairs.

Despite persistent quizzing in the cab on the way home, she couldn't get a word out of him. They pulled up in front of the house. Windows dark in the dusk, it looked the same as always. No sign of anything suspicious going on. "Why am I all dressed up?"

"Why not?" Gavin paid the cab driver. "Let's go inside and relax." He marched up the front steps and she followed as fast as her heels would allow. "Huh. I forgot my key—do you have yours?"

"Sure." She frowned and reached into her purse. Gavin never forgot or lost anything. Yet more to be suspicious about. She slid the key into the lock and turned it. As she pushed the door open, a blast of light filled her eyes, and she saw their modest hallway was crammed with people.

"Surprise!"

Bree might have fallen back down the steps if Gavin hadn't been standing there to catch her. "It's our wedding reception," he whispered in her ear. "A few months overdue, but better late than never."

"Oh, Gavin." Tears welled in her eyes as she recognized the faces of her friends from high school and college, even from nursery school, and her old nanny! All the people she would have invited to her wedding—if she'd had time to let them know about it.

Her father stepped forward out of the throng and kissed her on the cheek. "You look radiant, darling."

"Thanks. It's all Gavin's fault." She wiped away a tear. Then she glanced up. "The walls, they're painted!" She and Gavin had been painting—and plastering, and sanding, and varnishing—for several weekends. He'd insisted on doing most of the work himself and wouldn't let her pay for a thing. As a result the renovations had promised to take most of the next decade. Now, suddenly, everything looked perfect.

Gavin squeezed her. "I got a crew in today. Fifteen guys. They promised to knock it all out in an afternoon, and it looks like they kept their word." He led Bree through the foyer into the high-ceilinged living room, where, sure enough, the walls gleamed with new paint, the exact soft yellow they'd talked about. "It's beautiful."

They greeted friends and talked and laughed and drank and ate a fantastic catered buffet, then danced on the newly paved terrace until the sun started to peep over the horizon.

Gavin caught her and twirled her around. His breath heated her cheek as his strong arms wrapped around her like a cocoon. "Do you forgive me for keeping you guessing all afternoon?"

"I forgive you, my love. I forgive you for everything." Laughter and tears mingled together in a soft sweet kiss that lifted them above the merry crowd into a world of their own.

* * * * *

CEO'S EXPECTANT
SECRETARY

BY
LEANNE BANKS

Leanne Banks is a *New York Times* and *USA TODAY* bestselling author who is surprised every time she realizes how many books she has written. Leanne loves chocolate, the beach and new adventures. To name a few, Leanne has ridden on an elephant, stood on an ostrich egg (no, it didn't break), gone parasailing and indoor skydiving. Leanne loves writing romance because she believes in the power and magic of love. She lives in Virginia with her family and a four-and-a-half-pound Pomeranian named Bijou. Visit her website at www. leannebanks.com.

This book is dedicated to all the fabulous authors of the KINGS OF THE BOARDROOM books and my family—Betty Minyard, Karen Minyard, Jane Poff, Tony Banks, Adam Banks, Alisa Kline, Kevin Kline, Richard Turner, Amy Turner, Mason Turner, Julia Turner, Phillip Poff, Jennifer Little, Rex Little, Asher Little and Emily Pierce.

Prologue

He couldn't sleep.

Brock Maddox looked down at the woman on the bed beside him. Her eyelids were closed, her dark lashes hiding the warm sensuality of her blue eyes. Her brown hair splayed across his pillow and her wicked, wonderful lips were swollen from the lovemaking they'd shared just an hour ago.

The soft sheet sloped over her full breasts, which she'd tried to keep hidden; the dusky rose of a nipple peeked above the white cotton. His fingertips knew the feel of everything beneath that sheet—every rib, the curve of her waist and lower still, the wet, velvet secrets that encased him, stroked him and plunged him into another world.

Elle Linton had captured his attention the first time she'd walked into his office for a job interview. Fearing she might present a distraction, he'd chosen a different woman who had subsequently decided to quit just one month later. Elle was the natural next choice.

By far the most observant assistant he'd ever had, she had quickly taken note of his every preference, from his favorite sandwich and soothing music to who was allowed to interrupt him and who wasn't. A few late nights with sandwiches had progressed to wine and gourmet delivery. A couple of innocent brushes against her body had left him hard with longing.

He'd begun to smell her perfume in his sleep. He'd noticed her gaze lingering on him and seen the wanting in her eyes—he should have resisted. He remembered the night everything had changed between them as if it were five minutes ago….

Six o'clock. He should tell Elle she could leave, he thought, opening the door to his office. She had been standing right outside. Giving a smothered sound of surprise, she dropped the files on the floor.

"Sorry," he said, bending down at the same time she did. "Didn't mean to startle you."

Her perfume rose to his nostrils and he felt that same seductive tug. The one he always pushed aside. She stumbled and he instinctively pulled her against him.

Her eyes met his and irresistible electricity crackled between them. He was achingly aware of her breasts against his chest and the sensation of her thighs on either side of his leg as he held her upright.

"Sorry," she whispered, her gaze holding his.

She wore a black pencil skirt with a back vent, her legs were bare, her feet in a pair of black heels that made it difficult to tear his gaze from her backside throughout the day. If she were another woman, he would lower his head and take her mouth. He would pull her blouse free and slide his hands over her breasts, savoring the touch of her naked skin. If she were another woman, he would pull up her skirt and make her wet with wanting him, then thrust inside her until…

"I should—" he began.

She closed her eyes. "Should. Do you ever get tired of that word?" she asked. "I do."

Her response shocked him and a frustrated chuckle escaped his throat. "Elle…"

She opened her eyes and her gaze spoke to him, making wicked invitations.

"If I were responsible and sane, I would transfer you to another position," he said.

She opened her mouth in protest. "No—"

He put his fingers over her lips. "But I—" He rubbed her lips and she flicked her tongue over his finger. He swore. "Just tell me you want this as much as I do," he said.

She tugged his tie loose and pulled open his shirt, buttons cascading to the floor. "More," she said.

Then he'd pulled her into his arms and carried her upstairs to his private apartment where they'd spent the entire night burning up the bed.

Brock stared down at her as she slept peacefully. His gut knotted at the thought of the preliminary report he'd received from his private investigator. He would meet with the P.I. tomorrow, but the brief text message indicated that Elle might be the person leaking secrets about Maddox Communications to their biggest rival, Golden Gate Promotions.

He hadn't read the text until after they'd made love. Now he was stuck with a nauseating sense of betrayal. Was it true? He would wait for the hard evidence. He would need to see it with his own eyes. Was it possible that the woman who had warmed his heart and his bed for the last several months had secretly been stabbing him in the back?

One

Brock strode down the hallway of the cushy San Francisco North Bay condominium and cynically wondered how Elle could afford such luxury. He paid her well, but not this well. No, he knew exactly how she could afford it, he thought, tightening his jaw. Elle, his assistant—his lover—had sold him out. The time had come for confrontation. Brock wasn't CEO of the top advertising agency in San Francisco for nothing.

With controlled anger, he narrowed his eyes as he knocked on her door on a sunny Saturday morning. He counted as he waited. One. Two. Three. Four. Still in shock that the sweet woman who'd become his mistress had turned out to be a cold-hearted liar, he balled his fist as he waited. Five. Six. Seven.

The door swung open and the woman who had made love to him with no holds barred stared up at him with a pale face and plum lips. Her dark brown hair was sexy-sleep disheveled and her blue eyes rounded in surprise at him.

"Brock," she said, lifting her shoulders in the ivory silk robe she wore. "I thought you wanted to keep our relationship private," she whispered. "Is there a business emergency?"

"You could say that," he said. "I've found out who is selling our secrets."

Alarm shot through her gaze and she shook her head, an expression of dread washing over her face. Her skin paled even more and she covered her mouth. "I'm sorry," she said. "I can't—" She broke off and ran away from him, leaving the door wide open.

Disconcerted, he stared after her. *What the hell?* Stepping inside the small but elegant foyer, he closed the door behind him and walked a few steps down the hallway. He heard the unmistakable sound of Elle losing her breakfast as he glanced at his watch. Despite his overriding fury, he felt a twinge of pity. She hadn't appeared sick when he'd last seen her on Friday.

Minutes later, she came out of the bathroom, still pale. She spotted him as she lifted her hand to her forehead and sighed, looking away. Brock followed her as she walked down the hallway and turned into a moderate-sized kitchen decorated in shades of rust and cream. The contrast of the cream ceramic tile against her cherry-colored toenails emphasized her femininity. He remembered the sight of her naked from head to toe, whispering his name over and over as he made her his, driving both of them into pure pleasure.

He pushed aside the memory. "How long have you

been sick?" he asked as she reached in the refrigerator for a can of ginger ale and poured it into a glass with ice.

"I'm not sick." Her hand shook as she lifted the glass and took a sip. "It's just the mornings—" She broke off and took another sip. "It's nothing really."

Something in her voice tugged at him. Something wasn't right. *Sick. Mornings.* Realization shot through him like a round from a forty-five. He sucked in a quick breath. It wasn't possible, he told himself, yet his gut told him otherwise. His gut told him what he didn't want to know. Brock had learned long ago not to ignore what that churning sensation inside him had to say. It had saved him personally and professionally too many times to count. "You're pregnant," he said.

She closed her eyes and turned away from him.

"Elle," he said, his heart hammering against his rib cage. "Don't lie to me—not this time," he added, unable to keep a touch of cynicism from his voice. "Is it mine?"

Agonizing seconds of silence passed. "Elle," he said.

"Yes," she whispered desperately. "Yes. I'm pregnant with your child."

Brock felt his heart stop in his chest. He swallowed a thousand oaths. The woman who had betrayed him carried his child. He raked his hand through his hair. He'd walked into her building ready to throw the book at her. He still wanted to. No one got the best of Brock Maddox. No one.

He ground his teeth together. He'd protected his family business—he could do no less for his child. His child deserved his name, his history, his everything. There was only one thing to do. "You must marry me."

Elle jerked her head to gape at him. "Absolutely not. You didn't want our relationship to be public. Why would you want things to be different now?"

"Because you're carrying my child. Everything is different now."

Elle took a quick little sip of ginger ale as if to calm herself, then shook her head. "This is crazy. You made it perfectly clear that our relationship was a secret fling." She met his gaze briefly and he glimpsed a stab of pain in her blue eyes before she looked away again.

"If we want to do the right thing for the baby, then we have no choice. We must get married and raise this child together," he said, his jaw clenching with tension. Five minutes ago, he'd been ready to show Elle everything he had against her. He had trusted her. She had betrayed him and his company and he'd wanted to make her pay. His fingers clutched at the envelope full of evidence.

She gnawed at her lip, still avoiding his gaze. "I can't—" She broke off and lifted her chin. "I won't marry you. The pregnancy was unexpected."

He felt a sinking in his gut. "You're not planning to have an abortion."

She met his gaze in shock. "Of course not," she said. "I'll raise this baby on my own." She slid her hand protectively over her abdomen.

"You'll just want unlimited financial support, right?" he asked, unable to check his cynicism.

She narrowed her eyes. "I can take care of this baby

on my own. I don't want anything from you. Do you hear?" she demanded. "Not a thing."

"That's ridiculous," he said. "I can provide—"

"Get out," she said in a low, firm voice.

He blinked at the resolute expression on her face. "Excuse me?"

"Get out," she repeated. "You're not welcome here."

Stunned at the strength of her response, he shook his head. He hesitated only because she looked so fragile and he didn't want to upset her more. "I'll leave," he said. "But I'll be back." He strode out of the condo, already formulating a plan. He was, after all, known as the man with a plan. Always.

Elle held her breath as she watched Brock Maddox leave. As soon as she heard the front door close, she finally exhaled. The room seemed to turn sideways and she felt the alarming sense of her knees weakening. She quickly grasped onto the counter, her hands shaking as she set down her glass.

She just needed to get to a chair, she coached herself. If she could just sit down for a moment.… On wobbly legs, she made her way to a barstool and slid onto it. She took a breath, praying for her head to stop spinning.

How had he found out? She'd been so careful when she'd become Brock's assistant and been forced to spy on him. She'd been so careful—except for that minor matter of going to bed with her boss and having a scorching affair with him. Her intentions had been honorable. She'd needed the money for her mother's cancer treatments.

Her grandfather had offered her a way to do that while accomplishing his own, less honorable goal.

When she'd first started working for Brock, she'd told herself to treat the job the same way a man would. Compartmentalize. She would do an excellent job for Maddox Communications as she ferreted secrets for her grandfather, Athos Koteas. Elle felt a bitter taste form in the back of her throat. In one way or another, she had spent her entire life at the mercy of a powerful man. Elle might not like the cards that had been dealt, but she would damn well play them to the best of her ability. She wouldn't let her mother die as a result of her pride or a misplaced sense of ethics in a business completely without ethics.

The only thing she hadn't counted on was Brock. Meeting him had made her feel as if she were in an earthquake that was rocking her to her core. She'd never intended to be attracted to him, let alone go to bed with him. And she'd never dreamed she would fall for him.

Elle heard the sound of soft footsteps in the hallway and glanced up to see her mother walk into the kitchen. Though a bit weak and frail, Suzanne seemed to be improving with the help of the experimental cancer treatments. Elle immediately plastered a smile on her face to hide how upset she was over Brock's visit. "Good morning, Mom. Can I fix you some blueberry pancakes for breakfast?" Elle was always looking for a way to keep up her mother's strength and weight.

Her mother shook her head. "Never try to kid a kidder, kiddo. I overheard the whole conversation with Brock. It's obvious that you're in love with the man. I don't want you giving up your chance for happiness because of my illness."

Elle quickly pulled her mother into a hug. "Don't be ridiculous. You and I have always taken care of each other. Besides, I always knew things wouldn't work out long-term with Brock. I just let myself get carried away," she whispered.

"But the baby," her mother said, pulling back, her eyes searching Elle's face. "What are you going to do about the baby?"

"I'm strong," Elle said. "I can take care of myself and my little one." She lifted her hand to her mother's cheek. "You should know. You helped make me strong."

Her mother sighed, her gaze filled with worry. "But, Elle, the man asked you to marry him. Do you know what I would have given for your father to ask me to marry him?"

Elle's stomach clenched. "Brock didn't ask. He issued an order, the same way he would in the office." She shook her head, knowing that everything between her and Brock had changed before he'd walked through her front door. He clearly knew she'd been giving away the company's secrets. He would never forgive her, never trust her. She refused to bring her baby into a marriage of distrust and anger.

Taking a deep breath, she patted her mom's hand. "Come on, now. You and I have more important things to focus on. Like your health, the baby and—" she forced her lips into a determined smile "—blueberry pancakes."

Brock gunned his black Porsche down the freeway. At the speed he was driving, he should have gotten a ticket.

His heart wouldn't stop hammering in his chest. He'd been so ready to slice her to shreds. If he hadn't been intimate with Elle, he would have pursued her legally. She had betrayed him.

He sucked in a sharp, shallow breath. He still couldn't believe he'd trusted her. He still couldn't believe he'd given in to his urge to take her and claim her. She'd been so passionate in his bed. Making love with her had been addictive, had taken him to a totally different level than he'd ever experienced before. He wouldn't admit that to anyone but himself. He needed to go somewhere quiet, somewhere where he could figure out his next step. He was going to be a father.

On impulse, Brock took an exit and drove toward Muir Woods. The huge, mysterious-looking Redwoods called to him. The trees were almost as old as time. What advice would they offer? Not many knew he had a spiritual side, but deep down he did. Too often he'd pushed that element of his being aside because he was the one who'd been left in charge of Maddox Communications. Regardless of the odds, regardless of his adversaries, he was the one who had to keep it alive.

Brock pulled off the road and got out of his car. The shade of the trees surrounded him with a quiet he longed to feel inside. He took a deep breath, trying to inhale the peace, but his mind was racing at a breakneck speed. Every morning since his father had died, Brock had woken up in warrior mode. Except for a few stolen mornings with Elle. Being with her had provided a secret relief from his everyday pressures. She'd known what he was going through with the company and hadn't questioned the need to keep their affair secret. She'd welcomed him with warmth and passion, and she'd been the only person in his life who hadn't made demands on him. Now he knew why, he thought, bitterness burning through him like acid.

Until now, Brock's priority had been the company's success. Now his world had shifted. Soon enough, he would need to protect a child. In the meantime, he would protect his child's mother, Elle—the woman who had betrayed him and his company.

Brock knew, however, who was behind this. Athos Koteas. His lip curled in distaste. The man would stop at nothing to bring down Maddox Communications. And he had gone too far this time. Athos, the owner of Golden Gate Productions, Maddox Communications' biggest rival, was known as pure poison and would play dirty to get his way.

The peaceful solitude around Brock did nothing to calm his anger, which was only escalating. The time had come for him to confront Athos in person.

Returning to his Porsche, he started the engine and drove to the Koteas house, determined to bring the battle between Golden Gate and Maddox into the open. Ironically, Athos lived in Nob Hill, not far from Brock's own family home. Brock pulled in front of the large Edwardian mansion with lush cascades of bougainvillea, but the beauty was lost on him.

Climbing the steps to the front door, he stabbed the door chime. A moment later, a woman dressed in a black suit answered the door. "Hello. May I help you?"

"I'm here to see Mr. Koteas," Brock said.

"Is he expecting you?"

"He'll see me," Brock said. "My name is Brock Maddox."

The woman looked him over, then guided him to a formal sitting area. But Brock wasn't at all inclined to sit. His anger still burning inside him, he paced the carpet. He heard footsteps and glanced around to see Athos walking toward him. The short, stocky man still had a full head of silver-and-white hair, and a sharp glint in his gaze.

"Good morning, Brock," Athos said, lifting a dark eyebrow. "An unexpected pleasure."

Brock clenched one of his hands into a fist and released it. "Perhaps not. I know you've been trying to destroy Maddox Communications. I recognize that you have very little honor, but I never dreamed you would use your own granddaughter to do your dirty work."

Athos acted confused yet his face tightened. "Granddaughter? What granddaughter?"

"You can forget the pretense," Brock said. "Elle Linton is your granddaughter. But you wouldn't want to make that public, would you? She's illegitimate because your son abandoned her mother."

"It's not unusual for children to disappoint their parents," he said, shrugging. "Elle shows promise. She's intelligent."

"Crafty, like you," Brock said, the knot in his gut pulling tighter. "You don't mind getting anyone dirty as long as you get your way."

"I didn't become a success by avoiding a fight," Athos said, lifting his chin and narrowing his eyes. "You're a successful man, too. You and I are more alike than you think."

Brock felt his blood pressure go through the roof. He clenched his fist again, willing himself not to knock Athos off his almighty perch of pride. "I don't think so. I wouldn't force my grandchild to wallow in the mud for me."

"I didn't force—"

"And her pregnancy, was that part of your plan, too?" Brock goaded the man.

Athos's hard veneer slipped. "Pregnancy?" he said. "What are you talking about?"

"Elle," Brock said. "She's pregnant with my child."

Athos turned pale as he shook his head. "No, she wasn't supposed to—" He continued to shake his head, his skin color changing from white to gray as he began to fall.

Brock watched in disbelief, rushing toward the man, catching him as he collapsed. Stunned at the limp body of his adversary, he shook his head. "Call an ambulance!" he yelled. "Mr. Koteas is ill."

Elle rushed through the doors of the emergency room, her heart in her throat. The only other time she could remember being this upset was when she'd learned her mother had cancer. Although Athos had never been affectionate toward her, Elle still felt a debt to him for his financial support of her mother and her.

Brock stepped in front of her as she headed straight for the information desk and she faltered. Her breath hitched at the sight of him, so tall, so strong. Then she remembered what Athos's housekeeper had told her. Brock had been with her grandfather when he'd collapsed.

Brock reached for her and she shrank from him. "You," she said, every cell in her body accusing him. "You're the one who caused this. You caused my grandfather to have a heart attack."

Brock shook his head. "I never would have dreamed he was so fragile." He gently took her arm. "I won't let you handle this alone. I don't want you upset."

"Not upset?" she retorted, pulling her arm away from him. "How could I not be? Do you realize what you've done? I'll never forgive you for this. Never," she said, pushing away from him.

Her stomach in knots, she approached the information desk. "Athos Koteas," she said over the terrible lump in her throat. "Is he—" She broke off, unable to form the words. "How is he?" she whispered.

The nurse gave her a look of sympathy. "Your name?" she asked.

"Elle. Elle Linton," she said, holding her breath.

"Come this way. Mr. Koteas has been asking for you."

Her heart filled with dread, she followed the nurse to the last room on the hallway. Elle looked inside and saw her grandfather hooked up to monitors and tubes. He'd always seemed so strong, so much larger than life when she was a child.

The nurse nodded. "You can go in."

Elle tentatively stepped into the room, moving closer to the bed. Her grandfather's face was pale with strain, his usually neat hair mussed, his eyes closed. The green gown emphasized his ashen complexion. "Athos," she said, because she'd been instructed long ago not to call him grandfather. For a long time, she and her mother had only served to remind Athos of his disappointment in his son.

Her grandfather opened his eyes. "Elle," he said, lifting his hand.

She immediately wrapped both her hands around his. "I'm so sorry about Brock," she said, unable to hide her desperation. "When he called to tell me you were in the hospital, I was horrified that he would go to your house and accuse you." She shook her head. "It's his fault that you had a heart—"

"No, no," Athos said, shaking his head. His eyes were weary. "Brock Maddox is not responsible for my heart problems."

"I don't believe that," she insisted. "If he hadn't shown up at your house—"

Athos gave her hands a feeble squeeze and shrugged. "It would have happened sometime," he said. "It has happened before," he told her, meeting her gaze. "It will happen again."

Confusion and fear trickled through her, the combination burning like acid. "What do you mean? What are you talking about? You've always been strong and healthy."

Athos sighed. "My doctor has told me I don't have much time. I may have been able to fool people that I'm strong, but my heart is very weak."

"Well, surely there's something that can be done. You should get a second opinion."

"Elle," he said in a chiding tone. "I've received only the best care. There's nothing that can be done. The reason I asked you to spy on Maddox is because I wanted to make Golden Gate Promotions solid before…"

Elle's throat clenched and she shook her head. "You're not going to die," she said. "You just need to get your strength back."

Athos's mouth lifted in a sad smile. "I've faced this. You must face it, too," he said as he took a deep breath and closed his eyes. "I'm sorry for getting you involved in my scheme. Brock was right. I shouldn't have asked you to take care of my dirty work."

"Excuse me," the nurse said from behind her. "We'll be moving Mr. Koteas to the Cardiac Care Unit. We need you to return to the waiting room."

Elle quickly kissed her grandfather's cheek and walked to the waiting room. Brock was standing across the room. She was surprised he was still there. A rush of contradictory feelings surged through her. He had become so many things to her—boss, lover, enemy. Father of her child.

Her mind raced back to what her grandfather had told her. He was going to die soon, and her mother's future was uncertain. Was she going to lose the two most important people in her life? Sheer panic squeezed the breath from her lungs. She tried to force herself to breathe, but she couldn't. Her head suddenly felt light and Brock's image swam before her eyes.

"Elle," he said, moving toward her, his face tight with concern. "Elle," he said again and everything went black.

Two

Alarm slammed through Brock as he caught Elle. "Elle," he said, and swore under his breath.

Her eyelids fluttered and she moved her head as if she were trying to shake off her weakness. "Brock," she murmured and shook her head.

"I'm taking you home with me," he said firmly.

"No," she said, shaking her head again. "I shouldn't. I—"

"I won't take no for an answer. You've been hit with too much today. You need to rest without interruption. My home is the best place for that."

Elle sighed and bit her lip, her eyes darkening with flashes of different emotions. "Okay," she said, reluctance in her voice.

Brock tucked Elle into his car and drove to his family home in Nob Hill. He ushered her up the steps to the home of his youth. He spent most of his time in the apartment he'd built at Maddox Communications, but that didn't seem like the right place for Elle, especially in her fragile state.

"You never brought me here before," she said. "It's beautiful."

"I wanted things to stay private with you."

She stopped. "And now?"

He lifted his hand to push a strand of hair from her face. "Now it's different."

"Because of the baby," she said.

"More responsibility is required when a child is involved," he told her. "We can talk more later. Come on in. You need to rest."

He pushed open the door and Anna, his head house-keeper, quickly rushed to the foyer. "Mr. Maddox. How can I help you?"

"Anna, this is Elle Linton. She's had a difficult day. I'd like her to have a chance to rest," he said.

"The blue bedroom?" she suggested. "It's on this floor."

He nodded. "Perfect. Is Mrs. Maddox here today?"

Anna shook her head. "No, sir. I believe your mother is in Paris at the moment."

Thank God, he thought. He wished she would stay there, although he knew she wouldn't. He'd learned long ago that his mother was a heartless woman who'd married his father for money and given him two sons because it was expected of her. Since his father had died, she'd tried to find ways to extract money from Brock and his brother Flynn.

He guided Elle toward the blue bedroom at the back

of the house. "I think you'll be comfortable here," he said as Anna drew the shades and pulled down the covers.

"You know I can't stay," she said, sinking onto the bed. "I'm only here because it's been such a difficult, crazy day."

"I know," he said, but his intentions were entirely different. "Anna, can you please get Miss Linton some water? Perhaps juice," he added.

Elle shook her head. "Water will be just fine." She closed her eyes and took a deep breath, then opened them again as if she were fighting her weariness.

"Kick off your shoes and rest," he said after Anna left. "It will be best for you and the baby."

She took off her shoes and lay down on the mattress. "This is just for a little while," she warned him, her eyelids growing heavier with each second.

"Put your feet under the covers," he told her. "Your water will be on the nightstand. You need to rest, Elle. Close your eyes."

Closing her eyes, she sighed. "Just for a little while," she said.

He watched her and within seconds, her breathing slid into a regular rhythm. Unable to force his gaze from her, he stared. The sight of her in his home did something crazy to his insides. He'd thought his heart was dead after his fiancée left him. He'd planned to keep things low-key with Elle. Knowing she was expecting his child, though, changed everything, even his resentment toward her because she'd betrayed him.

He needed to move quickly. Brock had never been more certain of the right thing to do in his life. Taking in the sight of her lovely face, her parted lips inhaling even, measured breaths, he felt his resolve solidify.

Forcing himself to look away from her, he left the room and called his publicist.

Hours later, Elle awakened to a semidark room. The bed and furnishings were unfamiliar. Uncertainty rushed through her as she rose to her elbows, trying to shake off her grogginess. Then she saw Brock seated across the room with an electronic book reader in his hands.

He glanced up at her. "Okay?"

Everything came back to her—the terrible scene in the kitchen with Brock, her grandfather's heart attack. Panic raced through her. She threw off the covers and swung her feet to the floor. "I need to check on my mother and grandfather."

Brock was beside her in seconds, putting his hands gently on her shoulders as if to steady her. "Already done. Your mother is making an early night of it. She said you should do the same. You've been too stressed lately. Athos is resting comfortably in the CCU. If he continues to improve, he'll be moved to a regular room on the cardiac floor tomorrow."

Despite all the tension between her and Brock, she couldn't deny her relief at his touch and the reassurance of his confident voice. "You're sure?" she asked. "You're sure they're okay."

"I'm sure," he said, then glanced at the clock. "It's late, but you're probably hungry."

Elle gasped when she saw the time. "Oh, my goodness, it's nine-thirty. I can't believe I slept that long. I need to get home."

"Not tonight," he said firmly.

"What do you mean?"

"I mean I agree with your mother. You've been too stressed lately. You need to rest. This is the best place for you to relax."

"Oh, this is insane. I'm fine."

"Uh-huh. That's why you fainted in the E.R.," he said, his gaze holding hers in silent challenge.

It was hard to argue his point, she thought, sighing. Just as it had been hard for her to fight her attraction to him from the day she'd met him.

"Come on, let's get you something to eat," he said, pushing aside a stray strand of her hair. "An empty stomach is an invitation to faint again."

Her pulse raced at his fleeting touch, making her feel lightheaded. Heaven help her, she couldn't pass out again. "Maybe some toast," she conceded.

"That's all? You can have anything you want. Steak, chicken," he said, guiding her toward the door.

The thought of a heavy meal made her feel queasy. "Just toast, please. I can fix it myself."

"No," he said. "Anna's been waiting to fix something for you since you walked in the door. She said you looked terribly pale."

"There's no need to fuss," she said as she walked down the hallway beside him. She'd been too upset to notice much about Brock's house. Now that she was more composed, she took in the décor. Beautiful antiques stood on top of luxurious rugs. Heavy draperies lined the windows. Brass framed mirrors reflected over-the-top chandeliers.

"This is amazing. It must be like living in a palace," she said. "The antiques are—"

"—my mother's," he said with an edge of weariness in his voice. "As you know, I don't stay here very often. I feel more at ease in the apartment at the office."

"Oh," she said. "It's beautiful, but I can see why it might be hard to relax here. I'd be afraid I'd bump into something and break a million-dollar lamp."

He chuckled. "That would be one way to clear out some of this junk. Anna," he said as the housekeeper approached them. "Miss Linton says she would like toast."

Anna nodded, trying to hide her disapproval. "With beef tips, or turkey and mashed potatoes? Or perhaps crab?"

Elle shook her head. "Just butter and maybe jelly on the side."

Anna sighed. "If you're certain, Miss Linton. Would you like some wine?"

"Orange juice with ice and water," Elle said.

Anna nodded again. "I'll have it for you in the dining room in just a couple moments."

After Anna left, Elle turned to Brock. "I'm not really going to eat toast in a formal dining room, am I?"

He chuckled. "There's a breakfast table in the sun-room."

"Sounds wonderful," she said and followed him into a sunroom with a skylight that revealed the stars of the San Francisco night sky. Blinds were at perfect half-mast to showcase a courtyard with trees draped in white lights. She sank onto an overstuffed chair next to a glass table with a fresh flower arrangement. She looked around the room and breathed a sigh of relief. "I like this room."

"My father did, too," Brock said, sitting beside her. "He liked this room best. Got up before sunrise and read two newspapers here before going into work every day. Carol wanted to redecorate, but I refused. She has changed several rooms in the house, but not this one."

"Why do you call your mother Carol?" she asked.

"That's her name," he said.

"Still, most men call the woman who gave birth to them 'Mother' or 'Mom.'"

His gaze grew shuttered. "She's always been more Carol than Mother. Breeding was compulsory."

Elle gasped. "That's a terrible thing to say."

He glanced toward the entry. "Here comes your toast. Thanks, Anna."

Elle also thanked Anna and began to nibble the hot buttered bread. Anna had brought several different kinds. Any other time, she would have chosen wheat. Today she went straight for the sourdough. South Beach diet be damned. All she'd wanted since getting pregnant were carbs, carbs and more carbs. Thank goodness for prenatal vitamins.

Feeling Brock's gaze on her, she took a sip of orange juice. Something about him made her nervous in an exciting, forbidden way. Still. Even after that terrible scene this morning. She glanced away, frowning to herself.

"Jelly?" he asked.

She shook her head and took another bite of toast. "This is perfect."

His mouth lifted in a half-grin. Just as quickly, his smile fell. "How long have you known you were pregnant?"

Her throat closed around the bite of toast and she coughed, trying to swallow. She took another sip of juice. "Well, I haven't been regular lately."

"You didn't answer my question," he said.

She gnawed on her upper lip with her bottom teeth. "I suspected about six weeks ago."

His eyebrows shot up. "Six weeks?"

"I've been nauseous since then. At first, I thought it might be an intestinal virus." She shrugged. "Or stress. I avoided taking a home pregnancy test, but I made sure I was taking good vitamins. I was in denial," she confessed. She just couldn't believe she'd gotten pregnant by Brock, and she sure as heck had no clue what to do once her pregnancy was verified.

"So, how far along?" he asked.

"Three and a half months," she said. "I saw the doctor two weeks ago. He said the nausea should pass soon. I'm still waiting," she said, rolling her eyes.

"Why didn't you tell me?"

"I couldn't figure out how. I kept rehearsing all these different ways and none of them seemed right." Her stomach clenched and she dropped her piece of toast onto her plate. "I've had enough."

"You've hardly eaten anything," he said.

She shook her head. "I'm not hungry."

"But what about your health? What about the baby?" he demanded.

"I'm doing the best I can, and I'm taking prenatal vitamins. I have to believe that babies born with less food than I'm consuming have turned out fine, so I hope mine will, too." She pushed the plate away and stood. "I should go home."

Brock got to his feet, looming over her. "No. Stay here tonight."

She shook her head, but he gently put his hands on either side of her face and pushed her hair behind her ears. "You need rest. When you wake up in the morning, you'll feel better. Trust me."

Elle looked into his eyes and felt her heart twist and tug with opposing feelings. She trusted him, but at the same time, she didn't. She'd spent the last several months watching this man eat his competitors alive during the day and making her melt in his arms at night. He was passionate about the company. She'd never believed he could be equally passionate about her, yet when they'd been together, both of them had seemed to combust every time. She'd tried to tell herself it was just physical, but she'd known she was lying. She was falling for Brock. She *had* fallen for Brock.

Even though she'd slept for over five hours, she still felt exhausted. She couldn't fight her weariness and Brock at the same time. "Okay, but I'm leaving in the morning."

His gaze flickered with something indiscernible and she wished she could read him. She knew he could be a dangerous man.

"You're wise to give yourself a break, Elle. Let me walk you back to your room."

With his hand at her waist, she couldn't help breathing

a sigh of relief. It was temporary, the same way their relationship had been. Still, he'd been a respite for her as she had been for him. It was a shame the whole thing had blown up in their faces, but she'd always known there'd never been any other possible ending for their relationship.

Brock opened the door to the blue bedroom. "Anna refilled your water. Call if you need anything. Sweet sleep," he said and brushed his lips over her forehead.

Elle awakened the following morning when a sliver of the sun peeked through the curtains in the room. She savored the perfect cushiony firmness of the mattress and the cuddly cotton sheets. Even the pillow offered her head the perfect elevation. She sighed in contentment, inhaling the faintest whiff of eucalyptus and lavender.

Easing into consciousness, she thought about her mother. She should check on her. Three seconds passed and she thought of her grandfather. Frowning, she opened her eyes and realization hit her. She needed to check on him, too.

Sitting up, she remembered she was in Brock's Nob Hill home, and she definitely should be leaving. Sliding from the bed, she felt the padded carpet beneath her feet and rushed to the bathroom to shower and get on her way. By the end of bathing, though, she was fighting nausea.

Crap.

Taking deep, even breaths, she pulled on her clothes and walked down the hallway. She followed the sound of voices and found two people talking in the kitchen. "Good morning," she said.

Anna and a man she hadn't met yet turned to look at her. "Miss Linton?" Anna said. "May I get you some breakfast? Eggs, potatoes, bacon?"

Elle felt another roll of nausea. "Herbal tea and toast, please. Can you tell me where Mr. Maddox is?"

The woman smiled. "The sunroom. He likes to read the paper there in the morning when he's here," she said. "Would you like me to bring your toast and tea into the sunroom?"

"Yes, thank you very much," she replied.

As Anna had said, Brock sat in a chair in the sunroom, reading a newspaper. She felt a sudden attack of shyness. She'd stayed over at Brock's apartment at the company several times, but he'd never brought her here. Seeing him in the home he'd grown up in pointed out the differences between them. He was wealthy—and legitimate. She wasn't.

Silly, she told herself. She just needed to go home. "Brock," she said.

He immediately turned around and looked at her with those blazing blue eyes. "Good morning. Did you rest well?"

"Yes," she said. "I should go back home."

"How's your stomach feeling?" he asked.

"It's felt worse," she hedged.

"How's the morning sickness?"

She swallowed. "I'll be okay."

"Why don't you sit down and stop pushing yourself?"

"I have things to do," she said.

He pulled a sheet of paper from the table and handed it to her. "Here. Maybe this will help you take a break."

She glanced at the press release. It announced the engagement and subsequent wedding of Elle Linton and Brock Maddox.

Elle sank into a chair. "You haven't sent this out, have you?"

"It went out last night," he said.

She sucked in a deep breath and fought light-headedness. "Why?"

His gaze met hers. "You know it's the right thing. Do you really want to raise an illegitimate child? Doesn't your child deserve more?"

She closed her eyes, inhaling deeply, her heart torn. "We're not marrying for the right reasons."

"What could be a better reason than our child?" He frowned. "You look pale. Do you need water?"

She shook her head. "I feel sick," she said and raced for the bathroom by her room.

After her stomach calmed down, Elle wiped her face with a cool washcloth and brushed her teeth. Then she sank into a chair in the blue bedroom where she'd slept last night. She was trying to calm down but her mind was racing. *Marriage to Brock Maddox?* She shook her head at the possibility. At the same time she wondered how she could get out of it now that he'd released the news to the press. What choice did she have?

Hearing a tap at the door, she felt her heart race.

"Elle," Brock said. "Are you okay?"

Not really, she thought, but rose from the bed and opened the door. He looked down at her in concern. "If you're getting sick this often, you should see a doctor," he said.

"Well, you have to admit it's been a rough twenty-four

hours for me." She gazed at him, hard. "Why did you go ahead and announce our marriage when I'd already told you no?"

"Because I'm thinking of our child. Our child deserves the best I can give him or her, and I believe a real man doesn't shirk his responsibilities."

Like her father had. Elle had to admit she had never wanted the cloak of shame for her child that she had worn for most of her life. How many times had she been asked about her father and been forced to reply that she didn't have one? "This is too fast."

Brock's jaw tightened. "It can't happen fast enough, as far as I'm concerned," he said. "When news of your pregnancy hits, I want you wearing a wedding band and living in my home."

She frowned, feeling her stomach turn. "Is this all about image?"

"No," Brock said. "It's about doing the right thing for everyone concerned. I want you and our baby protected." He sighed. "You're right. This is fast, but it's necessary. If you were dreaming of a big church wedding, that's going to be difficult to pull off."

"I never pictured a big, fussy wedding for myself. Whenever I thought about it—and it wasn't often—I always thought a small beach wedding would be beautiful," she said. "But that wouldn't work now, so—"

"Yes, it can," he said, meeting her gaze. "I can make that happen. Would you like a new dress, and flowers?"

"No, it's not necessary," she demurred, looking away, feeling confused by his consideration.

"Let's schedule this for a week from now. Ask

someone you trust to go dress shopping with you, and choose some flowers. You can put it on my card."

"No, I—"

"I insist," he said, taking her hand.

Compelled by his tone, she met his gaze again.

"We're making a big commitment, Elle. It may not be what we'd planned, but it's going to work out. There's no reason for you to be miserable during the process."

But what about him? she wondered. He may be pushing forward on marrying her, but what were his real feelings? Especially since he knew she'd betrayed him for her grandfather. He still didn't know about her mother's treatments, and she found herself reluctant to tell him. Would he think it was just an excuse? Would he think she had tried to extract information from him in bed when in truth, falling for Brock and going to bed with him had *never* been part of the plan?

"How can we possibly make this work? With my family background and yours?" she asked.

"You and I will make it work," he said. "We have good motivation."

"But what about how I leaked company secrets?" she asked.

"That's in the past," he said firmly, his jaw locked. "We need to take care of the present and look toward the future."

Elle heard his words but his hard expression made her wonder if he would ever be able to truly forgive her.

Exiting the elevator in the Powell Street office of Maddox Communications on Monday, Brock felt a sense of responsibility hit him, as it often did. It was hard to believe, but even the seven-story Beaux Arts building built in 1910 would have been demolished by the wrecking ball if not for his father's determination to restore it. These days, the reception area looked totally different than it had during James's heyday. Continuing his father's tradition of embracing modern technology, Brock had arranged for two seventy-inch plasma screens to sit on either side of the reception desk, showing videos and commercials produced by Maddox Communications.

Nodding to the receptionist, Brock walked down the hallway, noting Elle's empty desk outside his office. He hadn't needed to fire her or ask her to resign. She'd known she wouldn't be welcome in the office any longer. He felt a twinge of longing followed quickly by a blast of impatience with himself. From the first day she'd begun working for him, Elle had inspired a strange combination of emotions inside him.

If he'd been smarter, perhaps he wouldn't have allowed himself to get involved with her so easily. But she was smart and warm, and her sultry blue eyes had distracted him after his fiancée had left him wondering if he should even try to get involved in a serious relationship with a woman. When they'd given in to their impulses, she hadn't asked him for more. That had only made him ravenous for her.

His need could have brought down the agency his father had worked so hard to build. How could Elle have tricked him like that? How could she have lied with her kisses and passion?

He thought of her grandfather and wondered if he would have done the same for his father if he'd been asked. Brock already knew the answer. He would have done anything his father asked because he'd provided Brock with unswerving love and loyalty.

Pushing aside his mixed emotions, he walked into the office that had belonged to James Maddox. Brock had changed it very little since his father's death. Somehow, keeping the same furniture made him feel as if his father were still nearby. The founder of Maddox Communications, however, would be turning in his grave if he knew Brock had gotten sexually involved with his assistant, let alone the granddaughter of Athos Koteas.

He called the human resources director to send up a temporary assistant. Someone trustworthy, he emphasized, feeling a surge of bitterness and tamping it down. Stabbing his fingers through his hair, he took some time to prioritize the work on his desk. Brock was still babying the deal with The Prentice Group. Marrying Elle would dispel any objections the conservative client would have about Brock's involvement with a coworker.

He swore under his breath. This week had been a nightmare. Finding out that Elle had betrayed him had been bad enough, but learning of her pregnancy had totally turned his head around. Even though he wasn't sure he could ever trust her again, seeing her in his house had done something to him. Having her there had made the house feel more like a home to him.

Brock had lost his fiancée because he'd ignored his personal life in order to focus on the company. Although he wasn't in love with Elle, he did have feelings for her.

Add that to the fact that she was carrying his child, and he was determined to make their relationship legal.

His BlackBerry rang and he checked the incoming number. His brother, Flynn. He'd probably gotten wind of the press release. Brock picked up. "Brock here."

"I suppose congratulations are in order," Flynn said. "This is sudden."

Brock felt a twist of discomfort. Since Flynn had gotten married and stepped down as VP at the firm, Brock had found himself wanting more camaraderie with his brother. "You know me. When I make a decision, I move fast."

"I'll say. Are you headed to the courthouse tomorrow?"

"We're getting married next week," Brock said. "It'll be a beach ceremony. I'd like you to come."

Silence followed. "Thanks. I'm honored."

"I'll give you the details later. How is Renee?" Brock asked, referring to Flynn's wife.

"Happily bearing my child," Flynn said. Brock could hear the contentment in his brother's voice—for once, he felt a sliver of envy. He couldn't honestly say that Elle was happy to be pregnant with his child.

"She's excited about attending the shower for Jason and Lauren Reagert's baby this weekend."

Brock nodded. It seemed pregnancy was in the water at his firm lately. Jason was a huge new talent at Maddox, and when he'd married his wife, Lauren, he'd done so to avoid a scandal. It hadn't taken long for Jason and Lauren to fall in love. Brock didn't expect the same for himself, but he was determined to make his marriage to Elle successful, at least.

"I'm glad things worked out for them," Brock said.

"Any chance your marriage will make you leave the office on time once in a while?"

Brock gave a cynical laugh. "On time? There's no such thing as a regular quitting time in my life until I'm sure Golden Gate can't do any more damage to Maddox." Even now, he wasn't sure exactly how much Elle had told Koteas, and he refused to grill her in her current state.

"Okay, bro, just don't forget to live your life. See you next week," Flynn said.

"Next week. Bye." Brock disconnected the call. He glanced out the window of his office at the shoppers and trolley cars in constant movement. He remembered the words his father once said when he'd been daydreaming instead of completing a school assignment: *The world won't stop just because you've got problems.*

So true, he thought, pulling himself out of his distracted state. He picked up the phone to call a jeweler.

Three

Elle spent the day visiting her mother at home and her grandfather at the hospital. When she'd broken the news to her mother that she was going to marry Brock after all, her mother had been ecstatic. Elle still couldn't believe it. The very thought of it locked up her brain, so she'd put off shopping for a dress or anything else. When Brock had called to invite her to dinner at his house, her mother had insisted she join him.

A chauffer picked her up at the condo and took her to Brock's at six o'clock, but he wasn't home yet. She wasn't surprised. She'd worked for him long enough to know his first, second and third loves were Maddox Communications. He was the most dynamic, complex man she'd ever met and despite every reason she'd had to not get involved with him, she couldn't stop herself.

At the time that she'd fallen for Brock, she'd just been glad to get a piece of him.

Now, everything was a mess.

She sat in the den, which was far too fussy for her taste, and sipped a glass of orange juice and sparkling water. Tired from the day, she sighed, slipped off her shoes and closed her eyes. It seemed like seconds passed and then Brock was standing in front of her.

He studied her with a cryptic grin hovering on his lips. "I should have known you were pregnant when I had to wake you up to go home after we made love all those nights."

Feeling her cheeks heat at memories of their intimacy, she straightened and pushed her feet into her shoes. "I have to be honest. For a while there, I was worried that something more serious might have been wrong with me."

"But you've been thoroughly checked out?"

She nodded. "The doctor told me it's not unusual to have a lack of energy. Supposedly that changes sometime during the second trimester."

"Good," he said and extended his hand. "Let's have dinner. Then I have a surprise for you."

"A surprise?" she echoed, feeling a secret rush of pleasure followed quickly by caution. "Is this a good surprise or a bad surprise?" she asked as he led her into the sunroom.

"I think most women would call it a good surprise," he said. "Don't ask any more questions. You'll know soon enough."

During dinner, he only made vague references to his work. Elle felt a stab of loss over his previous openness with her. She'd never realized how much she appreciated the way he'd shared his thoughts and concerns about the company. Of course, she couldn't blame him for being guarded since he'd learned she'd been spying on him. Still, the loss tugged at her. They would never be the same again. He changed the subject and asked her about her activities.

"You visited both your mother and your grandfather? I told you to rest."

"If I'd rested any longer, I would have screamed," she told him. "Can you tell me you would be happy to lie in bed all day long?"

A flicker of heat shot through his gaze. "Under the right circumstances," he said.

She felt a surprising sliver of arousal but shook it off. Even during their affair, they'd rarely stayed in bed more than an hour or two. "I would like to see those circumstances," she said.

The housekeeper poked her head inside the room. "Mr. Walthall is here, Mr. Maddox. He's waiting in the front living room when you're ready."

"Ah, the surprise," he said and glanced at her plate. "Are you sure you've had enough to eat?"

"Plenty," she said. "I was told to try to stick with small, frequent meals."

"Then we'll make sure that's what you get. I'll tell Anna." He stood. "Ready?"

"Brock, it's not your housekeeper's job to make sure I'm eating properly."

"She'll love it. My mother is on the twig-and-berry diet, so Anna will be thrilled at the prospect of fattening you up."

She shot him a dark look. "I don't plan to get fat. I just plan to be healthy."

He shrugged. "That's what I said."

Not really, she thought, but didn't say so as they turned the corner into the formal living room where a man sat with several large cases. He stood and extended his hand. "Mr. Maddox. Phillip Walthall. I'm happy we can be of service to you. And this is?" he asked, looking at Elle.

"This is my fiancée, Elle Linton," Brock said. "Elle, Mr. Walthall is a jeweler. He's going to show you some selections so you can choose something you'd like."

"An engagement ring," she said, unable to keep the dismay from her voice. She was still trying to pretend this wasn't going to happen. How in the world would she be able to avoid it if she were wearing a ring all the time? "I don't need one."

"Of course you do."

Mr. Walthall laughed. "Give me a chance to change your mind."

Brock urged her to sit while the jeweler pulled out a tray of diamonds that made her blink. Although she and her mother had lived in a nice place, they'd been careful with their money. Her mother had always worked and Elle had attended a state college. She'd never envisioned wearing a ring that looked like it cost more than her tuition had. "These are all so big," she said.

Mr. Walthall chuckled again. "That's not a complaint, is it?"

"I'm just overwhelmed," she said.

"What I like to ask my clients is, what is your dream engagement ring? All these years, you must have secretly dreamed about the ring you might receive from the man you chose to marry," Mr. Walthall said.

Elle closed her eyes and took a deep breath. Had she ever dreamed about an engagement ring? More often, she'd dreamed of having a father. Then, she'd dreamed of finding a man who would love her as much as she loved him. She'd known Brock would never love her like that, but she hadn't been able to resist him. If she was going to have a ring, why not make it meaningful, at least to her? "What is December's birthstone?"

Mr. Walthall lifted his shoulders. "It depends. Blue topaz, tanzanite or ruby, depending on your point of view."

"Why do you ask?" Brock asked.

"The baby is due in December," she said.

She saw sadness and something else she couldn't quite read in his eyes. "My father's birthday is in December."

Elle felt a riveting connection with Brock ripple through her. How amazing that their child would be born in the same month as Brock's father. "I'd like to see some options that would include blue topaz, tanzanite or ruby."

"Very nice. I always like it when a couple makes a choice that has personal meaning," Mr. Walthall said.

Within a matter of minutes, she had chosen a series of beautiful tanzanite stones to accent a solitaire diamond. "A half-carat diamond," she suggested.

Mr. Walthall's face fell. "A half?"

"Eight carats," Brock corrected.

Elle felt her eyes nearly bug out of her face. "I'll need a crane," she protested.

"You may not realize this, but your ring is not just a reflection of your taste. It's a reflection of me, too," Brock said.

She bit her lip, thinking he was spending an obscene amount of money. "You could feed a third-world country with this," she wailed.

"If it will make it easier for you, I'll send out a donation matching the cost of the ring tomorrow," Brock said wryly.

"Can we knock it down to three?" she asked.

"Five. That's final," he said.

Elle looked at the jeweler, who appeared totally bemused by their negotiations. "I guess it's five."

Mr. Walthall nodded. "It will be a beautiful ring."

"When can you have it?" Brock asked.

"When would you like it?" Mr. Walthall replied.

"Tomorrow," he said.

"As you wish, sir." Mr. Walthall put the trays into his suitcase and clicked them closed. "It's a pleasure to do business with you. If you change your mind and wish to increase the size of the diamond tomorrow morning, just give me a call and we can make the adjustment."

The jeweler left and silence fell over Brock and Elle like a blanket.

Brock cleared his throat. "I didn't realize the baby would be born the same month as my father's birthday."

She looked up at him. "Does it bother you?"

He paused a long moment and his gaze softened. "No. It sounds crazy, but I think it will be a comfort."

She stared at him in surprise. He was a strong man who never asked for comfort, who never seemed to need comfort. Unable to keep herself from reaching out to him, she lifted her hand.

He drew back. "I want you to stay here tonight," he said.

"Why?" she demanded, hurt by his rejection of her gesture. "There's no reason I can't stay with my mother until—" She stopped. "Until we're married."

His face turned to stone. "You're still doing too much. I can be sure you'll be taken care of if you're here."

Elle sighed. She considered arguing, but the truth was she was tired. It wasn't as if she would be sharing Brock's bed. The thought made her stomach clench and her skin burn. What would happen when they made love again? Would it be like before? Was it possible that they could share the passion they once had?

She forced herself to focus on the baby. "I do need the rest," she said. "But I want to stay at my mother's tomorrow night."

"I'll send a driver and mover to pack your things and bring them here," he said and looked at her with a possessive gaze. "Plan to stay here tomorrow night. The ring will be ready, and I'll want to put it on your finger."

By Saturday, Elle still wasn't accustomed to the weight of the engagement ring on her finger. She was thankful for the distraction of the baby shower for Jason and Lauren. One of Lauren's neighbors in Mission Hill was holding the party at her house. Brock had insisted that his chauffeur take her there. He didn't want her driving, which she thought was ridiculous.

She carried her gift for Jason and Lauren's baby boy

into the house. Blue balloons and decorations filled the foyer and the large living room had been made ready for the baby shower.

Lauren, with a big baby bump, glanced up as Elle walked into the room. "Elle," she said, rising to her feet. "I'm so glad you could come. Look at that gorgeous gift. Tell me what's in it," she said, beaming with pregnant radiance.

Elle couldn't help smiling. "You'll have to open it," she said.

Lauren made a face. "You can't give me a hint?"

"It's blue," Elle said.

Lauren laughed. "Come here and have some wine," she said. "I can't drink it but the rest of you can. I want to toast your engagement." She put her arm around Elle and guided her to a table. "How did you keep it so quiet?"

Elle bit her lip. "It just kind of happened. I don't think either of us expected it. Hey, that punch looks delicious."

"That's for me," Lauren said, "since I'm on no booze. But you can have some." Lauren poured a ladle full in one punch cup and then another. She lifted hers in a toast. "Wishing you the happiest, most wonderful marriage ever."

Elle felt her throat knot with emotion. *How could this marriage possibly be the happiest ever?* "Thank you," she said and took the teensiest sip possible. The last thing she wanted to do was get sick at the shower.

"Give me the scoop," Lauren said. "From the press release, it sounded like you two will be married soon. What's the rush?"

Elle felt her stomach turn. "You know Brock. When he makes a decision, he moves fast."

Lauren laughed. "You're so right."

Elle felt the rise of nausea in the back of her throat. "Excuse me. I need to use the powder room. Could you tell me where it is?"

"Oh, right through that hallway," Lauren said and pointed. "Go right ahead. I'll be here when you get back."

Elle rushed to the powder room. After she recovered, she splashed her face with water and rinsed out her mouth. Taking a deep breath, she tried to calm herself. She walked outside and immediately ran into Lauren, who studied her with concern. "Come here for a moment," she said and whisked her away to a private bedroom. "Are you okay?"

"Of course," Elle said. "I just feel a little off. It's probably a little virus or something I ate."

Lauren paused and shook her head. "You're pregnant, aren't you?"

Elle's heart leaped into her throat. She would have tried to lie but the sympathy in Lauren's eyes prevented her. "Please don't tell anyone. Brock insisted that we get married."

Lauren nodded. "I've been in your same situation."

"I'm not sure it's exactly the same," Elle muttered, thinking of her grandfather and how she had betrayed Brock.

"Close enough," Lauren said. "Just try to be open to possibilities. It could turn out much differently than you expect—I speak from experience. Most importantly, take care of yourself. You've got someone precious growing inside you."

Elle felt a sudden urge to cry. Her eyes burned with unshed tears. "Thank you," she said. "You don't know how much I appreciate that."

Lauren pulled her into an embrace. "Have you thought about names?"

"That's way in the future," Elle said. "I'm still just getting through today."

"The good times will come soon. Believe me," Lauren said.

Elle could only hope her friend was right.

Two days later, Elle put on the dress she and her mother had found on sale at an exclusive shop not far from Maddox Communications. Elle had thought about visiting Brock at the office at the time, then quickly dismissed the idea. He wouldn't have wanted her there.

"You look beautiful," her mother said, hugging her. "I'm so happy you're getting married. I'm so happy your baby will have the father you never had. You have no idea what a relief that is, Elle." Her mother sighed. "I wish I could have given you that."

Elle's heart twisted. "You gave me the best things in the world. You, attention and bubbles."

Her mother laughed. "You always did like bubbles." She put her hands on Elle's belly. "I bet your baby will like bubbles, too."

"You and I both will blow bubbles for him or her," Elle said, unable to resist a smile.

"Yes, we will," her mother said. "But first, it's time for

you to get married." She leaned toward Elle and brushed a kiss over her cheek. "You're beautiful, sweetheart. Your Brock is so lucky. Be happy, my girl. Be happy."

Elle could only hope. She forced her lips into a smile as her stomach turned somersaults. She looked in the mirror. Was that really her? That woman wearing ivory with baby's breath in her hair? Was she really going to marry Brock Maddox? And could they really make their marriage work?

She and her mother rode in a chauffeured car to the beach location for the wedding. The sun had burned off most of the morning fog, so at least there would be no rain. The car pulled to a stop in front of the private cottage where they would eat a meal afterward. Elle spotted Brock in the distance. Her heart stuttered at the sight of him. When she'd first met him, she'd never dared to dream they would be married. There were too many obstacles. She wondered again if this was a mistake.

"Elle," her mother said, lifting her hand to smooth the crease between Elle's brows. "Stop worrying. This is a happy day."

"But—" Elle said, fear twisting her inside like a vise.

"No buts," her mother said. "Remember. Never trouble trouble unless trouble troubles you."

Elle smiled at the saying her mother had quoted to her so many times throughout the years. She took a deep breath. Just for today, she would try not to trouble trouble. She followed her mother from the car to the cottage where the hostess greeted them.

"Everyone is ready for you," the woman said. "Especially the groom. The harpist is already playing."

"Harpist?" Elle said in surprise, craning to look out the window.

"Oh, I'm sorry," the hostess said. "Perhaps that was supposed to be a surprise."

Her mother's eyes danced with excitement. "I'll go first, like we planned," she said, smoothing her blue dress then lifting her hand to Elle's cheek. "I'm so happy for you, and for the baby."

Elle's stomach dipped. "I love you, Mom," she said.

Elle watched her mother walk down the stone path, then down smooth wooden planks over the sandy beach. The blue-gray Pacific rippled with white crests. Gathering her courage, she walked toward the door. A bouquet was pushed into her hands.

Blinking, Elle glanced at the hostess again in surprise.

The hostess smiled. "Mr. Maddox insisted. They're beautiful, aren't they?"

Elle looked down at the arrangement of white lilies and blood-red roses, and couldn't help thinking of all the bad blood that had flowed between her family and Brock's. Could their marriage sew together the jagged, bitter edges of competition?

Closing her eyes, she took a deep breath. One step at a time. The hostess opened the door and Elle stepped outside.

Brock watched as the door to the cottage opened and Elle appeared. The wind lifted tendrils of her hair and the hem of her lacy dress fluttered against her shapely upper calves. She had an ethereal look to her, almost angelic, but he knew different in every way. She'd been a sensual goddess in his bed, fulfilling his every need. At work, she had seemed like the perfect assistant, but the truth was she'd been tricking him every day, deceiving him.

He felt a stab of bitterness in his throat and swallowed it. There were more important things, he reminded himself. The baby. *His* baby. If there was anything his father had taught him, it was duty to the company and duty to his family.

His mother had been a dutiful but passionless wife and mother. Brock knew Elle would be different. He'd already experienced her passion and he knew, deep down in his bones, that she would love their child. Their child wouldn't be regarded as an obligation. Elle would receive their child as a precious gift and responsibility. As for their relationship, they would work that out along the way.

She met his gaze and though he couldn't see her eyes from where he stood, he guessed they were probably turbulent with conflicting emotions. She looked like a prized princess, her head held high, walking tall, only the smallest bump showing when the wind flattened her dress against her abdomen.

Brock couldn't tear his gaze from her. She'd been the lover who'd both comforted him and turned him upside down. And betrayed him.

Despite that last fact, he still craved her. He should have hated himself for it, but he knew that once she bore his name, he would be her first priority. There would be no more division of loyalties. Her loyalty would be to him.

She took the last few steps and stood next to him, searching his gaze. Just as he'd anticipated, her eyes were full of emotion. He took her hand in his and watched her inhale quickly. It gave him pleasure to know that he still got past her reserve.

He lifted her hand to his lips and kissed it, all the while looking into her eyes. "We're ready," he said in a low voice to the officiant, and the ceremony began. He repeated the vows he'd never made before and watched as she did the same.

"I now pronounce you man and wife," the minister said. "You may kiss the bride."

The sun came out from behind a cloud and Brock pulled Elle into his arms. She felt both strong and delicate against him. He lowered his mouth to hers and gave her a kiss of promise. He felt her tremble. "It will be okay," he whispered against her ear.

"It will," she whispered, but didn't look at all convinced.

Elle felt numb. The steak dinner arranged for her wedding celebration may as well have been sawdust in her mouth. Her hands were freezing, but she forced herself to nod and smile at Flynn and his wife, Renee.

"You look beautiful," Renee said.

"Thank you," Elle replied, feeling a stab of guilt for betraying the woman by using their friendship to get more secrets for her grandfather to use against Maddox. Renee had been a friend to her. She was surprised Renee was willing to speak to her, let alone extend her good wishes.

"I can't tell you how glad I am to see my brother get married," Flynn said. "He's been married to the company for so long, I was starting to wonder…"

"No need to wonder anymore," Brock said, lifting his glass of wine. "Thanks for being here," he said to Flynn. Then he turned to Elle. "To my wife—may our love grow, our commitment deepen and our joy overflow."

"I can only hope," Elle whispered under her breath, lifting her glass of sparkling water. The passion she glimpsed in his laser-blue eyes reminded her why she'd fallen for Brock. His passion for work, for life and, in the dark of night in his office apartment, for her.

Her mother and Brock's brother and sister-in-law clapped in approval.

"Honeymoon plans?" Flynn asked.

In one heartbeat, Brock's eyes turned to ice. He looked away. "Later," he said. "I have to dig the company out of its current crisis."

Elle felt her stomach sink to her knees and was glad she was sitting down. She knew she was the reason for the "current crisis."

An hour later, after their guests had departed, Elle left the cottage in Brock's limo. It was so silent she could barely breathe.

"You look beautiful," Brock said, but didn't meet her gaze.

She tried without success to take a deep breath. This was a huge mistake, she thought. Was there any way she could go back? Was an annulment possible? "Thank you," she said in a quiet voice. "The flowers and harp were very nice."

He nodded. "Every woman deserves something special at her wedding."

"Who told you that?"

He paused. "Renee."

"That was generous of her."

"I thought so," he said.

She bit her lip. "I don't blame everyone for being angry with me, and I don't blame you for resenting me—"

"I don't," he cut in. "Your loyalty was with your grandfather. Now it's with me."

It was so much more complicated than that, she thought. As the limo pulled up in front of Brock's grand home, he got out of the car and escorted Elle through the front door. His combination of good manners and primal strength had captivated her from the beginning. He could appear so smooth and civilized, but if necessary, he had the instincts of a street fighter and would go for the jugular to protect what was his.

She wondered how far his possessiveness toward her extended. Was it just for the baby?

The housekeeper approached them with a beaming smile. "Congratulations, both of you. I'm so happy for you. And you just look lovely, Miss Linton." She covered her mouth. "Oh, I should have said Mrs. Maddox."

Elle's heart skipped at the sound of her new name. Pushing aside her conflicting feelings, she took the woman's hands in hers. "Thank you, Anna. You're very kind."

"Please have Roger move Elle's things into my suite," Brock said.

"Right away. We'll have it done in no time," the housekeeper said and walked down the hallway.

Elle struggled with a surge of panic. "Your suite," she echoed, meeting his gaze.

"My suite has two bedrooms, two baths, a study, den and small exercise room. At some point my mother will return here, hopefully for a brief period," he said in a dry voice. "The less she knows about my private life, the better—she's been known to cause trouble. There won't be as many questions if you're living in my suite. Now, I need to go back to the office, but I'll be home later tonight. Roger will be on hand for you to move the rest of your things here during the next few days, but I don't want you to overdo it. You've had a busy day."

He looked deep into her eyes and she saw a glimpse of the passion they'd shared. But just as quickly, the fire was gone. "I'll see you later," he said, leaving her alone on their wedding night.

Most of Maddox's employees had left by the time Brock invited Logan Emerson into his office after hours. He'd hired the private investigator a short while back when it had become clear that someone was leaking company secrets. Brock's gut sank again as he remembered the exact moment he'd learned Elle had been the one. Elle, his uncorrupted island, had been twisting the knife at the same time she'd made love to him.

Logan sat across from Brock. "I just heard about your marriage. I was surprised."

"She's pregnant with my child," Brock said.

Logan, usually reserved, gave a low whistle of surprise. "I'm assuming that means you won't be prosecuting her."

"You assume correctly," Brock said.

"I understand. Well, it appears as if my job here is done," Logan said.

Brock frowned. "Perhaps not. Maddox is still at a critical point. There are several possibilities I want to explore. Quickly, of course. I'd like to keep you on longer until we see how things shake out."

"No problem," he said. "Just let me know what you need."

"Good," Brock said and stood. "That's all for now."

Logan extended his hand. "Best wishes on your marriage. It's not my place to say, really, but I don't believe Elle enjoyed the deception."

Brock just nodded. He was still coming to grips with how his life had been turned upside down in such a short time. "Thank you."

Brock reviewed his plans for the rest of the week, but it took longer than usual because he kept thinking about Elle's deception. He clenched his hands, then released them. The only thing that helped him was the fact that he would have done the same for his father. And he'd do anything for the sake of the company. It was his duty, his destiny, his heritage.

Hours later, after he left work, he climbed the stairs to his suite. He noticed one of the bedroom doors was closed but the one to the master bedroom was left open. The lamp on his bedside table was on, and the covers on his king-size bed were turned back. Walking through the doorway, he studied the room, catching the whiff of a sweet scent. His gaze caught on a small, clear vase on the bedside table. Inside stood one ruby-red rose. From Elle's bouquet. He saw a piece of paper sitting next to the vase.

Thank you. Elle.

It wasn't the first time she'd thanked him for giving her flowers, but still, he was touched. The rose reminded him of the passion they'd shared before everything had come to light. He lifted it and inhaled the fragrance, wondering if they would ever feel that sweetness they'd shared again.

Four

Elle set her alarm so she could join Brock for breakfast. She wasn't at all sure how to make their marriage work, but she knew that avoiding him wouldn't help. Shaking off her sleepiness, she beat him to the sunroom by a minute and a half.

His eyebrows lifted in surprise as he entered the room.

She felt a tiny surge of gratification and smiled. "Good morning." She lifted the hot pot of coffee. "Ready for your first cup?"

"Yes, thank you," he said, and she poured for him.

She felt his gaze skim over her as he took a sip. "Where's yours?"

She shook her head. "Coffee's not on my list these days."

"Why not?"

"Caffeine's a no-no during pregnancy," she said. "It helps that I've temporarily lost my taste for it."

Brock's eyebrows furrowed. "Ooh. That's tough. How does that affect your sleepiness?"

She laughed. "I'm still in the sleepy stage."

"Sleepy stage?"

"I want to take naps constantly. I've actually felt like this for several weeks and was hoping I wasn't coming down with something. But I guess in a way, I did. The nine-month flu," she said, chuckling to herself.

Brock smiled as he lifted his cup for another sip.

"The good news is any day now I'm supposed to start feeling a burst of energy and I'll be incredibly productive."

"As long as you don't plan on running a marathon," he said. "Your main job is to take care of yourself and the baby."

"At some point, I'll need to make some plans for a nursery," she ventured, watching his expression carefully.

He nodded and met her gaze. "Eventually, the child can be moved into his or her own room. My suite was originally designed for my wife and me to share the master bedroom, and the infant to sleep where you are currently."

Elle felt a jolt of heat as sensual memories flooded her mind. Did Brock want her in his bed again? What would be different between them? "Is that what you want?"

"We don't need to make that decision right now. You've been through a lot during the last couple of weeks. Make sure you don't do too much today when you're packing and unpacking your belongings. That's what Roger is for."

She nodded and a silence fell between them. How she longed for the easy conversation they'd once shared.

He glanced at his watch. "Time for me to go."

"So early?" The words popped out before she knew it.

"Breakfast meeting with—" He stopped as if he remembered he couldn't share that information with her. She'd shown him she couldn't be trusted. Elle hated that. She wondered if it would always be this way between them—oh-so-careful with edited information.

"Have a good day," she managed.

"You, too," he said and walked away.

Her stomach twisted and she forced herself to take a quick breath. *Give it time,* she told herself. *You haven't even been married twenty-four hours.*

Later that day, Elle's mother helped her pack. "This is the sad part," her mother said. "As happy as I am for you that you're married and moving to live with your husband, I'll miss you terribly."

Her mother's tone tugged at her heart and Elle gave her a hug. "It's not like I'm moving very far. We can see each other as often as we like. And you know you can call me for anything," Elle said firmly.

"I'm glad I finally joined that support group last year," Suzanne said. "We really do help take care of each other, and heaven knows I don't want to be a burden to you."

Elle held up her hand. "Stop that craziness. You know you're no burden. I just don't want you to push yourself too much, especially now that you've gone back to work part-time."

"Look who's talking," her mother said. "You're the one who's been working double time lately, preparing for the wedding and moving. Thank goodness Brock won't let you overdo any longer. I can tell he's a strong man."

"Yes, he is," Elle murmured, thinking Brock wouldn't let her within a mile of the office at this point.

"What I don't understand is why you didn't tell him about the baby as soon as you knew," her mother said, her brows knitting in a furrow.

"Aside from the fact that it was an office affair?" Elle said, even though it had been far more than that to her. She smiled and gave her mother another squeeze. "You know, things just get complicated sometimes."

Later that evening, Elle tried to help Roger carry a box upstairs but was brushed aside. He shot her an appalled glance. "Absolutely not, Mrs. Maddox. Mr. Maddox would have my head. I would have my head," the older man said.

"Okay, okay," Elle said, stepping aside. "At least let me get you something to drink."

Roger gave a heavy sigh. "Thank you."

Elle checked out the small refrigerator in the mini-kitchen and pulled out a bottle of water. She walked back to the smaller bedroom where Roger was stacking the last of the boxes.

"Now, you know not to lift these," he said, shooting her a warning gaze with iron-gray eyebrows over dark gray eyes.

"Maybe we should spread them out a little," she suggested.

He lifted his hand as she approached to help. "I'll do it, but only with the agreement that you leave a light on at night so you won't trip on your way to the bathroom."

"Excellent idea," she said, clapping her hands. "I see why Brock relies on you."

Roger's lips lifted in a half grin. "Thank you. I'm honored by the compliment."

A few moments later, she thrust the bottle of water into his hands and impulsively hugged the cranky man.

He gave a low chuckle of surprise. "Now, promise you won't try to do too much this evening. Rome wasn't built in a day, you know?"

During the next hour, Elle emptied four boxes into drawers and the generous walk-in closet. Glancing up, she noticed the late hour and decided to take a break with a hot shower. She wondered where Brock was. Was he staying at his office apartment tonight? In the bed they had shared so many times after work?

The notion twisted something inside her and she tried not to think about it as the water spilled over her. She tried to visualize the warmth washing away all her worries as she rubbed her belly. Elle couldn't overthink the future right now. Dealing with today was enough.

She dried off and pulled a comfy cotton nightshirt over her head. She combed through her wet hair and slid her arms into a long terry-cloth robe that tied at her waist. Her stomach growled, surprising her. It was late and she needed to sleep. What had she read recently about foods one should eat at bedtime? A banana. She'd seen a bunch downstairs. She would eat half of one, she decided, and headed for the stairs.

She took the first step, then the next. Her foot caught in the hem of her robe and she grabbed at the banister but she was too late. She fell headfirst down the stairs and felt the impact of the wooden steps against her chest and belly. A scream escaped her. She grabbed and clutched for anything to stop her. She screamed again.

Anna and Roger appeared at the bottom of the steps, their faces filled with horror.

Elle closed her eyes at their expressions. Oh, god, help her. The baby. The baby.

Roger rushed to her side. "Miss, are you okay? Are you awake?"

Elle took a deep breath, trying to take stock of her body. She felt sore in places she couldn't identify. "I'm conscious," she said, opening her eyes again. "But I'm afraid," she whispered. "I want to make sure the baby is okay."

Roger's eyebrows drew together. "We'll take you to the hospital immediately," he said.

Brock marched into the emergency room, his heart pounding against his chest. He stopped at the desk. "Brock Maddox. My wife is here," he said in a curt voice.

The receptionist nodded. "Please come this way," she said and led him down a hallway to a room. She opened the door and he spotted Elle reclining on a table with Anna and Roger by her side. The atmosphere in the room was grim.

All three of them looked at him.

"Mr. Maddox—" Roger and Anna said in unison.

Brock felt the twist in his gut tighten further. "Thank you for getting her here," he said, then turned his attention to Elle. "How are you?"

She bit her lip. "Waiting on the ultrasound," she said, her expression full of fear. "I wish I weren't so clumsy," she whispered, her eyes shiny with unshed tears.

Brock rushed to her side and took her hand in his. "I'll make sure you're okay," he said.

"But what about the baby?" she asked, her voice breaking.

Roger cleared his throat. "We'll be in the waiting room."

"I feel so horrible," Elle said. "What if my carelessness—"

He pressed his fingers over her lips. "You can't think that," he said.

A young woman dressed in white walked through the doorway. "Hello, I'm Dr. Shen." She extended her hand to Elle and then to Brock. "I understand Mom took a tumble. Babies are amazingly resilient, so your little one is likely okay. Let's check it out."

The doctor squirted some gel on Elle's belly and rubbed a device over her.

Brock watched as a jumble of a being appeared on the screen before them.

"Good, strong heartbeat right there," Dr. Shen said, pointing to the flicker on the screen. She moved the device. "Everything looks good so far. Placenta's intact."

She removed the device and handed it to the nurse,

then turned to Brock and Elle. "You might have some bruises tomorrow, but your baby is fine. Just be careful around stairs, okay?"

Elle gave a big nod of relief. "Very careful."

The doctor scrawled her signature on the notebook screen. "You're released. And we can give you a copy of the ultrasound video, if you'd like."

"Thank you," Elle said.

"Thanks," Brock echoed. Elle looked at his face, which was full of wonder and awe. She understood. The heartbeat, the movement of the tiny legs and arms—it was overwhelming. And amazing.

The nurse wiped the gel off of Elle's abdomen. "You can get dressed now," she said.

Elle took an audible breath. "Sorry to bother you with this," she murmured and moved to slide from the table.

Brock wrapped his arm around her shoulders. "You can't be serious."

Elle bit her lip. "I know you have other things to do."

"There's nothing more important," he said. "Nothing."

"It almost didn't seem real before," she said. "But it does now. We're going to have a baby."

He nodded and smiled. "Yes, we are."

Two days later, Elle couldn't stand her Brock-imposed exile from the outside world any longer. Now, she desperately needed to get out.

The housekeeper frowned as Elle put her hand on

the doorknob of the front door. "You're not going out, are you?" Anna said.

Elle turned to look at the caring woman. "Yes, I am. The doctor says it's fine. I haven't had any spotting. The ultrasound looked good. Some physical activity will be good for me."

"Mr. Maddox won't like it," she said.

"Yes, well, he would just as soon see me wrapped in a cocoon until my due date. That's not going to happen," Elle said firmly.

"I can't say I blame you, but you really did give us a scare. If Mr. Maddox should ask where you are, what should I tell him?"

Elle smiled. "Tell him I'm shopping for a shorter robe."

The housekeeper chuckled. "Good for you. Let me call Roger. He can drive you."

"Oh, that's not necessary at all," Elle protested.

The housekeeper shook her head. "Mr. Maddox would want you to go with a driver. It won't take but a moment."

Elle cooled her heels, then stepped into the town car and directed Roger to take her to an outlet.

"Outlet?" Roger echoed as if it were a foreign word. "Are you sure you wouldn't rather go downtown? That's where the senior Mrs. Maddox always goes."

"No, I love Nordstrom's Rack," she said, settling back in her seat.

Roger let her out at the front door and Elle walked into the busy store. She wandered through the lingerie section, admiring the silk gowns. She would be too large for them soon enough, she thought, sliding her hand over her belly. Finding a rack of robes, she flipped through the selection and pulled out a red one. "You'll look like a giant, mutant cherry," she muttered to herself.

Her cell phone rang and she saw Brock's number on her caller ID. Wincing, she answered. "Hello?"

"What are you doing at Nordstrom's Rack?"

"Buying a short robe," she said. "I assume your spies informed you?"

"Roger told me you insisted on going to an outlet," Brock said. "I can afford to get you a robe and anything else you need, for God's sake. You don't have to watch your pennies. And you sure as hell don't need to be shopping at outlets."

"But I like shopping in outlets. It's like hunting is for men. Bagging the one with the biggest rack in one shot."

Silence followed. "I've never heard it described that way."

"Well, I'm glad to know I've provided you with a new analogy," she said. "Maybe you can use it for a campaign."

"Hmm. That's not a bad idea."

"Shh. Better not tell me. I'm the enemy," she couldn't help saying.

Brock gave a heavy sigh. "You're not the enemy."

"Bet you'd never let me in the office again," she said.

"Sure I would," he said. "Just not right away. Dinner at home?" he asked, clearly changing the subject.

"If we must," she said.

"You hate it there," he concluded.

"It's so—" she searched for the right word "—full."

"I know," he said. "Maybe we could get rid of some of the clutter."

"How do you think your mother would feel about that?"

"It's possible she wouldn't even notice."

Elle snorted, then tried to cough to cover it. "I don't think so."

"Well, start with one room downstairs. Take it over and redo it the way you want. Put the old stuff in storage."

Elle felt a trickle of excitement. "This might work."

"Of course it will work," he said. "It was my suggestion."

She rolled her eyes. "You're so arrogant."

"That never stopped you before," he said.

She sucked in a quick breath. "No," she whispered. "It didn't."

"What do your want for dinner tonight?"

What she wanted more than anything was a quiet dinner in Brock's apartment at the office. But she knew that wasn't possible. He wouldn't let her near the office yet. She felt a deep sense of loss. They'd shared so many private memories there. "I'd like some good old American cooking tonight," she said, thinking of one of the few places they'd actually gone to together—a diner with a delicious defiance against the carb-hating trend of the day.

"Mashed potatoes," he said, and she heard the smile in his voice. "The Four Square Diner. Don't spend too much time at the outlets. I'll call later to firm up a time," he said and hung up.

Elle glanced at the sexy leopard-printed sheath hanging

on the end of the rack. She wondered if she would ever be able to inspire Brock's primal urges again.

After a jam-packed day, Brock stood to greet Elle at The Four Square Diner. He studied her face. "You overdid it today," he said. "You're tired."

She brushed her lips against his cheek. "Thank you. You look gorgeous, too," she said and sat down.

He couldn't keep his lips from twitching. "You're supposed to stay rested."

She picked up the menu from the table. "There's a difference between rested and going into a coma. How was your afternoon?"

"Good. The campaign for the Prentice account is going smoothly," he said.

"Great. How do you like your new assistant?"

"He isn't you," Brock said.

She nearly dropped her menu. "You have a male assistant?" she asked, surprised.

"Careful," Brock said. "You're edging toward sexist."

"The whole advertising business is sexist," she said dismissively. "I wasn't aware you'd ever had a male assistant."

"I haven't," Brock said. "But this one is competent."

"It might also negate any criticisms about your marriage to me," she said. "Good strategy."

Brock met her gaze, giving nothing away. The waitress arrived and took their order. After she left, Brock returned his attention to Elle. "What did you buy today?"

"Odds and ends," she said, wondering how much

of an embarrassment he considered her to be. She'd often thought her grandfather had considered her an embarrassment until he'd found a use for her.

"What odds? What ends?" he asked. "Just tell me you bought a new robe that you won't trip over."

She smiled. "Yes, I did, along with a few other things. Do you have plans for this weekend?"

Brock shrugged. "The usual," he said. "Work."

She nodded. "There's always that."

She noticed him lift his hand to a man across the room. She recognized the man as one of Brock's executives, Logan Emerson. The man nodded at Brock, glanced at her, then looked away. She'd always had an odd feeling about Logan. Brock hadn't discussed his hiring with her and she'd always wondered at Brock's motivation for bringing him into such a high-profile position at Maddox. Logan had never seemed to fit in.

"How's he doing with the other account reps now?" she asked.

"Fine," Brock said. "I've altered his duties a bit in the last few days. I think that will work out better."

"Oh, really?" she asked. "What will he be doing?"

"I've assigned him to work more closely with personnel and computer security," he said as their meal arrived.

"Wow," she said. "That's a big switch from sales."

He nodded but didn't make any further comment and a possibility occurred to her. "Computer security," she mused. "He always seemed better suited for security. So quiet, so determined to stay in the background—he could be a private investigator."

Brock's jaw twitched, but he still added nothing. It suddenly hit her.

"He *is* a private investigator," she said. "Was he the one who told you about me?"

Brock stabbed his fork into his meatloaf. "And if he was?" he asked her.

She bit her lip, feeling her appetite for the open-faced turkey sandwich disappear. She adjusted her paper napkin. "That's why you wouldn't talk about him with me," she said. "Did you already suspect me?"

Brock set down his fork. "You were the last person I suspected," he said, his eyes as turbulent as a stormy sea.

She felt a twist of guilt and looked away. "I was almost relieved when you found out," she confessed in a low voice. "Being pregnant made it even worse. If it hadn't been for my mother needing the experimental treatments—"

"What?" he asked, his voice hoarse. "What experimental treatments?"

She finally met his gaze. "I wasn't sure if Logan might have known something about my mother's illness," she said. "My mother is taking experimental treatments that are very expensive. There's no way she or I could afford them, and insurance wouldn't cover them."

"Are you saying that Athos agreed to pay for your mother's treatments as long as you spied on me?"

A lump formed in her throat. "Yes, he did. I'm ashamed of it, but I didn't feel as if I had any other choice. I couldn't risk losing her. She's all I've ever had."

The sound of stainless steel clanging against plates

and the conversation of the other diners was a roar compared to the absolute silence between them.

"Why didn't you tell me your mother was sick?" he asked.

She shook her head. "I didn't want to." She closed her eyes, thinking back to the times she'd shared with Brock. "I didn't want my time with you tainted with any of my problems. Those moments we shared together—it was like you and I were on a private island and nothing or no one could trespass." She opened her eyes and took a deep breath. "Afterward, I had my work and you had yours, but that time together was precious. It had to be protected."

Brock reached across the table, his hand covering hers. "I can take care of your mother's medical treatments."

She immediately shook her head, swallowing a quick taste of bitterness at the havoc her grandfather had created in her life. "No," she said. "Let him pay. It's the least he can do for all the trouble he has caused."

Brock's gaze gentled. "You're lucky you have such a good relationship with your mother," he said. "I admire your devotion to her."

Five

After a long shower, Elle wrapped a towel around herself and ran the blow dryer through her hair. She would clip the tags off her new robe in just a moment, she promised herself, looking forward to the luxurious sensation of silk over her skin. She suspected there'd be no sensual pleasures in her near future. They were, after all, sleeping in separate rooms.

Closing her eyes and mind to her thoughts, she concentrated on the warm air dancing through her hair and over her shoulders. A few seconds passed and she opened her eyes, finding Brock standing in front of her, bare-chested with a small tray in one of his hands.

Startled, she dropped the dryer. "Oh, my," she said, bending down to turn it off. As she leaned forward, her towel dropped to her waist. Swearing under her breath, she lifted it to cover her chest and stood.

"I knocked," he said, his gaze sliding across her towel-covered body.

"I didn't hear you," she said, sensing awareness twist and turn between them. She felt heat rush to her face.

"I was downstairs and the housekeeper thought you might like some juice and cookies," he said.

Elle smiled and took the small tray from him. Still holding on to her towel, she carefully set it on the dresser. "That was nice. She's so sweet, but she fusses over me more than my mother."

"Maybe because you're so busy taking care of your mother," he said.

"Maybe," she said, too aware of his presence so close to her. She knew his body intimately. At the moment, he wore a pair of pajama bottoms that dipped below his ripped abs and belly button. She remembered sliding her hands over his wide shoulders while he kissed her deeply. It was all too easy to recall the sexy gasp he made when she touched him intimately.

"Elle," Brock said. "What are you thinking right now?"

She bit her lip and looked away. "Nothing important. Nothing worth—"

He touched her arm and her denial stuck in her throat. It had been two weeks since they'd been intimate, and God help her, she'd missed him. Even through the morning sickness. She'd missed being with him, away from everything and everyone else.

"I can't believe you still want me," she whispered.

He pulled her toward him and the sensation of his strong chest against her nearly buckled her knees. She deliberately stiffened them.

"Why not?" he asked. He skimmed his hand down to the small of her back and pressed her into him.

The obvious strength of his arousal shocked her. She searched his gaze for clues to his emotions. "But after what I did," she said. "How could—"

He moved his other hand up to the back of her head, sliding his fingers through her hair, tilting her head so that her mouth was completely accessible to him. "Let's not overthink it."

He lowered his mouth to hers and kissed her possessively. Should she be asking for more than sex? she wondered. Maybe not, she thought as his tongue slid past her lips and caressed hers. Maybe he was right. Maybe she should stop thinking and concentrate on feeling. What did she have to lose?

Dropping the towel, she lifted her hands to the back of his neck and surrendered to the moment.

Brock gave a low, barely audible growl and pushed the towel to the floor. When her bare breasts pressed against his chest, she sighed. He groaned. He slid one of his hands over her nipple and she gasped, feeling a correlating electricity between her legs.

"Problem?" he asked, rubbing his lips over hers.

"I'm more sensitive since I'm—" He rubbed her nipple again and she sucked in another breath as she felt herself grow swollen.

"Should I stop?"

"Oh, please, no," she said, surprised at the speed of her arousal.

"Is this safe for you?" he asked, going completely still. "For the baby?"

She nodded. "The doctor said—" She licked her lips. "He said we can do anything we did before."

Brock swore under his breath and lifted his hands to her face. "Damn my soul, but I've missed you," he said and took her mouth in a sensual, ferocious kiss that matched the way she felt about him.

With each second that passed, she felt her temperature rise, her heart beat faster. She wanted more, so much more. Squeezing the muscles of his arms and drawing his tongue into her mouth, she couldn't keep still. She wriggled against him and he slid his leg between hers, lifting it high between her thighs, rubbing her where she was already wet and aching.

She slid her hands down over his ribs to his flat abdomen and pushed her fingers beneath the waistband of his drawstring pants. Brock lifted his hand to her breasts, flicking his thumbs over her nipples.

The sensation made her dizzy. She pushed his pants over his hips, wanting more of him, craving ultimate closeness.

"It's too fast," he muttered as she closed her hand over his shaft.

"Not for me," she said.

"Oh, Elle," he said, picking her up in his arms and carrying her into his bedroom. He set her on his big bed and pushed his pants the rest of the way down. His gaze fixed on hers.

"You don't know how many times I've dreamed about having you in my bed here," he muttered and slid his hand between her thighs, finding her secret wetness. His mouth dipped to hers, his tongue taunting and exploring the same way his fingers were teasing her femininity, making her breathless and almost shockingly needy for him.

The wanting in her tightened like a strong coil, pushing her higher and higher. She stroked desperately at his flexed arms and shoulders. His harsh breaths mingled with hers.

"Brock," she said, a mixture of a plea and demand.

One second later, he slid inside. His gaze, dark with arousal, held hers as he thrust. Unable to hold back, she arched toward him and felt herself come apart in fits and starts. He kept thrusting, driving her higher than she'd thought possible until one last time, he stiffened inside her and his climax vibrated all the way to her core.

She held on tight, stunned by the ferocity of their lovemaking. His heart pounded against hers and his breath blew over her bare shoulder. She felt his strength and power in every cell of her being and never wanted to let go of the sensation.

After a few more breaths, he let out a long sigh and eased to his side, still holding her in his arms. "From now on," he said, "you'll sleep in here with me."

The next morning, Elle was awakened by a sound. She opened her eyes to the sight of Brock dressed and picking up his BlackBerry from its charger. A tiny ray of sunlight peeked through the shade on the window.

Shaking off her sleepiness, she sat up. "Where are you going?"

He glanced at her. "Where I go almost every Saturday," he said. "To the office. I need to review some new suggestions that came in yesterday for one of our major accounts. No need for you to get up. I'll be back late this afternoon. Enjoy your day," he said and walked out of the room.

Elle stared after him, stunned at his perfunctory attitude. Frowning, she halfway wondered if he was the same man who'd made love to her with such passion last night. Last night he'd acted as if he couldn't get enough of her. Today he acted as if he couldn't get away from her fast enough.

She'd felt the enormous connection between them click back into place last night. She'd been sure their lovemaking represented a turning point. Now she wasn't sure at all. Brock was so distant. Even when they'd been having their affair in the office, he'd acted warmer than this. She instinctively wrapped her arms around herself as if she felt a sudden chill.

He still didn't trust her, she realized, feeling a knot form in her stomach. She shouldn't be surprised. Even though he had sold her on the idea that they could overcome what she had done for the sake of the baby, he clearly wasn't there yet. She couldn't help wondering if he ever would be. Sinking back down onto the bed, she dozed for a while, trying to escape her lost, afraid feelings. After some bizarre dreams, Elle threw off the covers and jumped out of bed. She refused to be a wuss. There were much worse things she could be facing. Now wasn't the time to cower under the covers. Now was time to try to make her marriage work, and she'd start with the house. Today she would work on redoing the den.

The first thing she ditched was the heavy drapes. The housekeeper gasped when she saw Elle on a chair, pulling them down.

"Mrs. Maddox, what on earth are you doing?" Anna asked.

"Brock told me to pick a room and redecorate it. I've chosen this one," she said.

The housekeeper's eyes widened. "Oh, my. Has he, uh, discussed this with the senior Mrs. Maddox?"

"I don't think so," Elle said. "But he said he didn't think his mother would mind if I redid one room. It won't be as if I'm taking over the entire house."

"True," the housekeeper said, nodding. The rest of her expression didn't agree with her nod.

Elle sighed. "Do you think I shouldn't? I don't want to offend her."

"Technically, the house belongs to Mr. Maddox. Mrs. Maddox has lived here since her husband passed away, but by all rights, Mr. Maddox is the master of the house and since you're his wife, your wishes should be respected."

"A roundabout way of saying there could be trouble," Elle said, then lifted her hand. "Don't worry. I don't expect you to comment. No need for divided loyalty." She turned her attention back to the room. "I'll try to tie in some of the colors from the other rooms, but I want to make this room comfortable for Brock. I want him to feel like he can relax here."

"I think that's an excellent idea," Anna said.

"The drapes have got to go, though," Elle said. "And most of the furniture and knickknacks."

"As you wish," the housekeeper said. "But please let Roger do it. Mr. Maddox would have my head if he saw you on that chair."

Elle spent the next several hours packing up knickknacks while Roger hauled away anything that weighed more than a tissue.

"I don't want to impose, but if you would like some suggestions, Mrs. Maddox used some decorators," the housekeeper said.

"Thank you. I could use some suggestions, but I know someone who has a great eye and I owe her a visit," she said, thinking of Bree Kincannon Spencer. Bree's friendship was another casualty in the dirty little corporate war her grandfather had instigated. Although Elle knew Bree might not forgive her, she needed to apologize to the woman who had trusted and befriended her. The prospect made her nervous, but it was necessary. "This is a lot of furniture. Are you sure you can find a place to store it?"

Roger nodded. "No problem. We'll find a place."

"Thank you," Elle said and smiled. "Both of you." Then she went upstairs to her room and dialed Bree's cell, expecting to leave a message that might very well be ignored.

"Hello?" Bree said breathlessly after several rings.

Surprised at the sound of the woman's voice, Elle temporarily lost her words.

"Hello?" Bree repeated. "Elle?"

"Yes, it's me," Elle said, pacing from one end of the bedroom to the other. "Listen, I know you probably hate me. If I were you, I would hate me, too, but would you be willing to give me a few minutes of your time to explain? Nothing will excuse what I did, but your friendship really meant a lot to me. I would just like you to know what really happened."

Silence stretched from the other side of the line,

making Elle's stomach knot. "I understand if you don't want to, and I know you're probably busy with Gavin today, since it's a Saturday—"

"I sent Gavin to play golf," Bree said. "He needed to take a break from his new business and I know he's missed playing but he didn't want me to feel neglected. I had to insist."

"You're so lucky," Elle said in a low voice, thinking of how Brock had left before she'd even made it out of bed that morning.

"I could probably meet you in an hour. Gavin won't be back until five. There's a little café down the street from us. Would you like to meet there?"

"Yes, thank you, Bree. This means a lot to me," Elle said.

An hour later, Elle walked into the café, spotting Bree at a table. The young woman stood and Elle immediately saw a new confidence in her. Elle remembered when Bree had enlisted her help with a makeover to get Gavin's attention. Bree had spent so many years without self-confidence that she hadn't realized what a true beauty she was. But now she was a radiant, happily married woman—and a woman who had been betrayed by Elle. Elle felt another twist of nerves ripple through her.

"Bree, thank you for coming." Elle's voice trembled, but she was determined. "I'm so, so terribly sorry for what I've done," she said, and then the whole story about her grandfather and her mother's illness just spilled out.

Fifteen minutes later, Bree reached for Elle's hand. "Oh, my God. How terrible. Why didn't you tell me?"

she asked. "I would have helped. You know I have the money."

"I couldn't," Elle said. "And I felt so trapped and afraid. Every day looking in the mirror, I just hated myself more and more. And then when Brock and I got involved—" Elle felt her voice break again.

Bree looked at her in sympathy. "Gavin told me Brock looked devastated when he got the news from the P.I."

Even though deep down, Elle had suspected that Brock would have been hurt by the news, part of her had wondered if it might have stabbed his ego more than his heart. Now, she couldn't be sure.

"Well, the good news is that you and Brock are married, so everything is fixed," Bree said cheerfully.

Elle didn't say anything, but Bree must have read her expression.

"What's wrong? Brock must have forgiven you, right?"

"It's not that easy," Elle said. "We're working on things." She bit her lip. "I'm pregnant," she whispered.

Bree's eyes rounded. "Oh, my goodness. Are you excited? Is he? I mean, I know it's been a muddy swim getting here, but a *baby*."

Elle realized more than ever how much she had missed Bree during the last few weeks. "I'm getting there," she said. "I'm just getting over morning sickness."

"As someone whose marriage didn't start out perfectly, the only thing I can say is hold on. Things can change for the better. They certainly did for me. For a while there, I never believed Gavin would love me, but I wouldn't doubt it for a second now."

"I'm so glad. You really do deserve happiness," Elle said.

Bree shot her a sympathetic smile. "You do, too, Elle."

"Do you think you can ever forgive me?" Elle asked.

"It's already done. But you're going to need to forgive yourself, too."

Elle felt a slight easing in her chest. She'd carried around the tight feeling so long it had become a part of her. To have Bree forgive her so freely gave her hope that maybe she and Brock could make their family work after all.

"Thank you so much, Bree," she said. "And now I have a favor to ask. You remember how I helped you with your little makeover?"

Bree nodded. "You definitely don't need a makeover."

"Brock's den needs a makeover. You have a wonderful eye. I was hoping you wouldn't mind helping me."

"I'm flattered," Bree said. "Of course I'll help."

After taking photographs of the den and talking about ideas, Elle and Bree decided to go shopping and found the perfect couch, a recliner for Brock and a sofa table. Unaccustomed to having things delivered at the drop of a dime, Elle blinked at how Bree arranged to get the furniture delivered immediately. Bree left with a hug and Elle went to an electronics store to purchase a huge television. As soon as she mentioned her address, the store manager agreed to deliver and set it up immediately.

By seven thirty, she was propped on the new sofa, watching a chick flick on the new television while she ate roasted chicken, green beans and macaroni and cheese. The sad thing was that Brock still hadn't come home. Elle consoled herself with the macaroni and cheese, even though she knew she would rue the effect later.

Just before eight o'clock, Brock strode into the room, glancing around in surprise. "Where'd the furniture go?"

"You told me to redo a room," she said. "This is the room I've chosen."

He glanced at the television. "That's a great picture. I bet you would feel like you're at the game when you're watching baseball," he said.

"That's the idea," she said, pleased with her purchase. "Do you mind trying out your new chair?" she asked, waving her hand toward the recliner.

He gave a short laugh and moved to the chair, sitting down and easing back. He let out a sigh. "Perfect," he said.

Elle beamed. "I think I sat in fifty chairs before I chose that one."

"I like the couch, too," he said. "The room looks totally different."

"I'm not done with it yet, but I think I've made a good start."

He shot her an inquisitive glance. "You've been a busy girl."

She nodded. "Yes, I have."

He glanced at her plate. "And you're eating well, too. I'm glad to see it."

Elle sighed, looking at her mostly empty plate. "I'm craving carbs. Heaven help me when it's all over."

"You'll be a beautiful mother," he said quietly.

"Do you really think so?" she asked.

"Yes, I do," he said.

She wanted to ask him if he'd missed her today, if he'd thought of her at all, but she knew the question would sound silly. "How was your day?" she asked.

"Good. Fuller than I expected. I had dinner with a prospective client. The owner of a cosmetics company based on the west coast." He rose from the chair.

"Sounds exciting," she said, hoping he would tell her more.

"It's the beginning stages, so anything can happen. You know how it goes." His gaze fell over her like a warm veil of heat. "Come upstairs and we can relax in the hot tub."

The desire in his eyes temporarily dissolved her questions. She gave a slow shake of her head. "Pregnancy and hot tubs aren't a good idea. Something about the high temperatures being dangerous for the baby."

He nodded. "I see."

"But a bath or a shower is okay," she said.

He extended his hand. "Come upstairs with me," he said. "I've missed you."

Those last three words were pure magic to her.

On Sunday, Brock didn't go into the office and Elle persuaded him to go for a walk on the beach and share a picnic.

Brock leaned back against the quilt they'd spread

out on the sand. "I can't remember the last time I did this."

"Maybe you should do it more often," she said, packing away the remnants of their picnic lunch.

"Maybe," he said, his gaze skimming over her, taking a long swallow from his water bottle. "How are you adjusting to being a Maddox bride?"

"I'm getting there," she said. "I'm just hoping my husband will be home more when our child is born."

He inhaled and nodded thoughtfully. "I'm working on it. My father spent a lot more time at the office than he ever did with us."

"What do *you* want?" she asked. "More time in the office? Or more time with your child?"

"I hadn't even considered it until now," he said. "I was always too busy protecting and growing the company."

"I don't really know what to expect of a father," she said and shrugged, "because my father left as soon as he found out my mother was pregnant."

"That must have been tough for both of you," Brock said.

She nodded. "It was, but my mother and I were always very close, so I'm lucky that way. Unconditional love between us."

"But something tells me you had to take care of her a lot," Brock said.

"True," she admitted. "But with her, I always felt good enough. Did you ever feel that way with your father?"

"Hmm," he said. "Good question. I was always pushed to do better, do more." He glanced at her. "In that way, you were lucky." He rose up and leaned toward her, pressing his mouth against hers. "What inspired you to be such a hard worker?"

"I didn't want to be at the mercy of any man," she said. The answer came easily to her lips.

He lifted his eyebrows. "Really?"

"Yes. I spent my entire life with my grandfather supporting us though he was ashamed of us. I didn't want that for my future. I studied and worked hard," she said, then closed her eyes. "Then my mother got sick."

She felt him stroke her hand. "When did Koteas approach you?"

Bitterness filled her mouth. "When my mother's improvement dipped and the only thing that could help her was the experimental treatment. Of course, insurance wouldn't cover it. And my grandfather wouldn't cover it without a price."

"Did you plan to seduce me?"

Elle laughed and opened her eyes to meet his gaze. "That's one of the funniest things you've ever said to me. I was terrified you wouldn't hire me. When you finally did, I was fascinated by you. You were this unstoppable force. I'd never met anyone like you."

"You went to bed with me without a blink of an eye," he said.

"I—" She broke off, feeing a stab of guilt mixed with a myriad of other emotions. "I couldn't miss out on being with you," she said. "Why did you decide to be with me?"

"Same reason, different words," Brock said, sliding his hand behind her neck and drawing her mouth against his. "I couldn't resist you."

Six

"Oh, my God! Vandals have struck," a woman's shrill voice called.

Just out of the shower, Elle quickly wrapped her robe around her. Alarmed, she pushed open her door and raced—carefully—down the stairs.

Another shriek sounded from the area of the den.

Elle finally made it there in bare feet and gaped at Brock's enraged mother, Carol. "Oh, my God," the sophisticated, elegant woman repeated.

"It wasn't a vandal," Elle said breathlessly. "It was me."

Carol looked at her and frowned as much as her Botox-treated brow would allow. "Who are you?"

Elle fought a flutter of nerves. "I'm Elle," she said. "Elle Linton—"

"Linton," Carol interjected. "That name is familiar.

Don't tell me," she said, lifting her hand when Elle opened her mouth to speak. "I know that name." She blinked in recognition. "My son Brock's assistant." Then she frowned again. "Why are you here? And wearing a robe? And destroying my den?" Carol said, looking around the room in complete disapproval.

Elle paused, then said, "Elle Linton Maddox."

Carol's eyebrows would have risen to her hairline if they could have. "Maddox? Oh, my God. Has my son married you?" Her gaze immediately dipped to Elle's belly. "Are you pregnant?"

Elle cleared her throat, realizing that Brock hadn't bothered to contact his mother about their marriage. "Brock and I were married just last week."

"Oh," Carol said, clearly at a loss for words. "He didn't tell me."

Although Elle understood why Brock resisted his mother's involvement in both business and his personal life, she felt a twinge of sympathy for the woman. It couldn't be easy hearing that your oldest son had gotten married—from the new wife herself. "I'm sorry. I realize this is awkward," Elle said. "Brock has told me a lot about you."

Carol's lips lifted in a cynical smile. "All good, I'm sure," she said, looking at the den again. "I don't suppose you could tell me what has happened to this room."

"Uh, Brock asked me to choose one room downstairs to redecorate." Elle shrugged. "I chose the den."

"Oh," Carol said. "I suppose I shouldn't be surprised. It was bound to happen someday." She returned her attention to Elle, studying her for a long moment. "So you're the new Maddox bride," Carol said, slowly strolling toward her. "I suspect you have no idea what you're getting into, but I can help with that. My flight from Aspen just arrived an hour ago—I made an extra stop there on my way back from Europe. Let me freshen up and the two of us can do lunch."

Uncomfortable at the prospect, Elle shook her head. "Oh, I couldn't. You just got in. I'm sure you want to relax."

"Nonsense," Carol said, lifting her lips in a smile that didn't meet her eyes. "I need to get to know my son's new wife." She glanced down at Elle's abdomen again. "You didn't answer my question. Are you pregnant?"

Elle thought about denying it because she knew what Carol would think—that the pregnancy was the only reason Brock had married her. Which, of course, was true. "Yes, I am."

Carol gave a knowing nod. She glanced down at a diamond-encrusted watch. "Will an hour give you enough time to get ready?"

"That's plenty of time, thank you," Elle said. "But if you need to do something else, there's no rush—"

Carol smiled again. "There's nothing more important."

An hour later, Elle joined Carol in the Bentley driven by a driver named Dirk. Carol peppered her with questions during the ride, and Elle did her best to sound as boring as possible. The car pulled in front of a posh restaurant in a pricey shopping neighborhood.

"Here we are," Carol said and led the way into the restaurant. Although there was a lunchtime crowd, the host wasted no time finding a table for them. "Now," she said. "Tell me all about yourself. All about your romance with my son."

Grateful for the water the server immediately poured, Elle shrugged. "It wasn't something either of us expected. There was just this special connection we couldn't ignore."

"Obviously, since you're already pregnant. How far along are you?"

"Over three months," Elle said, trying to ignore Carol's tone. "But I'd rather hear more about you and the family. What was Brock like as a baby?" Elle said. "I'm sure you must have so many stories to share."

"Not as many as you'd think. Being the wife of James Maddox was a full-time job. My husband expected me to be by his side for client dinners. I joined clubs and served on boards to keep the Maddox name visible. The company was always number one with my husband. As it will be with Brock," she said. "But I'm sure you already know that, since you've worked with him."

"But you must have some memories of Brock as a child," Elle said.

"He was a handful. Very physically active, very curious, ambitious from the day he was born. Of course, his father loved that about him. We had a nanny before he was sent to private school. His father had very strong opinions about Brock's upbringing. He always said he was raising the lead lion, and the word 'average' was never allowed in any discussions about Brock. Speaking of a nanny, I can get you in with the most exclusive agency in San Francisco."

"Oh, I haven't even thought about nannies yet," Elle

said, thinking her view of parenting might differ widely from that of Carol Maddox.

"Well, don't leave it until it's too late. I'm sure Brock will demand the cream of the crop. He's just like his father that way," Carol said. "Since you're no longer working for Brock, have you decided which clubs you'd like to join? I can help you with that, too."

Elle shrugged and smiled, trying not to feel over-whelmed. "I have to be honest. Between the marriage, the move and the pregnancy, I'm still taking it one day at a time."

"Oh, the pregnancy," Carol said and shook her head. "The most miserable times of my life. I was in bed half the time with both of them. Maybe you'll get lucky and have a boy the first time and then you can talk Brock into stopping at one. Having a second child was necessary for the well-being of my marriage," Carol added. "Never forget for a moment that women will compete for the attention of a wealthy man, whether he's married or not. There's always someone trying to take your husband away from you."

When Elle returned home, she felt like crawling back into bed and hiding. Marrying Brock was clearly the biggest mistake of her life. She should have quit Maddox and fled to Mexico or Canada or Paris. Anywhere but here with Brock's Cruella de Vil mother. Feeling suffocated, Elle snuck out of the house and drove to her mother's. They spent the afternoon talking and baking cookies together for one of the members of Suzanne's support group.

When the clock passed seven in the evening, her

mother slid her arm around Elle. "Sweetie, shouldn't you be with your husband?"

"He's working. He won't mind me spending time with you," Elle said.

"But it's getting late," her mother said. "Are you sure you shouldn't go home?"

Elle's cell phone rang. She winced, pretty certain she knew who was calling.

"Elle?" her mother prompted, when she didn't race to her purse.

Elle reached for her phone and answered it. "Hi," she said.

"Where are you?" Brock asked.

"With my mom," Elle said, forcing her lips into a smile. "Baking cookies. Where are you?"

"At home looking for my wife," Brock said. He paused a half beat. "My mother scared the piss out of you, didn't she?"

Elle laughed nervously. "Cannot lie. She's a little creepy."

"Come home," he said. "I'll protect you."

"You can't protect me during the day when you're at work," she said.

"I can buy her a new place," he said. "Let her fill it up with all the stuff that's in the house."

"She can't be all bad," Elle said. "She had you."

"Don't remind me," he muttered.

"I don't know," Elle said. "I bet you don't know everything about what went on between her and your father."

"You're not defending her," he said.

"No, but I think there may be more than meets the eye."

"I can't disagree. There's Botox, face-lifts, Resty-lane—"

"Give the woman a break. Her whole life was being Mrs. James Maddox."

"She sucked you in," Brock said.

"I can see some of her points," she admitted.

Silence passed. "You're joking."

"No. I'm not."

"That's it," Brock said. "I'm sending Roger to get you."

"I have my car," Elle said.

"I don't want you driving in the dark," Brock said.

Elle rolled her eyes. "Too bad," she said and hung up. Feeling her mother's gaze on her, she pretended to continue her conversation. "Of course, I'll come home darling. Right away," she said and turned to her mother. "I guess I should go home."

Her mother studied her suspiciously. "Are you sure everything is okay between the two of you?"

"I'm sure," Elle fibbed, making sure not to look directly at her mother because her mother could read her like a book. "We're newlyweds. We're working things out. Plus, I'm pregnant. It's complicated, but Brock is an amazing man." Elle wasn't shading the truth about most of what she'd said. "I'll see you soon," she said and gave her mother a hug.

Thirty minutes later, Brock heard the front door open. He knew it was Elle and breathed a sigh of relief. If he'd known his mother was returning today, he would have found a way to protect Elle. His mother was the most manipulative woman he'd ever met and he would have thrown her out of the house earlier except he'd never had a compelling reason. Until now.

He strode toward the foyer and met Elle just as she took her first step upstairs. "Elle," he said.

She turned around. "Hi," she said.

"I'm sorry you had to deal with my mother by yourself today," he said.

She made a face. "It's not as if she's a mass murderer," Elle said. "Although she clearly has issues."

"That's an understatement," he muttered. "I'll be moving her out as soon as possible."

Elle frowned.

"What?" he demanded.

"I hate to displace her," Elle said. "Something about her seems so sad."

Seeing the compassion on her face made something inside him twist and turn. Underneath it all, Elle had a good heart, but her sympathy for Carol was misplaced. "Giving Carol her own place isn't displacing her. It's not as if I'm kicking her out and telling her to live in a park."

Elle bit her lip. "Are you sure it's the most compassionate thing to do?"

"I'm sure it's the right thing to do, for Carol and our marriage," he said firmly.

Two days later, Carol was ensconced in a new home just a few streets over and all her things had been hauled away by a moving company. Unfortunately, she had taken very few of the furnishings from Brock's home, which meant that Elle would need to sort out what should be discarded and what should be kept.

Elle turned to Anna. "What if I throw away something important, something that belonged to James?"

Anna pressed her lips together in sympathy. "I'll help as best I can, but he did pass several years ago."

Elle groaned. "I'll run everything past you. If there are questions about something, we'll put it in storage."

Going through all the junk took over twelve hours a day for the next week. Elle fell into bed every night exhausted. When Brock awakened her one morning, she wasn't sure which day of the week it was.

"This has got to stop," he said. "It's bad for your health. Bad for the baby."

"It's almost done. It'll probably only take a couple more days" she said, still melting into the mattress.

She felt his sigh drift over her shoulders. "I still have a lot to do with Prentice, and we're on the brink of another big deal, but I'd like to take you away," he said, skimming his fingers through her hair.

"Really?" she said. "Where?"

"Somewhere quiet," he said. "Somewhere away from here."

"I tried to exorcise the demons in this house, but I'm not sure I did," Elle said.

"Demons?" Brock echoed.

"Bad karma?" she said. "Bad memories? I'm not sure what it is, but I don't want it contaminating our future," she murmured.

He took her shoulders and turned her over to face him. He looked into her sleepy blue eyes and found himself craving more. "There's no such thing as bad karma," he told her. "I told you I would protect you."

She let out a long sigh. "With our histories, it's going to take more than one warrior to make our marriage work."

He saw the steely determination in her gaze and felt a surge of something primitive inside him. He'd never met a woman like Elle, a woman who could match his passion and his strength. "You keep surprising me."

"Is that a good thing?" she asked, her blue eyes dark and moody.

"I'll let you know. In the meantime, pack a bag. You and I are getting out of here," he said, making an instant decision. If Elle was going to rest, then he needed to take her away.

Within hours, Brock was driving toward the mountains. "I have a house a few hours from town. I go there as often as I can, which hasn't been much lately."

She sank into her leather seat and relaxed. "I've never heard about this place. You never went when I worked for you."

"When you were working for me, I was spending every spare moment I could with you," he said, taking a turn up a mountain road.

She rolled her head toward him. "It's nice to know that I wasn't the only one who was half crazed," she said.

He shot her a glance, then chuckled under his breath. "Half crazed is under estimating it by a long shot."

"Yeah, yeah," she said. "At least you got to stay all night in your apartment. I usually had to drive home in the middle of the night."

"What are you talking about? My driver took you home," he said.

"Oops," she said.

He shot her a sideways glance, feeling his gut tighten with frustration. "Are you telling me Dirk didn't take you home all those times?"

She paused. "I'm not telling you that."

"Because you don't want him fired," Brock said. "How the hell did you talk him out of it?"

"It wasn't easy, but how was I going to explain arriving home at my mother's with a chauffeur, especially when I needed to drive myself to the office the next day? He followed me to make sure I arrived home safely."

"I guess I shouldn't be surprised. Dirk did the right thing by following you home," Brock said. "I never realized what a stubborn streak you have."

"When I worked for you, my job was to make sure I anticipated your every need to make your life as easy as possible," she said. "Now I'm your wife."

"You mean the job description has changed," he said, and chuckled.

Silence stretched between them and he shot a quick glance at her. She looked pensive. "Elle, what's wrong?"

"I worry about how we're going to negotiate everything. I'm not like your mother," she said.

"Thank God," he said.

"What I mean is, I'm not the corporate super-wife type. If you married me expecting me to agree with your every thought, then we're going to have some problems. Do you realize that you and I haven't even discussed parenting? Based on what your mother said, your father was determined to raise you as some kind of super Maddox CEO. I can tell you now that I want our child to have a much more balanced upbringing."

Offended by her assessment of his father, Brock tightened his hands on the steering wheel. "My father made sure I had the best of everything, the best education—"

"The best nanny," Elle interjected. "What if I don't want a nanny raising my child? What if I don't want my child sent away to boarding school?"

Hearing fear and panic in Elle's voice, Brock realized where all this was coming from and took a mind-calming breath. "Carol's got you all worked up for nothing. You should know that she loves causing trouble. I think she was just trying to intimidate you, Elle."

"She brought up some important issues, Brock. For one thing, I'm not going to sign on to a bunch of high-brow clubs and societies if it means our child will be getting leftovers from me. Tell the truth. When you married me, didn't you expect me to step into a role just like your mother did?"

Brock shook his head, feeling something inside him twist and tighten, angry that his mother had made an already challenging situation more difficult. "I honestly didn't think that far," he said. "I just knew that I wanted us to do the right thing for the baby, and that meant getting married."

Elle was silent again for a long moment. "Well, you can check that off your list," she said. "But there are other things we'll need to settle."

He raked his hand through his hair in frustration. "She's always causing trouble," he muttered. "Thank

God she's out of the house now. You'll see soon enough that everything will work out." Brock would make sure of it. He may have had one failed engagement, but there would be no failed marriage. "Relax. It's time for you to take a break."

Despite the worries sprouting like weeds in her mind, Elle dozed off. As they pulled into a clearing, she got her first glimpse of the mountain chalet, and the serene setting immediately eased some of her tensions. "It's beautiful," she said. "So peaceful."

"It was a mess when I first bought it. I redid the whole thing." He nodded toward the chalet. "A caretaker looks after it while I'm gone and stocks the refrigerator when I tell him I'm on my way. His wife usually prepares a couple of meals for me and leaves them in the freezer for reheating, so we won't have to cook."

"You've seemed so restless and busy since I've met you. It's hard for me to imagine you being able to relax enough to enjoy this. What's the longest amount of time you've ever stayed here?" she asked as he pulled to a stop.

"A week in the winter. There's a ski resort not far. I spent another week working on it during one summer. And then I came up here every weekend for a while," he said. "But I bought it more for short breaks. Come on. I want to show you inside."

He got out of the car and led her to the front porch, where a wooden swing hung from the roof. Two rocking chairs and a table echoed the cozy, laid-back ambience. She followed him through the front door to a foyer that was two stories high. Light spilled in through the tall windows onto the tile floors dotted with soft rugs. The natural flow of the house led her to a large room filled with brown leather couches and chairs, golden wood tables and an HDTV that bore a strong resemblance to the one she'd chosen for the den in Brock's home.

She met his gaze and laughed. "It's the same size as the one I got, isn't it?"

He smiled and took her hand. "You must know my taste," he said, lifting her hand to his mouth.

Her heart skittered at his charming maneuver. She knew he had plenty of charm, but he'd displayed little of it toward her during the last few weeks. Understandably so.

"Come outside," he said. "The view will take your breath away."

He led her out glass doors to a two-story deck that revealed peaks and valleys as far as the eye could see. "It's amazing. It's so wonderful, I'm surprised you're not up here nearly every weekend."

"There've been too many demands at work," he said, staring at the view. "Especially over the last several months."

Elle felt a stab and twist of guilt. "Because of me," she said.

His gaze flickered, but he didn't look at her. "It's water under the bridge," he said. "I have to focus on repairing damage and making sure the company is secure and ready for the future."

More than ever, she hated that she had made Brock's job even more demanding and difficult than it should have been. She put her hand on his arm. "I really am sorry," she said.

He shrugged away. "Like I said, we can't focus on that. We have to move on. Speaking of which, let me show you the rest of the house."

She slipped her hand inside his, wishing she could get beneath the surface of Brock's veneer. Although she'd suspected he'd let her closer than most, she still sensed that he kept a protective wall around his heart. For example, she knew nothing about his failed engagement. She hesitated to talk about it, but she was growing impatient with the secrets between them. Plunging into uncharted territory, she glanced up at him. "Did you ever bring your ex-fiancée here?" she asked softly.

He glanced at her in surprise and shook his head. "No. I thought about it, but there was never time. Claire didn't understand the demands of my position. She wanted a man who could take off and travel whenever she felt the urge. I couldn't be that man. It wasn't all her fault, though. Toward the end, I could tell things weren't going to work out between us and I buried myself in my job even more."

"Was the breakup difficult for you?"

He gave a wry smile. "I don't like to fail," he said. "At anything. I'd had a crush on her during college, but she was always in a relationship with someone else. We bumped into each other when she was finally single and I decided I'd finally gotten my chance."

Elle's heart twisted at the idea of Brock waiting so long for a woman. He hadn't had to wait any time at all for Elle. She'd tumbled head over heels for him right away. "If you had loved her so long, how could you let her go?"

"She wasn't happy. Besides, I'm not sure I would call

it love back in college. It was more a case of unrequited lust then. The dream and reality didn't match up. We weren't well suited."

Digesting his explanation, she smiled cautiously in return. "And you think you and I *are* well suited?" she asked.

"Things are only going to get better for you and me. Trust me," he said.

Walking into the large master bedroom with the same beautiful view as the deck downstairs, she watched him meet her gaze with pride. "Not bad, is it? I put money down on this place after I'd been working for my father for three years and had won a new account. He was pissed that I hadn't consulted him first."

"I don't think you needed to consult with anyone about this," she said. "It's your secret baby, isn't it?"

He lifted an eyebrow. "That's an interesting way of putting it," he said, glancing out the window.

"Well, it is. How many people have you told about this place?" she asked.

"Not many. My brother knows about it."

"Your one act of rebellion," she said.

"Oh, I rebelled more than once. This was just my most productive act of rebellion," he said.

"Did your father ever see it after you renovated it?"

His eyes narrowed. "No. My father was a great man, but he never liked to admit when he was wrong."

"You don't have that trait," she said. "That was one of the things that drew me to you. You are extremely confident, and can made decisions at the speed of lightning. So many of the decisions you made when we were working together, I would have second- or third-guessed.

But you went ahead and made them. In the rare moments when you were wrong, you admitted it and took another track."

"The ad business requires decisiveness. If you stay in the same place too long, you'll get run over. I have too many people counting on me to allow that to happen," he said, meeting her gaze with laser-blue intensity. "I can't let them down."

He would never allow himself to let them down, just as he would never surrender the responsibility of his child. His sense of obligation was fierce and steadfast. She felt a shudder ripple through her at his expression and she found herself wondering if he would be the compassionate father she hoped he would be, or the hard taskmaster his father had been for him.

"Are you hungry?" he asked. "I called ahead and the caretaker said he would put cold cuts in the refrigerator for us. After that, perhaps you'd like to rest again."

"A sandwich sounds good, but I'd rather go for a hike than take a nap. I can nap in San Francisco," she said.

"Not that I could see," he said. "According to Anna, you were barely taking breaks for meals during the last week."

"I'm surrounded by tattletales," she said in frustration. "You have these people watching me like hawks."

"I'm your husband now, Elle. It's my responsibility to make sure you're safe and well-cared for. "

Responsibility. Obligation. Duty. She didn't want to be any of those to Brock, but she was certain he wouldn't understand her gripe, especially since she was pregnant with his child.

"Sandwich and hike, then," she said, lifting her

chin. "You can take a nap if you're feeling tired," she suggested, unable to resist the urge to goad him a little.

He chuckled and pulled her toward him. "You've forgotten. You always fell asleep before I did at my apartment."

She lifted her hand in surrender. "I can't argue with that," she said as he planted a kiss on her mouth.

Several hours later, after lunch, hiking, and consuming a warmed-up chicken pot pie, Brock sat on the sofa and Elle brought him a scotch on the rocks. He noticed she did it as if she hadn't thought twice about it.

"Thanks," he said and studied her for a long moment. "It occurs to me that you may know more about my preferences than I know about yours," he said as she sank onto the couch beside him with a bottle of water.

"Hmm," she said and laughed with a self-satisfied smile. "You've never been anyone's assistant, let alone *my* assistant."

Brock took a sip of the perfectly chilled scotch. "You don't have to be arrogant about it," he said with a grin.

She slid a sideways glance at him. "I am not, nor have I ever been, arrogant. The concept is completely foreign to me."

"Okay, then you're a show-off," he said, taking another sip.

She dropped her jaw. "I am *not* a show-off. If anyone is a show-off, it's you," she said. "Look at you, with you laser-blue eyes and dark hair. You're charming when you're inclined…"

He frowned at her. "When I'm inclined?" he echoed.

"It's not every day," she said.

Brock shook his head. There were so many people who sucked up to him on a daily basis—but not Elle, and he liked her for that. "So what's your favorite cocktail?" he asked.

"Strawberry martini with sugar rim," she said and licked her lips. "Delicious."

The sight of her tongue on her plum-colored lips made his gut draw tight. "Noted. Favorite meal?"

"Depends on the day," she said. "Especially since I've been pregnant. Lately I've been craving macaroni and cheese," she said with a wince. "That's gonna do terrible things to my hips."

"Your hips are perfect. Favorite sandwich?" he continued.

"When I'm good, I'll take a chicken and vegetable wrap. When I'm bad, open-faced turkey with gravy and mashed potatoes or roast beef."

"I like that about you," he said, shooting her a smile. "I like that you are a red-meat eater," he said, remembering the way she'd once savored a steak with béarnaise sauce.

"Not lately," she said.

"Are you telling me you never want me to take you out for a steak?" he asked.

"No," she admitted. "Just later."

"Okay, I'll take a raincheck. Same for that strawberry martini," he said. "Favorite toy from childhood?"

She blinked. "My little pony," she said. "I always

wanted a pony, but I knew that was an impossible dream."

"Favorite dessert?" he continued, losing himself in her ocean-blue gaze.

"Chocolate anything," she said.

He smiled. "If you could travel anywhere, where would you go?"

"Europe."

"That's a whole continent," he said.

"And your point is?" she said, lifting her eyebrow.

He laughed, drinking in her audacity. "I wish my father had met you," he said.

"Why?" she asked. "I'm just an assistant."

He shook his head. "No, you're more. Observant, responsive and fascinating."

"Now, you flatter me," she said, flashing her eyes at him.

"Technically, I don't need to flatter you anymore. You married me, so I can coast."

"Oh, I think that would be a huge mistake," she said. "For both of us. Don't you?"

Seven

Brock made love to Elle through the night until she was too exhausted to continue. She curled up against his chest, slid her arms around his neck and fell asleep. The next morning she awoke to an empty place beside her. Elle lifted her head. She heard his voice, but not close by.

Pushing aside the covers, she rose from the bed and listened as she pulled on her robe. Was he downstairs? She crept closer to the bedroom door, and pushed it open.

"It's Sunday, for God's sake," Brock said, his voice carrying from downstairs. "Can't this wait?"

Silence followed. She heard Brock swear. "Okay, okay. I'll be back in town by this afternoon and in the office this evening." He swore again. "This better be worth it," he muttered.

Elle felt a twist in her stomach. The short, sweet time they'd shared together was over. Her chest hurt. Her heart hurt, but she didn't want him to feel bad after he'd made such an effort for them to get away. She bit her lip. "Hey," she called downstairs. "This has been wonderful, but I'm ready to return to civilization if you don't mind."

Brock walked out from under the second-floor landing so she could see him. Shirtless, he wore silk pants low on his hips. His bare chest was mesmerizing, his hair tousled by her fingers. He was the sexiest thing alive.

"You don't like the cabin?"

Her heart wrenched in her chest, but she forced herself to step up and give the response he needed. "No, I love it. But I have a ton to do and I'm starting to feel a little antsy," she said. "Do you mind?"

His gaze wrapped around hers for a long moment and he shook his head. "No," he said. "No problem. Let me know when you're ready. I'll load the car."

As soon as Elle and Brock arrived home in San Francisco, he returned to the office. Elle returned to redecorating the house. With the assistance of Bree, she'd found a decorator who helped her combine some of the older elements in the house with some of Brock's taste. Elle decided to retain a semi-formal tone for the living room and dining room for entertaining.

Brock was so busy he often didn't come to bed until after eleven o'clock, but he always rose early. She knew he was still feeling pressured by Golden Gate Promotions. Despite her grandfather's heart attack, he still hadn't given up his fight against Maddox. More than ever, Elle was aware of how much her deceit was costing Brock. It seemed as if all he did was work. She didn't see how they could possibly rebuild their relationship under the current circumstances, but she also couldn't exactly stomp her foot and demand he spend more time with her.

He surprised her one evening when he arrived home before dinner. She was eating a club sandwich in front of the television and debating whether to visit her mother again.

"Hey," he said, looking unbearably handsome in the doorway. "I like what you've done with the downstairs," he said. "You combined the old with the new and lightened it up." He glanced at her sandwich. "That looks good, too."

"I can fix you one," she said, standing, filled with the instant pleasure of just being with him.

He shook his head. "No, I can get the housekeeper. It won't take a—"

As if on cue, Anna stepped inside the room. "Good evening, Mr. Maddox. Mrs. Maddox." Glancing at Elle's plate, she shot her a disapproving glance. "Is there something I can get you?"

"I'll have the same thing she's having," Brock said. "With a beer."

"Club sandwich," Elle supplied with a sheepish smile.

"What was that about?" he asked curiously as he sat down beside her.

"Your staff gets really upset when I fix my own food. I think they consider it an insult," she said.

Brock chuckled. "Trust me, they're not used to anyone doing for themselves around here. Anna probably doesn't know what to do with you."

"How's work?" she asked, noticing that his lack of rest was visible around his eyes. "You look tired."

"You know I'm in the race for the gold against your grandfather. Can't take a lot of breaks."

Frustration filled her. "I don't understand him. I would have thought his heart condition would slow him down, or at least make him see reason."

"He and my father have a lot in common. My father was determined to leave the business for future generations of the Maddox family."

"Is that the way you feel?" she asked. "That you're building Maddox for your heirs?"

"At this point in the company's growth, it's more about taking care of the employees who are counting on me, and securing our growth for the future. I haven't spent a lot of time thinking about what my heir will ultimately do." Anna delivered the sandwich and beer. "Thank you," he said to her. "Why do you ask, Elle?"

"Just curious. Your father instilled in you a strong sense of family tradition and I wondered if you planned the same path for our child."

"You don't like that idea," he concluded, then shot her a sly smile. "You don't think I turned out well?"

"I didn't say that," she said, giving in to the urge to smile. "I just wouldn't want our child to feel locked in to only one choice."

"If it's a boy, he may want to play baseball," he said.

"Or sing opera," she said, choosing the polar opposite to watch Brock's reaction.

"Not if he gets my musical ability," Brock muttered, taking a bite of the sandwich and washing it down with a swig of beer. He let out a long sigh. "This is the most relaxed I've been since we left the mountain house. Thank God my dinner meeting had to cancel tonight."

Elle couldn't decide whether to feel offended or flattered. "Well, it's good to see you," she said. "I've missed you."

He glanced up and met her gaze for a long moment. "I can see how it would get lonely around here."

"It's not that," she said. "I was just used to seeing you at the office, so I spent most of my days with you."

He nodded. Something about him seemed restless, unsettled. "It won't always be this busy. I'll be around more."

"Will you really?" she asked, keeping her voice light even though her feelings were anything but. "That workaholic gene is pretty strong."

"You're not the first to notice," he said, his gaze turning moody. "After we get through this crisis, I want to shift things so that I can delegate more often. But in the meantime, you and I have received our first social invitation," he said, changing the subject. "Walter and Angela Prentice are having a cocktail party on Friday night and they specifically requested your presence."

The Prentice name was familiar to Elle—Walter's company was Maddox's most important client. "Do they know about the baby?" she asked, acutely aware that Walter was very image-conscious and wouldn't tolerate even a whiff of a scandal.

"I didn't mention it, but Walter's such a family man, I'm sure he'll be delighted with the news, since we're married."

"Family is everything," she said, repeating the Prentice slogan.

"Yes, it is," Brock said, taking a bite of his sandwich and leaning his head back against the sofa.

She felt a shot of sympathy for him, remembering the challenging days he'd endured when she'd worked for him. Finished with her dinner, she rose and stood behind him. "Take a deep breath and let the day go," she said, repeating what she'd told him in his apartment so many times.

"Hmm," he said as she sank her fingers into his shoulders.

"You can't work 24/7," she whispered. "You can't work right now, so you may as well rest. Rest and get stronger for when you *can* do something."

Brock inhaled and exhaled. "I remember how much I craved these massages at the end of the day," he murmured.

She gently rubbed his shoulder muscles with her thumb and forefinger. "Good?" she asked.

He groaned in response.

She continued to knead his shoulders as she brushed her mouth against his ear. "Does it feel good?"

"Yes," he said. "Too good. I want more," he continued. "I want to feel you every way I can. Inside and out," he said and turned around to meet her gaze. "Let's go upstairs."

"You haven't finished your sandwich," she said.

"I'm hungry for something else."

The next evening, Brock asked her to meet him at the Prentices' home, since he was running late. Elle dressed carefully, eager to convey just the right tone as

Brock's wife. After all, this was their first major public outing together. Fighting butterflies, she exited the car and climbed the steps to the Prentices' mansion.

With marble columns, a valet in the driveway and a man greeting guests in black tie at the door, the major clothing manufacturer's property oozed success, as it should.

"Good evening," the man at the door said. "Your name?"

"Elle Linton," she said, then corrected herself. "Elle Linton Maddox."

His gaze flicked over her in assessment and he nodded. "Welcome," he said and opened the door for her to enter.

Elle was immediately hit with the sights and sounds of an opulent party. The scents of gourmet food and wine filled the air. She heard a string quartet and smelled fresh-cut roses. Mirrors reflected guests dressed in couture fashions. She hoped the black gown with dark embroidered rosettes just below the bodice would pass muster. She brushed a strand of hair from her face and searched for Brock. She'd waited a few extra minutes to leave, not wanting to arrive before him.

A waiter offered her a glass of champagne and she shook her head. "No, thank you. Do you have water?"

He pointed to a waitress as the other end of the room where the chandeliers flashed light and brilliance that was reflected in the mirrors. "Thank you," she murmured, searching the crowd for Brock. She didn't see a soul she knew in the entire room, and wondered where the hosts were. She should at least be able to identify Walter Prentice since he had been in Brock's office before. Accepting a glass of water from the server, she nodded her thanks and backed against the wall. Perhaps she would be able to see Brock from here.

A group of men on one side of her discussed the terrible performance of the Giants. A group of women on her other side discussed plastic surgery. Elle caught fragments of each conversation.

"They need to trade the pitcher. He can't do anything," one man lamented.

"Have you heard about Dr. Frazier? He does amazing things with filler."

"If you ask me, it's not the pitcher, it's the management," another man said.

"I hear he worked on Carol Maddox. She looks a little too tight to me," a woman said.

Elle's ears perked up at the mention of her mother-in-law.

"She looks better now that he's plumped up her face a little. Speaking of Carol, did you hear about Brock? He's off the market," a woman said.

"Oh, no," several women murmured. "Who got him?"

"I hear he knocked up his assistant. The only reason he married her is because she's pregnant," the woman said.

Elle felt her face heat with embarrassment. Even though she knew the woman's words were true, the humiliation struck at the core of her. She wanted to defend her relationship with Brock. She wanted to tell the woman that she and Brock had experienced a closeness that neither of them had expected, yet both had cherished. But she wouldn't. Because the bottom line was, Elle had betrayed him and he'd married her because of the baby.

Taking a long drink of water, she strongly considered leaving. She could tell Brock she hadn't felt well…

"Well, well, Mrs. Maddox, what are you doing in the corner?" Walter Prentice said with a big smile and booming voice. "Come and meet my wife. She's been dying to see who finally slayed Brock Maddox and brought him to his knees."

Elle forced her lips into a smile and accepted the arm he offered. "Good evening, Mr. Prentice. You have a lovely home. And I wouldn't call it slayed," she said, referring to Brock. "I definitely didn't bring him to his knees."

"Oh, don't tell me Brock didn't give you a proper old-fashioned proposal?" he asked, ushering her through the crowd.

"Well, you know Brock. He's a breathtaking combination of tradition and cutting edge," she managed.

"Too true," he said. "Now, here's my wife, Angela. Angela, this is Brock's new bride, Elle."

The elegant woman gave her a warm, curious glance. "How lovely," she said. "Walter and I were so happy when we heard Brock had gotten married, although you two did a good job keeping it secret. Shame on you. Everyone loves a wedding."

"Brock wanted to keep it low-key. Neither of us expected our feelings to grow like they did," Elle said, working hard to keep the smile on her face.

"Brock has a good head on his shoulders," Walter said in approval. "Where is he?"

"I'm not sure," Elle said. "He was running a little late at the office. I'm certain he'll be here soon."

"He shouldn't keep his bride waiting," Mrs. Prentice said. "Let me introduce you to a few of my friends."

For the next half hour, Elle's head swam with new names. Mrs. Prentice, clearly an overachiever like her husband, introduced her to several people. When Mrs. Prentice emphasized the fact that Elle was Brock Maddox's new wife, Elle felt curious glances sizing her up. After fielding questions about their small wedding and nonexistent honeymoon, Elle managed to slip away to call Brock.

He picked up on the fifth ring. "Brock Maddox," he said curtly.

"Elle Linton Maddox," she returned just as curtly. "Where are you?" she asked. "The Prentices are asking for you."

"This cosmetics contract is a major headache," he said. "I'm running late."

"You said you were running late an hour and a half ago. What am I supposed to say to Mr. and Mrs. Prentice?"

"I'll leave now," he said. "See you in fifteen minutes."

He disconnected the call and Elle tucked her cell phone inside her evening bag. The house felt as if it were closing in on her. Desperately needing some fresh air, she walked outside to the patio where guests mingled, enjoying the beautiful night. She moved toward a column in a dark corner and sucked in the air. She looked up at the cloudy sky, shielding the stars, remembering a similar party that could have been a thousand years ago, or just yesterday.

Her grandfather had given permission for her to attend a Christmas party at his home. Elle had been eight years old and her mother had bought her a red velvet dress with lace at the hem and collar. Elle had been so excited. She'd hoped to meet her father, but he didn't show up. The other children had avoided her as if she were somehow less than them. The whole experience had been a disaster and she couldn't wait to get home and tear off her dress, put on her pajamas and go to bed. She remembered the feeling of not belonging all too well. She had the same feeling right now.

She stood there for several moments in the dark, wondering if she should leave, and if she did, whether anyone would notice. Then she heard a familiar male voice in the background.

"Walter, great to see you. You really know how to throw a party," Brock said as he walked within just a few feet of her. Her heart skittered at the sight of him.

"I met your wife earlier. She's beautiful. You shouldn't leave her on her own. Someone might steal her away," Walter said.

Brock gave a forced laugh. "You're right. Elle is beautiful. Do you know where she is?"

"I'm sure she's around here somewhere. The Missus was introducing her around," Mr. Prentice said. "I remember Elle was your assistant."

"Yes, she was," Brock said. "When I realized we had feelings for each other, I decided we should make our relationship official. I didn't want to muddy the professional waters."

"Good move," Walter said. "Keep business separate from romance. Congratulations again on your marriage."

"Thank you," Brock said. "Now, if you'll excuse me, I'd better go search for my bride."

Walter laughed and thumped Brock on the shoulder. "If anyone can find her, I'm sure it's you."

From the shadows, Elle watched as Brock pulled out his BlackBerry and sent a text message. Glancing around, he accepted a glass of wine from a server. He loosened his collar, looking impatient.

Elle wondered if she should step forward, but something kept her from it. Her wedding to Brock was all for show and she no longer knew if she could keep up the performance. Elle moved along the wall to the French doors and scooted through the crowd. All those years of being the Koteas's dirty little secret played through her mind, and here she was again, having been Brock's little secret. She felt like such a fraud. Brock didn't really want to be married to her. She couldn't help feeling like he resented her for the pregnancy.

Unable to bear the return of feelings she'd suffered since childhood, she dashed out the front door and asked the valet to hail a cab for her.

Although her mother didn't know the whole truth about her relationship with Brock, she did know Elle's history. She didn't know that Elle had accepted a deal with her grandfather to keep her mother well, but she knew just about everything else. Elle needed to see her.

"What a lovely surprise," Elle's mother said as she

rose from the sofa where she'd been watching television to greet her daughter. She studied Elle from head to toe. "You look lovely. What are you doing here?"

Elle flew into her mother's accepting arms. "What do you mean? Are you suggesting I usually look like a hag when I visit you?" Elle asked.

"Well, no," her mother said, pulling back slightly. "But you're not usually dressed to the nines. Want to tell me what this is about?"

"Can't we just enjoy the visit?" Elle begged.

"Hmm," her mother said doubtfully, dipping her head. "Sit down on the sofa and I'll pour you some green tea."

Elle made a face. "It smells like stinky socks," she said, but sat down, anyway.

"It's soothing," her mother retorted, heading for the kitchen, "and the antioxidants are good for both you and the baby."

Elle's cell phone rang and she frowned, fumbling in her small bag.

"Is that your cell I hear?" her mother asked.

Elle silenced her phone. "Oh, you're watching a Sandra Bullock movie. I miss our girls' nights together," she said.

Her mother reappeared with a cup of tea. "Who rang on your cell phone?"

"I'm not sure," Elle said, reaching for the tea. "It stopped."

"Uh-huh," her mother said and sat down beside her. "Elle, what's wrong? You know you can talk to me."

Elle's throat grew swollen with emotion. She'd carried so much during the last several months—the weight of her mother's illness, the deal with her grandfather, her secret affair with Brock and the pregnancy. And now, her misery over being married to a man who didn't love her.

"I just wanted to see you," Elle said. "I've been so busy I haven't had a chance to get over here during the last few days."

"Hmm," her mother said, but she slid her arm around Elle's shoulders and hugged her. Thank God for unconditional love. Elle felt the tears back up in her eyelids.

A knock sounded at the door.

Her mother turned, frowning. "Security didn't call. How odd."

Elle knew who it was. "Don't tell him I'm here."

Her mother stared at her. "Who?" she asked. "Elle, who?"

"Brock," Elle whispered and shook her head. "I just can't deal with him right now. I just can't."

Her mother sighed. "Elle, this is ridiculous. You can't hide from your husband."

"Please," Elle said.

"Is he abusing you?" her mother asked, grave concern on her face.

"Of course not," Elle said.

"Just a minute," her mother called and walked to the door. She opened it. "Hi, Brock. Elle and I were just talking about you."

Eight

"I searched for you at the party, but I couldn't find you," Brock said, looking at Elle. She was beautiful, dressed in a black, slinky gown that hid her pregnancy but accented her curves. Her eyes were smoky blue, her lips shiny and inviting. Her gaze, however, was cautious and guarded.

"I waited a long time, then I just followed a whim to visit my mother," Elle said, her smile forced, her eyes dark with secret emotions. He wondered what was going on.

"Prentice said he and his wife were happy to see you," he said.

"They were very gracious," she replied.

Brock wasn't quite sure how to approach Elle at this point. She clearly wasn't interested in seeing him. That was a first. When they'd been working together, she couldn't get enough of him. He'd felt the same for her. He still felt the same for her, although he didn't know when he would be able to fully trust her again. He had no doubt that she could sense that. Perhaps that was part of the problem.

He glanced at the television. "What are we watching?'

Elle's mother cleared her throat. "A Sandra Bullock movie," she said. "Would you like some green tea?"

Brock blinked. *Green tea?* He would rather drink dirty water. "Thank you," he said and sat down on the sofa. "I hear Sandra Bullock is up for an Oscar."

"Not for this movie," Elle's mother called as she walked toward the kitchen. "But she's my favorite actress."

"Why didn't you wait for me?" Brock asked Elle in a low voice.

"Do you have any idea how insulting it was to have to make excuses for you for almost two hours?" she said. "If you expect me to be a Stepford wife like your mother, you can forget it. We should just end it now."

"My mother," he echoed, appalled. "Why would I want you to be like my mother? Trust me, I have no oedipal urges. What happened at the party?" he asked gently. "Did something upset you?"

"Aside from waiting for you endlessly," Elle whispered, "I happened to overhear people say that the only reason you married me was because I was pregnant. Don't even try to deny it because we both know the truth."

Her desperation and vulnerability dug at him. "You and I both want the best for this baby," he said.

"Yes, but you and I need—" She stopped and lowered her voice. "You and I need to have a relationship," she whispered. "It can't all be about the baby or it's not going to work."

"We have never had a shortage of passion, Elle," he said.

"I want more than passion," she said. "I want compassion, companionship…" She took a deep breath. "I want love."

Brock felt his gut twist. "I can give you passion, compassion and companionship, but love is going to take a while. But I'll work at it. I promise," he said.

She stared at him with pain in her eyes. "I'm going to be blunt here. I don't want a marriage like your parents had."

Brock felt like she'd slapped him. "What the hell do you know about my parents' marriage? You've never even met my father," he said, a twinge of anger stinging a raw place inside him.

"You've obviously forgotten the earful your mother gave me," she said. "Besides, if you're a chip off the old block, then in a way, I *have* met your father."

"Here's the tea," Suzanne said as she brought Brock's cup to him, looking back and forth between Brock and Elle with concern. "It's still a little hot."

"Thank you," he said.

"This is…nice," she said, sitting down without taking her eyes off them. "Enjoying a movie with my daughter and son-in-law. Shall we watch the rest?"

Brock only made it through the chick flick because he was so distracted by what was happening with Elle that he could barely follow what was on screen. What had gotten into her? He'd thought she would be excited about attending the Prentices' cocktail party.

The interminable movie finally ended and Brock rose to his feet. "Time to go. Elle needs her rest and so do you," he said to his mother-in-law.

"How thoughtful," Suzanne said, taking his hand and looking directly in his eyes. "I'm so glad you're looking after Elle."

"I wouldn't have it any other way," he said to reassure her. "Thank you for your hospitality, Suzanne. Ready, Elle?"

Elle met his gaze with a hint of a mutinous expression that didn't bode well for the ride home. He could feel the chill already. "Yes," she finally said and gave her mother a hug. "I'll talk to you soon," she promised and joined Brock as they left the condo.

They walked to his car in silence and Brock ushered her into the passenger seat of his Porsche. He rounded the vehicle, slid in and started the engine. "I think we should start this conversation over. First, I apologize for being late tonight. This prospective cosmetics account is almost more demanding than the Prentice account."

Glancing at her, he noticed her arms were crossed firmly and her jaw was set. But after a long silence, she finally gave a heavy sigh. "Apology accepted. In the future, however, I would appreciate it if you would keep me better informed about delays."

He nodded. "I can do that. Now, about us…it's going to take time, Elle," he said.

"Exactly. With the schedule you keep at the office, it's going to be difficult for you to put in any time on our marriage."

Brock had heard something similar from his ex-fiancée just before she'd left him. His gut tightened at the prospect of Elle doing the same. He'd hoped that since she'd been his assistant, she would understand his devotion to the company. He'd also hoped that because of all the nights they'd shared, she would somehow know, deep down, that his drive for his company was part of his blood, part of his very being.

"Are you complaining about my work hours?" he asked.

She narrowed her eyes. "I resent that. I'm not complaining. But let's look at this a different way. If you were trying to build a business relationship with me, how much time would you put in?"

He blinked at her challenge.

"I'll take a wild guess and say you might want my relationship with you to last at least as long as your relationship with Prentice," she said.

He took a deep breath as he pulled into the driveway. "Of course I want our marriage to last," he muttered. He parked in the garage and turned to her. "What are you trying to say?"

"It's easy," she said. "If we both want our relationship to work, we both need to put in the time."

"We spend every night together," he said.

"Asleep," she said.

"We don't sleep for the first two hours."

She let out a quick breath. "We need to be about more than sex," she whispered, her eyes dark and tumultuous.

"Are you saying I don't satisfy you?" he demanded.

She bit her lip. "I'm not saying that, but maybe we

should put the emphasis in our relationship on something else," she said. "For a while."

"You want to date," he concluded, incredulous. But when he gave it some thought, it made sense.

She licked her lips and he felt himself grow hard. He had felt that mouth against his, sliding down his throat and chest, down lower, taking him to insane heights….

"We never did that, Brock," she said. "We never just…dated."

"Okay," he said slowly. "Does that mean we sleep together or not?"

"That's up to you," she said. "If we waited for a little while to—" She broke off. "Do you still want to sleep together while we figure this out?"

Brock decided to leave the ball in her court, since this was her idea. "I'll let you decide," he said, rising from the car and crossing over to open the passenger door. "Dinner tomorrow night?"

"I'd rather hike on Sunday," she said.

Brock swallowed.

"Is that okay?" she asked.

"Sure," he said. He could last. He'd suffered far worse than unmet sexual need in his life.

Less than an hour later, Brock slid into bed and Elle curled against him. "Thank you," she whispered, her lips against the back of his neck. He felt her breasts against him, her hand over his abdomen. He wondered if he would be able to stand this all night long.

Brock took a deep breath. He'd grown accustomed to making love to Elle every night. After all, she was his wife. She stirred his passions and was incredibly responsive. Why should he deny himself? Or her?

He knew, however, that she wanted him to use some restraint. It would take every bit of his determination, but he would damn well do it. Elle was worth it. And so was their marriage.

Sunday afternoon, Elle climbed up a trail behind Brock. She inhaled deeply, disgusted with her lack of physical fitness.

"You okay?" Brock asked, looking over his shoulder.

"Sure," she said breathlessly.

He turned around and came to a stop. "You don't sound okay," he said, searching her face.

She put her hands on her hips as she tried to catch her breath. "It's the altitude," she said.

He grinned. "Not the exertion?"

She scowled at him. "The climb has been straight up."

"I thought you could handle it," he said.

"I can," she replied and took a deep breath.

His blue eyes flickered over her. "Let's take a break and drink some water."

"You're just saying that because I'm pregnant," she said.

"I'm thirsty," he said, sitting down as he pulled out his bottle of water. "Aren't you?"

Elle sank onto a rock and also pulled out her water. She drank down the cool liquid quickly.

"You should make sure to keep hydrated," Brock said.

"I will," she said, downing almost all of the bottle.

"Want mine?" he asked.

"No, I'm good," she said.

He pulled an extra bottle from his backpack and offered it to her. "I want to make sure my wife and baby have plenty of water."

She finished hers and accepted his. "Thanks from both of us."

He enclosed her hand in his. "Let's go back down," he said.

"I feel a little like a wimp. I didn't expect to get this tired this soon."

"You're pregnant," Brock said. "You're feeding and breathing and doing everything for two."

Elle couldn't resist smiling. "Thanks," she said, drawing strength from the clasp of his hand. "Let's go back down."

"Good. Now tell me, when you were a little girl, what did you want for Christmas?"

Elle did a double take. "For Christmas? A father," she said, unable to keep the words from escaping her mouth.

Brock stopped midstep. "A father," he echoed. "I'll always be a father to our child," he promised.

"Will you show up at most of his soccer games or her ballet recitals?" she asked.

He took a quick breath. "Yes, I will."

She nodded and started to walk again. "That's good," she said, making her way down the trail.

"When you were a little girl," Brock said, "what kind of husband did you want?"

"I dreamed of Prince Charming sweeping me away to a fairytale kingdom with a huge castle with housekeepers and cooks. But I was in charge of the babies," she said. "We didn't have nannies because the prince and I took care of our children."

Her childhood dream moved him.

"Crazy, isn't it?" Elle said.

Brock pulled her against him. "Not crazy at all."

As they made their way down the last part of the path, Brock asked half a dozen more questions.

"What are your favorite movies?" he asked.

"I hate to say it," she said.

"Sandra Bullock movies," he said.

"Yes, and Julia Roberts. I like girl-power movies. Comes from being left in the shadow of my father and grandfather," she said.

"Understandable," Brock said. "Your favorite flower is the rose. And you especially love a multicolored arrangement."

She stared at him in surprise. "How did you know that?"

"I got you flowers a few times. I caught you smelling the roses more than once."

"I didn't know you'd noticed," she said, meeting his gaze.

"I didn't notice as much as I should have," he said. "But I noticed a few things. I'll notice more in the future," he promised.

She rested her forehead against his. "What's your favorite flower?"

Surprise rushed through him. "I've never thought about it."

"Think about it," she said, smiling.

He shrugged his shoulders. "I don't know. Wild flowers?"

"Hmm. I'm not so sure about that."

"You're not going to argue with me about my favorite flower, are you?" he challenged.

Elle sighed. "Okay," she relented. "So which sports event are you dying to attend?"

He laughed. "Lots of them, but I can't make time for them all," he said. "Would you go with me?"

"Of course."

"Good," he said, pulling her into a hug and sliding his hands down over her butt, lifting her against him. "You never quit making me want you," he said.

Elle brushed her lips over his. "Who, me?"

"Oh, yeah," he said. "You."

That night as she snuggled in his arms, Brock wanted her more than ever. His need for her alarmed him, but the sensation of her skin against his and her clean, sexy scent distracted him. He resigned himself to another night of frustration and forced his eyes closed.

Seconds later, he felt her hand drift over his chest, down to his abdomen. He caught that wicked, curious hand just before she touched him where he was hard and wanting her. "No teasing," he said in a low voice.

She lifted her lips to his, her eyelids fluttering to a sultry half-mast. "What if the teasing will be followed by satisfaction?"

"I thought you wanted us to take some time—"

She rubbed her mouth against his, sliding her tongue just inside. "I want you, too, Brock," she confessed. "It's hard for me to stay away from you."

"If you're sure," he said, loosening his grip on her

hand. Two breaths later she was touching him intimately and kissing him as if there was no tomorrow. He wondered if he would ever get enough of her.

They made love that night and when Brock awakened in the morning, he was caught between wanting to take her again and giving her a break. He wanted Elle too much. She got under his skin.

The following week, despite their discussion, Brock came home late every night. Elle refused to be a nag. She occupied herself by visiting her mother and grandfather, and continuing with redecorating the house. On Friday, Brock left before she rose, but Elle decided to take breakfast in the sunroom, anyway.

Yawning, she indulged in eggs, bacon and blueberry pancakes. The housekeeper brought her the newspaper and she scanned it as she ate. Just as she was finishing a gooey, delicious bite of pancake, she glimpsed a photo of Brock with a beautiful blonde. He was lifting a glass of wine and she was laughing

Elle's food lodged in her throat. "Oh, my God," she said, choking, coughing then swallowing. She read the caption beneath the photo. "Hot San Francisco Mad Man Brock Maddox charms cosmetics queen Lenora Hudgins."

Elle stared at the photo, absorbing every detail. Lenora was beautiful. Brock looked charming and sexy. She wanted to club him. She was staying home every night when he was out *courting* Lenora Hudgins. Or her account, anyway.

Twelve hours later, she was still steaming as she waited for Brock to return home. He finally wandered in at eight o'clock as she finished a BLT while watching her second Julia Roberts movie. Taking a deep breath, she focused on that big-screen TV instead of how furious she was with her husband.

"Julia Roberts," he said. "Did she win an Oscar for this one?"

"No. I watched that one earlier," she said.

Silence stretched between them. "How was your day?" he asked.

"Downhill after my second blueberry pancake," she said, "thanks to your photo with Lenora in the paper."

Another silence fell like a lead weight. "What photo?"

"The one in the paper this morning," she said, still not looking at him. "You didn't see it?"

He swore. "No. I didn't. You didn't read anything into that photo, did you?" he asked. "Because it was all business."

"Hmm," she said. "If I were the jealous type, I would have to disagree. I can't help wondering how you would feel if the roles were reversed and I were toasting a man with that kind of smile on my face." She thrust the paper toward him, her gaze focused on Julia Roberts on the screen. "You want to answer that one?"

"It isn't what it looks like, Elle. Come on. You worked for me. You know exactly what those dinners are all about."

"Again, how would you respond if that were me in the photo? And I said 'it isn't what it looks like?'" she asked.

"I would want to beat the guy to a pulp," he conceded.

She finally met his gaze. "I don't think Lenora would look good with a black eye," she said. "I also don't think you would get the account if I punched her."

"You want to join me the next time Lenora and I have dinner?" he asked.

"I think you might have a hard time winning the account with your pregnant wife along," she said.

"You didn't answer my question."

"Any chance I can get some free makeup samples?" she asked.

His lips twitched. "What do you want me to do?"

"Tell me how much she turns you off," she said.

"She does," Brock said. "Plastic. Over-Botoxed. Her skin is so tightly stretched she looks like she's permanently in a spaceship with a G-force blowing back her skin."

"You're exaggerating," she said.

He chuckled. "The woman is impossible to please. She's an alien."

"Does she want you to go to bed with her?"

"No, Elle, she's just incredibly difficult and demands a lot of attention," he said, irritation bleeding through his cool countenance.

His response aroused her curiosity. "In what way?"

"Do you really want to know?" he asked.

"Yes, I do. I miss the activity at the office. Hearing about your work is fun for me," she said and he sat down beside her. "Tell me about her. Is she married? Does she have children? How old is she?"

"Unmarried, one child, college-aged, she's fifty-three. She's had too many face-lifts and works out too much," he said.

"Scared, but gotta be tough to stay on top," Elle said. "Bring her here for dinner one night next week. We'll have roast chicken, mashed potatoes, string beans and biscuits."

"The only thing she'll eat is the chicken," he said.

"We'll see," she said.

He narrowed his eyes at her. "What makes you so sure?"

"What have you got to lose?" she countered.

He shrugged. "Good point."

They slept together for the next three nights, but didn't make love, even though their experiment was technically over. The lack of intimacy relieved Elle, then made her feel uneasy. She tried not to focus on it. On Monday night, Lenora was scheduled to arrive for dinner at six. By six-thirty, she still hadn't arrived.

"This is why I can't stand dealing with this woman," Brock muttered, pacing from one end of the den to the other.

Five minutes later, the doorbell rang. "I can't believe it," he said. "She finally showed."

Elle allowed the housekeeper to greet Lenora, then counted to ten and rose. She slid her hand inside Brock's and walked toward the dining room. He squeezed her hand and glanced at her. "Thanks," he muttered.

Lenora swept into the hallway. "I'm so sorry I'm late. Crazy Monday," the platinum blonde with smoky eyes and a too-thin frame said.

"Lenora, we're glad you could come. This is my wife, Elle."

"Nice to meet you, Elle. Something smells delicious."

"Just a little home cooking. I figure a hardworking woman could use a little home cooking every now and then," Elle said.

Lenora studied her for a moment, then sighed. "Comfort food," she said. "I never indulge, but I just might tonight."

"It won't hurt you," Elle said. "As my mother would say, you could use some fattening up. Come into the dining room. You've earned your dinner."

Lenora smiled. "I'll pay with the elliptical tomorrow, but you're tempting me."

"We all gotta live," Elle said, and the three of them entered the dining room.

After Lenora consumed chicken, mashed potatoes, stuffing, biscuits and green beans, she groaned as she sat back in her chair. "That was delicious. So bad, but so good."

"Give yourself a break," Elle said. "You obviously work like a dog."

"I like her," Lenora said to Brock. "Where did you find her?"

"In my office," Brock said. "I got lucky."

"So you did," Lenora said, one of her over-Botoxed eyebrows rising just slightly. "Tell me, Elle, how do you plan to approach aging?" she asked. "Not that you're anywhere near it."

Elle sighed. "I'm conflicted. I want to take care of my skin, but you know, Catherine Deneuve doesn't believe in staying too thin. We women have a tough road to hoe, but I don't think I want to kill myself after forty-five. I mean, the truth is, no one is paying me to look good."

Lenora gave a short laugh. "So true. So your theory is to look good without overextending yourself. Make it as easy as possible," the woman said.

"The kiss method," Elle said. "Keep it simple, sweetheart."

"Ooh," Lenora said. "I like that." She clasped her fingers together and leaned forward. "Okay, Mr. Maddox, I want to sign with your company. And our campaign will be 'Keep It Simple, Sweetheart.' It works for any age, from teens to young twenties to new moms to women of a certain age."

Brock shot Elle a cryptic smile. "I couldn't agree more."

Three hours later, after everyone—including Lenora—ate a slice of hot apple pie à la mode, Brock led Elle to bed. "I've missed you in the office," he said, taking her clothes off.

She felt her heart beat faster. "Are you ready to trust me again?" she asked.

"You did get me a new account tonight. Maybe I should hire you as a copy writer," he said, grinning. "Did I remove your fears about any possibility of attraction to Lenora?"

"I thought she was lovely," she said, lifting her hands to sift through his hair.

"She's a barracuda," he said. "You're very sharp, but you're also compassionate. I've always been drawn to you for those qualities."

"Hmm," she said, enjoying the way his hands slid over her skin.

"You are irresistibly sexy. I can't get enough of you," he said, skimming his hands over her belly. "Hey, Elle, I owe you one. You really did land me that new account, you know. She wasn't convinced until she met you."

His acknowledgement made her stomach twist. "Take it out in trade," she whispered. "For what happened with my grand—"

His mouth covered hers, keeping her from finishing the word. "In the past," he said, sliding one of his hands over her swollen breast.

She savored the sensation of his mouth on hers. "I want to please you," she said, even though what she really wanted to say was *I love you*. But she couldn't say that. Not yet.

"You do," Brock said.

"How?" she asked.

"Just by being here with me," he said.

The following Sunday was Father's Day. The day was always rough for Brock. Even though his father often had been out of town, the two of them had always talked on the phone. Brock would say how lucky he was and his father would laugh, but his gratitude and pride had been clear.

Since his father had died, Brock spent Father's Day remembering his dad. Staring out the window as he sipped a cup of coffee, he felt Elle come up behind him and wrap her arms around him. Something inside him eased. He covered her hands with his.

"What are you thinking about?" she whispered.

He inhaled deeply. "My dad," he said.

Silence stretched between them for several seconds. "Father's Day," she said.

"Yeah," he said, nodding.

"Do you have good memories of how your father spent the day with you and your brother?" she asked.

"Not really," Brock said. "But we always touched base by phone. I miss being able to give him a call."

"Hmm. Understandable." She gave him a squeeze. "I spent every Father's Day indulging in fantasies about how a father would teach me to pitch and catch. Or swing a bat. Or play golf. Or read the Sunday cartoons. Or just tell me super-wise things about life."

"Your father missed out by not getting to know you," Brock said, turning toward her.

"I missed out, too," she said.

"Have you ever met him?" he asked.

She shook her head. "He moved to Chicago and never came back. My grandfather stepped in to give my mother and me financial support, but—" She shrugged. "I was more of an irritation and burden than anything else."

"Irritation," he repeated, sliding his finger over her jawline. "You know that pearls are created by the irritation of a grain of sand."

"I've never been called a pearl before," she said.

"Can't imagine why," he said, rubbing his hands over her shoulders. "Seems obvious to me."

She smiled. "You're a charmer."

He shook his head. "I'm just calling it the way I see it."

"I have a small gift for you," she said.

"Why?" he asked.

"For Father's Day," she said.

"I'm not a father yet."

"Close enough," she said. "Check out your Black-Berry."

The smile on her face jacked up his curiosity. "What have you been up to?"

Her smile grew wider. "Don't ask me. Check it out for yourself."

Brock went to his phone charger and picked up the BlackBerry. Noticing there was a message, he pushed the button.

"Turn up the sound," she said.

He listened as a disco tune began to play and the ultrasound image of his child danced across the tiny screen. He felt joy shoot through him. "Look at him move," he said. "Or her." He watched, amazed at the sight of the tiny little combination of him and Elle. Unable to resist, he played the video again, staring at his dancing baby. When it ended, he played it again.

Elle gave a soft, throaty giggle. "You like it," she said.

He met her gaze. "I do."

"Here's your Father's Day card," she said, handing him an envelope.

Feeling a strange dip in his gut, he tore open the envelope and read the card. As he read, it hit him hard that his life was changing. Moved, he stared at the card and wondered if his mother had ever given his father such a card. And if she had, Brock wondered if his father had cared. He'd known his father wasn't particularly emotional. James Maddox had been determined to build the most successful advertising agency in San Francisco.

James Maddox had also wanted a beautiful wife. James Maddox had also wanted children. James Maddox got what he wanted.

He'd been a demanding man. At times, Brock had sweated meeting those high standards. He knew his brother had struggled with those standards, soared past them, and flipped the bird at them. Brock actually admired his brother for that.

As much as Brock had revered his father, he'd never felt close to him. Did he want that same kind of relationship with his own child? Brock frowned.

"What is it?"

"Just thinking," he muttered.

"About?" she asked, lifting her hand to his cheek.

"Being a father. Figuring out what kind of father I need to be," he said. "Different than the dad you didn't have. Different than the father I did have."

Elle swallowed audibly. "You're going to be amazing," she said, her eyes shiny with unshed tears.

"How can you be so sure?" he asked.

"I know you have an amazing mind and incredible drive. But I also know something a lot of other people don't know. You, Brock Maddox, have an awesome heart."

Nine

As Brock reviewed some new copy for the Prentice campaign, his intercom buzzed. "Yes?"

"Flynn Maddox is here," his assistant said.

Brock smiled. "Send him in."

Flynn burst through the door. "How's married life?"

"I could ask you the same," Brock said, standing and slapping his brother on the back.

"Couldn't be better," Flynn said. "I just want to thank you again for keeping those divorce papers out of my hands all those years ago."

"Your marital problems were partly my fault. I realized that," he said. "I'm glad you're happy now."

"Happy as a clam," he said. "How about you?"

Brock nodded. "It's going as well as it could."

Flynn rocked back on his heels and studied him. "Could be better?"

"I didn't expect to feel this much for her. I don't know how to handle it. Every time I try to guard my feelings, she finds a different way in."

Flynn's lips lifted in a half grin. "I like this. The woman has knocked my rock-solid brother off balance."

Brock swore at him.

Flynn chuckled, then his smile fell and he shook his head. "You're not sure about her because of her grandfather, right?"

"Wouldn't you wonder the same?" Brock asked, pacing to the other side of his office. His doubts made him feel like a caged animal.

"Now, with Renee?" Flynn asked. "No. It sounds corny, but love is rare. You shouldn't fight it, or you could miss your chance forever."

Brock felt a lump of emotion in his throat. "How did you let go?"

"After I lost Renee the first time, I knew I had to do everything I could to keep her when I got her back. But you don't always get a second chance. And it's not easy. If you need proof, look at Renee and me. Even though Mother has done her best to keep us apart, we've managed to overcome her this time."

"You're right about Mother," Brock said. "She tried to poison Elle against me. I decided she needed to live somewhere else. I paid for a new place for her."

Flynn whistled. "I'm sure that wasn't cheap."

"It was necessary," Brock said. "She's a bored and

unhappy woman. I just wish she would find a wealthy husband who would take her away and occupy her."

"You and me both," Flynn said. "You and me both."

When Brock was forced to work through the weekend on a project for Prentice, Elle decided to take action. Picnic basket in hand, she walked into Maddox Communications and smiled at the security guard. "Elle Maddox. I'm going up to see my husband," she said, pointing to her basket. "I want it to be a surprise."

"May I see your ID?" the man at the desk asked.

His request gave her pause, but she pulled out her driver's license. "Here it is," she said and smiled.

The man checked a list. "Wait just a second please," he said, picking up his phone as he stepped away.

Curious, she watched as he spoke on the phone. What was this about?

The security man returned and nodded to her. "If you'll wait just a couple moments," he said.

Her stomach tightened. "Isn't my name on the approved list?" she asked.

"Just a moment," he said, clearly hedging his response.

The elevator doors opened and Logan Emerson entered the foyer. He met Elle's gaze as he walked toward her. "Mrs. Maddox," he said with a nod. "How are you tonight?"

"I'm fine," Elle said, recognizing the man who had caught her in the worst deception of her life. She couldn't blame him, and yet at the same time she couldn't stop the heat of humiliation. "How are you?"

"Fine," he said, glancing at the basket she held in her hand. "Dinner?"

"A surprise for my husband," she said.

He nodded again. "Mind if I look?" he asked. "It's been a long time since I've had a home-cooked meal."

She didn't believe him for a second but she opened the basket. "Roast beef sandwiches with cheese and just a hint of horseradish on whole wheat of course, so we can pretend it's healthy. Whole wheat pasta with sundried tomatoes and pesto. And chocolate pie with whipped cream."

Logan winced. "Ouch. When was the last time I had homemade chocolate pie with whipped cream?"

"Do you want mine?"

"Is that a bribe?"

She narrowed her eyes in anger and lifted her chin. "You son of a bitch," she said. "If you haven't changed every computer code and key in that office, then you're not worth your fee. And I *will* tell Brock the same thing. I'm just here to see my husband for dinner," she said in a low voice, more desperate than she'd intended.

Logan held her gaze for a long moment. "I guess this means I'm not getting any of that chocolate pie," he said.

"You guess correctly."

"It's my job to protect Maddox and Brock," Logan said.

"You keep doing that," Elle said. "And it's my job to look after Brock and our marriage. Frankly," she said, lowering her voice, "I'm glad you caught me."

He blinked, a flicker of emotion flashing through his

eyes before his expression became inscrutable. "She's cleared," Logan said to the security guard.

"Just for tonight?" the guard asked.

"For anytime," Logan said. "Any questions from anyone, ask me." Logan turned to the elevator and swiped his card. Then he extended his hand. "Mrs. Maddox, your husband is hunched over his desk. He needs a break."

Feeling a strange combination of triumph and gratitude, she walked toward the elevator. She stopped just before she stepped into it. Sighing, she pulled out one of the pieces of pie and gave it to Logan. "No obligation. No payback. No bribe," she said. "Enjoy it and find a woman who will bake a pie for you every now and then."

She walked into the elevator and punched the button for Brock's apartment. Gripping the basket tightly, she counted the floors as she rose. Finally, she arrived on Brock's private floor and tiptoed into the darkened suite. She and Brock had spent so much time here. She smiled as she remembered sharing Chinese takeout, laughter and amazing sex. She remembered holding him and feeling him relax in her arms. Brock was always so tense; it gave her such pleasure that he could actually feel at ease enough with her that he could rest.

Tonight, she hoped she could help him the same way she once had. The room was actually a bit chilly. She glanced around, glimpsing a fine layer of dust and smelling the faint scent of mustiness. "Oh, my goodness," she murmured and turned on the light.

If she didn't know better, she would suspect that no one had been here since the last time she and Brock had shared a night together. That couldn't be possible, she told herself. She slid her finger through the dust on a table against the wall and walked toward the bedroom. The large bed was neatly made, the bedside tables empty. She walked into the bathroom and there was nothing on the counter. She rubbed her fingers over the bristles of the toothbrush. They were dry.

Elle couldn't deny the fact that the clear evidence of Brock's absence comforted her terrified heart. She hated the idea that he might have replaced her. Every indication suggested that he hadn't.

She pulled the bottle of red wine from the basket and poured it in a glass she pulled from the cabinet. Inhaling deeply, she savored the bouquet of the wine and then poured herself a glass of sparkling water the chef had packed for her. She pulled several candles from a different cabinet and lit them. After she set out the picnic, she took the backstairs to Brock's office and knocked on his closed door.

No response. She knocked again.

"Hello?" Brock's voice said from the other side of the door. "Who is it?"

"Your evil wife," she said.

The door immediately opened and Brock stared her, his shirt loosened, his tie discarded, his expression stunned. "What are you doing here?"

"Dinner," she said and kissed his cheek.

"Where?" he asked, looking at her empty hands.

"Upstairs," she said and smiled. "If you can spare a few minutes."

Brock met her gaze and his lids lowered in sexual

response. "I haven't been to my apartment since the last time you and I were together," he said.

"I know," she said. "Time we changed that, don't you think?"

He took her hand and slid his fingers through hers. "Sounds good to me."

She led him up the back stairs to the apartment where she'd left candles glowing in the darkness.

"Nice," he said.

"It gets better," she said and led him to the low table in the small den where they'd shared so many meals before.

"What made you do this?" he asked as he lowered himself to the floor.

She followed him to a sitting position. "You've been burning the midnight oil too much lately."

"Just one night," he said, reaching for his sandwich. "Oh, my favorite."

"Try three nights," she corrected.

"That long?" he said, surprised. He took a bite. "This is heaven. Oh, and pasta salad." He took a long sip of red wine and sighed. "You are my dream come true."

"Anyone could have brought you a roast beef sandwich with horseradish, pasta salad and red wine," she said.

He shook his head. "Nobody but you could be sitting across from me. Nobody," he said, "but you."

"How can I resist that?" she asked.

"I damn well hope you can't," he said and chomped through the rest of his sandwich, washing it down with wine. "How's the bedroom?"

She shot him a demure look. "How would I know?"

"Are you saying you don't know?" he demanded, pouring more wine into his glass.

"I think the bed needs to be exercised," she said, sipping from her own glass.

"Any chance you'll exercise the bed with me?"

She leaned across the table and pressed her mouth to his. "I thought you'd never ask."

As dawn broke through the curtains the next morning, Brock struggled to bring himself to a wakeful state. He fluttered his eyes open and tried to focus. Groaning, he started to get up.

He felt Elle slide her hand over his waist to his abdomen.

"It's too early," she whispered.

"Can't argue with that," he said and turned toward her, pulling her warm, sexy body against his. "I can't decide if it's totally bad or totally good that you came to see me at the office."

She ran her fingers through his hair. "You better say it's totally good," she said.

He chuckled and slid his hands down her waist to her bottom to pull her against him. "Totally good," he said and groaned as he felt himself grow hard. He swore under his breath.

She rubbed her sweet lips against his mouth and wriggled her honey-soft nether regions against him where he was hard and already wanting. "Oh, Elle, I can't get enough of you."

He pulled her against him and slid against her wetness, seeking, wanting, needing. He found her swollen opening and thrust inside her.

She gasped and the sound aroused him even more.

"Brock," she whispered. "I need you."

"You've got me," he promised, thrusting inside her. "In every way."

She enclosed him with her wet velvet, gasping and begging. The sound of her breath and voice made him crazy. He craved her with every inch of his being. The sensation of her silken warmth drove him over the edge. With just another thrust, he felt his climax roar through him, sending him into a spasm of pleasure.

"Elle," he whispered, sinking down on her.

"Oh, yes," she said, clinging to him. She rubbed her lips over his ear. "This almost makes me want to move into this apartment."

A chuckle rumbled up from his gut. "I'd never get any work done."

"You did before," she said.

"That was tough. You were a major distraction. I couldn't wait for the end of the day when you and I would escape," he said. "Now that you're pregnant and you're my wife, it's just as strong as ever."

"Really?" she asked, her gaze puzzled as she stared up at him. "You don't seem to have a problem coming home late."

"The company's in a transition period. That will change," he said. He was trying to put the pressure on Golden Gate, but he couldn't tell Elle about it. He wanted to, but she was too close to the situation emotionally. He knew she felt some tug of gratitude toward her grandfather. The knowledge dug at him, but soon enough, he would remove that obstacle between them.

She gave a sigh. "Until then, I guess I'll have to rescue you every once in a while."

"Rescue me?" he echoed, wondering what she meant.

"From work," she said. "I'll bring you a meal and use it to lure you up to your office apartment. And then who knows what else will happen?" she said, grinning up at him.

That day, as Elle began work on a picture display for Brock in the sunroom, the doorbell rang and Anna appeared. "Mrs. Maddox is here."

Elle lifted her eyebrows. "Which one?" she asked, hoping it was Renee.

"Oh, I'm sorry. Mrs. Carol Maddox," the housekeeper said.

"Oh, there you are," Carol said, coming from the hallway. She smiled at the housekeeper. "No need for formal announcements. We're family here. You've made a lot of changes in a short amount of time. The house has a more sparse feel to it," Carol said. "How does Brock like it?"

"Very much. I'm trying to create a combination of new and traditional. Bree has helped me," Elle said.

"I didn't know she was an interior designer," Carol said.

"She has an amazing eye," Elle replied.

Carol stepped closer and studied the photo display. "What's this?"

"A surprise for Brock. I know his memories of his father are important to him, so I wanted to display them in a meaningful way."

"Oh, look, there are even a few of me in there," she said with a bite in her tone. "At the hospital and at Brock's graduation. Don't mind me. I'm just the mother," she said and gave a brittle laugh.

"The focus of the subject is Brock's father. I see it as a memorial of the best of him," she said.

"That will be a challenge," Carol murmured. "But that's not the reason I came. I realize it's last-minute, but I, too, have been hard at work on my new home. Of course, it will never be as large or as impressive as this, but I like to think I've turned it into a stylish place. I'm having a little housewarming tomorrow night from seven to nine, and I insist that you and Brock join me."

Elle blinked. "Tomorrow night?"

"I can't believe you're booked. I know Brock has only made one public appearance with you, so—"

Elle felt the stab of shame. Carol was insinuating that Brock was embarrassed by her, embarrassed that he'd married her. "I'll have to ask him. He's been swamped at work."

Carol shot her a sympathetic but knowing gaze. "As he always will be. Do try to drag him away for just a little while tomorrow night. I'd like him to see my new residence. It would be embarrassing to me if he didn't attend. I'm counting on you," she said and smiled. "Good luck on the photo memorial. Such a sweet gesture. Ta-ta for now."

Elle broke the news about his mother's "invitation" when Brock finally arrived home that night and was eating a late dinner.

He paused, midbite. "You've got to be kidding. Of

all the ways I want to spend my nonexistent spare time, that is not one of them."

"I know," she said. "But she's your mother and it's not as if we'll have to stay the entire time."

He clenched his jaw. "Nothing good ever comes of being with her."

Elle laughed under her breath. "You can't say that. After all, your father created you and Flynn by being with her."

Brock rolled his eyes. "Well, since then," he amended. "I don't understand why you're taking her side on this."

Elle shrugged. "It's not a side. She's your mother, your only living parent."

Brock was silent for a long moment. "It makes you think about your mother and her health issues."

"I don't want you to have regrets," Elle said. "Your mother may be a pain in the butt, however, she did give birth to you. And who knows what really went on between your father and mother? Even you've said he took her for granted."

"Okay, we'll go for a half hour," he said.

Elle nodded, thinking about the little stabs Carol had taken at her during their conversation.

"You're too quiet," Brock said, studying her.

She took a sip of sparkling water, not wanting to reveal her insecurities.

"What is it?" he demanded. "What else did she say?"

"She wasn't here that long," Elle said.

"Long enough to cause trouble. What else did she say?"

Feeling pinned against the wall, Elle lifted her

shoulders. "She just made a point of saying that you and I hadn't made but one public appearance. I was probably reading something into it."

"Such as?" he asked.

"That you're embarrassed by me," she said and bit her lip.

Brock rolled his eyes. "You've got to be kidding."

"Well, you have to admit we married quickly. And I'm pregnant. And I used to be your assistant. These are all the kinds of things that make for conversation," she said.

"Gossip, you mean," he corrected. "The reason I've turned down invitations was to give us a chance to get used to the idea of being married. I especially didn't want you to have any additional pressure. You've gone through enough during the last few months."

"So, you're not ashamed of me?" she asked.

He shook his head. "Just very protective."

A ripple of pleasure and excitement raced through her at the hard expression on his face. Elle had never had a man in her life so determined to protect her, and it was something she'd secretly longed for as long as she could remember. Brock's devotion touched a core part of her and she wondered how much longer she would be able to keep herself from expressing her love for him. And when she did, would it be a treasure or burden?

Elle dressed carefully as she prepared for her mother-in-law's housewarming. She didn't want to feel self-conscious, but she had a feeling that nothing she wore was going to change that. She fixed her hair for the third time and dabbed on some lip gloss.

"You look beautiful," Brock said from the doorway. "Can we get this over with?"

Elle smothered a laugh at his impatience. "Thank you and yes," she said, walking toward him.

She liked the way her blue silk dress flowed over her body. It felt like a lovely whisper echoing down to the tops of her knees.

"You really do look nice in that dress," Brock said. "It brings out your eyes."

"Thank you," she said. "So does your tie."

He shot her a disbelieving glance. "Yeah, sure. My white shirt does amazing things for my eyes."

"Actually, it does," she said. "Because you're dark-complected. The white shirt provides a contrast against your complexion, and your blue tie emphasizes your blue eyes."

"So you say," he said with a shrug.

"One more thing that makes you hot," she said.

He did a double take. "Really?" he said.

"Yes, really," she responded. "With your tanned skin and dark hair, you're expecting brown eyes. Instead, yours are a shock. A compelling shock."

"Nice to know I have a genetic predisposition toward keeping you attracted," he said and extended his arm. "Ready to go?"

Just fifteen minutes later, Dirk pulled up in front of Carol's new condominium. A desk with security and a concierge stood just inside the beautiful building.

"By the price I paid, I knew Mummy wasn't slumming," Brock murmured as he showed his ID to security.

"Do you regret getting this place for her?" Elle asked,

knowing that she was a big part of the reason Brock had bought his mother the condo.

"Are you kidding? I would have paid twice as much to get her out of the house," he said as they stepped onto an elevator. "There's a reason I spent so many nights at the apartment. But you've made the house feel more like a home for me," he told Elle.

A warm feeling surged inside her. "I'm glad. I wanted to make you feel comfortable there."

The elevator dinged their arrival on Carol's floor. "Here we go," Brock said. He glanced at his watch. "Thirty minutes to go."

Less than a moment later, the door opened and a butler dressed in a tux greeted them. "Welcome to Mrs. Maddox's home. We're so glad for your presence. Please come in and enjoy the food, beverage and company."

From across the room, Brock's mother called out. "Brock, darling, bring your lovely wife here. I have some people I want her to meet."

"Warned you," Brock said under his breath as he slid his arm behind Elle's back.

"Hello, Mother," he said. "Your home is incredible," he said, looking around. "You never cease to amaze me with what you can do in such a short time."

Elle swallowed a chuckle, noticing his careful word choice. "I have to agree," she said. "It's amazing what you've accomplished."

Carol preened under the praise. "Thank you both. Of course, I've been working day and night to make this happen. I'd like you to meet my new neighbors, the Gladstones. Eve and Bill, this is my son Brock and my new daughter-in-law, Elle. Elle is going to give me a grandchild soon," she said in a stage whisper. "I'm so excited, I can't find the words."

Brock squeezed Elle's shoulders. "We're very excited, too, Mr. and Mrs. Gladstone. It's nice to meet you. I'm glad to know my mother has some wonderful neighbors."

"Nice to meet you," Elle said, extending her hand, a bit off-balance from Carol's announcement of her pregnancy.

"Our pleasure," Eve said. "And when is the little one due? Next year?"

Elle opened her mouth to reply, but Brock moved forward. "Again, nice to meet you." He nodded to his mother. "I'm going to get Elle something to drink," he said and guided Elle away. "Ready to go now?" he asked.

"It wasn't that bad," she said. "I just didn't expect her to mention the pregnancy."

"That's part of her charm. The unexpected," he said, lifting a glass of red wine from a server's tray. "Could you bring some sparkling water for my wife?" he asked the man.

The server nodded. "Just a moment," he said and swiveled to go to another room.

Brock glanced around. "Some of this stuff looks familiar."

"It should," Elle said. "She took some of it with her."

"But she sent me an astronomical bill for decorating," he said.

Elle shrugged. "Sorry. Not my area. I'm accustomed to shopping at outlets."

"And I'll take you away from all that," Brock said, his expression softening.

"I hope not," she said. "There's nothing wrong with taking a pause before you spend a lot of money."

He tilted his head to one side. "How refreshing," he said.

The waiter returned with a glass of fizzy water. "Here you go, miss."

"Thank you," Elle said to the man. "She hired excellent staff," she murmured after he left.

"As if my mother would have done anything else," Brock said with dark humor.

"Brock, it's been so long," a feminine voice said from behind them.

Elle glanced at Brock's face as she turned and saw his expression twist in pain just before it shuttered and went blank. "Claire," he said in the most neutral voice Elle had ever heard him use. "What a surprise."

Elle looked at the tall, beautiful blonde with a perfect shape and felt a sinking sensation in her stomach. "Claire?" she echoed, searching her memory for the name and unfortunately coming upon it.

Claire was Brock's ex-fiancée.

Ten

The ravishing specimen of beauty flicked her gaze over Brock. "You're looking good," Claire purred. "I've missed you."

Elle bristled at the woman's obvious seductive tone.

"I didn't know you and my mother were still in touch," Brock said.

"She insisted I come tonight. She told me you would be here."

Brock cleared his throat. "Claire, this is my wife, Elle."

Claire blinked and parted her lips as if in surprise. "I thought I'd heard a rumor, but I wasn't sure," she said in a sad voice, then turned to Elle. "Congratulations, Elle. You got a wonderful man."

"I know," Elle said, forcing herself to extend her hand. "Thank you. Lovely to meet you."

"She's so sweet," Claire said to Brock. "I never would have expected you to choose someone so—" She broke off and shrugged her bare, glimmering shoulders. "It's coming back to me now. Are the two of you expecting?"

Silence stretched between them, against the background noise of social conversation and tinkling glasses.

"Yes," Brock said. "Elle and I are very much looking forward to our first child."

Claire stared into Brock's eyes and her gaze seemed to say, *I could have been the mother of your child instead of her.* Claire nodded. "Congratulations. How exciting," she said. "I see an old friend. Please excuse me."

"Of course," Brock said and took a long swallow of wine. "I'm ready to go."

"Me, too," Elle said, every bit of social courteousness sucked out of her.

Brock's mother stepped in front of them just as they approached the door. "Leaving so soon? You just arrived," she said with a practiced pout.

"Perhaps if you hadn't invited my ex-fiancée and also neglected to tell her that I'm married, we might have stayed five minutes longer," Brock said, clenching his jaw in obvious anger.

Elle's stomach began to churn. She didn't know what upset her more—Brock's fury, his mother's manipulation or the memory of Brock's stunning ex-fiancée.

Carol's eyes rounded in mock innocence. "But I

thought you two would enjoy seeing each other. Time to let bygones be bygones now that you're married," she said, shooting a glance at Elle before she looked at Brock again. "Unless it stirred up old feelings—"

Elle swallowed a gasp.

"Not from me," Brock said. "The only thing you're stirring up is trouble. You invited Claire to intimidate Elle."

Carol shook her head. "Oh, now, really. How could Claire intimidate Elle?"

"Exactly," Brock said. "Elle is my wife and the mother of my child. Claire is history. You might want to remember that. Good night," he said, and ushered Elle through the door.

Fifteen minutes later, Elle and Brock walked inside the house. The housekeeper greeted them. "May I get something for you?"

"No, thank you," Brock said.

"I'm fine," Elle said.

"Are you sure you wouldn't like some sparkling water?" Anna asked with a gentle smile.

"No, thank you," Elle said, feeling as if she'd lost every bit of her sparkle. "I'll just get a bottle upstairs. You're kind to ask, though. Thank you."

She and Brock climbed the stairs and Elle stared into the mirror as she removed her earrings and necklace. She felt like such a fool. She'd tried so hard to look pretty, but Brock's ex was at a totally different level. The woman was breathtaking.

"You okay?" Brock asked.

"She could be a model," Elle said.

"That doesn't mean she was right for me."

"But she was perfect, gorgeous. I bet she's intelligent. You wouldn't tolerate anything less. How could—"

"She was extremely demanding. I knew it wouldn't work," he said.

Her heart sank to her knees. Elle turned to him. "And I'm not demanding," she said. "I'm grateful. So maybe it will work."

"Elle, come on, this is exactly what my mother wanted you to worry about," Brock said, walking toward her.

She put her hands out in front of her. "No, no. I need a few moments. Hours, maybe." She shook her head and fought the pain that wrenched inside her. "I know you married me because I got pregnant. But are you really counting on me to be the grateful little wife who doesn't ask too much of you?"

"Of course not," he said. "You always challenged me. That was part of the reason I couldn't resist you. You affected me that way from the beginning. I broke all my rules for you, Elle. If I'd followed my own policies, I would have had you transferred. But being with you made me feel like…I'd found home." He shrugged. "You can believe me or not. It's your choice."

She stared into his face and saw the raw truth. He loved her, even if he couldn't say it yet. It shocked and comforted her at the same time. "I believe you," she whispered, and flew into his arms.

He held her tight. "Listen, the next two weeks will be a crunch. But after that, you and I will take a break and go away."

"The mountain cabin?" she asked.

"Anywhere you want," he said and pressed his mouth

against hers. He slid his hand to her belly. "I never had so much to live for before," he said. "How'd I manage this?"

"You got lucky," she said and smiled.

"Yeah, I did."

Brock breezed through his morning, accomplishing tasks far faster than usual. Lunchtime came and he called Elle. She was eating a sandwich with her mom and planned to visit her grandfather that afternoon.

The latter gave him a twinge, but he ignored it. "I'll see you tonight," he said.

"Don't work too hard," she said, and the smile in her voice flooded him with warmth.

He roared through the afternoon. The only thing that stopped him was the sight of Logan Emerson walking into his office with a solemn expression on his face. "There's been a leak."

"About what?" Brock demanded, frustration soaring through him. He'd already eliminated one threat. What else could be at work here?

"The Prentice account," Logan said. "Someone got your files and shared them with Golden Gate."

Brock frowned. "I still don't understand what information you're talking about."

"Did you take anything home?" Logan asked.

"A flash drive and one file, three weeks ago," Brock said.

Logan lifted one brow. "Enough to give Golden Gate an edge."

Brock pictured the flash drive and file sitting on his

desk at home, right after he and Elle had gotten married. His stomach fell to his feet.

Elle put the final stamp of approval on dinner, which consisted of Brock's favorite red wine, beef burgundy, potatoes, broccoli and bread. Even though one of the staff would gladly do it, she lit the candles on the table and arranged the roses herself. She had never felt more hopeful, more in love. Maybe, just maybe, it would all work out. Her heart skipping a beat, she took a deep breath and laughed at herself. *Calm down,* she told herself. This was just another night of married life. The best kind of married life, a little voice inside her said.

She heard the sound of footsteps and her heart raced again. Brock was home. She looked up, unable to keep from beaming at him. "Welcome home," she said.

His face was blank, but anger blazed in his eyes. His mouth was set with bitterness, his jaw clenched. "When did you tell your grandfather about the new plans for the Prentice account?" he asked.

Elle felt her blood drain to her feet. She shook her head. "What are you talking about?"

"Weeks ago, I brought home a file and a flash drive. I left it here for one day. One day," he repeated. "Convenient for you."

"I have no idea what you're talking about, Brock," she said.

"There's no need to lie. You've got me. You've got our marriage. It's not as if I can do anything about the fact that you stole information from me again. I just want to know when you did it. That's fair, isn't it?"

Elle felt nauseous. "I didn't tell anyone anything

after that day you came to my mother's house. I don't know what you're talking about. You wouldn't even discuss the new Prentice campaign with me. Don't you remember?"

"I remember," he said. "I also remember I made the huge mistake of leaving work at home. I'm sure that would have been too tempting for you to resist."

Elle shook her head. "You're wrong. I didn't even see that file or your flash drive. And if I had, I wouldn't have touched them. I couldn't stand any more deception. I wanted things to be clean and honest between you and me. You have to believe me. You have to."

"Why should I believe you now?" he asked. "You spent months deceiving me while you went to bed with me. I'm starting to wonder if the pregnancy wasn't some part of your plan. If you tied yourself to me with a child, I couldn't possibly prosecute you. Right?"

Elle lifted her hand to her throat, feeling it close, nearly depriving her of oxygen. She shook her head. "Brock, you can't possibly think that. Not about our baby. Not about me."

His gaze dipped to her still-small belly. "I know that when it came to a test of your loyalties, you chose your grandfather."

"No, I chose my mother," she cried. "What else could I do? Can you honestly tell me that if your father had been ill and you had been put in the same situation, that you wouldn't have done the same thing I did?"

"I would never have been in your situation because I would have made sure I was never at someone else's mercy like that," he said.

Elle gasped at his words. Somewhere beneath her

pain, anger roared to the surface. "Well, how nice for you that you've never been vulnerable. How nice that you were born to privilege, educated at only the best schools and eased into a high-profile job."

"I fought for that job," Brock said. "My father didn't give me any passes for my work at Maddox."

"Like I said, good for you," she said. "I'll tell you this much. If I had it to do all over again, I would make the same horrible choice because my mother's life depended on it. I'm sorry I hurt you because I did fall in love with you. Helplessly, hopelessly. Then the pregnancy took me by surprise."

He stared at her without an ounce of compassion. "It's convenient for you to bring up love at this point when you've never mentioned it before," he said. "I'm staying at the apartment tonight. Congratulations on fooling me twice, Elle. Sleep well. It must be nice to be able to lie and sleep as easily as you do." Then he turned and walked out.

The knot of emotion in her throat threatened to choke her. She wanted to call after him and defend herself, but her voice completely failed. How could he believe she had gone behind his back again?

Because she'd done it before, just as he'd said. For months.

So why should he believe her? What evidence had she given him to believe the contrary? The answer made her so nauseous she dashed to the bathroom and was sick to her stomach. Leaning against the sink, she rinsed her mouth and pressed a cool, wet cloth to her head.

She put herself in Brock's place. With their history, would she have believed him?

Even though she knew in her heart of hearts that she loved Brock and would never deceive him again, she could see why he wouldn't believe her. The reality made her eyes burn and her chest hurt as if someone had torn out her heart. A sob bubbled up from somewhere deep inside her and she began to cry huge, wrenching sobs. She cradled her arms around her chest to hold herself together, but she felt as if she were splitting apart.

Of all the things she'd had in her life, she'd lost the most important. The promise, the dream of something different for her and Brock and their baby.

Elle didn't eat one bite that night. She couldn't have forced it down her throat. She was in such terrible emotional pain and shock that she didn't know what to do. Should she leave? Should she stay?

She took a hot, calming shower, dressed in a soft nightshirt and crawled into bed in Brock's room. She could still smell just a trace of his scent when she closed her eyes. A tidal wave of memories swept over her and she couldn't stop herself from crying again. She'd thought there wasn't one more tear she could shed tonight, but she was wrong. Finally, she exhausted herself and fell asleep.

Awakening in the morning with swollen eyes, she immediately remembered everything that had happened the previous night and pulled the sheet over her head. Was there any way she could turn back time and fix everything?

Not unless she was a genie or a witch. Brock seemed bent on believing she was the latter. She pulled back the sheet and gazed out the windows. Another gray, foggy morning in San Francisco. Natives knew the truth about the bay's climate. Fog, fog and more fog. She slid out of the bed and peeked through the blinds at the gray day.

Her heart still hurt as if she'd had major surgery. Biting her lip, she knew she needed to figure out what to do. If Brock despised her as much as he seemed, then he would never trust her. What kind of marriage could they have? What kind of parents would they be together?

Elle refused to have the same kind of relationship with Brock that his parents had appeared to have. That couldn't be good for anyone. No matter what happened between her and Brock, at least the baby would have a father. That was more than she'd ever had.

Her mind was spinning and she couldn't stop it. Scenario after scenario flew through her mind. What would she do? How would she live? She didn't mind going back to work. In this situation, she would welcome it. But would Brock try to take the baby from her? She'd never, ever let that happen.

Her stomach growled despite the fact that she couldn't imagine eating. She needed to eat, she told herself, for the baby if nothing else. She took another shower in hopes of cleansing herself of the dirty feeling that covered her like a veil of pollution.

Possibilities, choices chugging through her mind, she went downstairs. The housekeeper greeted her with a concerned expression. "Is everything okay? Your meal was left untouched."

"Mr. Maddox had a crisis at work," Elle said and heaven knew it was the truth.

"Oh, what a shame," the housekeeper said, folding

her hands in front of her sympathetically. "Can I get you anything for breakfast?"

"Thank you," Elle said. "I'd like something bland. Toast and jelly."

"I'll bring a scrambled egg on the side and some oatmeal just in case. Perhaps a little fruit," the house-keeper continued. "And just a couple of slices of bacon. Protein for the little one."

Although her stomach seemed the size of a pea, Elle managed to down a few bites of egg, toast and even a strip of bacon. She swallowed several sips of icy fresh-squeezed orange juice and said a mental goodbye to the notion of having staff at her beck and call. That wasn't the worst of her losses, she knew.

She decided to explain her plans to the housekeeper later, after she had packed. Upstairs, on the bed she'd shared with Brock, she pulled out two suitcases and began to put clothes inside. She found a box for her favorite books and keepsakes she'd brought from her mother's.

She heard the doorbell ring but ignored it. Elle knew she couldn't stay under the circumstances. Brock would never trust her and she wouldn't subject him, her or her baby to the life of misery their enforced togetherness would create. She wouldn't be able to bear his bitterness and resentment and the effect of his hatred of her on their child. The thought of it wrenched at her again.

"Oh, hello," Brock's mother said from the doorway. "Anna said you were napping, but I heard sounds. I hope you don't mind that I came upstairs," Carol said. "I just wanted to thank you and Brock for attending my little open house the other night." Carol stopped, finally taking in the sight of Elle's suitcases and boxes. "Oh, my goodness, you're not packing, are you?"

Elle bit the inside of her lip. "Brock and I have realized we're not well suited, so I've decided it's best if I leave."

"Oh, dear," Carol said, her voice oozing sympathy. "I'm so very sorry." She walked into the room, dressed in her couture of the day. "But I totally understand. Not everyone is cut out to be the wife of a Maddox. I'm not sure I really was, either," Carol confessed in a soft voice. "If I'd known in the beginning what I learned just after a year, I'm not sure I would have—" She broke off and shrugged. "Well, you know what I'm saying. Can I help you pack?"

Elle blinked at the woman's offer. "Uh—"

"I'm sure it's difficult for you," Carol said, moving to Elle's side and picking up a book. "Is this yours?"

"Yes," Elle said, watching as she put the book in a box.

"I'm so sorry that things didn't work out with you and Brock, but again, I understand," Carol said. "Between the Prentice account and the threat from Golden Gate, Brock just can't see straight. It seems the Prentice account is a twenty-four-hour-a-day job. Maddox is always having to come up with a new campaign."

Elle's antennae went on alert. "New campaign for Prentice?" she asked, pasting a bland look on her face. "What was wrong with the old one?"

"With an account like Prentice, they're always demanding something new. Brock's most recent idea may cost some bucks, though," Carol said, picking up a stuffed monkey. "Is this yours?"

"From my mother," Elle said. "I've had him since I was a child."

"How sweet," Carol said and put the monkey in the box. "Is this everything?"

"Not quite," Elle said. "I'm curious. How did you hear about the new campaign for Prentice? I didn't know a thing about it."

For a microsecond Carol froze as if she knew she'd been caught. Then she shrugged. "I thought everyone knew."

"Of course everyone didn't know," Elle said, her anger growing. "Only someone who'd looked at Maddox's plans would know about the changes. Only someone who'd had a chance to look at papers and a flash drive left at home by the Maddox CEO."

Carol gasped. "Whatever are you saying?"

"Hello, Mother," Brock said from the doorway, shocking Elle with his entrance. She gaped at him, wondering what had made him return home so early. He shot a glance at her full of forgiveness and repentance that made her heart turn over.

"Why, hello, Brock," Carol said with forced happiness. "What a surprise."

"You were the one," he said, walking toward his mother.

Carol gave a one-shoulder shrug and steadied herself on an end table. The woman suddenly appeared frail to Elle. "What are you talking about?"

"You looked at my file. You made a copy of my flash drive," he said.

Carol shrugged again, but this time she backed away. "What's that? What file?"

"The file for the Prentice account. You sent it to Golden Gate," he said. "You wanted me to believe Elle sent it, but all along, it was you."

"It could have been her. She lied to you before you married her. She could have brought down Maddox Communications," Carol said, her eyes glinting with fear and fury.

"Why did you do this?" he demanded. "It would only hurt you in the end."

"I knew you would find a way to top Golden Gate Promotions, but your marriage was ruining my future. Look at what it's already done to me. I've moved into a small condo! And I know the terms of your father's will. My income has been cut as a result of your bastard child."

Elle stared at the woman in shock. How could one person hold so much vindictiveness and evil? She almost couldn't comprehend it.

Brock's eyes blazed with fury, but his voice was deadly calm. "I'm done with you. I never want to see you again. You won't get one more penny from me. I'm sorry you've turned into such a bitter woman, but I won't have you contaminating my marriage. Now, get out."

Carol narrowed her eyes at him in impotent rage, then stomped from the room. Her heavy footsteps echoed down the stairs and the sound of a door slamming vibrated throughout the house.

Brock took a deep breath and looked at Elle. "I was wrong."

Elle nearly laughed. "You think so?"

He walked toward her. "I am so very, very sorry. I

should have believed you and from now on, I will," he promised.

Elle tore her gaze from his to glance at her luggage, trying to hang on to her plan to move away from him and make a new life for her baby and herself. "We have so much baggage," she whispered. "How can you ever trust me?"

"I already do," he said. "I trusted you when I shouldn't have. When I was told by a professional that you were deceiving me."

"What do you mean?"

"I forced the P.I. to give me evidence that you were selling secrets to Golden Gate. Not until he provided me with ironclad proof did I believe it."

Elle felt her eyes burn with tears. "I hate it that I lied to you. I hate myself for it."

"You need to forgive yourself," Brock said. "I forgive you."

Elle looked up, searching his gaze. "How can you?"

"Because I know you were doing the best you could. I know you were tortured about it," he said.

"I was," she agreed. "When I met you, I fell so hard for you. In my grandfather's plan, everything was supposed to remain business, but you blew me away. You were everything I'd wished for in a man, but had never found."

"And you were everything I wanted in a woman, but felt I'd never find. When I made love to you, I felt like I was coming home," Brock said, pulling her into his arms. "I never knew what love was before I met you."

Elle's heart stopped in her chest. "Love?"

He nodded. "Love. I was willing to risk it all for you. Even Maddox Communications. Logan tried to talk me into prosecuting, but I refused. It wasn't just about the baby. It was about the connection you and I shared. I knew I'd never find that again. When you told me that you'd agreed to spy for your grandfather so that your mother would get her treatments, I could only hope you felt that strongly about me."

"I do," Elle said. "I would do anything for you, Brock. I love you. More than anything. I want to build a life together."

"Then stay," he said, pressing his mouth against hers. "Stay forever."

Epilogue

The jazz band played in the background of the Maddox Communications party. They were celebrating the merger of Maddox and Golden Gate Promotions with Brock as the CEO. Elle slid a hand behind her grandfather's back and gave him a hug. He felt so frail to her. "Are you okay?" she asked.

Her grandfather smiled. "It was meant to be. Your husband is the future of both Maddox Communications and Golden Gate Promotions. My sons didn't have the drive, but Brock, he does."

Elle glanced at Brock across the room as he chatted with his brother and felt a rush of love. Their relationship had grown by leaps and bounds during the last few weeks.

"I should sit down," her grandfather said.

"Of course," she said, feeling remiss. "Can I get you something else to drink?"

"This water is fine," he said and nodded as he sat. "Go see to your guests."

Elle dropped a kiss on his forehead. For all the pain and suffering Athos had caused, he had led her to Brock and she was thankful for that. She had walked just a few steps when she was stopped by Evan and Celia Reese.

"How is life with the CEO of the newly merged Maddox Communications and Golden Gate Promotions?" Evan asked. "Are you keeping him in line?"

"Ha," Elle said, but smiled because Brock had made a special point to spend more time with her lately. "You two look like you're doing great. I'm so happy you could come to the party."

"Wouldn't miss it," Celia said, pushing her red hair behind her ear as she gazed affectionately at her husband. "This is actually a stopover. We're going to the French Riviera. Evan is determined to give me a honeymoon I'll never forget."

"It's hard being married to an overachiever, isn't it?" Elle joked.

Celia laughed. "You bet. Good luck with the baby."

"Thanks," Elle said and moved toward Brock. She noticed he and his brother were looking intently at their cell phones.

"What are they doing?" Elle asked as Flynn's wife appeared at her side.

"It's the battle of the ultrasounds," Renee said. "We may know the sex of our baby, but yours is set to disco. I think it's a draw."

Elle laughed. "How are you feeling?" she asked.

"Excited," Renee said, stroking her full pregnancy bump. "The doctor says my due date will be here before I know it, but it feels like forever."

"Any names yet?" Elle asked.

"We're still playing with the first name, but I want Flynn for her middle name," Renee said.

"I love that," Elle said.

Renee nodded. "It's good, isn't it? What about you and Brock?"

"We find out the sex for sure at the end of this week. If it's a boy, we'll include Brock's father's name somehow," she said.

Renee tilted her head. "Your mother looks great."

Elle's heart squeezed tight as she looked at her mother standing several feet away, tapping her foot as she enjoyed the party and the music. "Thank you. She's come a long way."

"There are our brides," Flynn interjected, clinking his beer against Brock's beer bottle. "We did good, didn't we?"

Brock met Elle's gaze and she felt a melting sensation. "I couldn't agree more," he said. "I won the ultrasound contest."

"That's a lie," Flynn said. "I know the sex and my baby is going to beat you to the punch."

Before Brock could dispute his brother, Jason Reagert and his very pregnant wife, Lauren, approached them. "If we're going to talk about winning the time game, Lauren and I will beat both of you," Jason, newly promoted to vice president, said.

Lauren, in her ninth month of pregnancy, glowed

with love and happiness. "That's right," she said. "Our baby boy could make his appearance any minute."

"Stop making me nervous," Brock said. "Do we have a doctor in the crowd?"

"Trust me. I'm on the edge of my seat," Jason said. "I have a packed bag for her sitting in the car."

Gavin Spencer, the former ad executive for Maddox who had started his own business, stepped forward and extended his hand. "Congratulations," Gavin said. "I can only hope I'll give you some competition in the future."

Brock gave a loud chuckle. "You dog."

Bree smiled at her husband. "Don't underestimate Gavin," she said.

"Or you," Brock said. "Elle tells me you helped with redecorating the house. Thanks," he said.

"My pleasure," Bree said.

Brock took a deep breath and exhaled, squeezing Elle's shoulders. She could feel his excitement emanate from his body, and she knew that when all was said and done, he would come home to her, seeking her love and affection. The knowledge made her feel more complete than she'd ever dreamed.

"It's time for a toast," Brock said as someone dinged a spoon against a crystal champagne flute. It took several moments, but silence finally descended over the crowd. "This has been a long time coming," Brock said. "Golden Gate Promotions has been a jewel in the crown of San Francisco ad agencies, always raising the bar for their competitors. I'm pleased to announce the merger of Golden Gate Promotions and Maddox Communications. The combined force of the two companies will create an unbeatable alliance of power and talent. To Athos Koteas," Brock said, lifting his glass to the man seated on the other side of the room. "I will always honor your spirit of creativity. To my father, I will always honor the gift of Maddox Communications that he built from the ground up. To my wife, Elle," he said, taking her by surprise.

She blinked at him.

"Yes, you," he said. "You have given my life meaning beyond work. You have given me a home whenever I'm with you. I love you."

Elle's eyes filled with tears. "I love you, too," she whispered.

The room echoed with applause.

"Hear, hear," Asher Williams, CFO of Maddox Communications said. "Melody and I have some news, too," he said, pulling his lovely wife against him. "We're having twins."

The group crowed with approval and applauded again.

"Congratulations," Brock said, extending his hand. "You've been busy."

"No more than you," Ash said with a broad smile.

Walter Prentice, Maddox's star client, stepped forward and patted Brock on the back. "You're doing a good job. More than ever, I can tell we signed with the right firm."

"I'm glad you feel that way," Brock said. "We'll work to make sure you continue to feel that way. Mrs. Prentice," Brock said, nodding toward Walter's wife. "Thank you for coming tonight."

Angela looked strained and unhappy, which was

highly unusual for Walter's beloved wife. "Congratulations on your success," she said. "And on the baby. Never underestimate the importance of your wife and children."

Brock sensed a sadness beneath the surface, but he knew now wasn't the time to comment. Instead, he took her hand in his. "I won't," he said earnestly.

Brock felt his brother, Flynn, draw him aside. "Excuse me," he said to Angela.

"We have something else to toast," Flynn said, giving his brother a fresh beer.

"What?" Brock asked.

"Who isn't here tonight?" Flynn asked. "Who is missing?"

Brock glanced around the busy room and shrugged. "I don't know. Who?"

"Mother," Flynn said with a dry smile.

"Oh, my God, you're right," Brock said.

"Renee tells me she has found a man willing to keep her in the style to which she has become accustomed," Flynn said.

"How could we possibly get that lucky?" Brock asked.

"I don't know, but I refuse to question good fortune." He bumped his bottle against Brock's again. "Ding-dong, the witch—"

"Is gone," Brock said and slapped his brother on the back. "I never would have pictured this last year. Would you?"

Flynn shook his head. "Some things turn out better than you expect," he said.

Brock latched his gaze onto Elle as she walked

toward him. She was his home. He'd never known true love until her. Thank God he'd found her. "Better than I could have dreamed," Brock said and opened his arms to his wife.

"Are you having a good night?" she asked, smiling up at him.

"I'm having a good life," he said. "Because of you."

* * * * *

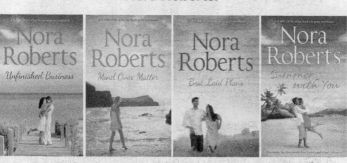